Vicious

To

Jade

[signature]

[signature]

Vicious

A novel of punk rock
and
the second coming

Michael Forester

PARALIGHT

PRESS

First published in Great Britain in 2018
by Paralight Press

www.michaelforester.co.uk

The right of Michael Forester
to be identified as author of this work
has been asserted by him in accordance with
the Copyright, Designs and Patents Act 1988

ISBN: 978-0-9955248-6-6

Cover Image © Michael Forester

Printed and bound by TJ International, Padstow, Cornwall

BY THE SAME AUTHOR

Fiction :
Dragonsong
The Goblin Child *and other stories*
A Home For Other Gods

Life Writing:
If It Wasn't For That Dog
Forest Rain

Poetry Chapbooks:
Love
Light
Peace
Forest Meditation

Further details of these publication appear at the end of this book

Prologue

Rule Two:

The Game will be initiated upon the occurrence of an event, outside the control of the players, that establishes a tear in the curtain ("a random tear"). Players are free to observe the occurrence of the event if they wish. A player who initiates a tear in the curtain will forfeit the Game and may, at the discretion of the Arbiter, be excluded from any future Game.

Saturday 5th April 2008 9.00 pm GMT

A Dream (maybe).

Twenty-one men,

Seven women

(covertly gathered).

Two Ethereals

(observing; concerned).

A machine.

A switch,

thrown.

A hum.

An audible sigh of relief.

But not from the Ethereals.

One looks worried.

The other is more animated.

Henry

Rule Three:

The Arbiter will confirm the existence of a randomly established tear in the curtain by passing through the tear onto the field of play.

It all started on a Spring Sunday Morning – 6th April to be exact. I know the date is right because it was the morning following my twenty-first birthday. I rolled over in bed and straight off the edge, my eyes still closed. Hitting the floor on all fours is my favoured methodology for shaking myself awake. In fact, mum says, I've been doing it since the day I learned to jump out of my cot. Except this time, as I hit the carpet my left knee landed squarely on something small, irregularly shaped and extremely hard. I yelped in pain, suddenly very wide awake. As a method for dispelling sleep it was effective. In view of the pain involved, I can't recommend it.

"Aw ffffffff……" I started, still sufficiently the subject of parental influence not to permit the whole of the forbidden aphorism escape my lips. I reached down under my knee and pulled the offending article from the indentation it had made. The object was the size of a golf ball – just small enough to fit completely in the palm of my hand. I lifted it towards the light and uncurled my fingers. For a moment, I couldn't focus, still seeing two of whatever it was… black… carved… hard. When my eyes finally did stabilise, I realised that what I was holding in front of me was a small intricate carving in what appeared to be ebony. It reminded me of a Voodoo doll (not that I'd ever seen one, you understand, having had a particularly sheltered childhood – but that's the power of daytime TV for you). The item was, above all else, indescribably ugly. Squat to the point of being fat, its facial features were a distorted caricature of a human's. With a stubby nose and a wide mouth, it rather put me in mind of an Egyptian god, yet, somehow, managing to lack the grandeur and elegance. Beneath the face, the merest hint of a neck joined directly onto a bulbous body. Underneath folded arms that carried a tiny spear protruded a distended stomach and an enormous roll of fat that cascaded inelegantly into equally obese thighs and calves. Finally, the whole body was perched upon disproportionately small flat feet that were webbed like a duck's. The eyelids of the carving were closed in a way that suggested a comfortable, slothful sleep. The term that came to mind for it was 'Talisman'.

Presuming that this was my father's less than subtle comment on my previous evening's excesses, I tossed the carving down on the bed, turned to the wardrobe and began to strip off last night's clothes. I was down to my underpants and in the process of pulling on my dressing gown when there was a noise behind me that sounded for all the world like an old gas kettle hissing. I turned. Another hiss, this time clearly emanating from the bed. Creaking... Cracking... a high-pitched hum. I looked down at the little carving. It was vibrating. I stood there in my underpants and unfastened dressing gown, disconcerted, but mesmerised nevertheless. I was just wondering what the hell kind of trick my father was playing when the inconceivable happened. The grotesque little Talisman opened an eye. It looked up at me, left eye open, right eye closed, its left eyelid blinking rapidly as the eye adjusted to the light. After a moment, the right eye followed. Then the head began to move, turning on the squat little neck. The Talisman surveyed the room with a nonchalant kind of gaze until its eyes alighted on me with an expression that I could have sworn was fascination... or admiration... or love. Finally, the rest of the body shook itself loose. In a motion that parodied mine precisely, the creature jumped from the bed to the floor onto all fours, screamed a little high-pitched scream as if in pain and clutched its left knee. Then giggling in fits of laughter, it ran to my leg and tried its best to throw its arms around my ankle. I would have been relieved to have discovered that I was still dreaming, but the sunlight streaming in through the window and a warm breeze rustling the curtains indicated otherwise.

Being newly turned 21, a student of Philosophy, and until quite recently, an avid reader of Marvel ™ comics, it's fair to say that my take on reality was perhaps, a little more malleable than that of my parents. In short, I was prepared to suspend my disbelief long enough to consider the possibility that what I was seeing was not a hallucination, but a genuine, experimentally verifiable, reality.

As the little creature clung to my ankle I reached my hand down towards what I was now thinking was perhaps not so much a Talisman as a Talis-*Man*. Immediately, it looked up into my face as if to reassure itself of my intentions, then, hopped onto my palm and clung to my index finger. I lifted it towards my face to study its less than attractive features more closely. Despite being intellectually aware that it was never going to win a beauty contest, I felt no distaste for it and certainly nothing as strong as revulsion. Rather, what I actually experienced was a certain nervous perturbation that simply by the fact I was not resisting it, I was engaging in something intensely personal, intimate, possibly even quasi-sexual – in short, something I would not wish others to know. For its part, the Talis-man studied me just as intently. Then, it smiled an unengaging smile that revealed a row of uneven, rotting teeth. It was obvious that the smile was intended to convey warmth. Whatever mother had given birth to the creature must once have loved it but I couldn't imagine anyone else doing so. The Talis-man seemed unaware of or at least unconcerned about my mixed feelings for it. To this creature, love was clearly a one-way street and it was behaving as if it had found its soul mate. Though I had never been the target of such devotion before, I wasn't at all sure I wanted to be from this particular entity under these particular circumstances. I sat on the bed looking at it and wondering what on earth to do with it while it continued to cling desperately to my thumb. As I reached out to put it down on the bedside cabinet, the creature's expression changed from love first to wariness and then to suspicion. With a movement faster than my eye could see, it twisted its spear round and stuck it in my finger.

"Oww!" was my predictable response. "All right! I won't leave you," I said quickly and with irritation. The suspicion on the creature's face turned back to caution and then again, to affection. Clearly, we were not to be parted if the Talis-man could possibly avoid it. I slipped it into the pocket of my dressing gown and went off to the bathroom to shower. Inside, I turned the key in the lock, hung my gown on the back of the door and switched on the shower. The Talis-man peered over the edge of my pocket cautiously. When it saw the water cascading down into the bath, an expression of sheer joy came over its face and it squeaked excitedly. "You want to join me?" I asked with some amusement and lifted it carefully into the bottom of the bath. There it proceeded to swim solemnly up and down in the shallow water, spear still in hand, its little webbed feet propelling it surprisingly efficiently from one end to the other. As I looked down on it, I had the strangest sense that it looked slightly larger than before; at least egg sized; that it wouldn't fit as comfortably in my palm as when I had first picked it up. "Naah. Trick of the light," I said under my breath. The Talis-man giggled.

The main event for the day was my date with Laura.

We had arranged to go walking on the less well frequented paths around Minstead, an area off the main tourist routes of the New Forest that we particularly liked, about twenty minutes' drive from where I live in Brockenhurst. Laura was fourteen months my junior and had just turned 20 back in February. I'd been taking things very cautiously with her. We'd started going out the previous March, but it had been an on/off thing, chiefly because I was pushing her too hard. She'd had a strong moral compulsion and I'd not made enough space for it. When she finally ended the relationship on Christmas night last year, I was devastated. Then, quite suddenly, she started it again on New Year's Day. I didn't worry too much about why. I was just grateful she had and resolved not to make the same mistake twice.

The question I had to address now was what to do with the Talis-man while I was with her. Judging from the creature's reaction when I had tried to leave it in the bedroom, I decided I had better take it with me. I would slip it in my pocket and do my best to keep it concealed from Laura for the afternoon. The Talis-man watched in loving fascination as I put on my summer uniform of t-shirt, denims and open sandals. Then, I slipped it into my breast pocket and headed downstairs. I was careful to lock up on my way out – there'd been a burglary last month, just after I'd started work at Matthis. Strangely, nothing had been taken and the damage done was minimal. But what had left mum in tears was that the bastard had torn up her favourite photo of her and me from last Christmas Day. The half of it with her on was left screwed up in the bin, smeared with some black stuff. The half with me on was missing. Gay burglar? Bloody perv, I say. I didn't want that to happen again. Double-checking the lock, I then headed out to the car, a rather elderly Ford Fiesta. The Talis-man remained in my pocket throughout the journey to Laura's house in Southampton, stirring only when I parked and got out to knock on her door. As I did, it poked its head up over the edge of my pocket and looked around curiously. Anxious that it should not be seen, I pushed it gently back down. Fortunately, it did not resist.

Laura arrived at the door looking fragrant and glamorously sexy in matching white t-shirt and jeans. A green scarf was hanging loosely around her neck as if she had just brushed it from her head. I looked admiringly at her curvaceous body and was rewarded with a peck on the cheek and "Come on slow-coach!" as she sauntered down the path on low-heeled walking sandals, her shoulder bag and hips swinging in perfect time. In the best male tradition, I complied with her instruction and trotted after her, my eyes glued to her backside.

As she got out of the car at Minstead, Laura picked up the rug from the back seat. I tried not to raise my eyebrows at this encouraging gesture, since for virtually the whole of our relationship so far, she had barely let me do any more than kiss her, insisting that even this was more of a compromise with her principles than she really wished to make. Admittedly, though, she had shown a little more inclination to normal romantic behaviour over the last few weeks. Nevertheless, I wasn't about to risk screwing things up a second time.

For its part, the Talis-man seemed content to remain in my pocket. Only an occasional shifting of its weight as we walked reminded me it was still there. Maybe it would not prove to be such an inconvenience after all. Laura and I chatted about nothing in particular for the first mile or so of our favourite walk until, by series of less and less well-defined paths, we reached a remote clearing that we knew but no one else seemed to. We both remembered it well as the place of our first kiss. Moving purposefully to the sunny side, Laura spread the car rug carefully on the ground. Clearly in an amorous mood, she turned to me, put her arms round my neck and kissed me long and deep, her body pressed tantalisingly against mine. To be more specific, her right breast pressed against my t-shirt pocket. Now, I acknowledge that this may not have been entirely normal for a 21-year-old man being kissed by a lovely 20-year-old girl, but I have to say my attention shifted from the kiss. And although it focussed on her breast pressing against me, it wasn't for entirely the normal reason. My concern was for the fact that the Talis-man was squealing and fidgeting around in my pocket under the pressure. And I was even more concerned as to how Laura would now react to the presence of something clearly animate pressing back against her breast. But surprisingly, she showed no initial reaction at all. Evidently, my powers of seduction were sufficient to drive all other thoughts from her mind. This apparently continued to be the case for the next few moments as Laura began to indicate by shifting her weight that she wanted us to drop down to the rug – without breaking the kiss. Who was I to argue? I allowed myself to be drawn slowly earthward until we were both sitting, still locked in the delicious embrace. Then, just as firmly, she drew us both down until we were lying on the rug.

Under just about any other circumstances this would have been precisely what I wanted – and not before time, too, in my opinion. However, the pressing matter of the Talis-man remained, well, literally, pressing. As Laura snuggled closer into my open arms and pressed her body more urgently against me, she showed the first sign of being aware of its presence. Indeed, she was more than simply aware, for while still locked in the kiss, she reached inside my pocket, took hold of the creature and dropped it to the ground beside me. At this point matters were, I felt, rather taking their natural course and I left the Talis-man to fend for itself while I devoted myself to more urgent priorities.

Bad decision.

My hands were now sliding under Laura's t-shirt and I was enjoying the sensation of the soft curves of her back when, oh joy! The wonderful girl's own hand began undoing my belt and the top button of my jeans.

"Oh, Henry," she murmured. "I've tried so hard to resist this. But I can't. It's too powerful. I truly, truly love you with all my heart. And I want you so much."

Well, I wasn't too fussed about the 'being in love' part. In my experience, for girls, loves equals commitment, equals wedding bells, equals responsibility. But nevertheless, what was happening at this moment was exactly what I wanted. I wasn't about to let the small matter of my entire future get in my way. However, my joy was short-lived. At precisely the same moment as Laura's hand began to ease back the elastic top of my Calvin Kleins, I felt something enter the bottom of my right trouser leg. Under normal conditions I would have been anything but concerned about this, assuming this action to have been initiated by the delectable Laura's left foot. However, I was just a tad bothered that the movement on my right calf might be the responsibility of an altogether different, though equally determined, individual. As if in confirmation, the movement persisted rapidly up the inside of my trouser leg well beyond the reach of any normal person's foot until it, too, arrived at my underpants. Said individual then lifted the material of said garment and started rearranging my personal parts to suit his comfort and convenience. Perhaps, even this might have been manageable if it hadn't been for the fact that at precisely the moment that the Talis-man was making his way into my pants from the lower end, Laura's left hand entered the same garment from the upper end. Now, I ask you, which normal 21-year-old man would not have enjoyed the sensation of something moving around his penis whilst he was locked in an embrace with a beautiful girl? Well, actually, this one. And my deepest fears were confirmed when the shitty little bugger began sticking its spear firmly and repeatedly into my right testicle.

"Oi!" I said involuntarily, "Piss off you!" Pretty well any other phrase uttered in pretty well any other tone of voice would, at that moment, have taken me closer to my long-desired objective, inside Laura's own underwear, that sunny Sunday afternoon. But I can hardly blame the girl for assuming this wholly negative aphorism to have been directed at her. In a nanosecond, all her warmth and yielding evaporated and she petrified in my arms. A moment later, she pulled back from the embrace and sat up instantly. Equally instantly, the Talis-man stopped sticking his spear in me. The look on Laura's face was a mixture of anger, embarrassment, surprise and fear. For a moment, she simply stared at me. Then, enormous tears began to roll down her cheeks from both eyes. Her lip quivered. Still sobbing, she screamed at me.

"You bastard! You, rotten miserable bastard." You've spent the last year making it clear that you want to make love to me. I get all ready to give myself to you – my very first man – my only man. I get all steamed up wanting you then... then... this! You sod! You rotten sod!"

I tried to interrupt. "No, Sweetheart. I didn't mean you. I wasn't talking to you. I was yelling at the shitty little..." And then, I stopped, realising simultaneously that on the one hand, there was no way to explain to her exactly who I was talking to without showing her, and on the other, that the little bastard who had so effectively interrupted the proceedings was now nowhere in evidence.

"Yes?" she managed to ask through the tears, "the shitty little who?" I knew I was beaten by a lethal combination of the sodding little creature – who I could now see was going to be nothing but trouble – and the oldest weapon on earth: a woman's tears.

"Nothing," I said sadly. "I'm really, really sorry Laura. I don't know what came over me. Come back here and let's carry on. It's lovely." But even as I made the suggestion, I knew the situation to be beyond redemption. Without answering, she wiped her tears, adjusted her clothing, picked up the rug and marched stiffly back in the direction of the car. I zipped up my jeans and followed, some twenty or so paces behind her and somewhat less stiff. I couldn't say for sure at exactly what point on the route back I became aware of something animate, the size of a small light bulb, moving around just a little inside my right trouser pocket.

Sunday 6th April 2008 3.04 pm BST

Not a word passed between us on the journey home. Not a word was spoken as we arrived at Laura's house. I was bursting to know if she had decided it was all over between us. But I knew that if I put the question to her at that moment there could be only one possible answer. It was wiser to let her emotion dissipate and then try to repair the damage in any way I could. As her hand reached out for the handle of the car door, she turned and looked at me silently – a long, eloquent look. After several moments of this guilt-inducing gaze, she simply got out of the car and walked up the path to the front door. There, she turned and held my eyes once more with precisely the same expression before opening the door and letting herself inside. Honestly, I couldn't have felt more at fault if she'd stood on the doorstep and burst into an unaccompanied rendition of 'I will survive'. And all this, for something I didn't do.

Tolly

Rule Six:

Players are free to invite Tangibles to observe play. Observers will not interfere with the chain of events.

Saturday 15th March 2008 4.00 pm GMT

"Because you won't fuckin' let me, Dad!"

Well, that's what it sounded like anyway, but we can't be sure, because the words, though roared in unquestionable anger, are muffled by more than the distance between us and the speaker, who is somewhere out of sight.

We have entered the hallway of a small flat, in Shirley, Southampton, constructed circa 1975. It is barely wider than the front door. The herringbone teak block floor was once highly polished and buffed to a shine. Years of shuffling feet have ground the dust into the grain, so that the floor shines only around the edges and a dirty oval shaped depression runs the full length of the hall and across most of its width. Hanging over a small mahogany hallstand to our left is an oval gilt-framed mirror, which sways whenever the door is opened. The motion has long since rubbed through the flock wallpaper to gouge an arc into the plaster.

"It's got fuck all to do with you anyway, Dad!"

As we move quietly down the hallway so as not to disturb the occupant or occupants of the flat, we notice a pile of newspapers on the floor, standing perhaps a third of a metre high. The name of the publication is clearly visible in tabloid red: 'The Worker's Hammer'. The headline in 140-point typeface reads: 'Tories Routed – Workers Beware *"New"* Labour.' The date, too small for us to see at this distance, reads 3rd May 1997.

"And damn your fuckin' Marxist-Leninist, Wigan-Pier, International-Socialist-Red-Flag-Flying *Cause*. I've had it up to my tits with you and your friggin' Socialism. What I want's been gone fer nearly thirty fuckin' years and all the fuckin' commies in Cuba won't fuckin' bring him back. It's my fuckin' life, Dad, so fuck off pesterin' me."

There is a silence broken only by muffled sobs. We take the opportunity to move a little further down the hallway. And as we do, the speaker starts to mumble. We need to get closer to hear her properly.

"Oh, Sid," she sobs "twenty-nine years, Sid. Thirty next February. Why did you do it? It weren't yer fault, Sid. If only you'd know that. You didn't top 'er. An' it was me, Tolly, who was yer li'l baby girl, Sid. An' it was my tears you wanted to kiss away. Not fuckin' Nancy's, the cheatin' lyin' witchbitch. She promised me you was mine, Sid. Promised me she'd leave you alone. An' she never, ever loved you like me. That's why I 'ad to get rid of 'er, Sid. Surely you see that now, don't you? It was fer you I done it." She continues to mumble incoherently, barely audible now. But the words seem not to be her own; a poem, perhaps?

You were my little baby girl…
But now you're gone
There's only pain…
And I don't want to live this life
If I can't live for you.

Now, her voice rises, her head turned towards the ceiling and she screams at full volume again. "Nancy fuckin' Spungen! Can you 'ear me up there, Nancy? Yer good 'n' dead an' I'm glad. 'Cos now, he's mine. I've waited twenty-nine years for him, Nancy. An' he's cumin back. So, you keep yer fuckin' 'ands off him up there 'til 'e does. You hear me, Nancy? He's mine an' one day he's cumin back to be wif me."

As we reach the hinge side of the bathroom door, we can see the speaker in profile through the crack. Mascara runs in streams like volcanic lava down the side of the face that is visible to us and drips onto her enormous breast which itself is spilling out over a sky blue, Ann Summers bra (Sky Blue for Sundays, Canary Yellow for Mondays, Sun Kissed Peach for Tuesdays. We have not been informed of the colours for Wednesday to Saturday).

"I fuckin' hate you. I was never good enough for you, was I?"

In a motion that seems unconscious, she reaches down with her left hand to a white, eight-inch plate balanced precariously on the edge of the wall-mounted avocado sink. On it stands the remains of a large chocolate cake, somehow vaguely reminiscent of the crumbling ruins of a once great city. Like some enraged deity bent on obliteration of an errant Sodom, she grabs a handful of cake and lifts it towards her face, dark brown butter icing oozing between her fingers as she compresses it and forces it into her wide-open mouth. Most of the cake finds its way back out through alternating sobs and angry roars. To fill the resultant void, she reaches with her right hand for the Old Holborn roll up that is smouldering on a shelf above the sink next to an open can of Castlemaine 4X export strength lager. As she draws on the cigarette, she pauses. She is alone. She has been talking, if indeed it can be described as talking, to the mirror.

11.00 am 12ᵗʰ June 1959 BST

I sense your confusion. Let me alleviate the discomfort for you. Slide back a few decades with me, if you are minded to, and we will emerge into the bright, bright sunlight of the summer of 1959. Is it my imagination, or were the summers really warmer and the rainfall really softer back then? There was certainly something more hopeful, more noble, about England in the years following the Second World War than the weary, struggling nation it has become in the twenty-first century.

Recognise where we are? Yes, clever you! Got it first time. Hampstead Heath. See that couple walking hand in hand over there? No, I don't expect you to recognise them and yes, they do look a little odd together, don't they? Her friends call her Sophie. Don't you agree that there's something about her even at this distance that betrays her pedigree? She has a poise, an elegance that reaches beyond her 19-year-old beauty to speak of careful breeding over generations. Her bearing suggests that she has been taught from birth that she is entitled to a certain deference from her social inferiors. In their turn, those around her unconsciously respond to that intuitive self-confidence and defer without even realising what they have done. Such behaviour is unremarkable to her and she barely registers it. And that, perhaps, is precisely why her companion caught her attention some months ago – for the simple reason that he did not defer; that he gave not so much as one emotional, intellectual or social inch to her; and this, despite the fact that his accent and his cultivated Angry-Young-Man presentation speak in eloquence of his working class, son of toil origin.

And that is why it happened – why the honourable Sophia Montagu-Curzon, first daughter of the Marquis of Netley, prospective antique dealer, met and fell in love with Frank Jones, first-born son of Mary Jones and one of three possible fathers (well, three that Mary could remember when she was sober), foot soldier of the Class War. In a poorly lit corner of a dusty shop in the docks area of Southampton, they had each laid a hand on the same table at the same moment. No matter that it would not have suited Mary's need for the kitchen table Frank was looking for. No matter that it had no particular provenance or likely worth for Sophie to impress her parents with. Each staked claim to it, he by iron grip, she by vitriolic stare and neither would relinquish it willingly. But as is so often the case in matters of the heart, something unexpected afflicted both claimants at the same moment. The outcome, quite out of character to both, was that each immediately and inexplicably relinquished their grip on the table in favour of the other. Inevitably, neither purchased the item and both walked away from the shop empty-handed. Not hand in hand, you understand, for this was 1959 and the real world, not some awful Hollywood tear-jerker. Nevertheless, a bond was formed that day. And with each fully aware of the social ravine that separated them, neither disclosed to their respective families that they were together constructing an emotional viaduct to cross the chasm.

So here we find this rather unlikely couple, preoccupied now by the impending evolution of post-war, post-empire Great Britain into an inevitably Socialist State (or not as the case may be), and preoccupied now by the precise length of time it takes for the female nipple of the left breast to harden under the manual and oral attentions of a hitherto inexpert male, whose sexual dexterity is growing in a manner most satisfactory to the owner of said breast.

So, for what noteworthy purpose are we observing this private event? I'm surprised you have not already guessed. This corner of Hampstead Heath, and this quiet Sunday afternoon are the time and place at which Tolly enters this universe, this time around.

Monday 17th March 2008 5.45 pm GMT

We are back. We now stand on a street corner in Shirley. Look! Coming up the road from Southampton; that little Austin Allegro. Recognise the driver? Yes, that's right. It's Tolly. Well, you could hardly fail to recognise her with that red Mohican haircut, could you? Flotsam of the 1970s punk rock era, I'd say. I don't like to waste my time on riff-raff like this, but needs must.

We slip over the road just as the driver of the old Allegro turns into the forecourt of the same 70s block of flats we entered yesterday. She pulls up across two parking spaces, parallel to neither, kills the engine and opens the door. She edges her right buttock off the seat and it sags towards the door sill. The motion of her right leg out of the car brings to mind the slow swing of the arm of a large crane on a small building site. But quite unlike a crane, it drops heavily to earth with an audible thud. Now her large right hand reaches out behind her, searching for the door frame, and makes contact. Slowly, she pivots herself round to bring her left leg parallel to the right, then leans her weight forward until it is borne by both her legs instead of the seat. Slowly, she rises to an approximation of the vertical. From the rear of the car, she takes two Asda plastic carrier bags in one hand, while patting her right hip with the other. "Permanently low prices," she whispers to herself in an exaggerated northern accent that resonates back to the store's 1980s advertising campaigns. Then, she turns from the car and makes her way with a swaying gait to the front door of the block. She will wait for the lift and take it to the third floor, where flat 301 is first on the left out of the lift car door. She blesses the flat for the advantage it conveys of not requiring her to walk down the long corridor once she has exited the lift. She curses it for the noise of the lift gear each evening which is always audible over the TV. By experience, she knows the only means available to her for blotting out the sound of the lift gear is her 'Sid Sings' albums (she has seven copies that she rotates so as to ensure none ever becomes too worn to play) and the dulcet tones of Sid Vicious screaming his rather memorable version of 'My Way'. Years ago, when she was feeling particularly Devil-may-care, she would open the windows and play them full volume with stereo speakers facing out over the car park. But now, they are for her pretty ears alone. "If only... if only," she sighs whenever she hears his voice. But for now, it is not to be. Death took him from her in 1979.

We will leave Tolly to make her way up to the flat while we appear there at the speed of thought. I want to show it to you properly before she arrives. If we move around too much in the presence of Tangibles like Tolly, there is always a danger that they will feel us passing or catch a glimpse of us out of the corner of an eye.

We'll look at the kitchen and the lounge today. The educational tour of the bedrooms we will reserve for another time. On second thoughts, you might prefer to avoid the kitchen – unless of course, in a former incarnation you had a professional interest in the worst excesses conceivable to the world of culinary hygiene – cockroaches, salmonella, e-coli – you know the kind of thing I mean. We'll pass on into the lounge, it's a tad less stomach-churning – not that we have stomachs to be churned, of course. Brace yourself anyway – it's going to be a bit of a shock.

It's a bright sunny afternoon outside but the curtains are closed. Tolly can't actually remember the last time she opened them, but it wasn't in this century. At first, she told herself there was no point, she was so rarely in the flat during daylight hours. Then, after a while, the nagging little voice in her head (her mother's voice, actually) that had once offered her a modicum of discipline, finally gave up entreating her to maintain some *Standards*. Now, it simply berates her for the complete and utter shithole she's made of her life (the voice's words, not mine, you understand). Now, it simply talks to her from the mirror, along with everyone else she hates. And sometimes, Tolly is not quite sure which side of the mirror and the line of hatred she is on herself.

Anyway, when our sight has adjusted to the light level, we realise that there is another impediment to our vision – a thick fog of hand-rolled cigarette smoke lingers in the air. Tolly is a chain smoker. In fact, she has perfected the art of one-handed cigarette rolling which permits her to draw freely on each cigarette whilst rolling the next. She was pleased with herself when she pioneered the technique during a particularly uneventful episode of EastEnders. Now, the action is automatic and repeated incessantly in front of Corrie and the More-4 re-runs of Deal or No Deal (she dreams of winning that quarter mill herself one day, but hasn't applied to go on yet... something tells her she might not be accepted, but she can't quite pinpoint exactly why she thinks so).

Tolly gets a mite worried when occasionally, she becomes aware of how many packets of Old Holborn she is getting through, not to mention cigarette papers, but she confronts the concern aggressively and drives it from her mind. And anyway, a mate at the local union branch gets them for her VAT-free so long as she doesn't ask any questions. Tolly thinks that her employer gives *Fuckin New Labour* more than enough of her money anyway, so she doesn't see why she should add to Alistair Darling's money bags. As far as she's concerned, once the class war was won, he'd be on the executioner's list somewhere between Gordon Brown and Tony Blair.

If we blow some of the smoke away, we can at last see the lounge in all its glory – a twenty by twelve-foot monument to all that was worst in the 1970s' interior design, tempered by one or two strangely out of place antique pieces which are actually surprisingly good. There's an early colour TV, except the colour control's almost gone and most of the time it only shows black and white. That's next to a reel-to-reel tape recorder on the floor which might even have a bit of value itself now. Next to that is a radiogram, 1960s vintage. Tolly still uses it to play Sid's records on. And next to that is a particularly fine Queen Anne corner commode. I'd put that at around 1720 – nice example, probably worth a couple of thousand. On the other side of the room from where we're floating, there's a large bookcase stuffed with old Socialist literature – New Left Book Club, International-Socialist magazines, George Orwell novels and so on. Then, next to the bookcase is Tolly's sofa. There is no other seating in the room. But don't go thinking she has her guests sit on the sofa with her. Firstly, she takes up all the space herself and secondly, it has been over eight years since another person entered this flat. In fact, to be more precise, it is a little over eight years since the last person left this flat: her father, Frank – horizontally. The last item in the room is the shrine. A shrine, you ask? Oh, yes, indeed. The shrine is the centrepiece of the room and Tolly's prized possession. In the very centre of the room is an oval teak coffee table. Once it had a glass centre to it but this has long since been removed. Now, standing on the floor and rising up through the centre of the table, is a large plant stand. On the stand is an urn.

Friday 7th January 1977 2.00 am GMT

"What was Colorado U like, Nance?"

The older girl takes a long draw on her joint before answering. She inhales deeply and blows the smoke high up towards the ceiling.

"Shit." Nancy lies back on the pile of damp mattresses at the other end of the room and sucks on her joint again.

Outside, the snow is falling in uncharacteristically large flakes. Inside, the air is growing rapidly colder since the fire went out. The girls wrap their sweaters closely around themselves. There is no seating in the room save for the old mattresses piled up to chair level. Tolly is sitting on one pile, Nancy on another. Some of the windows are missing panes. Though the occupants of the house have sealed them as best they can with cardboard and pieces of plywood, the wind has an unfortunate habit of finding its way around the edges and into the room, some would say into the soul. All in all, it's an unremarkable squat in an unremarkable South London back street. And these are two unremarkable girls.

Tolly is 17 and has decided to rebel. Her mother's family (who never met her, you understand) would say it was inevitable that she would turn out to be Southampton street trash. Well, what with the death of her mother when she was 6 and her father's complete preoccupation with those awful unions and those dreadful strikes. In fact, it was amazing that Social Services hadn't taken her into care when Sophie's mother, who received regular reports from a retained private detective, had arranged for them to be called. But there's the Welfare State and the Socialist Local Authority for you. I mean, My Dear, really. The country's gone to the dogs.

But Tolly was a nice enough kid as far as her father was concerned. He'd truly loved her mother and was devastated when she died. Frank had tried to do all the usual things any loving father would do – sent her to a comprehensive, hadn't he? Taken her to the International Marxist Group meetings when she played truant; arranged her very own subscription to *Young Socialist* for her; taught her about the struggle of the working class and given her every possible advantage in fighting the class war that a young girl could ever hope for.

They'd continued to live in the nice new flat in Shirley that Sophie had bought with the last of her inheritance, and it had been a good life as far as Frank was concerned. In fact, when Social Services had stuck their noses in, after receiving the tip off from some anonymous busybody, the flat was pretty much the factor that swung their decision to let him keep her. But that was back in '67. Since then, the nice little girl with pig tails had grown up into some teenage minx he didn't recognise. She'd renounced the International Socialist Cause. I mean *renounced the cause*, for God's sake. Can you believe that? Well, there was nothing else a committed Socialist could do but tip her out, was there? And she'd gone to London, as far as he knew, chasing after them new 'Punk Rocker' groups. Christ only knew what she saw in the music and as for the people… a disgrace to the working classes, they were, with their funny hair an' their safety pins an' their bin liners. So, Tolly had gone and Frank had continued with his daily routine of IMG meetings, factory disruption, wildcat strikes and the like.

And Tolly? Well, Tolly had followed her dream. She had seen a new group perform the preceding year, 1976, in a club near the Docks. A band called The Sex Pistols. They had this bass guitarist – Sid. And oh, my God! Sex Pistol wasn't the word for it. Tolly had to have him. And she did have him. That night. In a dark corner, right behind the stage – the area euphemistically called the dressing room. Well, there was a bit of dressing after they'd finished, she supposed, when she giggled about it afterwards. But Sid was no laughing matter. This was real. Sid was *The One*. Tolly had decided to love Sid for ever. And Tolly, you understand, was a very, very decisive person. But there was just this little bit of uncertainty, this nagging doubt. She'd known the moment he tore her knickers off that this was her one true love; known as he shoved himself roughly into her with not the slightest concession to foreplay that this was the only man for her. Known as he held her hard by her Mohican and squeezed her tit so tight it hurt, that this was the soul mate she wanted to be with for ever. But… but… was she absolutely sure he felt the same? As he released his flow into her crying "Aww fuck," could she be confident he felt as deeply as she did? And as he immediately withdrew, did up his jeans and spat in her face, was she *absolutely certain* he was as committed to her as she was to him?

"Tolly, yer bein' a tit," she told herself over and over. "Of course, he fuckin' loves you. How couldn't he?"

So, she followed her soulmate back to London; found a squat as near to where she'd been told he lived that she could; waited at the stage doors and back entrances for him every night after the gigs. Of course, she understood that it was important that he didn't acknowledge her when he came out. She understood that he was the infamous Sid Vicious and had an image to maintain. She understood that, for the moment at least, they couldn't be together. But Tolly was patient. Tolly knew how to wait. Tolly was committed.

Nancy had told Tolly very little of her life in America. Only that she was expelled from school at 11; only that she'd been in psychotherapy and had attempted suicide several times and attacked her mother with a hammer; only that she'd been diagnosed as having Bipolar disorder and Borderline Personality; only that she graduated high school at 16; only that she dropped out of Colorado

U within the first Semester; only enough to ensure that Tolly worshiped the latrine she shitted in and would willingly trust her with her life. Tolly also trusted Nancy with her absolutely biggest and most important secret in all the world – her love for Sid Vicious and her certainty of his love for her. Of course, Tolly knew she was completely safe in doing so, 'cos Nancy had eyes only for Jerry Nolan of the New York City Dolls and wasn't that why she'd come to London anyway? So, when Nancy decided to go with Tolly to a Pistols concert, that was just fine. And when Tolly pointed out Sid to Nancy and Nancy gave that funny little shiver, that was fine too, 'cos Tolly knew Nancy was just bein' 'appy for her. And when Nancy said they should go to the stage door to see if they could meet him, that was fine too, 'cos she knew her new American friend was just tryin' to help her through this difficult time when Sid couldn't acknowledge her. But when Nancy pushed through the crowd of screaming teenagers and leapt the barrier and shoved the security guards aside just as Sid was comin' out the door, maybe that wasn't quite so fine. An' when she threw herself against him, wiv' 'im looking so surprised an' all, maybe that wasn't too fine, either. Then, when Sid had grabbed Nancy by the arm and said, "C'mon darling, you're wif me," and when they'd got into the big black car together which sped off in the direction of Sid's hotel, then that wasn't fine at all.

It wasn't Sid's fault. Tolly knew that for certain; knew that it was she, Tolly, who Sid truly loved. Hadn't he proved it time and time again in every gig the band had played, snarling as he caught her eye, screaming "Fuck you" for her and no one else? And then, there had been that night; that amazing night; that precious night behind the stage when they had proved their eternal devotion to each other with screams and snarls and an animalistic copulation in which each had touched the deepest reaches of the other's entities. No, it was utterly inconceivable that Sid did not love her with all his heart.

The explanation was simple. It was that Yankee witchbitch's fault. The bitch must have had it all planned from the first moments. She must have come to England just to steal Tolly's lover; must have planned that meeting with Tolly in the squat; must have groomed her relationship until the younger girl trusted her. Well, who wouldn't have trusted someone with Nancy's background? Nancy, who had seen so much more of the world at 20 than Tolly had at 17. Nancy, who knew that the System was "out ta git ya" and that the only person you could trust was yerself. Nancy, who knew when to curl up to protect herself and when to lunge in an attack. Nancy, who knew how to seem to give without giving and how to take without seeming to take. Nancy knew all these things and lost no time in teaching her younger protégé all she knew. And now, the reason for those lessons was obvious. They were for the sole purpose of gaining Tolly's trust in order that Tolly would lead Nancy to her man.

And Sid's culpability in all this? Well again, the answer was simple. Sid had obviously seen Nancy standing there next to Tolly that night outside the stage door and could see immediately they were friends. That was it. Now she thought about it, wasn't it definitely a look of relief Tolly had seen on his face as he saw them standing there? Relief that Tolly had found a friend to confide in while Sid himself, for a short time, could not look after her? And then, he had obviously thought it was ok to trust Nancy when she leapt the barrier. In fact, he must have thought that Nancy was doing it so that Sid and Tolly could be together again! He must have been expecting Nancy to take him to Tolly that very night! Yes! That was it! She could see it now. It was all so completely understandable. Anyone would have made the same mistake. Sid, darling Sid, wonderful Sid, was completely innocent of any fault. His heart was still true to Tolly!

And maybe… maybe, she had it now. Maybe, Nancy wasn't a

Yankee witchbitch after all. Maybe, she really was making it so that Tolly and Sid could be together. Maybe, she'd be getting in touch really soon. Maybe, she was on her way to the squat even now. And if that was true, Tolly had to be absolutely ready for her the moment she arrived. Dear Nancy! Wonderful Nancy! She was going to reunite Tolly with her man! At long last, they would be together!

So, after the week it took Tolly to work all this out, she picked herself up from the pile of mattresses, sniffed back her tears and smiled a shy little smile at her fellow squatters. She was sorry. Sorry for the worry she'd caused them all. But she was ok now. She could see the truth at last and everything would be just fine. Tolly didn't see them raise their eyebrows at one another and sigh "Nutter" under their breath. She was too busy making herself perfect for Sid. Nancy would be along for her any day now.

Of course, she was a little perplexed when she read old headlines in the café newspapers that referred to Sid Vicious being attached to a new American girlfriend. But she reassured herself that it was all part of the cover that Nancy needed to build up in order to make sure that Tolly and Sid could be together forever. As the winter of 1977 melted slowly into the spring of 1978, Tolly left the squat less and less. She even stopped going to Pistols gigs, not wanting to distract Nancy and Sid from their ingenious plan. Tolly had to wait in for Nancy. Occasionally, as her body grew more and more emaciated, hunger would drive her out for a few hours in order to beg or steal or earn a little money in the quickest way a girl can, in order to buy just enough to eat so that she could keep going for Sid. But she never gave herself properly to those men. She'd ensure she was paid first and then run off, or give only the briefest of blow jobs to get rid of them. Tolly's body belonged to Sid alone. No one else would be granted proper access to it.

The most challenging moment came in July 1978. Tolly was sipping a lukewarm cuppa in a café, trying to make the tea last a little longer so that she could get warm, hoping against hope that Nancy wouldn't call at the squat while she was out. She had been trying to make eye contact with that fat bald bloke of about 50 sitting two tables away, in the hope that he might be good for a few bob. But he must have been a homo, 'cos he didn't look back at her. When he got up abruptly to leave, he left his Daily Mirror on the chair – and it was today's. Tolly made a lunge for it, reaching it just before the old biddy who had the table on the other side of the homo. She smiled at her in superior triumph as she drew the paper protectively towards her. The ol' girl slipped back into her seat, muttering. Tolly needed the paper more than any ol' crow possibly could. Tolly was hungry for news about her beloved. Today, she was to be rewarded. She breathed in sharply. Her heart felt funny for just a moment. Staring out at her from page 5 was her lover. And sure enough, there stood Nancy next to him, obviously still working on arrangements to get Tolly and Sid together. Tolly didn't recognise where the picture was taken. But the paper said it was outside a nightclub in New York. Christ! New-fuckin'-York! Why hadn't they told her? Surely, they could have got a message to her somehow. If the plan had changed and she and Sid were to be reunited in the States, surely, they realised she needed to know?

Tolly got up from her seat, dazed, leaving the paper open. The old woman made a leap at it and shrieked in triumph as she carried it back to her table like some decrepit hyena claiming the discarded remains of a lion's prey. Tolly wandered out of the café without even hearing the middle-aged waitress behind the counter calling "You all right, love?" as the door swung shut behind her.

She found her way back to the squat on autopilot. She had to think. Had to work out how to get a message to Sid and Nancy. Then, slowly, it all began to fall into place. Maybe… maybe the newspaper article was deliberate. Yes, that was it! Sid and Nancy had arranged for their picture to appear in the paper, so she'd see they'd gone on to New York ahead of her to prepare for Tolly and Sid's reunion. An'... an' they must have paid that bald homo to leave his copy of the paper for her. Yes! That was it! Christ, she'd almost lost the paper to that ol' bird.

"Tolly, yer a stupid tit," she whispered to herself, smiling and shaking her head a little. "You've got to keep yer eyes open to look for the clues, girl. That's how they're communicating wif yer. Get yer bleeding act together." It was so obvious now she had worked it out. This was Sid's way of telling her it was time for her to come to New York to be with him. "Tolly, girl, the wait is almost over! You've got to stay calm now, an' work out how ta get yerself to the States. He's *waitin'* fer ya, girl."

She slept little that night. But then Tolly slept little most nights, if at all. However, this night her reasons for staying awake were different. This night, she was planning how she would get to New York to be with Sid. And after considering and dismissing many options, the solution became obvious to her.

Sister Serenity

Rule Five:

Players will not commence play until the Arbiter has made physical contact with a Nominated Proxy of each player's choice. The Arbiter will then declare the Game open. Prior to this point, Players may initiate contact with their Nominated Proxies **only** in non-incarnate form. Any physical manifestation before the Arbiter declares the Game open will result in immediate forfeiture of the Game by the offending party.

Sunday 6ᵗʰ April 2008 3.07 pm BST

Laura slams the front door closed behind her, so hard it makes the wall shake. Colours of emotion bob up and down in front of her eyes like carousel horses. The reds of anger morph to dark blues of disappointment. The deep greens of sorrow swirl into the sharp pink of fear. Grey frustration merges the other colours into a spinning top, a muddy off-white haze that settles over her head as she stumbles forward into the hall. She touches the fingertips of her right hand to her cheek and forehead as if seeking to stop the spinning and reaches with her left to the stair post. Her mother emerges from the kitchen in response to the sound of her entry as Laura steps onto the first tread of the stairs and then, the second, falling upwards towards the first floor of the little semi-detached house.

"Laura? Sweetheart?" a mother's questioning concern.

"No! Not now, mummy, not *now*!" she manages, though she cannot smother her sobs. Paula stands at the foot of the stairs watching her daughter struggle towards her room, remembering her own hopes and fears of twenty years of age. Without needing to hear the specifics of what has passed, she knows the source of the pain and knows that there is nothing she can do to offer comfort. Misery espouses solitude.

Laura enters her room, closes the door behind her with her own body weight and stands leaning against it. The folds of salty pain creep upwards, a rising tide from her heart to her head and back down to her soul. She slips to the floor, incapable of motion now, as dejection wraps itself about her. She sits sobbing, her head in her hands, her long blonde hair falling like a curtain to shroud what is, and should remain a very private hell. And here, she sits for… how long? An hour, perhaps? Certainly, it feels like all of that and more before she is ready to face her failure. Through the soft layers of her weeping rise the sharp peaks of memory. And though she is impaled on stakes of sorrow, Laura knows there is an act of contrition that must now be undertaken before it is too late, before her sin of failure renders her forever reprobate. She rises from the floor and makes her way to the window, stooping, shaking, as if she were closer to ninety years old than twenty. From the window ledge, she takes two items – a photograph and a book. These she carries to her bed; her single bed; her bed designed for one; her bed that states to all who enter the room, that this room is occupied by a child, awaiting the fulfilment of her purpose. She sinks to her knees by the side of the bed, and holds these items in front of her on the bedspread. The photograph is of a man of perhaps 25, tall, thin, with a receding hairline that predicts forthcoming premature balding. He is dressed in t-shirt and denim jeans. He stands with his arms folded, smiling, evidently for the camera. On the back of the photo, written in ink are the words 'Sunday 7th August 1994'. The book is a small, black bible (Why are bibles always black? What are they trying to hide?). Her head falls to the bed and her hair splays out, covering the bible and the photograph that she still holds in her hands.

"I'm so sorry," she whispers.

Is she praying, or is she talking to the man in the picture? If there is a difference, does she know it? "I'm so sorry, I let you down. Oh, Father… I don't know what to say. I wanted so much to do your will. I tried so hard to obey you and Pastor. All I ever wanted was to serve you; to love you. I have let you down, Father. Will you forgive me? Will you give me another chance? I promise I will do better. Please, Father, give me a sign of your forgiveness… that you still love me… that you will let me try again."

Laura does not leave her room again that evening, but falls asleep on the bed clutching these, her most prized possessions. Sometime during the night, she wakes for long enough to undress and slip between the sheets.

Then, with dawn reaching to her through the window she rises through the layers of sleep, examining her soul at each stage, remembering sorrowfully her sin of the day before. Now, reaching a full waking state, she stretches and is surprised to find herself more refreshed than she expected. She throws back the covers and rises. A little later, she will look back at the bed and see blood. She will not notice the slight, throbbing pain in her left hand. She will assume her period has started. She will be mistaken.

Henry

Rule Four:

The Arbiter will initiate the Game by establishing a bond with a Nominated Proxy.

MICHAEL FORESTER

I drove part way home and pulled over into a lay-by. There, I took the Talis-man out of my pocket and put him down on the passenger seat. He (Was it a him? I wasn't sure but that was how I was starting to think) looked up at me guiltily, like a dog that knew he had engendered his master's displeasure, without understanding the reason why. As I looked back at him, I noted that he was quite definitely bigger now – maybe twice the size of an egg.

"What am I going to do with you?" I asked, not knowing if I was talking to Talis-man or to myself. "I like that girl a lot; an awful lot. And she was all set to make today just about perfect for me – until you managed to screw it up, you little bugger." I didn't know if he had any comprehension of my words, but he certainly understood the tone of my voice. "You've done a very, very bad thing," I said, wagging my finger at him as if he were a small child, "and I certainly can't keep you if you're going to do this kind of damage," I continued, my anger growing by the moment. Talis-man started to shiver. Then, he dropped his spear onto the seat and jumped straight on to my left knee. My reaction was as much in shock as anger – I swiped him away with the back of my hand. He flew back over the gear lever and landed back on the passenger seat in more or less the position from which he had jumped. I recoiled slightly. I hadn't meant to hurt him – it was more a reflex action as anything else. But Talis-man, too, was shocked. As he picked himself up, he looked at me in disbelief, then, fell to his knees and began the deepest, most soulful wail I had ever heard in my life at a volume that was completely disproportionate to his size. His whole body shook and the tears fell rapidly from his eyes, making a noticeable damp patch on the seat. I groaned inwardly. What the hell was I supposed to do with this little creature that was, on the one hand, clearly bonding with me rapidly and on the other, already so devoted as to be causing disruption in my life? If I had focussed my attention inwardly at that moment, I might also have asked myself

42

what I was going to do about the connection that was beginning to form with Talis on my side. But at that moment my thoughts and emotions were outwardly addressed. I didn't think about my side of the bond at all. If I had, and I'd got rid of him at that moment, matters might possibly have worked out differently. But once we make a consequential choice, even if we are unaware at the time of its importance, nothing is ever the same again. We live with its effects forever.

Definitely aware that it was probably a bad decision, I picked Talis up and held him until he stopped weeping. "OK, OK," I said gently. "I didn't mean to hurt you. I'm not going to send you away." He looked up at me. The whites of his eyes were red. I looked down sympathetically. Then, I reached over to the passenger seat, picked up his spear between my thumb and forefinger and held it out to him. "Here you are," I said. "Take this." His face broke into a little half smile as he took the spear from me. Then, clutching it in one hand, he again threw both his little arms around my thumb in a gesture of complete devotion. With a sigh, I placed him back in my pocket and drove home. It was while I was actually driving that I had the sense that he was, once again, slightly bigger than before.

Monday 14th April 2008 8.00 am BST
Little had happened the following week. I'd scheduled it to be at home for studying, which was probably just as well, since our being confined to the house largely kept Talis out of trouble. He had been relatively well behaved, if a little inquisitive – I had needed to drag him out of the fish bowl several times where he seemed intent on playing with the fishes. He'd also developed a fascination with flushing the loo. He obviously enjoyed the sound of the cistern refilling and watching the water cascading down into the pan. But when my mother called up the stairs to me enquiring whether I had a waterworks problem, I had to put an end to his fun. He sulked a

bit, but otherwise, was unaffected. All the week, he refused every offer of food that I made to him, so that I eventually wondered if he needed to eat at all.

As regards Laura, I honestly didn't know what to do. Thanks to Talis, I'd completely and utterly screwed up the first opportunity to have full sex with her and given her every reason to think I'd rejected her once and for all. Did I let it go at that? Plenty of other Fish in the Sea? Well, not really. Irritatingly, the girl was on my mind and didn't seem inclined to get off it. I concluded in the end that the best thing was to give her a few days to calm down then send her an apologetic text that made absolutely no reference to Talis. This, I had started on Friday evening, followed by repeat exercises on Saturday and Sunday when the first had received no response. By Monday, I'd pretty much concluded that she wasn't up for a reconciliation – not just yet, anyway.

But come Monday, it was time for me to do some paid work again. Every university vacation, I had tried to gain employment in Matthis and Son PLC, known for its positive employment policies and relatively high wages. I'd consistently failed to get accepted until this vacation. This Easter was my last vacation before my final exams – 'Schools' as Oxford calls them – and it had been a major decision as to whether to spend the time studying or working. The former would undoubtedly have given me the chance of a better exam result. The latter would keep my student loan, parental loans and blood pressure slightly lower, as well as contributing to the all-important drinking fund. Laura and I had started working there together a couple of weeks back. Matthis had been really good about my 'booked holiday' last week, but now the reality of work returned.

I woke to the alarm in good time and sat up, immediately fully awake and looked down the bed to where Talis lay snoring. I had a decision to make. Would I try to get out of the house before he woke and leave him at home for the day or would I take a risk on taking him to work with me? There was danger either way. I knew that if I left him, he was capable of doing considerable damage and that mum would almost certainly see him. But if I took him with me, it was quite possible he would be disruptive. On balance, I thought it safer to take him. So, we went through the same bathroom ritual as the previous day and I donned the jacket, trousers and tie that were almost obligatory at Matthis. At least the presence of a jacket meant bigger pockets to keep the growing Talis in.

We took the train uneventfully from Brockenhurst to Southampton and from Southampton station walked the five minutes or so to Matthis' building where I swiped my card through the entry control point. I took the lift to the fourth floor and entered the office. I was one of a number of temporary staff who worked in Matthis' personnel office under the watchful eye of the departmental supervisor, Tracey, age circa 48.

Now, before going further, there are four matters I have to draw to your attention concerning Tracey. Firstly, Tracey is to intellectual achievement as HGV engine oil is to book-binding. Secondly, I wouldn't describe Tracey as overweight, exactly. It's just that to pass her in the corridor, one does not so much move to one side as enter into a high-altitude orbit. Thirdly, Tracey seems to hanker after the old Punk Rocker days of the 1980s – judging by her red Mohican haircut. Finally – and this is really, really important – Tracey likes men. Tracey particularly likes younger men. Tracey particularly likes younger, intellectually able men. Tracey particularly likes younger, intellectually able men who are undergraduates at Oxford University. And if the younger, intellectually able men who are Oxford undergraduates also happen to have Tracey as their supervisor *and* their names also happen to be Henry, then Matthis & Son should definitely, definitely, issue those younger men with a health and safety warning about Tracey.

You may ask why I'd continued to work at Matthis & Son given these somewhat challenging circumstances. The answer's quite simple really. I'm a penniless student. You can pluck us from the Job Centre more easily than you can pick bluebells in the Forest. This is a temporary job available in the vacation. They are about as plentiful as truffles. And it pays well. And that makes it unique. QED. Could I complain to the union or an employment tribunal about her? Tracey is also the Shop Steward, and runs the union's regional employment law training. Tracey never, ever does anything in public for which it would be possible to complain. So, I had decided to swallow hard, accept that I was going to get ogled and occasionally touched up. I also do everything open to me to ensure that I am never in a room alone with Tracey.

As I entered the office that Monday morning, I patted my jacket pocket to ensure that Talis was still there. I froze momentarily when I discovered he was not, but thawed almost as quickly on realising he had managed to move to my trouser pocket without my noticing. I wasn't greatly bothered. I should have been, but my attention was needed elsewhere. I swallowed hard in anticipation of being greeted by the delectable Tracey and walked into the office with a less than confident step. Two or three other student employees were standing by the coffee machine, postponing the inevitable attack on the filing pile. I was just about to join them when a voice accosted me from behind my left shoulder.

"Good morning Henry." Tracey was attempting to sound sultry. I was reminded of a squeaky wheel turning on sandpaper. "How was your break?"

I turned and smiled my best polite, non-inviting, non-misinterpretable smile at her. "Good morning, Tracey. It was fine, thank you," I lied, "and yours?"

She attempted a flutter of her eyelids and a sexy little shoulder shake. An image of vibrating refuse lorry parked itself in the top left-hand corner of my mental visual field and put on its handbrake.

"Not nearly as nice as it would have been with some lovely male company," she responded. The refuse lorry revved its engine.

"Yes… well… excuse me. I have to make a start."

"Don't worry about that just now, I have your appraisal forms to go through with you. Your ratings are very good – I don't think you're going to be disappointed." She was smiling broadly. Her voice speeded up a little. The refuse lorry's engine rose to two thousand revs and it started vibrating. "Let's go straight up to the staffroom. There'll be no one there at this time of the morning and we can talk quietly." Without waiting for my reply, she waddled out of the office and took the lift to the fifth floor. I considered my escape options. There weren't any. Houdini would never have established a reputation if he had had to work for Tracey.

I contemplated the empty staffroom over Tracey's shoulder with mounting concern. Matthis' philanthropic attitude to its staff had barely waned since its Victorian origins. The generously sized room was furnished with comfortable sofas but no single chair seating at all. Tracey motioned towards a sofa at the far end of the room, its back to the door. I walked the Green Mile. Eat your heart out, Percy Wetmore. Reluctantly, I sat – as far into the corner of the sofa as it was possible for me to get without disappearing into it. Tracey sat – as close to me as it was possible to get without disappearing into me.

"Well, Henry, isn't this nice." It was not a question. I nodded slowly; numbly. "I've wanted to talk to you for quite some time, Henry." Her earnest eyes fixed on me in a forlorn, almost pleading expression. Her hand nearest to me dropped from her lap to the tiny amount of space just between us and began stroking the fabric of the cushion with a disturbingly up and down motion. The refuse lorry's engine went up to three thousand revs and it began shaking. The next sentence came out at breakneck speed: "In fact, I should tell you that your performance ratings are very high and we don't really need to talk about them at all..." Then, she hesitated, momentarily unsure if she was playing this the right way. "The thing is, Henry... the thing is..." I think that at that moment, her confidence might have finally fled and I would have been free to leave but for the coincidence of two unfortunate events. The first was that Tracey's gaze dropped from my face in embarrassment, presumably in case I did not reciprocate the feelings she was about to declare. Regrettably, that event coincided with the precise moment that Talis, formerly motionless in the corner of my trouser pocket nearest my crotch, decided he was uncomfortable. In fairness, he really didn't move all that much; well, not at first. But in her desire not to look me in the eye it was enough of a motion to attract Tracey's attention; and more than enough of a motion to be misinterpreted. Tracey gasped. Tracey looked into my eyes with an expression of pure joy. Tracey looked back at my crotch. Talis stretched and applied his spear to my trouser pocket, presumably intent on getting into an even warmer spot between my testicles and penis. Tracey beamed like a new-birthed star. The refuse lorry's engine rose to six thousand revs. Its headlamps exploded. It began bouncing up and down on all four wheels.

My verbal response was as involuntary as my choice of words were unfortunate. "Oh fuck!" I groaned.

Regrettably, I realised how my aphorism might be interpreted only at precisely the same moment as Tracey screamed out, equally involuntarily, "Yes! Yes! Yes!" and threw herself across the whole three inches between us and into my arms. The refuse lorry blew all its remaining gaskets, leaked a big puddle of oil under its engine and collapsed on top of me.

"Tracey!! No!!! You've misunderstood," I said. Well, actually, it was more a case of trying to say it than actually getting the words out, you understand. If your respiratory system has ever been impeded by the presence upon your chest of a five-foot woman weighing at least nineteen stone whilst your voice was muffled by her size 46F breasts, you will know precisely what I mean. Predictably, Tracey was having none of it.

She took my face in her hands. "Oh Henry! I want you so much! (kiss, kiss) I've known who you really are since the first day you came to work at Matthis (kiss, kiss, kiss, kiss). Take me Henry, take me!" This last was said as she flung herself backwards to the opposite end of the couch, arms and legs spread wide open. I didn't have long to deliberate before Talis moved again, this time inside my pants. Tracey's eyes were on the movement in a moment. "Oh Henry! I just knew you wanted me tooooo! We've waited so long. Please, please, let me see him. I just know he's going to be wonderful."

She didn't wait for permission. Leaning forward, she brought her hands and her face right up in front of my crotch. In a movement that indicated considerable experience in such matters, she instantly had my button undone and my fly unzipped. Eagerly, she pulled the elastic of my pants forward and reached down inside. Her face took on a look of sheer ecstasy, as her fingers closed around… well, it certainly wasn't any part of me that they closed around. Tracey gradually began to withdraw her hand in order to feast her eyes upon her newly claimed prize. Talis emerged, between Tracey's fingers. Tracey gazed down longingly. Talis peered up and smiled – a big, broad, rotting teeth kind of smile. Tracey fainted and flopped backwards towards the other end of the sofa.

I had a number of choices at that moment. I could have cut and run – but I'm not a cut and run kind of guy. I'm more the feel-a-sense-of-responsibility-and-get-yourself-in-over-your-head kind of guy. So, I stuffed Talis into my jacket pocket, rushed over to the kitchen area and dampened a J-cloth to use as a cold compress. Then, I took the cloth and a glass of water back over to Tracey who was just beginning to stir. As I put the compress on her forehead and looked down anxiously, she opened her eyes.

"It was wonderful!" she blurted out. "You're so masterful. I've waited so long for this day. You'll never know how glad I am that I kept myself for you. It was hard, my love. Waiting all these years was so hard. But I promise no one else has ever touched me in all that time. I promise. I was ever only yours and I still am." Now, this misapprehension looked to me like quite a lucky escape and I wasn't about to inform her that no such act had taken place. That was the good news. "You're the only man I ever wanted. I love you with all my heart," she continued gushing. That was the bad news.

"Well," I said cautiously, not wishing to waste my advantage, "Love is a very serious matter, Tracey. I think we should go back to work now and reflect long and hard on what's just passed between us."

I only realised how misinterpretable were my words when she giggled. "Ohhhh! Yes, yes!" she replied, gushing with enthusiasm. "Let's get together again this evening to do some *long hard passing* again."

"Actually, Tracey," I replied, cutting her off, "I meant that we should each do some thinking *alone*."

Her face fell. "Oh. Well, yes, I suppose you're right." She paused. "So, when can I meet your mother?"

I groaned. Tracey was not getting the message. "Well, not just yet, I'm afraid. My parents are on safari in Kenya," I lied.

"Ooooh! So, I can visit you at home on your own then?"

"Errrr, well actually no, on account of my little brother. He's only 6 and I have to look after him in the evenings." It was the first time I'd invented a sibling, but under the circumstances, it was the best lie I could come up with.

"Oh, Henry!" she said, reverting to some kind of normal awareness. "You're such a wonderful man to take responsibility for your little brother. I just love children. What's his name? When can I meet him?"

I hesitated and looked out of the window for inspiration. Literally, the only item in my field of vision was a billboard containing a sexually charged advertisement for chocolate flake.

"His name... his name is... his name is er... er... Cadbury!" I blurted out, smiling hopefully.

"Cadbury?" she said in surprise.

"Err, yes, Cadbury." We're distant relatives of the chocolate manufacturing family and it's traditional for every generation to name one child with the old family surname," I continued. "And he's an invalid in a wheelchair... and... and... he doesn't like meeting people and... and... I should really get back to work now." And with that, I made a dash for freedom while she was still suffering the tactical disadvantage of being supine on the couch.

I reached the door and was out safely, with the sounds of "Noooo... Henreee... come back, Henreee. I want you again..." coming faintly to my ears as I took the stairs four at a time. I had just made it to the entrance foyer of the building when Tracey burst out of the lift, waving her ample knickers high above her head. "Henry! Henry! Come back, Henry. I want you Henry." I was fortunate enough to make it through the main entrance door and out to the relative safety of the street from where I sprinted towards the station, casting worried glances behind me from time to time. The sight of Tracey puffing determinedly up the street, waving her knickers high above her red Mohican hair, put me instantly in mind of a nineteenth-century battleship in full regalia trying to steam sedately up the Solent in severely choppy waters.

By the time I reached the station, I was exhausted. But God was good to me that day. The Brockenhurst train was on the platform, ready to pull out and I leapt onto it through the last open door. The guard's flag was down and we were pulling away towards the safety

51

of the New Forest just as Tracey appeared on the platform, wailing "Henreee…" as we disappeared down the westbound track. I knew that absenting myself during working hours without good medical evidence would be terminal to my casual employment at Matthis. However, there's a short list of things I simply will not do for money. In fact, come to think of it, there's really only one item on the list. It starts and ends with having sex with Tracey.

Tolly

Rule Ten:

Interaction between Proxies is a matter of free will. Players will do nothing to stimulate or retard it.

The father and daughter reunion in Shirley was, shall we say, a little muted. One of the very few sensible things Tolly had done on leaving home was to keep a key to her father's flat. So, quite simply, one afternoon in August 1978, she let herself back in and waited, feet up on the sofa, for Frank to return home. When he did, a man of deeds rather than words, Frank managed an "Oh. You're back," and a nod in Tolly's direction.

For her part, she reaffirmed that very special bond that exists between daughter and father with, "Got a fag, dad?" The intense joy of the reunion was sealed with his mumbling something inaudible and tossing her a single Players Number Six before heading off to the kitchen. He just had time to make a cuppa before having to leave for the regional Convenors' meeting.

Tolly stayed long enough to get his signature on her passport application.

And to receive the passport.

And to steal £207.48 in union subs that Frank had collected and kept in a teapot under his bed, ready to send to the branch when the total had climbed to £250.00

The flight to New York was uneventful.

Wednesday October 11ᵗʰ 1978 4.00 pm Eastern Standard Time
Tolly is standing on the sidewalk, shell-shocked.

The air hostess had been quick to recognise her immaturity and took a particular interest in looking after her. She admired Tolly's Mohican. Tolly liked that. Tolly liked the airhostess. And Tolly trusted her just a little. She told her she was going to New York to meet Sid Vicious. Had the air hostess heard of Sid Vicious? The air hostess glanced at Tolly's hair again, smiled and said she had. Tolly thought that when things were settled and she and Sid had a home together, then, maybe, at some point, she might like to become an air hostess too. But there again, that would mean being separated from Sid, and Tolly didn't want that. They were to be together forever.

As the flight nears its end, Tolly asks the air hostess how she might get from JFK to Sid's hotel. The air hostess doesn't actually know where he is staying, but says if she herself were looking for someone in downtown New York, she would take a yellow cab to Time Square and maybe find somewhere to stay first. Does Tolly have any money, the hostess asks? Yes, she does. Do her parents know she's doing this? Tolly does not answer. The hostess suggests she changes some of her English money into dollars to pay for the cab and whatever else she might need. Tolly smiles her thanks as she passes the hostess and makes her way down the aircraft steps. She does not see the hostess' worried look.

But Tolly takes her advice anyway, changes some money in the airport and asks the man behind the glass screen where she can catch a cab to somewhere called Time Square. The man looks at her hair, smiles an American smile and directs her to the cab rank.

So now, here she is on the sidewalk gawping at an astounding six lanes of traffic crawling past, complete with the vocal and car horn accompaniment that only New Yorkers can make.

Tolly doesn't know what to do now. For want of any better alternatives, she starts to walk. She walks a long, long way, turning randomly this way and that, until her small suitcase begins to feel very, very heavy and her feet begin to feel very, very sore. Tolly walks until her case is too heavy and her feet are too sore to walk any further. Are there benevolent gods in New York on 11th October 1978? Perhaps. For now, she finds herself outside a hotel on West 15th Street where, too tired to go any further, she spends some of her fast dwindling cash on a night in a tolerably private room and a bed more comfortable than the one she had grown used to in the squat in London.

Thursday 12ᵗʰ October 1978 3.00 pm Eastern Standard Time

She wakes late. Something to do with this 'jetlag' thing the woman in the seat next to her on the plane mentioned? The priority of the day is not ablutions, not food, not even fluids. Just one thing now dominates Tolly's waking mind and her sleeping mind: how to get to Sid.

How, Tolly? How will you find your beloved?

"Easy!" She replies with ignorant confidence. "He'll have left a message for me in the newspaper."

But which newspaper, Tolly?

She considers a moment. "All of them!" she replies defiantly, with the unwavering certainty of youth that assures her all will now be well. She makes her way out of the hotel, past the sleazy, suggestive grin of the counter clerk, looks to the left and looks to the right.

Which way Tolly? Which way to Sid?

She hesitates a moment and then replies triumphantly, "Neither!" She has seen a street newspaper vendor. Darling Sid or Dear Nancy will have arranged a message for her in the newspaper right outside her hotel of course! She takes some coins from her bag and examines them carefully; hands a coin – that she does not yet know to be a nickel – to the boy with the newspapers, hoping it is enough. He stares at her hair for a moment, then decides she is pretty despite it and gives her a long suggestive look. Finally, he holds out a copy of the paper, just out of her reach. She snatches it from his hand and runs back into the hotel. Sitting on the bed, she turns the pages excitedly… and… YES! Here it is! Darling Sid and Dear Nancy have arranged a message. It's a story about an altercation at a Pistols' gig. Christ, how she misses the gigs. The atmosphere… the music temporarily deafening her… the spitting… the "fuck yous" from crowd to stage and back again… and yes, the wonderful, unforgettable eye contact with her Darling Sid. But it's not long to wait now. Soon, she will be driven to the gigs in a limo. Tolly skips the part of the article about the police... the arrests... misses the superior critical tone. She is looking for... looking for... YES! YES! YES! Here it is. Sid and Nancy are staying at the Chelsea hotel. Good ol' Nancy! Still pretending to be Sid's lover to protect him from the fans. There is no gig tonight, so, obviously, they will be at the hotel. Tonight, she, Tolly Jones, will go to the hotel to be reunited with her one, true love, with her beloved, Sid. And this time, it will be forever.

Thursday 12th October 1978 10.45 pm Eastern Standard Time
So, this is it. At long, long last, this is it. All the planning, all the preparation, all the support from Dear Nancy, all the effort by Darling Sid culminates at this one focal point in space and time. Tolly stands outside the hotel, a little nervous, now that she is actually here. But she feels certain, Sid will have meant her to come before midnight. She realises nervously, that though he is undoubtedly waiting for her, she does not know which room he is in. Darling Sid! In all the confusion, he has forgotten a crucial detail. Her heart melts at the thought of how much he needs her to take care of the little details for him. No matter. Tolly will find a way to cross these last few yards to be with him. Be patient, Sid, Be patient for your beloved Tolly! So, she enters the hotel trying to look like someone who should be there and walks nervously up to the reception desk.

"'Scuse me," she says, sounding terribly English. She senses intuitively that she must be polite in an establishment in which official looking people stand behind highly polished chest-high desks wearing impeccable uniforms. "Which room is Sid Vicious staying in?"

The woman has her auburn hair tied back into a bun as severe as the industrially chilled smile she gives Tolly. "I'm sorry," she says in a soft New Jersey accent that Tolly thinks might be intended to be just a little patronising, "We don't release information concerning the hotel's guests under any circumstances." It takes years of professional training to be able to look this helpful, yet remain so condescending at the same time. "Is there anything else I can do for you at this time?" Tolly rather thinks the severe looking woman probably doesn't really want to do anything whatsoever for her, at this time or at any other time. Tolly thinks she probably wants her to turn around and disappear out through the revolving door as soon as humanly possible. So, she withdraws to the sidewalk, nursing a small but painful emotional bruise. But Tolly will not be daunted! Oh no! This is meant to be! True love will reunite her with her beloved Sid. She makes her way to the side of the hotel, to the service entrance. She holds a vague intention of asking a maid or a bell hop or some other person she might feel intuitively more comfortable with where she might find Darling Sid.

But Heaven itself is supporting Tolly tonight! She has no need of asking. Mr. Vicious' presence in the hotel is the talk of the chattering staff. As she secretes herself in the shadows outside the service entrance, a Bronx accent wafts through the door. A Queens accent replies. The room number is mentioned. She misses it. It is mentioned again. Yes! Now she has it! Tolly waits for the voices to fade and slips into the service entrance.

Checking the corridor quickly, she hears voices approaching and slips through the first open door she can find – a broom cupboard as it turns out. There, she waits in the darkness, afraid to come out until she is absolutely certain there is no one around.

Friday 13th October 1978 3.07 am Eastern Standard Time
Midnight glides on oil into 1.00 am, 2.00 am, until Tolly finally finds the courage to leave her sanctuary. She makes her way to the service elevator and presses the button. The door slides instantly

and soundlessly back. Can she get any more fortunate? This is SO meant to be. The gods are SO with her! God is with her! FATE is with her, rushing like a raging river to take her to her love. She presses the button for floor 7. The elevator rises; arrives; stops. Again, the door slides silently back. Tolly steps forward, stomach churning. Just a few more paces now. Where is the room? As it turns out, she can follow the voice. "Screw You!" reaches her ears. A woman's voice? Maybe… Nancy's voice? A welcome party? Yes! That's it!! They've mounted a surprise welcome party for her. Darling Sid and Dear Nancy, and who knows who else, are waiting for her, just a few final steps down the corridor. She'll not spoil their fun. She'll play along, just as if she hasn't guessed. Tolly creeps quietly along the corridor, following the sound of the voice. "C'mon you Shit! Wake up! Don't you fuckin' pass out on me now." A smile passes over Tolly's face. Has her beloved fallen asleep from the exhaustion of waiting for her? No matter. He must have had so much worry on her behalf all this time. But now they can be together and she can kiss away his tears. She is standing now, beside the door, which is slightly ajar. "Fuck you! Wake up!" But doesn't the voice sound angry? And it really is Dear Nancy's voice, isn't it? Whatever could be wrong? The sound of a slap. Tolly is confused. How does a slapping sound fit in with her welcome party? No matter. Tolly takes a deep breath, pushes hard on the door and strides in, a huge anticipatory smile spread across her face.

Tolly looks around the room.

Tolly's smile petrifies.

Tolly sees no streamers. No music. No funny hats. No welcome party.

Tolly sees two bodies on a bed.

A man; naked; supine.

A woman in bra and knickers pulled to one side astride him, trying to ride an erection that has collapsed with his consciousness.

Tolly does not see the Johnnie Walker bottle on the carpet by the bed.

Tolly does not see syringes on the bedside cabinet next to a hunting knife with a carved handle.

Tolly does not see the clothes strewn haplessly over a chair.

Tolly sees only Sid's face.

Until the woman hears her gasp and turns in her direction.

Then, Tolly sees Nancy's face.

Friday 13th October 1978 6.40 am Eastern Standard Time

There is a sound each city makes as it awakens, that is characteristic of that city alone. Of all the cities in the world New York's awakening cries are the most easily distinguished. The shallow will hear the accents of the deliverymen, the hiss of steam from the pavement grilles, the horns of the early shift Yellow Cabs. But beneath that, for those that have ears to hear, there is a substructure, a soul song of harmonies, its aria of passion and pain and of tears for the cold and the dying and the hungry and the loveless.

Of course, were I myself awakening after some hours spent curled up on the damp ground behind the trash cans in Greenwich Village, I might have as little concern for the city's soul song as Tolly has this morning. I might be more preoccupied firstly with the fact that I cannot straighten my stiff neck properly. Then I might be forced to consider how cold and wet I am. Then, I rather think I might begin to focus on the question of why I was here at all… and wasn't there something I was supposed to have done last night… and wasn't there somewhere I was supposed to have been? Then, I would probably remember a severe smile and a head of auburn hair tied up in an elaborate bun and a revolving door and a broom cupboard and a service lift. And then, I might very well remember a sight that would stay with me for the rest of my life – that of a trusted best friend attempting to steal from me, the only thing I care about in all of this world, by seducing my poor sleeping Darling, who knew nothing of the awful act of betrayal that was being perpetrated upon him. Then, I am sure that I would feel the anger rise within me again, resonating back to how it had risen within me in just the same way last night. Then, I would wish, I would truly wish, I had done more than simply run from the room as... I... think... I remember doing. In fact, I would be so consumed with anger and the memory of anger that I would wish that last night, I could have found a knife... a great... big... hunting knife with a jaguar carved into its handle. 'Cos if I could have found a great big hunting knife, I just know I'd have dragged that Yankee witchbitch into the bathroom by her bleach-blonde Yankee witchbitch hair and I'd have stabbed her with that great big hunting knife and I'd have pushed it right down til the jaguar carved on the handle was clawing into that betrayin' lyin' Yankee witchbitch's stomach and I'd have held onto it so tight that the Yankee witchbitch couldn't get it out of her betrayin' lyin' Yankee witchbitch stomach no matter how hard she tried. And I'd have looked into her eyes and seen how frightened she looked and I would have known how sorry she must have been for what she done to me and my Love and I'd have watched her Yankee witchbitch blood slip out of her stomach and down the blade of the great big hunting knife and onto the carved jaguar and onto my hands 'cos then, I know that I'd paid that Yankee witchbitch back just a little bit for what she done, so's she'd never do it to anyone no more no matter how long she lived. An' then, I'd let go of the great big hunting knife and watch the Yankee witchbitch fall to the floor with her hands around the handle and I'd not care whether she was alive or dead or neither or both and I just know I'd never forgive her for what she done to me no matter how much she pleaded with me and my Darling for forgiveness an' we'd never be friends with her again no matter how much she wanted to come an' visit with us an' we wouldn't come to the phone or come to the door or return her calls ever again no matter how much she was cryin' an' no matter how sorry she said she was ever again.

And then, all I would have wanted would have been to get the fuck out of there to just about anywhere to get away from the Yankee witchbitch and the scent of betrayal that I could still smell hanging over that room no matter how far or how fast I ran and then, I'd run and run and run and run – north, south, east or west, I wouldn't care, until I couldn't run any more and then, I'd find an alleyway without noticing I was somewhere called Greenwich Village 'cos all I'd care about would be to be anywhere but where the Yankee witchbitch was squirmin' an' groaning' an' bleedin' and dyin' all over the bathroom floor with the scent of betrayal still hangin' over the room and my poor dear Darling Sid still lyin' in the bed in whatever kind of drunken drug-filled stupor the Yankee witchbitch had tricked him into just to get him into bed and just to ride his poor sweet cock and just to take him away from me and just to… just to… just to…

And then, I would look down. And then, I would wonder why there was blood on my hands.

Friday 13th October 1978 6.40 pm Eastern Standard Time
Tolly has been walking today. Tolly has walked a long way. First, she needed to find something to clean her hands with. She finds some waste tissue in a dumpster at the back of a café (well she thinks it's a café – the place is called 'McDonald's') and when her hands are presentable, she goes into the café and asks for a cuppa.

Behind the counter the waitress in the funny hat looks at her strangely and says "Sawrie," but they don't serve 'cuppas' here. Would she like "cawfie, pecan pie?"

Tolly doesn't know what cawfiepecanpie is, but says yes anyway, and "Where is the Ladies please?" The waitress looks at her strangely again and asks did Tolly want the Restroom, 'cos if she did, it was outback and here was the key 'cos they couldn't leave it open or the bums an' the junkies would be in and out all day. Tolly nods and takes the key on the big key fob that the waitress offers her. And when she discovers that the restroom is in fact exactly what she had wanted, and when she has cleaned up, she returns to the seating area to eat her cawfiepecanpie. As she does so, and just as she is realising how hungry and thirsty she is, the news item on the TV in the corner catches her eye. She recognises the front of the hotel first. Then, she sees the flashing lights and the police cars and Darling Sid being led away in handcuffs.

And now, the monster rises up in front of her, and looks into her eyes and stares her down so that she wants to turn away but she cannot turn away and she wants to close her eyes but she cannot close her eyes and she wants to shut everything out but everything is unwilling to be shut out.

Nancy: Tolly gave her a good telling off last evening, didn't she? She warned her if she ever made a play for Sid again, Tolly would never forgive her and would stop being her friend immediately. And Tolly had left the hotel, right then, hadn't she? Just to give Nancy time to think about the situation and see how bad a friend she was being to Tolly. And as she was going out of the door, hadn't Tolly seen a great big hunting knife with the jaguar handle on the table? And hadn't she passed comment that Nancy should put it away before someone got hurt? And hadn't Nancy said that Tolly was right and that she would deal with it right away and that she promised to think about the things that Tolly had said? Tolly thinks long and hard now. Nancy... Nancy must have... picked up the knife... must have been more upset than Tolly had realised... must have gone into the bathroom... with the knife... must have somehow... fallen against the knife. Oh Christ! Poor Dear Nancy, Tolly's best friend, Tolly's only really true friend ever *must have fallen to the floor and onto the knife* and with Tolly gone and with Sid asleep from exhaustion she would have called and called and called for help and no one would have come. And Tolly is so sorry now for leaving her best friend and Tolly is crying now and Tolly is wondering now, how Darling Sid could ever have been held responsible for what was clearly a tragic accident and Tolly is so afraid, now that it might be quite some time before she and Sid can be together again.

Thursday 1st February 1979 8.50 pm Eastern Standard Time
We've all cried, haven't we? We all know what it is to cry until there are no more tears, Ethereals and Tangibles, there's no difference when it comes to tears. And we all know that when the tears have finally discharged we feel better, even when we do not want to feel better. Now, some four months later, Tolly has finished crying and feels better even though she would rather not feel better. Now, she knows there is nothing she can do right here and right now in New York City to help Darling Sid who continues to languish under the unjust accusation of a crime he did not commit. And as Tolly considers the matter over and over, she realises that Darling Sid would want her to go home to England now, to be safe with her loving family. She counts the remaining money she has, the money that her dear father so selflessly pressed upon her when she last saw him, and feels true love for him once again. The merciful gods are still with Tolly. She has sufficient money for one of those Yellow Cabs back to the airport and for the flight home. Perhaps the same air hostess will be on the flight. If she is, Tolly will tell her about the terrible accident that has befallen her very dear and closest friend and how through a terrible misunderstanding, her Darling Sid has been suspected of being responsible in some way of some minor carelessness that contributed to the accident. And while she is explaining all this to a rather confused air hostess, Tolly, being in

mid-air, will miss the newsreels that would have disclosed to her that Sid has been released on bail and that while on bail his mother has supplied him with sufficient heroin to end his own life. But not before he manages to write a poem to his lover; a poem that Tolly will come to treasure all her life, a poem that Tolly knows proves beyond a shadow of a doubt that Darling Sid was thinking of her, Tolly, right up to the very end; a poem that starts:

You were my little baby girl…
But now you're gone
There's only pain…

When Tolly lands, she will feel a little uneasy about the possibility of returning to Shirley and her father's flat. Though she knows how her father would welcome her with open arms and fatherly love, she feels she needs some time to work out what to do next in order to help Darling Sid best. Tolly is good at thinking. She is certain that she can resolve the predicament if only she has long enough to think about it.

It is when she arrives at Heathrow and walks through into the arrivals hall that she learns from the headline of the Evening Standard that not everything is as she anticipated it would be for Sid and the future they have planned together. So, Tolly cries again. Tolly is good at crying. And it takes a long, long time before those tears have discharged. And when they have, Tolly does not feel even a little bit better.

Thursday 8th February 1979 7.00 pm GMT
Tolly has returned to the Squat and found it to be full of people she does not know and who are ill-disposed to make space for her. She has tried her luck at the café in case she can catch the eye of the bald homo and touch him for a few quid, but he has not been there any time she

67

has checked. She has tried her luck on the streets some more and now, with Darling Sid finally gone, she does not feel quite the same about the access limits she previously placed on her body. And because she is willing to sell a higher priced commodity, quite naturally, she can expect to be paid more. Well done, Tolly, you have become well versed in the rudiments of commerce, if not the very principles of capitalism themselves. Surely, Karl Marx and Frank would both approve of this considered evaluation of the ways of the enemy.

Consequently, Tolly has found that it has been possible for her to put aside just a little money. Not a fortune, you understand, but enough to pay the rent on a room with a real bed and real sheets and enough to buy (though she did have to think about this extremely carefully) one of those new portable colour TVs. But then, now that Darling Sid is on the Other Side, Tolly knows that the easiest means for him to communicate with her is through the hiss and static of the un-tuned TV. So, she now spends her evenings and nights "trading in the market" as she likes to think of it, and her days alternately watching the BBC news and detuning the TV in order to listen for messages from Sid. It is on one of those days, when she has been listening to the news most closely, that she learns that Sid's mother, Anne, is returning to Heathrow with her beloved's ashes. Tolly becomes most attentive. Excitedly, she de-tunes the TV to await any message that Sid might now wish to send.

Tolly listens. Tolly listens harder to the static than she has ever listened before. But there is still nothing. Tolly feels disappointment – an emotion to which she is no stranger. But wait… is she mistaken or… is that a pattern she can see on the screen?… the outline of a man's head and shoulders?… an outline of Darling Sid's head and shoulders? Yes!! Yes, yes, yes!!! She is sure now. Why on earth hasn't she seen it before? "Oh, Darling, Darling Sid, Tolly is so sorry she's not seen until now what you've been trying so hard to show her for all this time! But now, yes, she has it. Darling Sid's mother is bringing the ashes back to Heathrow for Tolly! Tolly is to meet her at the airport to take custody of Darling Sid and to look after him for all time. This is how Darling Sid has determined they can still be together – through the static and through the ashes. Darling, Darling Sid is so very, very clever. Tolly is humbled and feels deeply privileged that one so inestimably high has stooped to love her.

Friday 9th February 1979 10.15 am GMT

So, here is Tolly at Heathrow, standing outside the First Class arrivals lounge. She staked her claim to this piece of space early this morning, determined that nothing will impede the historical handover of the ashes. Since she arrived, the photographers have been gathering and now, there is minimal elbowroom since the flight has landed and Anne is clearing customs. The photographers try to push Tolly out of the way but she is having none of it. Tolly is a veteran of innumerable gigs where cohorts of screaming fans vie for space at a barrier. Heathrow is nothing to her by comparison and any reporter who gets too close finds himself nursing sore feet or ribs or jaw, very quickly indeed. But no more distractions please, because the doors are opening and… yes! Here comes Anne. Tolly steps forward. The photographers surge forward. Tolly holds out her hands to Anne. But there is no recognition. Anne shrinks back… draws the urn closer to her breast. Is there some misunderstanding? But Tolly has no time for explanations. She will justify her actions later if called upon to do so. For now, though, only the urn matters, only that she should take Darling Sid home with her where they can be together forever. With determination, Tolly reaches forward for the urn and grabs hold of one of its handles. With equal determination, Anne holds fast to the other handle. The photographers jostle… flashbulbs pop. Tolly tugs hard. Anne tugs hard. There is a cracking sound. The urn splits and the contents are flung, not down to the floor but upwards, high upwards to the air conditioning vent and are blown by the rush of air far across the room. Tolly and Anne stand back from each other, each looking upwards, each oblivious to the presence of the other travellers, the photographers, the airport staff. Darling Sid wafts gently through the air, like a celestial snow cloud, like a troupe of pantomime fairies (yes, children, you *Do Believe*, don't you? You simply *Must Believe* or Darling Sid will die!), some parts of him rising, some falling, most sucked directly back into the air conditioning system.

Before Anne has time to gather her thoughts, Tolly is gone. This is her moment. She will not be cheated of a future with Darling Sid. She has noted the presence of a janitorial door in the corner of the arrival hall. She must save Darling Sid now or never. Tolly passes swiftly through the door. Immediately on the other side, she finds herself standing in front of an airport employee. Brown coat, mop and bucket suggest he is a cleaner. Tolly will never know his name is Arnold Frobisher. Arnold himself does not know he is a fourth-generation descendant of the illegitimate offspring of a Viscount. He will never know that if he were to trace that lineage back, it would reach to recorded unparalleled acts of bravery under Henry V at Agincourt.

"Quickly!" Tolly hisses at the surprised janitor. "Wanna fuck?"

Arnold does not know how to respond. Rarely in his fifty-nine and a half years have such offers been made to him. He slides his hand over his bald pate, an unconscious gesture that he will never know is exhibited even to this day by most male members of the family, including the titled ones. He will never know that were he to do this in the correct office of the correct probate solicitor, he would probably, even now, be able to assert ownership over a material proportion of a long unclaimed inheritance. All this, Arnold will never know. But he does know he is standing in front of an opportunity of a lifetime.

"Well do ya?" Tolly is impatient. She knows she does not have long. Arnold nods his head vigorously. "Then go get me the dust from the air conditioning vent," Tolly hisses and for good measure lifts her skirt to reveal an absence of under garments and a God-gifted allocation of pubic hair that would not have shamed a Yeti.

Arnold's feet are spot-welded to the floor. His eyes are just as firmly attached to Tolly's crotch. "Go, Go!" Tolly hisses. "Get me the dust first. Then you can have anything you want."

Arnold shakes himself free of his supernatural cohesions and reluctantly removes himself from the spot in the general direction of Tolly's flapping hands. His biggest problem is now that he does not know where the air conditioning system's dust filters are located. But in the tradition of his bellicose ancestors, he is a quick thinker. He realises that what he does know is where the vacuum cleaners are stored and that they have dust bags. If this lady wants dust so badly and offers so much in return, then Arnold is not one to assess the extent of dental decay in the oral cavity of such an enviable gifted equine.

He disappears momentarily, to return with a brown dust bag, almost full, and hands it to Tolly. He cannot help but lower his eyes to the general area of the Promised Land a little below her waist. But Tolly has no time now. She has what she needs. Tolly has lied. She will not be granting anyone Nirvana between her legs today, least of all Arnold Frobisher. In a manner as treacherous as that of the French in hand-to-hand combat upon St. Crispin's day 1415, she pushes him roughly aside and makes her escape with what she is certain is a meaningful amount of Darling Sid.

Arnold has learned something new about life today. We might even be inclined to say the day has gentled his condition. Tonight, as he thinks back over the day's events, perhaps he will hold his manhood cheap. Or maybe, there again, he will just hold his manhood tight as he dreams of what might have been.

Tolly is literally flush with elation and success. She celebrates by taking a taxi back to her room. She does not notice the taxi driver looking at her in the mirror as she hugs the bag of Darling Sid to her breast and softy sings "God Save the Queen" – Sex Pistols' version – to him. For this is all perfectly normal, all quite understandable, is it not?

Tolly arrives at her room, locks the door behind her and drops, exhausted, onto the bed. And now, there begins a cleansing ritual which will in due course become refined into an annual celebration. For she must cleanse her body from all the defilement she has permitted to be perpetrated upon her. She must prepare herself for what she now knows to be inevitable: the bodily return of Sid Vicious. And on his return, her body must be perfect for him again. To this end, Sid himself will assist in cleansing her. Tolly knows *exactly* how Darling Sid will help her to purify herself for him. And when he deems her ready, he will appear.

Monday 17th March 2008 5.45 pm GMT

As Tolly enters the flat, we might be anticipating some variation on the theme we saw yesterday – weeping, anger, stuffing herself silly – that sort of thing. But what's this? There's a spring in her step. She pushes the door open rather more energetically than we might expect and it bounces back against the wall. The mirror cowers, rocking back and forth in terror. Tolly positively saunters in and drops her two carrier bags in the hall, then heads straight into the bathroom.

She leans forward towards the mirror, eyes shining, lifts her finger and points it directly at her reflection. The reflection backs off a bit, but still has the presence to lift her finger towards Tracey in a broadly similar manner.

"Right!" she says in an uncharacteristically confident tone. "Tracey Boudicca Tolpuddle Jones! Grieve for Sid no more. You've done it, girl!" The reflection looks confused. "You've done it," she says more emphatically. "He's back!"

Henry

Rule Sixteen:

In all other matters, the decision of the Arbiter is final.

During the fifteen-minute train journey home I received no less than 30 texts from Tracey. Though I had no intention of responding to any of them nor ever phoning her, I thought it prudent to enter her number into my phone's memory. That way, I would at least have some advance warning when she tried to get in touch again, as she inevitably would. I contemplated my next move. There was now really nothing to keep me in Brockenhurst, and judging by the events so far, it would only be a matter of time before Talis began to cause me difficulty at home. I decided to return to Oxford a few days early. That night, I packed my bag and mumbled something to mum about needing the extra study time as Schools were fast approaching. She was fully understanding and simply ruffled my hair and mumbled back "poor baby" in that infuriating way parents have when they've simply failed to recognise that you've grown up.

Tuesday 15th April 2008 9.08 am BST

I was out of the house early the next morning and down at the ticket office at the station in good time for the 9.08 am train to Oxford. Talis? He was his usual energetic self, snoozing peacefully away in my pocket. I paid for my ticket and slipped it into the same pocket. Bad decision, but old habits die hard. Inevitably, about twenty minutes into the journey the guard came round. You'll not be surprised to hear that I reached innocently into my pocket, to retrieve the ticket, naive creature that I am, only to find that Talis had decided that, if shredded, it would make an extremely comfortable pillow. I brought it out a piece at a time, to a series of objecting squeals from my pocket and a malevolent stare from the balding, bespectacled guard. I smiled up at him in what I hoped was a placatory manner. "I'm sorry about this," I found myself saying, "but look, you can just see the date on this piece here, and this other piece has got 'Brockenhurst' on it... and oh, look, you can just see the 'Ox' of Oxford on this last piece here." The malevolent stare continued long and hard over the horn-rimmed spectacles without verbal comment. How is that people in authority all manage to look exactly like my old headmaster about to administer punishment unspeakable for some small childhood misdemeanour?

"Well... that is..." I continued, "how about I stick it back together while you're checking everyone else's? I promise it will be readable before we get to Oxford." I watched his blue uniform and shaking head disappear silently down the carriage. I applied myself during the rest of the journey to reassembling, as best I could, the remains of the ticket. I counted 47 pieces in all. I will be making a small but heartfelt donation to the Sellotape Plc Benevolent fund.

On arrival at Oxford railway station, I was sorely tempted to leave Talis behind on the train. But I am not a cruel man and some overblown sense of obligation caused me to pat my pocket gently as I alighted, to reassure myself that he was still with me. The sense of obligation was directed at least as much to the unfortunate souls on whom he would wreak undoubted havoc if abandoned, as it was to Talis himself.

We walked the mile or so from the railway station to the little alleyway that runs down between the Sheldonian Theatre and Blackwell's Art Shop. It's a quiet spot. For some reason, the tourists all seem to manage to miss it. This unnamed little walkway opens onto a cobbled square called Nazarene Place, where, if you are so minded, you will find the understated portals of St. Joseph's, the smallest and least significant college in Oxford. I made my way past the Porter's Lodge and on into the quad where my room lay off staircase three. I climbed to the first floor and opened my door, then pulled it closed behind me, throwing the holdall onto the floor by the wardrobe. Then, I took Talis out of my pocket and set him down on the bedside cabinet. Looking at him sternly, I said, "Don't move," in what I hoped was an emphatic tone, pointing my finger at him. He looked up at me quizzically and shook his head. Then, I flopped down on the bed and settled into a deep sleep. Awaking at just after four in the afternoon, I discovered that Talis had not heeded the instruction.

"Where have you got to now, you little bugger?" I asked no one in particular. Searching the room produced no Talis but it did indicate his means of escape. The catch on my sash window had never worked properly, and the little creature was clearly stronger than he looked. The lower frame was raised up about twenty centimetres and wedged open with my netbook. I lifted the window slightly and gingerly removed it, taking care to ensure it didn't fall to the ground below. Funds would definitely not stretch to a replacement if it were broken. Then, I lifted the window and leaned out to see if I could detect where he had gone. There was no need to call Inspector Morse. Immediately beneath the window, a large wisteria covered the whole of the area of wall between my window and the window of the next room along. Talis was swinging gleefully on one of the longer strands of the plant in a plausible imitation of Tarzan. This in itself would not necessarily have been a problem, if it were not for the fact that approaching rapidly from around the corner was the college Master and a small group of what appeared to be dignitaries undertaking a tour of the college.

"You sod!" I said under my breath. I meant Talis, not the Master of course. But I had little time available before the Master and his guests reached the wisteria, when who knows what might happen. I tore out of my room and down the stairs, arriving at the wisteria seconds before the Master and his guests arrived. It was only then I realised that Talis was swinging just out of my reach. I leapt up several times straining to grab him. Each time, Talis managed to evade my grasp. Finally, I caught his webbed foot and we both tumbled to earth. I let out a cry of triumph – "Got you, you little bugger," – just as the Master and his party rounded the corner to see me sprawled on the ground holding Talis in a rugby tackle grip. The Master looked down questioningly. I looked up imploringly. Talis tried to let out a cry. Mercifully, it was muffled by the weight of my body on top of him.

"Ah, Tallison," said the Master. "Good to see you practising for the college first XV. But you're going to need more than a mustard-coloured cushion to practise on if you're to qualify. Still, carry on." And with that, he stepped straight over me and Talis, followed by his party, each of which stared down disdainfully at me in turn, as both metaphorically and literally, they passed over me. Without a word, I stood up and, clutching Talis under my arm, mounted the stairs back up to my room.

Entering the room, I bolted the door firmly behind me and placed Talis on one of the chairs by the fireplace as I sat in the other. I looked at him long and hard. Talis looked back enquiringly, innocently. I said, "Can we just get clear over something here, please? He did use the word *cushion*, didn't he?"

Talis' expression turned to sadness. A large tear built up in his left eye, then rolled down his face nonchalantly. Mournfully, he nodded.

"A cushion?" I asked again.

Talis nodded again.

"So... he didn't see you... ebony-coloured creature, stubby nose, small webbed feet, rotting teeth?"

He shook his head, the tears welling up faster in his eyes.

I looked at him without speaking for a full minute... "You are there, aren't you?" I finally asked him. "Please tell me I haven't hallucinated you for the last four days. Everything I believe in depends on you not being an hallucination."

Talis' tears stopped. He looked at me quizzically. Then, he put down his spear and stood up on my lap, balancing quite competently on his small webbed feet. He ran his left hand down his right arm. Then, he ran his right hand down his left arm. Then, he patted both thighs with both hands simultaneously. Then, he sat down and examined each foot in turn, paying particular attention to the webbing between his toes. Then, he looked back at me, smiled his wide smile, and, nodding vigorously, gave me a thumbs-up.

But somehow, he wasn't in the least bit amusing. I took him onto my lap and sat there cradling him for the rest of the afternoon and on into the darkening evening.

Philemon

Rule Eight:

Players will undertake play through Nominated Proxies and other Tangibles only. Any player who compromises this rule will account to the Game Maker for their conduct.

Sunday 28ᵗʰ September 2008 8.17 pm BST

"I want so much for you to see what I am seeing now. With aaaall my heart, I want you **to** know what it means to be in the *arms* of the Risen Saaaaviour."

The short man is standing at the front of a darkened auditorium, capacity 5,224 (fire regulations forced the number down from the planned 5,500). Every seat is taken. The height of the room, somewhere way above in the darkness, creates cathedral echoes. Surely, God is in this place. The podium on which he stands is built across almost the full width of the room, little short of a hundred metres wide, leaving a narrow gap at floor level only to enter each of the doors that stand at either side of the stage.

His shoulders are hunched. He holds his hands closely together in a gesture of intense supplication. His eyes close momentarily, almost as if he is in pain, and the words come slowly, emphatically, each carefully weighed. Leaning slightly forward now, his mouth almost touches the microphone. Eyes still closed and brow deeply furrowed, those mesmerising hands swing gently forward and back in time, emphasising each word. "If *only* your heart could be *warmed*… if only your eyes could be *opened* to see the *Light* of *Heaven* that shines beyond the brightest morning sun." Now, his head rises and with it his voice until he is almost shouting. "The Morning Star of **HIS LOVE** that shines into the darkness of **YOUR SIN**."

He leaves a moment's silence to let the meaning of the words sink in. Then, the voice returns, but softer this time, impossible to ignore. "But *oh*, my dear one, you can *not*. Your heart is *stone*. Your eyes are *blind* and it is *so, so cold* where you are now, in the infinity of your *dark, sinful night*." The voice drops still lower and he is almost whispering into the microphone. "My dear, dear child, can you not *see* that you are separated from the Risen One, from the Bleeding Lamb of God by a *chasm*?" A little louder now. "A chasm of darkness that is *your sin*?" He leans across the lectern and reaches his right arm forward, index finger raised, knowing that this almost-point will be taken by many to mean he is addressing them individually. It is for the same reason that he speaks only in the singular. "*You!*" His voice stops as his raised finger passes from left to right, almost-pointing across the whole width of the auditorium. "You stand upon one side of this **great, deep chasm**, yearning, hungering, desperate to be warmed by the Sunshine of his Love. *Oh, my child!* You are so **hungry**. You are so **cold**. You are so **alone**. See how you shiver, my dear one!" His voice is almost pleading now. "And yet, beloved, The Bleeding Saviour stands upon the other side of the chasm of *your sin*, arms open, welcoming you with his *everlasting love*, waiting for that day, that wonderful day when you will see the bridge that he has laid down across the great gulf that separates you from him." Again, he whispers, sensing he has broken through. He has them now. "Can you see this bridge, beloved one?"

There is a second lectern towards the left of the podium. As the sermon approaches its climax, slowly, almost imperceptibly, a back light begins to rise upon a figure standing silently behind it. If they were not transfixed by the hypnotic voice, by the inescapable terror he preaches, they would gradually be able to discern the silhouette of a woman in a long dress and headscarf.

"You say to me, 'No, Pastor, I see only an old wooden cross, and I cannot trust that it will **bear** my **weight**. The chasm of my sin is so **deep**, Pastor, and I am so weighed down with such **burdens**. What if this burden I bear should make the old wooden cross crack while I am crossing over to the Saviour? What if it should **break** and I should *fall* into **that deep dark chasm**? What will happen to me, Pastor? What will befall me if I should fall *into the darkness*?'"

He pauses again, presses his hands together in front of mouth in his trademark gesture of prayer, waits as his words take effect. He can feel the Energy (some would say of the Holy Spirit) rippling back over the rows of the folding chairs before him in the darkness; listens for the tiny sounds of restlessness as the Burdened move uncomfortably and shuffle under the weight of their sin. He gives them a moment longer to contemplate their fate (carefully unspecified) should they be unfortunate enough to fall into his deep dark chasm. He will let them suffer a little more before he calls them Home. For is it not essential that Sinners confront their damnation face to face, that it stare them down into the abject terror of utter misery in order that they properly understand the inescapable necessity of Salvation? It is as if he knows, knows with a conviction that makes discussion irrelevant, that there is but one hope for them. And it is his task, his God-inspired vocation, to offer it to them.

As the backlight continues to rise behind the woman, a second spotlight, tinted yellow, now also begins to illuminate her from the distant ceiling with a halo effect reminiscent of sunshine. She looks young, but there is not enough light yet to enable an accurate estimation of her age. She has long, straight hair cascading down onto her shoulders from under an emerald-green headscarf. Her hands are held together in front of her. Her eyes are closed and her lips are moving silently. Looking at her brings to mind… who? Mother Theresa? Joan of Arc? Maybe… but perhaps… someone more spiritual; someone still closer to God than any of the female saints whose images they have grown up with.

He turns in the only direction that they can face if they seek Salvation. His head rises. His eyes face heaven. His arms reach up and out as far as he can stretch them. "*Ohhh, Jay-sus*! Will you *save* these sinners, Lord?" (His change to the plural at this point is, of course, quite deliberate.) He pleads as if to change the mind of an immutable God and cause Him to redeem the irredeemable. "*Ohhh, Jay-sus*! Will you hold that wooden cross steady as these dear ones traverse the chasm of their sin to reach your love? Will you bear them up, Lord, as they walk to you upon *Your Cross*, as they trust you to bear them to the *Heaven of your presence*?"

Without turning, he gestures, almost imperceptibly, to his left. An organ begins to play softly. In his mind, he repeats the old familiar words to the hymn tune as it plays:

Just as I am, without one plea,
But that thy blood was shed for me.

The warm yellow spotlight illuminating the young woman is fully brightened now. She is indeed very young – nineteen? twenty? Those in advantageous positions towards the front (and some have queued for these seats since before dawn), if they are observant enough, might be able to tell that the woman is showing by posture the signs of second trimester pregnancy. And now, of course, it is clear who it is she puts them in mind of. There is a whisper, almost an incantation from the congregation. "Blessed is she among women"

"Come, dear ones," the Pastor whispers softly into the microphone. "Come and be blessed by the Lord's Handmaiden. Come, let Sister Serenity mark you with the Blood of the Lamb, so that on that great day when *He* is brought forth among us again, He may welcome you into His kingdom. Come, let the Lord's Favoured *touch* you, that when He leads the righteous to Heaven He will know *you* by *your* touch. Come, beloved. There is no other way."

They are rising from their seats now, reaching their arms towards heaven, weeping, weeping uncontrollably for their Sin and for their Separation and for their Degradation and for their Damnation. At the ends of the rows where there is space, the most deeply affected begin to fall to the floor and to crawl towards the front, weeping, weeping, pouring out their pain in the tears.

And that Thou bid st me come to Thee,
O Lamb of God, I come, I come.

Pastor Littlemann nods to the young ushers on his left who stand aside to let the wheelchairs forward. And now, finally, he looks across the podium for the first time to make eye contact with the young woman. He nods to her. She lifts her left hand out in front of her and begins to unravel a bandage, wincing in obvious pain, and passes it to an assistant standing next to her who kisses it and places it on a maroon cushion. The innermost folds of the cloth are facing upwards and are stained red. Ushers stand positioned so as to guide the repentant and the halt in a single line towards her. The first approaches, wheeling himself forward in his chair with evident difficulty. He looks up into Serenity's face to her closed eyes, her soundless, moving lips. She senses the presence in front of her and reaches out her hand. As the young man reaches for it and presses her palm eagerly to his lips, he sees, for the first time, that the rumour is true. A hole perhaps the diameter of a pen, or a drill bit, or maybe of a large, rough-cut iron nail, penetrates from her palm to the back of her hand. Though it is not bleeding profusely, its issue is sufficient to mark any surface upon which it is pressed – if the pain of pressure can be borne, of course. And as the wheelchair-bound man presses her palm to his lips, Serenity shudders in pain. She slowly withdraws her hand, leaving a smear of red across his face. He seeks eye contact, recognition. But her eyes are closed in prayer and her lips continue to move soundlessly. The usher touches his shoulder and he wheels himself away, the tears flow down his cheeks, whether from disappointment of remaining unable to rise from his chair, or whether from having been touched by the Handmaiden of the Returning Saviour, we do not know. Or perhaps, as some would be inclined to think, it is simply part of the mass hysteria Philemon Littlemann has whipped up over the last hour and a half. As the wheelchair reaches the end of the open area beneath the pulpit, another usher holds out a fluorescent orange collecting bucket. The colour is reminiscent of B&Q... Orange Mobile Phones... Easyjet. The wheelchair-bound man drops into the bucket a bundle of notes held together in an elastic band.

Sister Serenity turns to the next in the line, a young man who has approached her on his knees. He reaches in evident anxiety for the stigmatum. As he presses her palm to his cheek she winces again. Not from the pain, which is starting to numb a little, but from the movement of the *SecondCome* Christ child she is carrying inside herself.

Sunday 28th September 2008 11.52 pm BST

The Pastor is standing inside the locked group of rooms right at the front of the auditorium and behind the podium. All are banished from this Holiest Inner Sanctum, save only the Pastor himself and Sister Serenity. Some of the members of the Church of the Body of Christ hold that this area is sanctified and that it contains the re-discovered Arc of the Covenant. Others say that angels have borne the cross-piece of the Cross of FirstCome itself from heaven to place it in the Pastor's care awaiting *SecondCome*. Some and Others are both wrong.

The building is dark and silent, save for this one room. Serenity has fetched herself a folding chair from the front row of the auditorium and is sitting with her head lain on her arms upon a trestle table in front of her. Her emerald-green headscarf has fallen from her head and her long blonde hair cascades over her shoulders and over the table. Exhausted, she drifts in and out of a light sleep. The Pastor glances at her disapprovingly. He is unshakable in his opinion that a woman's Glory should at all times be covered. He makes a mental note to remind Serenity of this most important Truth when he has finished the prioritised task of the evening.

Methodically, working as if he were alone, he counts the contents of each of the eighteen orange buckets, gathering the notes into appropriate bundles and throwing the coins into a sorter which totals and stacks them. It is well past midnight when this demanding task of spiritual intersession is complete.

"£16,246.77," he whispers under his breath. Then, he leans towards the sleeping young woman, grabs her bandaged hand hard and snaps, "Serenity!" She sits bolt upright, confused by this wrenching awakening and the pain in her hand. "Sixteen thousand! It's not fucking good enough! You're going to have to do better."

"Yes, Pastor," she manages as she shakes off sleep, "I'm sorry, Pastor. I was so tired tonight. I will do better tomorrow. There will be healings tomorrow. You'll have healings. I promise." Inside her uterus, she feels the kick and knows that *SecondCome* is confirming the Pastor's reprimand.

Tolly

Rule Twelve:

The free will of Nominated Proxies may be influenced but never withdrawn.

Monday 17th March 2008 5.55 pm GMT

Don't laugh! Don't you dare laugh at Tolly's names! Tolly had enough derision over them at school without you adding your puerile mirth, thank you very much. Pathetic, immature bitches, mocked her for her names. They're perfectly understandable names when you realise where they came from. Tolly's mother wanted to bless her with the name of a strong feminist leader from English history and Boudicca was the perfect choice. Her father wanted her to bear proudly a name that would remind her and everyone around her of the sacrifices that generations of workers had made on her behalf without ever knowing who she would be. Tracey? Well, Tracey was a concession to the way the rest of the world organised itself and gave her a backup should she ever need to be more restrained about the names her parents preferred for her.

Through childhood and adolescence, Tolly bore her names with profound pride, the diminutive "Tolly" being settled upon as an intimate family familiar term. But the events that took place in New York in 1978 proved to be so consequential, so momentous, that Tolly began to feel her age and her separation from the life she had lived hitherto. After much consideration, she decided to revert to her back-up name, Tracey. It was under this name that she moved forward into adult life, taking on her father's predilection for union matters and her mother's eye for spotting quality antique furniture, then ultimately, joining her father's company, Matthis & Son, as a part-time union convenor. Tracey knew in her heart that Darling Sid loved her for herself. Her name was unimportant to him.

So, now, we return as she busies herself in the little flat in Shirley, Southampton. Tracey Boudicca Tolpuddle Jones has much to do given that she has just witnessed Darling Sid's return to her. There are salads to be prepared (but perhaps not eaten), exercises to be undertaken (she really, really does have to strengthen those pelvic floor muscles, she knows she does), new shades of lipstick to be tried (all subtle variations of black, of course). And then, there is that unutterably important box on top of the wardrobe; the one in which she keeps her most treasured possessions; the one that comes down each year on the evening of 1st February and that stays down until the early hours of 2nd February. Thus, at 7.00 pm precisely on each 1st February, she balances precariously on the kitchen stool, gently lifts the box down and blows off a year's worth of dust before opening it carefully on her double bed. She is careful to place it towards the edge of the bed, so as to avoid the enormous indentation in the centre. Each year, for the last 29 years, with racing heart, she has gently eased back the tissue paper to behold the contents of the box in all their glory. Each year, she has stood and gazed in reverential awe before reaching forward and drawing from the box the bin bag and safety pins she was wearing the night the Pistols first came to Southampton; that night when it happened; that night Darling Sid first caught her eye; the night the connection was made, when their hearts became one, when he sealed their union by spitting three times (or perhaps it was only twice – Tracey prefers to remember it as three times) onto her bin bag and repeatedly roaring "FUCK YOU" directly into her face. It was then that Tracey knew. How could she not have known? How could anyone not have known? They were soul mates, she and Darling Sid, in the truest sense of the word. He had sought her; singled her out; made her his own. And now, their conjunction would be eternal. He would forever be the sun around which she orbited. He would forever be the reason she drew breath, or lit a fag, or smoked a joint, or swallowed a cheeseburger. By this single act of unprovoked degradation, this deliberate dehumanisation that she had never dared to hope or dream could possibly be hers, by this, and this alone, he had sealed it. For Tracey, the backstage visit after the gig, the fuck itself, was but the sweet culmination of what had already been sealed in spittle, front of house.

Tonight will be the very first occasion on which she takes down that box other than on an anniversary of Darling Sid's death. Tonight, she will, for the very last time, re-enact the ritual which first took place in that little room of hers on 9th February 1979 and which she has gone on to mark every 9th February since 1979. First, she will remove her clothing. Then, like an acolyte before the altar, she will carry the bin bag and safety pins into the lounge and lay them down in front of the urn in the plant stand. She will take the urn from its stand and shake onto the bin bag the remaining contents, the very last of Darling Sid's precious body. She will not need to be as sparing tonight as she has been in the past. For 29 years, she has had to be careful, sprinkling the minimum necessary quantity of the precious dust that she required for *The Cleansing*, as she has come to call the ritual, since she never could be sure how long it would have to last. But now, there is no more need to be sparing, for Darling Sid has a new body and she does not need to commemorate him with the dust of his last one any longer. This will be her final act of *Cleansing* before she moves on to consummate her relationship with Darling Sid Reincarnate. She will place onto the radiogram her least worn copy of 'Sid Sings'. Then, she will kneel in front of the altar, directly over the bin bag and the dust. She will close her eyes and sway to the music, massaging her breasts and clitoris until she is close, very close. Finally, when the moment of climax is almost upon her, she will reach for a handful of the precious dust and force it up inside herself, as deep as she can reach until, just as Sid is coming to the end of *I wanna be your dog*, she climaxes, screaming "FUCK ME, SID, FUCK ME."

Later, she will wake, lying spreadeagled on the bin liner, a safety pin penetrating her right buttock. In front of her will be the coffee table, knocked over by the violence of her and Darling Sid's love making. The plant stand will have buckled by the weight of the table on top of it. The urn will have shattered. But none of this will matter anymore. She has no more need of the sacraments, now that her god himself has returned to her. She will sit on the sofa naked, biting off large mouthfuls of reheated frozen pizza, the salad forgotten and unopened in the kitchen.

And now, her mind will turn to strategy, for Tolly is no fool. She knows that Darling Sid, in this new body, does not know yet who he is. Tracey knows he has reincarnated with his old memories buried deep in his unconscious. She knows that in this incarnation he calls himself Henry and that he is a student at the Posh People's university as well as a temporary worker at Matthis & Son. She knows it to be her appointed task to wake him from this trance, to remind him who he really is and regenerate his awareness of his eternal birthright of her devotion to him. She also knows that there is little time. She has made enquiries. Henry will have to return to university no later than 20th April. She has less than five weeks to wake him up. And from this time, she must deduct the weekends, for she can only be certain of seeing him on work days. This leaves her a total of 24 days in which to bring him back. Alone amongst the pizza wrappers and ketchup bottles, Tracey smiles and plans her strategy. And though she does not know it, for the first time in her life, she is conducting herself in a manner of which both her mother and father would have been very, very proud.

Tuesday 18th March 2008 3.55 am GMT

Tracey has been quite unable to sleep this night. Frequent waking due to indigestion is second nature to someone of her size. But this is different. This is a matter of pure unbroken wakefulness as she turns over and over the events of the day that led to her seeing her lover in the flesh for the first time in nearly 30 years. It's enough to give a girl goose-pimples, it really is.

Tracey is reflecting how the morning had started, with a batch of student workers waiting to come into the training room. The little sweethearts were only there for a few weeks at a time but the union had negotiated that they were to become automatic temporary members for the duration of their stay, with the company paying their subs directly. And that meant an induction to union as well as the company – in practice a DVD, a talk from Tracey and a tour of the factory – before they settled into their various roles.

So, she's in the training room waiting for the little darlin's to come in. She can see one or two of them in silhouette outside already, their chairs backing onto the opaque window between the training room and the reception area. Room's all set up. Blinds are drawn at the windows, chairs round a horseshoe table, DVD player connected to the TV at the front, TV on stand-by. Tracey presses the remote – a perfectly ordinary remote – to make sure it's working. Doesn't do to look technically incompetent in front of the iPod generation, does it? Tracey reckons that if a Sony Walkman was good enough for her it should be good enough for everyone. But then again, she's found it near impossible to locate Walkman-playable copies of punk era music, so maybe the march of technology wasn't to be resisted after all. As her right hand smothers the remote control, she glances again through the opaque window – a perfectly ordinary window with a perfectly ordinary, if somewhat heavy, pattern in the glass designed to obscure what was going on inside the room from the waiting area outside. Tracey sees a perfectly ordinary silhouette of a perfectly ordinary head and shoulders seated on a chair immediately on the other side of the glass. Then, there follows a perfectly ordinary hiss that you get when a TV aerial's become disconnected. She looks up sharply at the screen, a reflex action generated from the nightly ritual of listening out for Sid's communications from the *Other Side* (not that there have been any messages from Sid for many, many years.

Tracey's all but given up hope of him ever speaking to her again. She's pretty much concluded that his test of her faithfulness is to observe from heaven as to whether she can maintain her devotion for a lifetime without communication from her bodiless lover).

Then, a somewhat less than ordinary shimmering pattern forms on the screen – but only if you're someone who knows how to look for it; only if you're someone who has a Mohican haircut; only if you're someone who's had Sid Vicious spit in your face while he fucks you; only if you're someone who's loved him for well over a quarter of a century; only if you were someone who'd taught a Yankee witchbitch a fucking good lesson for trying to steal him; only if you'd spent a night a year for the last 29 years cleansing yourself ritualistically with precious Sid's cremated remains. Only then would you see how the dots on the hissing screen are rearranging themselves. Only then could you watch, held to the spot, on legs like tree trunks that have driven their roots from that second-floor training room right down into the ground ten metres below. Only then could you see that precious head of moving dots slowly turn on those beloved shoulders of shimmering static, to reveal in profile the face you know so well. Only then would you see those worshipped electronic lips silently mouth the words you've waited half a lifetime to hear again: "Fuck you bitch." If that was all there was to it, it would have been enough to engender in you a perfectly ordinary panic attack and no more. But if at the very moment those beautiful lips formed the words so long longed for and you simultaneously heard the words "Oh Fuck!" waft from the head and shoulders on the other side of that opaque glass, then you would know that your life had just changed forever. Because at that moment, you would know with a certainty beyond any other you had ever experienced before that your long dead lover had reincarnated and was waiting *right now* for you on the other side of the window. And at that moment, when it was all you could do to stop yourself from fainting, the last thing you'd be thinking about is that, maybe, the voice on the other side of the window was simply one Henry Tallison expressing frustration at having forgotten to bring his ID with him on his first day of employment; because it wouldn't be something as boring and coincidental as that. Not on this day. Not on the day when you and your lover were to be reunited.

But 29 years is a long, long time, isn't it? A girl's bound to feel some nervousness after all that time, isn't she? So, here Tracey is in the training room and there Sid is just on the other side of that window. And now, as she looks directly at him, her awareness of the enormity of the event growing inside her moment by moment, she can see it clearly at last. "Tracey, you big tit, how could you have missed 'im even through that fuzzy glass? You'd know that outline anywhere. It's him, darlin', it's *him*."

Tracey does not run for the door. She does not evaluate options. She does not reach for her shoulder bag to put on black lipstick and scent. She simply stands there, incapable of moving, looking through the window as the minutes tick steadily by, until at 9.40 am the administrator outside starts to notice Tracey is running late and decides to come see what's holding things up. And she knocks on the door and she opens the door and puts her head round the door. And she sees that actually nothing at all is holding things up. And she sees that nothing at all is holding Tracey up. Because Tracey is lying on the floor, her grey blouse and her red skirt billowed out evenly about her, and a bottle-worth of spring water that she has knocked over flowing evenly round her. The whole scene is somehow reminiscent of a well-framed early evening photograph of Mount Eiger from Lake Thurn. The administrator calls for a first-aider and then phones 999. The first-aider arrives and cannot revive Tracey. The ambulance arrives and the paramedics strain to place her voluminous frame onto the gurney.

They take her down in the lift and drive her away to A&E at Southampton General. The student workers are sent home for the rest of the day.

Monday 17th March 2008 8.45 am GMT

At 8.45 am sharp that day, four temporary student workers had, as instructed, reported for their first day of duty at Matthis & Son. All had brought their P45s. All but one had brought personal ID, the one being one Henry Tallison of Brockenhurst, Hampshire, situated some fourteen miles to the west of Southampton Docks, in the New Forest. All but one was female. The one who wasn't was acutely aware of that fact and in any other circumstances would be straining to do something about his good fortune in being thrown in with three attractive young ladies. But he was actually with his girlfriend, who was also starting work at Matthis that morning, so he was restrained. In addition, the job was particularly important to Henry and for once the emptiness of his pockets took precedence over the bulge in his trousers. So, for now, all he's going to do is listen.

Monday 17th March 2008 11.45 am GMT

Given the excitement at Matthis & Son this morning, the place has been buzzing and the grapevine positively throbbing with stories of Tracey's faint. The administrator's been in touch with the hospital and it turns out that the paramedics erred just a teensy-weensy bit on the side of caution. Apparently, our heroine woke up in the ambulance with the phrase "Where's My Sid?" booming forth from her voluminous lips. And it further seems that when she didn't get the answer she was looking for, she discharged herself immediately on arrival at the hospital. Don't worry, though – something tells me she's not going to come to any harm. She does have a bit of a dilemma as regards getting back, given that her car is still at work.

Taxis are an unwarranted expense and on buses she tends to get the chattering classes, well, chattering. She considers making a move on an unsuspecting hospital car park user like the one she executed on Arnold Frobisher all those years ago, but decides the strategy is no longer acceptable now Sid is back. In the circumstances, she opts instead for a taxi on grounds of speed, for there is no time to lose in getting back to her darling Sid. She makes it back to work by 11.45 am, only to be told that at 11.30 am the Head of HR had sent the students home for the rest of the day in light of the morning's commotion. They will not be returning until tomorrow. Tracey, too, is sent home with some admiring comments ringing her ears from the Head of HR concerning the dedication to work that has brought her back from the hospital. He doesn't mean it but it's as well to keep relations with the union buoyant. Tracey knows he doesn't mean it and she doesn't give a shit about keeping relations with management buoyant. But she does care about preparing for Sid. Tomorrow, she will arrive early and access the personnel files for the name and personal details of her newly reincarnated beloved. For now, all she has to do is prepare herself. A trip to Asda with its 'permanently low prices' will be called for, to be accompanied by slap of rear right buttock pocket and followed by a little ritualistic celebration, all of Tracey's making, back in the flat in Shirley.

Tuesday 18th March 2008 6.55 am GMT
Terry Jones, night porter at Matthis & Son, lives a sheltered life. His is a world of silent nights, one might almost say *holy nights*, peppered with periodic rounds of the silent offices, a silent two am tuna-and-cucumber sandwich lovingly wrapped in foil by his wife of 34 years followed by two not quite silent fingers of Kit-Kat ("Only two, my darlin'; Dr Jones says you have to watch your waistline. You're only eighteen months off retirement and our Caribbean cruise. Let's not miss it because of heart trouble from

too many calories") and a silent 40 winks in the porter's office which is completed without fail by 4.00 am, so no one's the wiser and what the eye don't see the 'art don't grieve, as Mrs. Jones is wont to say rather frequently.

Which is why Terry is rather surprised to find himself rousing from a dream at 6.55 am. Of course, it has to be a dream since it centres around the improbable phenomenon of a morbidly obese woman with a purple Mohican haircut carrying her strapless sandals in her right hand while she tries unsuccessfully to tip-toe silently across the polished granite floor of the foyer. Quite certain he must still be dreaming, Terry turns over and goes back to sleep. He's got another 45 minutes before the earliest of the day staff begin to arrive.

Tracey makes her way to the second-floor HR office, lets herself in with a legitimately held key and accesses a computer terminal with the illegitimately held access code of Barbara Smith, HR processing clerk ("Course you can 'av it, darlin'. Nuffink I wouldn't do for the union, you know that. Anyfink that 'elps you keep one step ahead of the bastard management is good by me."). The computer blinks at her as if irritated to be disturbed out of hours, then obligingly displays the HR department home screen. Tracey accesses the folder on staff data *("Matthis & Son complies fully with the requirements of the Data Protection Act and will not permit your personal data to be accessed or utilised without full and proper authorisation.")*, locates a file called 'Joiners' and looks up the date for yesterday. Four names; only one male. Tracey's heart rate increases as she sees the name her long-time lover has adopted in this new incarnation. But now, she is troubled. She scratches under her left breast, reaches towards her shoulder bag for a roll-up, then remembers where she is and snorts in disgust. She has his name. But will he recognise her? Her appearance has changed just a smidgen since those concert days back in the '70s. Her hairstyle alone might not be enough to jog his memory. And what if he doesn't even remember who *he* is? Have you ever met a reincarnate before, Tracey? Are you sure they do remember? And what happens if you make a move on him and he doesn't remember? The last thing you want to do is drive him off with your attentions.

She nods silently at her own admonitions. For now, she takes down the name, address and mobile phone number onto a scrap of paper (so much more reliable than all this soddin' electronic crap), and turns off the computer. She leaves a note for Barbara – "Babs, I'm still feeling crap. Not coming in today. Love, Tracey" – without concern for the question of how the note has arrived on Barbara's desk today, when she's feeling too unwell to be there. Babs won't mind. Anyfink for the union. Then, strapless sandals once more in hand, Tracey wafts (her word, not mine) down the stairs, silent and light of foot as a little sprite (best not to disabuse her just at this moment, I think).

As she passes through the entrance foyer, this time Terry does wake up – but only in time to see his former apparition of an extremely large woman with a purple Mohican haircut exit the main door and disappear into the half-light of a chilly March morning. Terry is aware that there are matters in this world for which he will never have an explanation; matters that, if you want to keep your street cred as Captain of the Lamb and Flag darts team, you must never, never mention to anyone.

Tuesday 18th March 2008 11.45 am GMT

The morning sun is struggling to enter at the place where the curtains join. The curtains are firm in their resolve to prevent it from doing so. The TV is on in the corner, spilling static into the room. The floor is strewn with empty 4X cans, boxes carrying the remnants of home-delivered pizza and several plates of untouched salad. Tracey is leaning back on the sofa, roll-up in one hand, breakfast in the other (Greggs Bakers in Shirley do this fantastic double cheese croissant). On the broken table in front of her is her scribbled note:

Henry Tallison,
42 Beaufort Close
Brockenhurst
07982 709581

The build-up of ash at the end of her roll-up indicates she has been motionless for a good five minutes. Unusually, she is silent. Tracey and silence are not the closest of acquaintances but she is too sober for a screaming match with Nancy Spungen (RIP) and the matter in front of her is far too serious to argue over it with her long dead father. It represents, after all, her whole future happiness.

Tracey remembers what happy feels like. She remembers black bin liners, and black lipstick, safety pins protruding through her cheek (so much more efficacious than cutting your wrists when you need to tell the world what you think of it), and screams of ecstasy when the Pistols entered the stage. She remembers the boom, boom, boom of the base drum and just once, the thrust, thrust, thrust of her lover inside her. But for Tracey, happiness is strangely detached, as if she is looking at it through a diaphanous curtain blowing in the wind. She reaches for the images. The curtain shimmers, the folds now too thick to see through, now affording just a glimpse of scenes from so long ago. Tears roll slowly down her cheeks as if savouring the feeling of her skin before falling onto yesterday's food-stained blouse under which we can see the canary yellow of yesterday's Ann Summers bra. Personal care, always more of an obligation to Tracey than a pleasure, is becoming less and less of a priority. She is looking at the world through a microscope. Each twist of the focus wheel brings what is important more clearly into her myopic field of vision. Simultaneously, it excludes more and more of the rest of the world. Take care, Tracey! This way lies madness. Step back a little before it's too late. But Tracey cannot hear. She is lost in the microscopic universe she has named Sid Vicious.

Wednesday 19th March 2008 7.50 am GMT

Reconnaissance!

It came to Tracey in the night as she slept soundly on the sofa, empty Old Holborn packets and 4X ring pulls strewn comfortingly around her. She woke at 3.15 am to the realization that blundering into Henry's life without proper research would risk losing Sid for ever. She knew instantly that the solution would lie in proper research of her target and the development of a military-like strategy for achieving her *outcome*. (Tracey heard about *outcomes* on a union training course in negotiating skills. For her, the word has always been slightly suggestive of something vaguely sexual, which, under the circumstances, is perhaps appropriate.) That's why she is here on a wet Wednesday morning, opposite a semi-detached house in a cul-de-sac in Brockenhurst. Tracey has been sitting in her rusting Austin Allegro a few yards down the road from number 42, where the lights have just gone on. She has been listening to Wave 105 but has just turned the radio off right in the middle of Leona Lewis singing Bleeding Love. The irony is lost on her. She will now sit waiting for her first glimpse of Henry as he leaves the house to catch the train into Southampton.

And here he comes… right on time. Tracey sits up sharply as she sees the front door being opened. An ancient pair of service binoculars, liberated by her dearly beloved father at the end of National Service, have been gathering dust in the may-come-in-useful-one-day cupboard and now, justify the entire concept of such a treasure store. She raises them to her eyes and takes her first unimpeded look at Henry. All 2.1 metres of him, athletic build preserved by reasonably regular visits to the gym, and a face that looks nothing whatever like Sid Vicious. Henry has Celtic colouring – short, tidy, light brown hair and blue eyes (though not visible to Tracey from this distance of course), with too sharp a chin for him to be regarded as classically good looking. Not that the girls have been too bothered about that so far. Henry has enjoyed considerable success with the fair sex since he has been mature enough to appreciate them. Tracey is disappointed. Where is the spikey black hair she so loved? Those chubby boyish cheeks? And there's no way the 2008 version of Sid would ever fit into that red Swastika t-shirt so beloved of her darling (Tracey has acquired a replica of said t-shirt – it is one of the great disappointments of her life that she has been unable to locate and acquire the original). She steadies herself; reminds herself it is the man inside that she loves. She will adjust to his new body in time. She is Sid's and Sid is hers, no matter what. If he's been born without arms and legs like them *the-lid-off-mine* babies, it wouldn't matter to Tracey. She loves him. End of conversation.

But now, Henry is hurrying to the station to catch the 8.05 that will get him to the front door of Matthis & Son just on time for an 8.30 start. Tracey starts the engine of the Allegro and rolls gently forward at a walking pace, unnoticed by her beloved. She follows him to the station, watches him disappear up the steps that lead to the platform and then returns to Beaufort Close where she continues to watch the house. Drastic action is now called for to support the *Reconnaissance* and achieve the *Outcome*. Tracey will step up to the mark. She will not be found wanting.

At 11.00 am, she has been sitting outside the house for a further two and a half hours or so. Before 9.00 am, a man and a woman exited, both middle-aged, whom she supposes to be the mum and dad. Since then, there has been no further movement from the house. By 10.00 am, the local mother-with-pushchair brigade had left for school with children in tow. Some have returned. Since 10.30 am, the street has been quiet and Tracey thinks it's time for stepping up to the mark. The particular mark to which she is now stepping up is the side gate of number 42 which is conveniently unlocked, affording her entry to the back garden. From here it's a small matter to break a single glass pane in the back door and turn the key from outside, giving her ludicrously easy access to the Tallison household. She enters surprisingly quietly given her size and looks slowly round the kitchen.

She eyeballs the usual range of fridge, complete with magnets, a monoblock tap dripping irregularly over a double sink, a dishcloth hung over it, a washing machine on spin. There is nothing special to catch Tracey's attention. Except, except on the notice board by the door to the hall, a series of family photos pinned up in no clear order. Tracey steps over to the board, looks more closely. She sees several shots of various members of the family and other unknown individuals in a variety of happy-type poses. Several show Henry. Tracey raises her right hand towards the board and points her index finger, circling it slowly around the photos, almost as if it were a wand. She fixes on a particular image showing Henry with his arm round his mother in front of a Christmas tree and stabs at it with her wand/finger. Tracey is not to know that this was only taken last Christmas. Neither is she is to know that it is a particular favourite of Henry's mother. She reaches for it, pulls it gently off the board and raises it to her lips. "Hello Sweet'art," she says as she kisses it. She does not notice that her black lipstick kiss lands on the image of Henry's mother more than it does on Henry. She is about to pocket the photo. Then, quite suddenly, she looks critically at it, tears it in half, taking only the part with Henry's image on it. The other half she drops to the floor.

Now, she wanders from the kitchen into the through-lounge that, unsurprisingly, bears little comparison with her own. No Old Holborn packets; no 4x cans; no pizza detritus. Just a tidy purple suite and plumped-up mustard-coloured cushions on a vacuumed red carpet, a teak coffee table complete with neatly organised magazines on the lower shelf and a TV on a chrome stand in the corner. She notices a large chip in the stand as if someone has thrown something at it. She knows how that one goes.

Tracey exits by the door into the front of the hall and places her foot uncertainly on the first step of the stairs. She feels an unseen barrier to the more private upper floor of the house but makes a specific decision to proceed as if breaking through a tape. She climbs the stairs slowly; then, at the top. There is a sound downstairs. She stops dead. A key in the door? No. Exhales relief. Post coming through the letterbox. She listens for the postwoman's footsteps dying away and the swing of the front garden gate. She proceeds across the landing, glancing round the door to what is evidently Henry's parents' room. No interest. She passes the bathroom. The only door left must lead to her target destination. She raises her hand towards the handle, then thinks better and reaches into her pocket for a tissue. Her hand lights on an old and rather overused one which she brings out, opens as best she can and uses to wrap round the door handle, depositing mucus on it in the process. "Smart girl, Tracey," she mumbles to herself. "Fingerprints." So, now, the door slides open and Nirvana lies before her. A single bed (Hallelujah! He has kept himself for her. He is as pure for her as she is for him). Recessed shelves on both sides of a closed-off fireplace. CDs by the hundred on the one side. Vinyl records by the dozen on the other. She begins to leaf through the CDs of band after modern band, meaningless to her. Begins to swear under her breath. "Fuckin 'ell, Sweet'art. Wot's this crap you listenin' to?"

Then, she sees it: the edge of a sleeve she'd know anywhere.

"Recorded at Wessex Studios, London, March 1977. Sid Vicious on Bass, and FUCK anyone who says it wasn't 'cos I know that man's playin.' Originally called 'No Future' but dumped by the bastards at A&M records before release. Finally issued by Virgin Records (blessed be the holy name of Richard Branson) on May 27th 1977. Went straight to number one, but that wasn't admitted by the BBC fascists until March 2001. Bastards never played it anyway, not ever, not never." She draws the vinyl record reverentially from its place on the wall and looks round for the record player; finds something called 'Bang & Olufson 4600' on a table in front of the blocked-off fireplace; presses where it says start and the machine's lights flicker on; lifts the opaque plastic cover; places the record on the turntable; selects 45 rpm; lifts the arm so, so carefully and eases it down onto the plastic. The room explodes with the sound she has loved for thirty years.

'God Save the Queen' unquestionably changed music history. It may arguably have changed the culture of a nation as well. Tracey had thought hers was the only surviving copy of the seven-inch disk cut onto ten-inch one-sided Townhouse acetate. She was wrong.

Tolly is sitting on her lover's bed squeezing the bedclothes in her fists.

She is weeping uncontrollably.

Through great heaving sobs, enough to move the Earth's own soul, she manages to repeat two words over and over.

"Thank you. Thank you. Thank you."

Thursday 20th March 2008 9.50 am GMT
"An' that's why we're running this programme as a joint 'nish'tive between management and the union."

Back in the training room at Matthis & Son, Tracey is delivering the induction programme for the Student Initiative only four days later than originally planned. Surely, this is British industry operating at its world-beating best. She is at the front of the room. She is poised professionally, if a little precariously, on the edge of a desk, which is looking rather as if it feels that what is being asked of it is beyond the call of duty. She is freshly attired in long multi-coloured skirt and flowing black blouse. Where it stretches at the buttons, we can see that the favoured colour of Ann Summers underwear for Thursday is actually red. She has evidently washed her Mohican hair and head and may well have been under the shower within the last 24 hours. Naturally, she is made up in the style that these days is referred to as 'Goth' but to Tracey is merely the same 'Punk' as she has always presented to the world all her life – black lipstick, black eye shadow, black eye liner and extended black eye lashes. She had briefly considered the possibility of a black bin liner as attire of choice for the day but decided that for her first face-to-face encounter with her long-lost lover, a fractionally more demure approach would be appropriate. She arrived at work with a smile on her face, humming. Yes, you did hear that correctly. Tracey was humming on her arrival at work. That one got the grapevine rumbling, believe you me.

So, here she is addressing a group of four fresh-faced students who are seated on a row of upright chairs in front of her. To her left are two females, appropriately professionally dressed, whose personal details need not concern us today. To her right sit Henry and the remaining female, a young woman with high cheekbones, pretty blue eyes and long blonde hair that falls about her shoulders like a waterfall. She is wearing a white blouse under a hand-knitted pink cardigan and navy blue trousers. Her chair is just a little closer to Henry's than Tracey might expect of newly introduced professional colleagues.

Tracey has a clipboard with each student's name on it. It is lying face down on the desk beside her. She has not referred to it, since she already knows the only name on it that matters to her. Her eyes have barely moved from Henry since she entered the room. So absorbed is she with him that she is failing to read the warning signs that would ordinarily disclose to her the danger of a possible connection between him and the attractive girl to his right – the glances, the little half smiles as they catch each other's eye, the unnecessary brush of hands as one or other of them reaches down to draw something from a bag. All is lost on our besotted heroine.

DVD-watching and welcome speech completed, the time arrives for the site tour. "OK, everyone," starts Tracey, "Hi-vis jackets on. We're about to take the site tour. Henry, you come up front and walk with me as you're the man (such sexism would never even occur to Tracey under normal circumstances). You others follow on behind, and don't dawdle and especially don't touch anything." She sounds exactly like the schoolteacher of Class 7 from 30 years ago, whom she is unconsciously trying to emulate. She finally reaches down for her board to look at the names. "So, that's Henry with me. Come over here, Henry." She reaches for his hand in a pre-planned manoeuvre that achieves exactly its objective of first physical contact. A shiver runs up her arm from her fingers that are touching that beloved hand right up to her shoulder. Momentarily, she is distracted by the pure joy of touch that oscillates back over 30 years of memory. Then, she rights herself, reluctantly lets go and looks down at the board again. "Right. So, it's Amanda and Vicky following behind us and bringing up the rear…" Her voice trails off into silence. She has just read the final name on the list. The Given name is Laura. But it is not the name of Laura that Tracey has stopped at, though. It is the first initial and surname that have rendered her totally immobile. The name she is looking at is Spungen. N Laura Spungen.

Involuntarily, she falls back. Reaches for the desk to steady herself. But it is not quite where her hand remembers it as being and she finds herself feeling around empty air. She is off balance once again. The last thing she remembers is falling backwards.

Sunday 23rd March 2008 9.50 am GMT

Tracey is supine; comfortable in the darkness; she could be floating. Is she floating? Is she dead? Has she reverted in time to her mother's womb? Tracey doesn't know. All she knows is that she wants the comfort to continue forever; because this is perfect; because the world is perfect; because Tolly is perfect. And Tolly is Tracey and Tracey and love are perfect and love is wonderful and being in love is… is… is… The stasis is broken by a bright stab of pain, long and sharp as a Stone Age flint knife, jabbing down at her. She recoils into the pillow that she now discovers is under her head. She opens one eye to discover the stab of pain is actually being caused by the entry of light into her darkness.

The room is clean and clinical, with a slight aroma of antiseptic. A low hum of conversation and movement is filtering under the door from just outside. Tracey doesn't know it yet, but she's been lying here for the last three days. Over the course of the next four hours, without any help from us, she will learn the following:

1. She hit her head on the side of the desk in the training room as she fainted.
2. She appeared to have concussion and was taken to Southampton General Hospital where she has been sleeping for three days since admission.
3. Babs and the girls in HR have sent her a big box of expensive Swiss chocolates as a get-well gift. They are open and about a third of the chocolates have been removed. This unquestionably means Babs has visited, probably at least twice.
4. The card accompanying the gift has been signed by everyone in HR; including Henry; including Laura. On the card, their signatures have been conjoined into Henry & Laura.
5. She loves Sid-Henry more than she can possibly express in words.

6. If that fuckin' Yankee witchbitch thinks she's gonna have Tracey's man a second time, she can fuckin' well think again. Tolly sorted her out once before, didn't she? And she'll bleedin' well do it again if she has to. This time, she's gonna fight for her man, an' this time, she's gonna win.
7. The moment she tries to lift herself from the bed with a view to discharging herself, she falls back on the pillow exhausted.

Babs comes to visit again in the afternoon with another box of chocolates. "You 'ad us really worried, Sweet'art. Everyone at work's really concerned, Darlin'. Everyone, and I mean *everyone including the managing director* is asking if you're ok."

"Babs, Darlin'," says Tracey, wincing with the pain on the rear left of her skull, "Do us a favour, will ya? That nice new boy and girl have signed my card – Henry and Laura, isn't it? And they're an item already. How sweet is that? Get me theys' addresses and mobile numbers, will you, Sweet'art? I know you ain't s'posed ta, but I just wanna thank 'em for being so thoughtful. An I ain't got no way a doin' that from an 'ospital bed 'less I can text 'em, do I? Go on, Sweet'art. I'm going bonkers wif boredom 'ere. You know I am."

Babs smiles her usual slightly parental smile at Tracey, suppressing the urge to tell the woman about her own true feelings for her. Babs has been married for centuries and sometimes thinks she has more great-grandchildren than the union's got members. She knows people are outin' themselves all over, but wif 'er upbringin' and the family lookin' up to 'er like wot they do, well, it just ain't written in the stars, Darlin'. An' wot's written in the stars is wot's gonna be lived out on the earth. So, she simply smiles again and nods her head.

Tomorrow, Tracey will have the information she has asked for. Of course, she already has one address, but she needs both phone numbers, and it wouldn't do to let Babs know she already had Henry's address.

The day after that, she will be sufficiently recovered to walk around the ward.

We'll fast forward to Wednesday, when she is permitted to wander off the ward down to the *Friends of Southampton Hospital* coffee shop in the entrance foyer. Watch her put on her warm and welcoming face and strike up another friendship with an ol' biddy by the name of Marjory Crooks. With Marjory in her blue-rinsed bun and twinset and Tracey looking like, well… looking as only Tracey can look, they make a most intriguing couple. But Marjory's in need of company and Tracey's already invited her out to her equestrian holding (all fifteen acres of it) just outside Bramshaw, where they can ride a couple of Tracey's horses through the New Forest to their hearts' content ("not ridden before, Darlin'? There's nothin' to it. I'll teach you in a few minutes and you'll love it"), before returning to tea and crumpets that will be laid out for them by Tracey's domestic staff in front of a roaring log fire in the Churchill Room ("Yeah, Sweet'art. He came there in the '40s to plan the war 'n that"). You can see Tracey's smiling inwardly after delivering that little lot. She almost believes it herself.

"Oh, just one more thing, Marjory," she says with a backward glance as she leaves the shop. "Could I borrow your mobile phone overnight please, Darlin'? I promise to tell your callers to ring back an' I'll be ever so nice to them. Go on, Sweet'art. It would really 'elp me out of a fix."

Marjory stiffens ever so slightly. You can tell she is hesitating, weighing up the value of this new friendship against the uneasiness she is even now trying to supress somewhere down in her gut. Intuition is telling her all is not well. But Marjory really does not want to listen to intuition just now. She'd much rather listen to tales of horse riding and afternoon tea in front of log fires and Mr Churchill's war planning. And Marjory knows for a fact that there will be no calls this evening. Not this evening or any other evening. Marjory will receive no calls because there is no one to call her. She only bought the phone because she was worried she might find herself stranded in the car somewhere late at night. In fact, truth to tell, she doesn't even know how to use it.

A vision rears up in front of her of herself and a new dear friend (my goodness, Marjory, an honest to goodness, real genuine friend! How exciting can life become?), galloping across open heathland, breathless with excitement, throwing their heads back and laughing together like those people on the Cadbury's chocolate flake commercials, then falling exhausted onto the sofa in the Churchill Room where tea and crumpets have been served and where later when everyone's gone home and they're alone and they look into each other's eyes and… NO! Marjory stops herself just in time. Not again. She can't let this happen again. So, no, definitely no! But friendship? What could be more natural than a pure, caring friendship to help her through the long, quiet days that melt into dusky loneliness and a cold single bed. Marjory knows that friendship could start with the smallest act of generosity – such as the lending of a mobile phone that isn't going to ring anyway. She smiles shyly at Tracey and the bargain is sealed.

Now Tracey has the phone in her hand and walks rapidly off in the direction of the ward she has told Marjory she is on, which happens to be precisely the opposite direction to the one she is actually on. She reaches a corner and turns it. When she's sure Marjory isn't following, she reverts to her normal swanking gait, proceeds down two more corridors, takes the lift up three floors then down two, finally exiting by her own ward. Here she gets dressed, and throws the hospital gown on the bed in contempt. She picks up the remaining chocolates and, with the newly acquired mobile phone poking out of her pocket, saunters off. It doesn't occur to her to tell anyone she is discharging herself. She has a number and she has someone else's mobile phone to call it from. What more could a gal want from life?

"Tracey, Darlin'," she mutters as she opens her front door, "you are about to become one seriously dangerous doll."

Thursday 27th March 2008 9.00 pm GMT

Tracey is sitting; comfortable in the darkness; she could be floating. Is she floating? Is she dead? Has she reverted in time to her mother's womb? Sid Vicious is sitting next to her, holding her hand, whispering softly in her ear. She can't quite catch what he's saying. All she knows is that the world is perfect and this moment is perfect and she needs so much for it to continue for ever.

Sid takes out a long-bladed hunting knife with a jaguar carved into its handle and stabs Tracey through the left eye, right into her brain.

"Aw, Sid, what did you wanna do that for?" says Tracey in surprise.

Sid smiles at her, says "Fuck you, Doll," then slowly recedes towards the ceiling where Nancy Spungen is standing in a party hat, holding a black balloon, giggling and pointing at Tracey.

Tracey lifts her hand to her eye at the centre of the stabbing pain as the dream fades. She has slept for over 24 hours after returning home. She shuffles forward on the sofa with a view to getting up, finds she cannot and allows herself to fall slowly backwards. Her hand encounters something hard and oblong: protrusions… buttons.

Remember, Tracey? Here are Marjory's phone and Laura's number. Her head is throbbing so hard now. The pain repeats every few seconds. It's hard to think when it's like this, isn't it Tracey? But come on girl, you've got work to do. Remember, Tracey! Remember a mate from a squat in London who vaulted a barrier to steal your lover, then told you she was looking after him for you. Remember the messages in the bald homo's newspaper. Remember the Chelsea Hotel in Manhattan. Remember an open bedroom door, Tracey. Remember a girl astride a boy, a dear sweet boy, who's too high on coke to realise what she's doing to him. Remember a Yankee witchbitch, Tracey. Remember a long-bladed hunting knife with a jaguar carved into the handle. Remember blood on your hands and Cawfiepecanpie and a long lonely flight home and a long lonely lifetime without the man you love. Com'on, Darlin.' Get up! It's payback time.

Thursday 27th March 2008 9.00 pm GMT

Tracey programmes the number on the slip of paper into the memory of the mobile phone. That's sensible. There's no point in re-dialling it every time, is there? She smiles with satisfaction when she enters next to it the name, 'Witchbitch'. Then, she leans back and closes her eyes to think carefully about the exact form of wording she needs to start *The Campaign*. Tracey likes to think of this as a military exercise, like she was one of those generals she's heard about such as Napoleon or Darth Vadar or Genghis Khan. Then, she sits bolt upright. She has it! A message of such terror-inducing sophistication she'll drive the cheatin,' betrayin' witchbitch to her knees in fear. She types WITCHBITCHWITCHBITCHWITCHBITCHWITCHBITCH on and on until her finger is sore. She presses Send. Exhausted, she falls back onto the sofa and swallows a handful of energy-reviving chocolates.

Thursday 27th March 2008 9.02 pm GMT

Laura is sitting in Starbucks in Southampton waiting for Henry. They've planned to see *Cloverfield*. Laura would have preferred something romantic like *Definitely Maybe* but Henry's into horror movies and she wants to please him. She knows she has some ground to make up having treated him pretty poorly over the last few months. When her phone registers a text, she groans, thinking its Henry telling her he's going to be late. When she finds it's a repetition of the same two words from an unidentified number, she thinks some stupid kid's playing a childish prank.

She thinks the same thing at 9.04 pm when the next message arrives. This time, it's YANKIEWITCHBITCH repeated endlessly.

At 9.05, Henry arrives, all smiles and full of admiring looks, so she forgets the stupid texts.

At least, she forgets them until 9.06. This time, it's FUCKINYAN-KEEWITCHBITCH and suddenly, Laura doesn't like it. Henry tells her to switch her phone off but her parents have told her not to do that in case they need to reach her urgently.

At 9.08, it's GETYERFRIGGINANDSOFFMYMANYOUYAN-KEEWITCHBITCH again repeated endlessly and that makes Laura cry.

At 9.10, it's GETYERFRIGGINANDSOFFMYMANYANKEE-WITCHBITCHORILLGETCHA and Laura is still crying from the last text.

At 9.12, it's HEY WITCHBITCH! REMEMBER WHAT IT'S LIKE TO BE STABBED WITH A HUNTING KNIFE WITH A GREAT BIG JAGUAR ON THE HANDLE? Only this time, it's not repeated.

And Laura isn't crying.

She's hysterical.

Friday 28th March 2008 9.02 am GMT

"I'm so sorry, Miss Spurgeon," says Babs into the phone. "Yes, entirely my mistake. *Spurgeon* not *Spungen*. Yes. Like the Victorian preacher? I'll correct it on the computer immediately, Miss Spurgeon. No, I assure you it won't affect your pay. We'll let you have that in cash within the next two weeks. Yes, someone will bring it round to you. I'm so sorry you won't be coming back, Miss

Spurgeon. I hope nothing has happened here to upset you? Perhaps, we'll see you back here during the Summer vacation then? Yes, goodbye, Miss Spurgeon."

"No need to report this," Babs mutters to herself. She types the correction into the computer. "No one even saw the mistake, did they?"

Saturday 5th April 2008 11.15pm BST

It's been a week since Laura felt safe enough to leave the house. Her parents informed the police of the texting, of course, being as how it was stalking, really. The police traced it to a phone owned by an elderly lady who'd lost it whilst in hospital. The young constable who visits is sympathetic, but there's nothing else she can do. Police resources are stretched and it's unlikely she will get a budget from the Inspector to do any more work on a case with no leads. But if the Spurgeons were able to tell them who was responsible, they would definitely be able to arrest the culprit on a charge of intimidation. As he closes the door behind the polite young policewoman, Haddon Spurgeon mumbles something about having a dog and barking.

Monday 7th April 2008 9.00 am BST

Tracey has woken with an idea of such enormous potential, she's shaking in excitement. She has just put the phone down from calling Babs to say she'll be off sick at least another week. "But Babs, Darlin'," she said, "keep that nice boy Henry's appraisal for me to do when I'm back next Monday, will ya? I reckon he's union material."

"No problem, Doll," said Babs, and books an appointment for Tracey and Henry on Monday 14th April.

Tracey turns her attention to *the Campaign*. Suddenly, there's no chocolate cake or pizza in evidence anywhere in the lounge of the

Shirley flat. Tracey has also virtually run out of rolling tobacco and the thought of screaming into the mirror hasn't occurred to her in days. Is this called 'Motivation'?

Tracey would have much preferred the climax of *the Campaign* to have taken place in the Chelsea Hotel back in Manhattan where it started all those years ago. But she's realistic enough to know that she'd probably not get that same room up on the seventh floor at such short notice and definitely not be able to get *the Mark* (as she's started to call the Yankee witchbitch) to New York in the time available. So Tracey settles for a little holiday facility she has located a few miles outside Worthing, called *the Chelsea Guest Cottages*. When she phones, she's in luck. With Easter having fallen over two weeks ago, the Cottages have a vacancy for next weekend.

"Yes, Madam, a delightful little one-bedroom cottage just right for a secluded holiday for two, with marvellous walking from right outside the door. No, Madam, there's no public path near the cottage. You and your daughter will have all the peace you require and the sea air will unquestionably assist her speedy recovery from the glandular fever. In fact, if you would prefer not to see anyone at all, Madam, we can leave the key under the mat and a welcome pack in the kitchen, so long as Madam is in a position to discharge the account in advance? And yes, Madam can park Madam's car immediately outside the cottage. Er, no Madam, we would not normally place Old Holborn rolling tobacco in the welcome pack, but that can easily be arranged if Madam wishes. Yes, and pizza. And chocolate cake.

"Yes, Madam, cash is entirely acceptable and if you are in a position to bank it to our credit today, there will be time for our account to be in funds before the weekend."

Tracey puts the phone down and shuffles off to check she has enough in the union subs box to cover the payment.

Tuesday 9th April 2008 10.00 am BST

Tracey has just put the phone down on another call to Babs, this time to say she's feeling a bit better and wants something to do. And how about she takes that nice girl's P45 and pay packet round to her. That would cheer both of them up. And maybe, she can persuade her to come back and work on a bit of union business? Babs had no objection. But then again, Babs never has any objection to anything Tracey suggests. Babs would have no objection to a whole lot more, if only Tracey would suggest it.

Friday 11th April 2008 11.15 am BST

So, here's Tracey signing for Laura's pay packet.

And here's Tracey clambering into the old Allegro for the short trip to Deacon Road as arranged with Laura on Tuesday. And what a nice phone chat she had had with the dear girl. Laura told her all about her family. Little brother Jamie? No, he'll be at school on Friday. Mum and Dad? Dad's an accountant and Mum's a midwife at Southampton General so no, they'll not be there either. But they'd definitely like to meet Tracey on another occasion. And yes, of course, Laura will be delighted to help Tracey out with a bit of union paperwork for an hour or two. Laura's been getting bored. No, not ready to return to work, and thank you for being so understanding. But, dear girl, that's what unions are for! Tracey is delighted to help. So, yes, she'll see you at noon on Friday complete with pay packet. "Bye for now, Sweet'art."

Friday 11th April 2008 12.00 noon BST

And here's Tracey arriving outside the house in Deacon Road.

And here's Laura opening the door, smiling.

And here's Laura going out to the car with Tracey to collect her P45 and pay.

And here's Laura sitting in the passenger seat for a moment to sign the receipt.

And here's Tracey getting back in beside her.

And here's Tracey stabbing a hypodermic into Laura's upper arm.

And here's Laura with a look of horror on her face as she falls unconscious.

Friday 11ᵗʰ April 2008 5.00 pm BST

The lounge-kitchen of the little bungalow at the Chelsea Guest Cottages near Worthing. It's furnished pretty much as you'd expect of a two-roomed holiday cottage. Chintz suite, little pine coffee table, TV in the corner. Carpet's a bit threadbare, mind. Tracey will put that on the feedback form. Through the door, over on the left, is the bedroom and off the bedroom is a little bathroom. Tracey has already looked in there and was delighted to discover that the bathroom is en-suite. That's going to help with the authenticity later this evening.

Of course, Tracey's already personalised the lounge just a little for the weekend. There's her portable record player and one of her 'Sid Sings' albums. She agonised over which copy to bring, but opted for the least worn one in the end. There are the two trays of Castlemaine 4X (no time to get it discount from her mate, so she's opted for Asda's permanently low prices). And the Chelsea Cottages management has been as good as its word. On the kitchen table (drop leaf, perfect size for two) is the welcome pack: bread, milk, tea, coffee, pizza, chocolate cake, Old Holborn.

What makes it feel most like home is that Tracey has drawn the curtains and put the lights on. The TV's on too, but the aerial's disconnected. She's not certain that there will be a message, being as how Sid has reincarnated and doesn't yet realise who he is, but the familiarity of the hiss is such a comfort to her. And anyway, he did manage to send her that picture in the static on the TV at work the other day that set all this off, didn't he? Tolly is not totally comfortable Sid would approve of what she is doing.

There on the pine coffee table is her lovely big hunting knife with the carved jaguar on the handle. She will remain forever disappointed that she has been unable to locate the original, but the copy is excellent – indistinguishable, really. No one but Tolly would know it was a copy – no one on the blade end of it, anyway. She turns her head in the direction of the bedroom just as a muffled groan emanates through the open doorway as she puts 'Sid Sings' on the record player – just quietly, like, 'cos she knows the last thing she needs to do right now is to attract attention to the cottage. She's tugging on the ring pull on the first can of 4X now. It looks like she's settling in for a long enjoyable evening.

Tolly would want you to understand what this is really about. Tolly has never had a proper opportunity to explain to Nancy just how much she hurt her by trying to steal Sid. So, the biggest benefit of this weekend is that at last they have a proper opportunity to discuss it in a calm, adult to adult fashion. And Tolly is really glad that Nancy agreed so readily to take this little girls-only weekend break with her. She feels that there may now be an opportunity for mutual understanding. Perhaps, in time, there might even be friendship – so long as she can be sure Nancy won't make another play for Sid now he's back. As she tilts her head back to let the golden liquid flow soothingly out of the can and down her throat, she feels a sense of encouragement, real encouragement.

A second 4X can goes the same way as the first. Now, Tolly feels as ready as she ever will be for the *big conversation* with Nancy. So, she's up and approaching the bedroom doorway with two more cans of 4X in her right hand and the big ol' hunting knife in her left. Not that she intends to do any harm with it, you understand. It's simply a talking point to get the conversation started with Nancy

– almost like a Talisman, you might say. She stands in the doorway momentarily, looks into the room and smiles. It's quite large as holiday accommodation goes. Plenty of space for a pine double bed, matching dressing table and bedside cabinets. The curtains (how sweet – the same pattern as the lounge curtains and suite) are drawn, of course.

"Hey, Nance," says Tolly. "Good to have you back, girl."

The girl on the bed lifts her head a little. There is a pleading look in her deep blue eyes, but she says nothing, nor does she move her body. Of course, that may have something to do with the duct tape over her mouth and the fact that she is tied, spreadeagled, to the four posts of the pine double bed. Tolly puts her head to one side and frowns a little. Something isn't quite as it should be. Ah, got it, Babe. The girl is dressed in day clothes – sweater and denims. That wasn't how it was in Manhattan. And Tolly knows, because she has a very, very clear recollection of how it was in that room at the Chelsea Hotel in the small hours of 13th October 1978. "Aw, Nance," she says, "This won't do, Darlin'. We gotta get you lookin' right. No point in all this if you don't look the part, is there, Sweet'art?"

Tolly puts the two cans of lager down carefully on the bedside cabinet and reverses to the bottom of the bed. The girl follows her with her eyes. Is that terror we see in there? Tolly doesn't think it is. Surely, Nancy knows she has nothing to fear from her ol' mate Tolly. Especially as they're only just getting started on their very own girls' weekend away.

Tolly lifts the big hunting knife.

The girl tries to draw back, but cannot.

Tolly swipes the knife straight across the bottom of the bed.

The girl tries to scream, but cannot.

Tolly looks at her in surprise.

All she has done is cut the ropes.

Friday 11ᵗʰ April 2008 6.00 pm BST

Tolly sits on the edge of the bed and smiles at the figure lying on it. The curtains being drawn, we can see that their rather fetching rosebud pattern is echoed on the bedspread. You can't see many rosebuds on the bed though. The bedspread has been pulled right back to reveal the matching white fitted Egyptian sheets in a 1200 thread count. But Tolly isn't counting threads today.

"There we are Sweet'art," she says. "That's better, ain't it?" The duct tape is as it was, but the girl has been unbound, her outer clothing removed and she has been rebound back in her original spreadeagled position, her legs and arms inelegantly pointing to the four corners of the bed. If we wanted to be unkind we might say her posture is reminiscent of an oversized starfish. Tolly clucks at her non-matching underwear. "Sweet'art, I gotta tell ya, yer lingerie just don't 'ack it, Darlin'. See, Sweet'art, we never know when our modesty's gonna be challenged, do we? You might be taken to 'ospital, or have a big night out wif a boy that ends up wif yer clothes off, or ya might even be in a situation like this. You gotta be ready at any time, Darlin'. Now, personally, I recommend Ann Summers. I got different colours for every day of the week. Look." And with one hand, she strips off her own blouse to reveal a midnight blue bra. The girl on the bed has not been listening. She's being paying much more attention to the knife Tolly has been drawing up and down her torso from the top of her knickers to her bra, all the time she has been talking.

Now, Tolly stands and removes her own voluminous denim jeans. She sits in her matching midnight blue Ann Summers underwear, looking down on the girl.

"See, Sweet'art, we really gotta get this sorted out, you an' me. We can't go on like this. Thirty years is just too long to be bearin' a grudge, Darlin'. You just got to face it. You've lost him and you ain't getting 'im back, Nance. Sid's been mine ever since the first time you died."

126

Tolly continues to slide the tip of the knife up and down the girl's abdomen, pausing just below the navel where Laura has a birth mark – a single horizontal red line. Hmm... isn't that just at the point where Nancy Spungen's knife wound was? That one's got to be coincidence, surely. Hasn't it, Tolly?

She continues, "Now, I gotta tell ya, Darlin', I'm a bit concerned. See, I'm not really sure how much of all this you actually remember. I've been reading up about this 'recarnation' thing on the Internet, and it seems folk like you don't always remember the last time they was 'ere. But don't worry, Doll. It's gonna be alright, see, 'cos I heard of this really cool way of getting people to remember who they was last time. And that's what we're here to do, Darlin.'" She smiles brightly at the hapless girl on the bed. "All you gotta do is remember, Nance, then we can talk it through like grown up people and put it behind us an' be friends again. You do see that, don't you, Sweet'art? You do want our friendship to come back again, don't you Darlin'?"

Laura is shivering now. Tolly continues to talk in an even tone as she traces the tip of the knife blade nonchalantly up and down Laura's body. The girl's pants are stained and the sheets are wet where she has long since lost control of her bladder. But hey, Tolly doesn't mind about things like that. To her, it's all part of the *outcome* that has to be achieved.

Tolly has drifted away into her memories now. She continues to look towards Laura, but she doesn't seem to see her. She continues to slide the blade mechanically up and down the shivering girl's abdomen holding the handle by its tip so that the motion is reminiscent of a pendulum. She is not really present in the normal sense of the word. She is back in 1978 in Manhattan. Then quite suddenly, she shakes her head and she is back in the room again.

"See, Doll," she starts, her voice faltering, "I don' really wanna hurt you, but I 'ave to. 'Cos all the web sites say I've gotta shock you or you ain't gonna remember. You do understand that, don't you, Nance? Tell you what, Sweet'art. I'm gonna make it as easy as possible for you an' then, if you do remember, maybe the knife won't have to go in again. Maybe, you'll remember before it does, Babe. Or maybe, it'll only need to go in a little way. And then, maybe, you won't die again, Darlin'. Lord knows, it took you long enough last time." She smiles brightly as she presses the knife down a little harder on Laura's birthmark. Laura squeals and wriggles, trying to recede. The skin remains unbroken. Laura remains unharmed, as yet. At least, she remains unharmed physically. As far as psychological harm is concerned, it is too soon to say.

Friday 11ᵗʰ April 2008 11.00 pm BST

At some point Tolly has made her way back into the lounge and passed out on the sofa, where she is snoring peacefully. The TV is hissing happily away to itself in the corner and 'Sid Sings' is on the turntable, poised for its next spiritually uplifting performance.

Laura still on the bed in the other room, still tied, still duct taped. She is also sleeping, but not nearly so comfortably as Tolly. The cottage is in darkness save for the slither of light from the lamp over the front door that is elbowing its way between the curtains, which do not quite join.

And now, here comes Tolly, making her poised, thespian-like entrance, as if from stage left, rubbing her eyes and scratching her rolls of excess fat. She flicks on the light switch as she enters. "Ello, Nance," she says, as if bidding a colleague good morning. "Sleep well? Warmer 'ere than it was at the squat, ain't it?" Laura wakes, blinking her eyes against the sudden penetration of the light. "It's good we've slept, Darlin'. Helped to pass the time, didn't it? See, we can prepare a bit, but we can't really get started properly till just after 3.00 am, can we, Sweet'art? You remember 3.00 am, don't you, Nance?" says Tolly, spacing her words slowly and precisely, never once breaking eye contact with the terrified girl on the bed. 3.00 am. Thursday. 13th October. 1978. Does she see recognition in Laura's eyes? "Yes, that's right, Doll!" she continues, "last time we met, wasn't it? Well, not counting the day last month you came into work to try 'n steal my man again." She tilts her head to the left and frowns a little. "If you want to be exact, it was prob'ly more like quarter past three, by the time I got to the room an all. That's why we gotta wait a bit, Doll. The more righter we get it, the better chance you got of really remb'rin', see?"

Laura mumbles through the tape, trying to speak.

"Tell you what, Darlin'. If you promise not to call out, I'll take the tape off your mouf. D'you fink you can promise me that, Doll?"

Laura's eyes are as full of fear as they were five hours ago. But she nods her head vigorously. Tolly waddles up to the bed, reaches down and snaps the tape back across her face in single movement. Laura gives no sign of feeling it.

"Please," she says. Her first word is 'please'. Now, that's a bit trite even for a situation as tense as this one, Laura. You're going to have to do better than that if you want to survive the night, you know.

"Please, Tracey. Please don't... hurt me... any more. I'll do anything you want. Just tell me and I'll do it." There is an undeniable tone of fear laced with misery in the voice. But underneath that, the educated, slightly plummy accent is still audible. "I promise. And if... if you let me go, I promise I won't tell anyone and... if you want money, my dad's got lots and if you want anything else, just tell me, only please, don't hurt me any more, Tracey."

The older woman looks down disdainfully. "Aw, com'on, Nance," she says in some evident irritation. "Stop the stallin'. If you don't wise up and tell me, you know, who you really are, this is really gonna end up hurting you, Doll."

Laura looks back in fear and confusion. Her long blonde hair is dishevelled and matted. Some falls over her shoulders and some sticks to itself on top of her head. Her high cheekbones that usually give an attractive definition to her pretty face are tear-stained and red. Her body, usually the target for active male imaginations even when fully clothed, looks no one's idea of sexy now. Still rendered immobile by the ropes, she is a figure of pathos – to everyone except Tolly, that is.

"I... don't understand... what you want, Tracey... just tell..."

Tolly leans forward over the girl, her face just a few inches from Laura's, the knife brandished high above her in her right hand. "Babe, if you call me Tracey once more, I'm gonna have to hurt you. It's TOLLY, Doll," she roars, "TOLLY! Fink you can remember that, Sweet'art?" And on the last word she brings the knife down hard onto the bed, the blade driving without pause through the pillow and into the mattress, just as it might into a young woman's flesh.

Laura screams.

Saturday 12th April 2008 3.03 am BST

"Right, Doll. I fink it's about time we got started, don't you?"

Three hours back, Tolly left the room in frustration after the incident with the knife and the mattress, flicking the light switch off as she went. She'd played 'Sid Sings' through two or three more times. Laura had heard her singing and cursing along to it from time to time. Then, despite herself, she had slept again – a defensive reaction, I would think. Either way, she had not called out. I think she reckoned the gain of being tape-free to be too valuable to risk in a probably fruitless attempt to attract attention from outside.

There comes a point where fear has done all it can to you. When you've finished with psychological and physiological reactions, the power of fear diminishes, sometimes quite rapidly. That is why people who've been there say that the only thing you have to fear is fear itself. So, if ever you find yourself alone and tied up by a schizophrenic, knife-wielding, homicidal, middle-aged, punk rocking psychopath, you will remember that, won't you?

Back here in the present it is 3.03 am and Tolly has just flicked the light switch back on in the bedroom. There in her right hand is the big hunting knife, the jaguar sleeping undisturbed on the handle. She has also locked the door behind her and slipped the key down between her voluminous breasts where it nestles in the midnight blue Anne Summers bra (Midnight Blue for Fridays). So, let the games begin, as those rather cute Roman Emperors used to say before the Coliseum ran with rivers of blood.

"Well, Doll, it's time." Tolly's tone is once again nonchalant, almost patronising, reminiscent of how one might speak to a small child. She looks directly into Laura's eyes. "We're gonna make everything as much the same as we can. Now, remember, I came in the door of the hotel room. And where was you, Sweet'art? Go on. You remember, Doll. You was sitting on 'im, trying your damnedest to give him a hard on, weren't you, Doll? Well, sorry to disappoint, Babe, but we ain't got no real cock 'ere for you tonight. So, what I've done... what I've done, Nance," she says, moving towards the bedside cabinet, "is I've bought you one!" She pulls open the drawer and with a broad smile and a flourish pulls out an Ann Summers, Flesh-smooth 6" Realistic Dildo, purchase price £12.50 (*looks just like the real thing, and feels just like the real thing. From tip to base, this superbly crafted dildo will satisfy you totally*).

Laura lets out an involuntary scream and draws back on the bed as far as her bonds will let her. "Aw, com'on, Doll, don't be like that," says Tolly, "I ain't gonna hurt ya, Sweet'art. But I gotta make you remember, ain't I? So, what we're gonna do, Babe, is you're gonna twist around onto yer knees, Babe, and you're gonna ride this dildo, just like you was trying to ride my baby boy that night. That'll be fun, won't it, Babe?" Her sentence ends on a bright, upbeat note and is accompanied by a cheerful smile.

Laura is about to scream again when she catches Tolly's warning look. She suppresses it instantly, knowing it will only result in more duct tape. And Laura knows she has to preserve each tiny gain she makes towards freedom. Tolly swipes the knife across the bond to Laura's left wrist, then does the same with her right. Laura blinks at her in confusion, not knowing quite what to do with her newfound freedom. "An' no trying to get away, Nance, ok?" The upbeat tone continues. Who knows whether it's mockery or whether she means it? "We got work to do 'ere, Babe, and I can't be chasing out after you into the night somewhere now, can I? So, just turn around an' we'll get the show on the road. Oh, an I'll tell you what, just for atmosphere, we'll put Darlin' Sid back on, shall we?" Laura notices for the first time that Tolly has brought the record player into the bedroom. Tolly leans across the machine and switches it on. Sid launches obligingly into 'Born to Lose'.

She turns her attention back to the girl weeping silently on the bed. "Right, Doll, up you get." She prods her with the tip of the knife. Laura supresses another scream and struggles around onto all fours. "Right, Sweet'art, get this inside you." Tolly's tone is more serious, aggressive, as she throws the dildo down onto the bed by Laura's right hand. Shaking and weeping, Laura reaches for it, kneels over it. She struggles to pull her knickers to her right side. "Com'n Darlin'!" Tolly's voice is harsher now. She sounds more hurried, more intense. "You was much keener on this when it was my poor baby's cock you was trying to ride. But then, you couldn't get that inside yous either, could you, Babe? 'Cos 'e was fuckin' sleepin' wasn' 'e, doll?" she screams, snarling out the words.

Laura is shaking violently now. "I'm... sorry Tracey..."

"Tolly!" the older woman screams back at her. "It's fuckin' Tolly! You could remember it well enough when we was in the squat, 'an when I took you to see Sid for the very first time, an' you jumped the barrier an' you made him take off wif you and you cheated him away from me, *you lyin cheatin Yankee witchbitch. You 'ad no fuckin trouble rememberin ol Tolly back then, did ya, Nance?"*

Laura is weeping hard now, but still she manages to keep the sound low, fearing the consequences of aggravating the older woman even further. "I'm… sorry… Tolly," she manages between sobs, "I don't know what I've done to hurt you. But I'm so, so sorry and I'll do anything I can to put it right."

"Nah, that's OK, Babe." Quite suddenly, Tolly's voice loses its cutting edge. She speaks almost softly "I knew we'd have to go the whole way before you'd remember, Doll."

On the record player Sid switches into 'I Wanna Be Your Dog'.

Tolly reaches back into the drawer of the bedside cabinet.

Slowly, very slowly, she draws out a hypodermic syringe.

"Remember this, Darlin?" Laura, head bowed, does not answer. "See, I always knowed you done it 'cos of this. If you'd never got him hooked on this it would never 'ave 'appened and he'd still be right here with me today, Doll. See, I know you can't blame junkies for what they do when they're high. And you was high outta your mind, Babe. No question of that."

Suddenly, Tolly sits on the edge of the bed. Laura recoils automatically.

Tolly isn't even looking at the girl when she drives the syringe into her thigh. And this time Laura does scream, a long hard scream, pitched so very, very high.

Saturday 12th April 2008 3.37 am BST

Sid's reached 'My Way' (second play round, of course). Tolly's never been able to decide if this is her favourite track on this album or whether she actually prefers 'I Killed the Cat'. It doesn't really matter. She listens to them both the same amount of times, anyway. She's a bit puffed out and red in the face now, though, because she's been working hard. Oh, and by the way, she's now in the en-suite bathroom. She's puffed out, because she's dragged Laura's semi-comatose body in here.

Have you ever noticed how much heavier people are when they're unconscious or dead? It really makes a huge difference when you're trying to move them. Anyways, with an enormous effort she's managed to get the girl propped under the sink for the final act of *the Campaign*. I think Tolly's got the quantity of junk just right, because Laura's beginning to stir.

Tolly's kneeling just in front of her on the floor, looking intently into her face, waiting for her to come properly awake.

Laura opens her eyes, blinking, still distant.

Tolly smiles at her. "Hi, Babe! Good trip?" she asks brightly. "We'd best be getting on. Time's marching and we need to get the job done." Terror returns to Laura's eyes as she remembers where she is and what's been happening for the last twelve or more hours. She struggles to rise, but Tolly's bound her hands together around the sink pedestal. "Aw, sorry 'bout that, Sweet'art. I know it ain't quite authentic, tyin' you like this, but I couldn't take a risk on letting you go. So, what we 'ave to do now is see our little story right through to the end. Then, you'll remember. You do see why we gotta do this, don't you, Babe? All the recarnated people remember who they are eventually, Sweet'art. It just takes enough stress til you get there."

Quite suddenly, she stops talking. She kneels, unmoving, looking into the young girl's eyes, looking for… what? Who knows? Perhaps it is some sign of recognition that this poor pathetic creature is never going to be able to give her. She stays that way for a full minute or more, her face no more than six inches from Laura's. Then, at last, it starts to happen. The jaguar on the hunting knife stirs beneath her hand. He is waking and he is hungry. Better feed him, Tolly. You know how he gets if you don't feed him.

Laura sees the movement of Tolly's right hand as she brings the knife forward. Her eyes widen in fear.

She pulls fruitlessly on the rope that secures her to the pedestal of the sink. "Sorry, Babe," says Tolly softly, as she raises the knife to the place just below Laura's navel. The place with the red horizontal birthmark. The birthmark that is no wider than the blade of a big ol' hunting knife with a carved jaguar on the handle. Tolly begins to press it slowly forward, her motion consistent, insistent. She is still looking intently into Laura's eyes.

Laura sobs… screams.

Then, without warning, she pushes back against the wall, pulling her legs from under her in a tendon-tearing twist and kicks the older woman hard in the stomach with both feet.

Tolly lurches back in surprise and falls onto her back, arms and legs kicking out like a helpless beetle.

Laura pulls hard on the rope and drags the pedestal away from under the sink.

In a moment, she is up.

With her right foot, she kicks the knife out of reach.

Then, she places the same foot on Tolly's huge stomach.

Leaning low over her, she spits in her face. And in an accent that most would easily mistake for New York, smiling, she says, "Not this time, you Limey Bitch."

Sister Serenity

Rule Seven:

Players are free to move around in time and space at will.

Sunday 3ʳᵈ July 1988 9.11 am BST

"Penny for 'em, Denny?"

The tall, muscular Irishman continued to lean over the safety rail of the ship's stern and gazed down at the white foam fanning out behind the vessel as it chugged its way out of Dublin harbour. His thoughts were worth considerably more than the proffered sum.

He was musing on the incessant rows and beatings administered by his father over more years than his memory could retain. The terror in which he, his mother and his siblings had lived had been seared into his brain with a branding iron.

He was thinking of his mother's growing tension each night as the clock drew its hands inexorably round to closing time; the slam of an angry front door; the silent pauses that followed; then, the thuds, reminiscent of the butcher's meat mallet beating down on a carcass; his mother's muffled screams as she bit down on her arm, trying to prevent her own cries of pain from waking her children.

He was thinking of the slow, deliberate footfalls on the stairs that preceded the nightly visitations of their tormentor to their bedroom; the rough hands that would wrench him and his brother from their bed as they pretended to sleep; the clenched fists applied to their heads and bodies for some imagined crime that was long forgotten in the haze of the morning's hangover; then, worst of all, the ominous creak of the door to their younger sister's bedroom as he and Sean lay nursing their rapidly forming bruises; the cries of "No Da," sharply curtailed; then, the silence; the wretched, squirming, captious silence that screamed his own powerlessness into his face, simultaneously requiring he act while mocking his inability to do so.

He was thinking of that last night; his sister's single high-pitched scream that he could not endure, demanding that finally, bruised and bleeding, he rise from his bed to approach his father silently from behind with the wooden chair from the landing; the sound of vertebrae snapping as he brought it crashing down, his mother watching with terrified eyes from the doorway.

He was thinking of the fear in those eyes as together, they looked down at his father lying motionless and silent on the floor and his sister lying foetal on the bed, whimpering.

He was thinking of how his mother changed seamlessly at that moment from victim into rescuer when she realised the implications of her son's act; how that night, she had packed him and his brother off from Galway in the direction of Dublin; how she had given instructions and enough money for them to make their way to London.

Denny gave a last backward glance to the seagulls that hung suspended over the quayside. He turned to his brother and smiled gently. "I was just thinkin' of home," he said shyly, as if admitting to some shameful weakness that should be hidden from a younger sibling. "Home and Mam, Sean, home and Mam."

Sean was oblivious to the events of that night, less than a week previous. All he knew was that his mother had woken him and told him to follow his brother's instructions to the letter. Presented with the opportunity of leaving a home and country which, at eighteen, he was desperate to escape anyway, he needed no second instruction. He had packed a bag and was ready to leave within minutes.

"Sure and there's me thinkin' you're dreaming of the girls of London town," he said, "and how they's going to be linin' up to dance wit' you, seein' as Andrew's already been claimed by Fergie an' there's no good men left in England except you and Matt Gross." Denny drew himself up to his full six foot two and gave his brother a warning glance. Though superior in height by four inches and in age by three years, he had failed to inherit their mother's gift for quick repartee which came so naturally to Sean. As he often reflected, he could always think of a suitable answer, but not until at least ten minutes after the end of any given conversation. The moral high ground offered him little protection from his younger brother's hunger for fun and excitement. "Aww, come an' have a pint, will you, Denny, and stop mopin'. Do you not think that Mam will want you to have a grand time? And d'you not think she's sent me along to look after you so's you don't land yourself in a pile of trouble? Sure an' it's me job t'see you enjoys yerself, 'cos you surely won't do it wit'out me." Denny smiled wryly down at his brother and allowed himself to be led to the bar.

The ship's saloon had been full since it opened as the vessel left Dublin port. Groups of men played cards or chatted idly at tables strewn carelessly around the room. A cloud of grey smoke and greyer conversation hug over the crowd that stood several bodies deep between the brothers and the bar. Unassumingly, Denny tapped the first person in his path on the shoulder. The man swayed under the motion of the ship and the influence of six pints as he turned to face the affronting individual who had dared touch him. His mouth was already open in readiness for the curse that was rising in his throat and the aggression flowing into his fist when he came face to face with Denny's chest. He stopped in mid motion and froze like the frame of a broken film on a cinema screen. Slowly, his gaze rose from Denny's chest, to his neck, to his mouth and then to his eyes. For a moment, he stood without making a sound, weighing up his chances against the dark, good-looking man in front of him. All the while the tall Irishman stood gazing enquiringly down, as if ignorant of the effect his height and frame had upon others. The shorter man's face broke into a submissive smile. It emphasised a scar, which ran from the right corner of his mouth to the edge of his jawbone. He had decided against picking so ill-matched a fight. "Sure, and can I be buyin' you a pint?" he asked. It was always that way with Denny.

"Very kind of you, sir. An' would it be too much trouble to be askin' for one for me brother as well?"

The shorter man winced and forced another smile. "No trouble at'll. It's me pleasure to be buyin' for friends from home. Sure an' we're all going to have to stick together when we get to Liverpool, for the English'll spare us no time of day. Me name's Connor." This last was spoken with more genuine warmth and a hand extended to Denny. Connor's temper had boiled down as quickly as it had risen.

"Pleased to meet you, Connor," Denny replied solemnly as he shook the other's hand up and down in time to the motion of the vessel. "And here's me brother, Sean," he said, as he eased his sibling in front of his new friend. Denny never thought to question why he made friends so easily.

Saturday 7th May 1988 6.11 pm BST

"How was the funeral?" Fredrick blew a column of smoke vertically above him as he looked at the ceiling. The light was beginning to fade now, and as darkness descended, the traffic outside growing quieter. A gentle breeze troubled the faded curtains at the open window, as the last shafts of sunlight gave way to the coming night.

"All right," came the muted reply from his right. Lying naked on her back, she stared nonchalantly up at the ceiling. Then, without moving her body, she reached out her arm and took the cigarette from his fingers. He offered no resistance as she drew it towards her own lips. Filling her lungs with the calming smoke, she allowed the images of the day to pass, single file, across the parade ground of her inner vision: trying to get into the bathroom in the morning as her family scrambled to ready themselves for the events of the day; applying lipstick and eye shadow in the mirror while she wished her eyes were blue and not brown; walking behind her parents as her little brother made faces at her and tried to pinch her; the vicar droning in the pulpit over some obscure lesson she was supposed to learn from the death of her grandfather; the graveside and the words of misery – "man that is born of woman hath but a short time to live"; the wake, populated by offensively opinionated and interminably boring maiden aunts; a decision to make a tactical withdrawal without her parents seeing; the call to Fredrick, holding her breath as she wondered if it would be he or his wife that reached the telephone first; the bus ride from Bootle into Anfield; climbing the stairs to the rented room he kept exclusively for their meetings.

Paula counted herself fortunate. After she left school at sixteen, her parents had been prepared to fund her through secretarial college. By eighteen, she had found her first job in the office of a local engineering company, a considerable achievement in the perpetual depression that was 1980s Liverpool. When she found herself making tea and running errands, she had decided within a matter of months that a better future beckoned and she took a position as a junior typist at Caldwell and Hollingsworth, an august firm of solicitors based in the docks district.

So, why was she so fortunate? Because there, she had come to the attention of Fredrick Dickinson. Where else could a girl like her have expected to meet a man of sophistication and learning? At 35, he was a junior partner in the firm and tipped for higher office. The one blot on his canvas, of course, was the wife who had tricked him into marrying her; who had made his life a perpetual misery; who sucked him dry of every penny he made; who held him, bereft of comfort, but nevertheless imprisoned in a loveless union.

Fredrick had passed her in the corridor. At first, she had noticed the way he leaned on his cane, favouring his left leg. When a file had slipped from under his right arm, she had stooped to retrieve it in order to save him bending. Their eyes had met and they had smiled at each other before each turned away, suddenly conscious that the intimacy of eye contact breeched the unspoken protocols of the firm. But the attraction was as mutual as it was instant. Later, she heard he had enquired about her. She had consulted Suzie who sat next to her in the secretaries' room. At the age of 23, Suzie had worked for the firm for three years and was the acknowledged Delphic Oracle on the ways of the great and the good. "Oh, 'im," Suzie had said. "You want to watch that one. Eyes for the girls 'e 'as. Not a good idea to get mixed up with him at all." The words had slipped across Paula's awareness like butter in a hot pan before melting to colourless irrelevance.

She had noticed instantly, when Fredrick's work came her way for typing. It was no surprise to her that he found excuses to visit her desk in connection with that work, by-passing the normal protocol of placing queries through the secretarial supervisor. It was only a matter of weeks before he had called her to his office when his own PA, Brenda, was off sick. Paula had been thrilled with the sense of importance that his attention bestowed on her. She had been overcome with pride when he had complimented her on the speed of her shorthand and the accuracy of her word processing. She had been flattered and tempted beyond her powers of resistance when he invited her out to lunch. She had been touched when he began to reveal the details of his private life to her and seek information about hers.

Within days, he was on her mind perpetually. Brenda had returned from her short period of illness, but Fredrick still found excuses to come to the secretaries' room. When the PA was again absent, he once more asked Paula to stand in for her. His request that she work late that Wednesday also came as no surprise. Nor was she perturbed when the evening's work extended into an invitation for a drink. She telephoned her parents and made an excuse. They found their way to a quiet little pub on Sparling Street where he had taken the bold step of declaring that he had feelings for her. She wasn't sure how to react, her own feelings a breath-stealing jumble of excitement and fear. He had walked her back to the bus stop. And there, he had turned her to face him, placed his hands on her shoulders and settled a gentle kiss upon her lips. She was lost for words. All she could do was look into his eyes and wait for his next move, stretched on the rack between the instilled fears of a religious childhood and the long-denied calls of an adult body. There was nothing more that night. He had simply smiled, turned her towards open the door of the bus and walked away.

The man's next move had come the following day. He openly asked her to spend the evening with him. Her agreement was instant, unadulterated by circumspection. She made another excuse to her parents, and at six o'clock, he shepherded her into a gently lit restaurant just off Jamaica Street, where the walls were shrouded by mute-coloured tapestries and the waiters ingrained with obsequious respect. Paula had never been in such a restaurant before. She had never been addressed deferentially before. She had never tasted fine wine before. She had never drunk too much of it before. When, at around eight o'clock, Fredrick proposed they next go somewhere she would be able to relax more comfortably, she had agreed eagerly.

Paula had found herself in the room they were lying in now. She had been under the influence of the alcohol, surely. But she had also known clearly what was to happen and acquiesced willingly. Fredrick took her coat and bag gently from her and laid them on a chair. Then, with an expertise that seemed to belie his claimed limited sexual experience, he led her to the bed where they had become lovers.

Now he lay to her left, each of them unclothed and supine, looking up at the shafts of dying sunshine that exposed the cracks on the ceiling and toyed with their exhaled smoke as it swirled upward. Paula knew, instinctively, they would be sharing much more than just cigarettes for a long, long time to come.

"Just all right?" he enquired. "Seems to me that you ought to have more to say for your dear departed grandpa. Or weren't you two that close?"

Paula took a final draw from the cigarette and watched the ash lengthen as she passed it back to Fredrick. "No, not close," she said with a touch of regret in her voice. "We've never been a close family. We all seem to live in our own little worlds, going about our own business. We come together for all the formal things – weddings, funerals, Christmases. But no one ever has anything good to say about anyone else. Aunt Maude reached the limit today, though. The ol' man wasn't even cold, an' she was moaning about what an awful childhood he gave her. Said she wouldn't wish it on a dog. Said no child of hers would ever suffer the way she did. Not that anyone's going to marry her and give her a baby to prove it though." She paused for a moment, then added, "I couldn't rely on my family to be there if I needed them. That's why I've learned to look after myself, see? Anyways, I've got you to love me now, haven't I?" As she rolled to her side, her breast fell against his right arm that lay regimentally rigid, parallel to his torso. She eased her hand across his midriff, running her fingers lightly over his stomach muscles. She was no more aware than he that middle age would shortly entomb the dying youth of his body under creeping layers of fat; that his full dark hair would soon begin to lose its density and yield the edge of its colour to invading grey. At 35, Fredrick himself had only a limited notion of what it would mean to grow old; at 19, Paula had none whatsoever.

Her hand glided gently down to his right thigh and along a six-inch scar that ran parallel to the muscle. She had seen it before of course, and was inquisitive. "Tell me about this, darling." As she spoke the words tenderly, she gazed intently into his face, searching for some means of thawing the emotion that she knew lay inside him. Her only chance of reaching him lay in melting her way into his heart with her love. At 19, Paula's knowledge of the ways of men was untainted by rationality and experience. She knew with an unalterable certainty that love conquers all.

His eyes flickered a little, then closed. He was silent for a time, reliving history.

"28th May 1982, Goose Green," he finally replied, eyes still squeezed together. "Herbie led the battalion straight into the Argies' guns." He paused, the contortions on his face betraying the recurrent nightmares that still bounced themselves against the edge of his consciousness.

She slid her hand reassuringly up his body and gently ran her fingers through the thick hair on his chest. He continued. "We took 'em out, of course. It turned the war around. But it could have been done with artillery and air support instead of handguns and gung-ho glory. No one knew what a total fuck up it was; what a total fuck up he was. And no one ever will – except the seventeen of our boys who didn't get up after the shooting finished. Herbie got a VC for it." He fell silent. Paula wished she hadn't asked. She felt awkward now, sensing she was on dangerously personal ground. There were matters on which she should not yet tread too brazenly. A change of subject and posture was required.

With a level of energy possessed exclusively and unconsciously by the young, she bounced herself swiftly from the bed to a kneeling position, tucking her ample legs under her. Her breasts hung freely now, moving almost imperceptibly with the rise and fall of her breathing as she looked into his face. Fredrick opened his eyes and gazed up at her vacantly. He reached to caress her, the back of his left hand brushing lightly at the base of her right breast. She took his fingers in her own right hand, the ring on her third finger hard against his skin.

"Tell me about this." It was an instruction, not a question.

"The ring? Oh, it's nothing special. It was my grandmother's. My mother inherited it when she died; gave it to me on my sixteenth birthday. It's just about the only thing of value she's ever given me.

Fredrick looked into her eyes. He took her hand in his own and slipped the ring from her finger to examine it more closely. He read the inscription inside. 'Let him kiss me with the kisses of his mouth.' "Bit graphic, isn't it?" he said. "Remarkable workmanship, nevertheless."

"What, the inscription? Never thought about it really. Grandad must have been a bit of a goer!"

Paula returned the ring to her finger where it sat snugly in an indentation it had already made in the three years she had possessed it. She smiled at him. "Come on then. Better come and kiss me with the kisses of your mouth!"

He drew her down towards him and kissed her hard.

"I love you, Fredrick." It was a simple statement, unaffected and without further agenda. She waited for a moment, hungry for reciprocation.

He smiled up at her. "I know you do, darling, I know you do."

"When will you be able to leave your wife?" Promises had been whispered in this room. Their shared plans had seeped into the walls and lay between the cracks of the floorboards. The room was aware that before long, he would leave both his business partnership and his marriage and flee Liverpool with her. They would go south, he had said: not London; maybe Reading, maybe Southampton. There, they would be able to make a life together, free from interfering eyes.

"I'm not sure," he replied.

She waited for more. There was none. She prompted with another question: "By the end of this year?"

He didn't answer. Instead, he raised himself from the bed, rather more slowly than she had done, and dropped his legs to the side. Reaching for his clothes, he began to dress.

She continued to kneel, looking at herself in the mirror opposite. She liked the way her hair curled to her shoulders. She knew she was beautiful. She knew that she loved him. She knew he would love her back. Soon, very, very soon, he would love her back.

Thursday 7th July 1988 12.55 pm BST

May gave way to June. June gave up the ghost to July. Paula had not expected to see much of Freddie over the summer. Nevertheless, she harboured a secret disappointment that he had not taken her to lunch much... not at all, in fact. And there was something she needed to talk to him about; something that she was beginning to become concerned about.

"Come on, you!" Paula felt a prod on her left arm. "Stop daydreaming or ol' Po Face at the front there will be having your wages docked." Paula's mind lurched back into the room at Suzie's desecration of her daydream. "Come on – lunch." Suzie grabbed Paula by the sleeve and marched her out of the door and down the stairs. The two young women emerged from the grey Victorian building into the midday sunshine "Chavasse or King?"

Paula thought for a moment. "Chavasse," she said, "It's closer." They made their way through the lunchtime crowds and the traffic, to the open, grassed area between the law courts and the police station. Although it was early, the space was becoming populated, as the office workers on lunch break joined the shoppers laden with carrier bags.

They located a spot and, laying down Suzie's blanket, staked a claim to it as personal territory for the next twenty minutes. Suzie sniffed as she looked at the expensively clad women passing them, bags and dog leads in hand, their pampered pets enacting unmentionable rituals upon trees and gate posts and sleeping gents' legs. "It ain't fair, is it?"

"What isn't fair?" asked Paula, genuinely surprised.

"Oh, life," replied Suzie, nonchalantly. "I mean, you take 'er over there." She pointed to a corpulent, grey-haired woman in her fifties, twenty yards away. She carried an air of innate superiority, crafted by generations of genetic memory and an upbringing of consciously imbibed presumptuousness. "Look at 'er. Never had to struggle in her life. Money to burn. More time than she knows what to do with. Then, look at me an' you, slavin' away in the likes of C&W 'til some man comes along and makes an honest woman of us. Then, we got a life of making babies and bottles and husbands' teas. Now, you tell me how fair that is."

Paula thought for a moment. "I quite like the idea of being made an honest woman, now you come to mention it. And babies... yeah, that would suit me." The girls giggled. Paula swapped her Appletiser for Suzie's Capri Sun.

"So, you going to tell me what's trublin' ya or what then?" The words were unexpected, escaping captivity before Suzie had taken the time to consider the wisdom of asking a question to which she already knew the answer. Paula looked at her silently, gazing her reply to her friend from her troubled face. Suzie was quiet for a moment, then, "How long have you known, Sweetheart?"

Paula's eyes filled rapidly with tears that overflowed, meandering their way down her cheeks until they dropped from her chin. "Come here, Darlin'," said Suzie. Paula acquiesced as her older friend drew her head to her shoulder.

Paula finally spoke. "I've missed two now." The statement was non-committal, but the implication expertly communicated.

"Who?" The question was an obvious one. Again, Suzie had a fair idea of the answer. When none was forthcoming from Paula, she answered on her behalf. "Fredrick Julian Angus Dickinson."

"How do you know his name?" Paula managed between sobs.

"Because he told me, Sweetheart... in bed... shortly after I enquired about the war wound. Did he give you the story about Goose Green? Pack of lies. He wouldn't know which end of a gun to point if you handed it to him loaded.

"So… so, how did he come by the scar?" asked Paula, challenged for the first time with the possibility of her lover's dishonesty.

"Not certain, Darlin', but I was told it was a shotgun wound from an irate farmer in Knutsford whose daughter Mr Charmer had been seeing. Been lots of others, of course, me included. That's not what matters though. The important question is what are you going to do now?"

Paula was quiet again, crying softly, her head on her friend's shoulder. Their allotted hour was almost up now but neither of them was inclined to move.

"Oh Suzie," she finally managed, "what *am* I going to do now?"

Her friend hesitated, then replied, "Get rid of it, Darlin.' It'll all be over quick and you can have your life back."

"No!" Paula sat bolt upright, her eyes burning with aggression. "It's mine! No one's gonna take this baby from me!"

Suzie recoiled in surprise at the vehemence of the outburst. "All right, all right, Sweetheart," answered Suzy. "I was just tryin' to help. Don't upset yourself." She paused, then added, "Well, there's only one thing for it then. You're going to have to tell Mr Charmer and see if he'll stand by you." The pigeons gathered around the bench now, as the girls' discarded bread and cheese became a battle of Goose Green in microcosm, engaging one another over the spoils of war. "Look, Sweetheart, I have to go, or ol' Po Face will be docking my wages. You stay here a while. I'll cover for you. I'll tell her you've been taken poorly. Give it some thought. But remember, I'll always be here for you." Suzie rose to leave, brushing the crumbs from the lap of her dress. Paula sat for a moment as her friend walked away and reflected on lies and trust and naivety. Then, without warning, she kicked at the bread, scattering the crumbs and the crusts over the path in front of the bench like a mechanised military intervention into a Stone Age conflict. Still weeping, she rose and submerged herself in the afternoon crowds.

Friday 8ᵗʰ July 1988 4.10 pm BST

"You little fool!" The words were harsh and were spat venomously from lips that had once kissed her tenderly. "How the hell did you manage to get yourself in that condition? You've bloody well ruined everything now, haven't you? Just when I was set to finalise plans to leave here and make a new life for us down south, you have to go and wreck it." He was in full flow now, his anger pouring uncontrolled over the edges of his composure, his body shaking violently.

She sat mutely on the bed, looking at him in growing fear. He'd never been angry with her before; never shouted at her. The most he'd ever been was silent and moody. She didn't know how to handle him this way. It shouldn't be this way. It wasn't her fault, or at least not her fault alone; That she ought to be able to expect a little comfort or even support from him. But all that had disappeared into the boiling sea of invective in which she was now drowning. Freddie got up from the bed naked. He paced the room rapidly, drawing on the cigarette in short, sharp bursts. "How could you do it? How could you do it?" He seemed almost to be talking more to himself than to her. His voice reached a crescendo, then fell to a threatening silence within moments.

She tried to interject. "But darling…"

"Don't you *darling* me," he snarled back at her, the uncharacteristic ferocity unabated. He twirled round and leaned across the bed to where she lay, his red, angry face just inches from her. For the first time, she saw something new, something fearsome in his eyes. She tried to identify it… not fear… not irritation… hatred? Surely not hatred? He loved her. How could love turn to hate over a piece of news that in other circumstances would bring joy and happiness to both of them.

"You've brought this on yourself. No one but you is responsible for your condition, Paula." The edge of the anger was blunted a little now, as his tone turned to parental judgement. Now she was a little girl again. He sounded like her class teacher when she was 13, Paula's feet frozen to the schoolroom floor, having been discovered in some monumentally minor misdemeanour. Then the harshness returned to his tone, wrenching her back to 1988. "Well, I'm not..." he slammed his fist down on the bedside table, "...going... to..." More thumps of his fist resonated on the wood just inches to the left of her hand. She was terrified of his anger, unable to process what was going on. Now, she feared for her safety as a side of him she had never before witnessed took control. "...take... responsibility... for... it." He sprang back as fast as he had leaned forward. The act was equally intimidating.

"I'm tipped for a senior partnership when Anderson retires this year. I'm not going to throw it away on the likes of you, you, worthless little bitch."

And now, her tears flowed. She covered her face in her hands and sobbed in fear and pain and for what she had done that had made him so angry. Her nakedness, so recently a source of attraction to him, was now an offence to his eyes. Grabbing her clothes from the chair, he flung them across the room at her. "Get dressed!" he screamed. "Get your damned clothes on. I should never have let you tempt me into bed. I should have known better. I've been with your kind before. You see an emotionally vulnerable, well-off man and you make him a target for whatever you can get from him. It's not mine. It can't be. And anyway, how do I know you're even pregnant? Are you lying to me?" This last screamed over an outstretched arm and an accusing finger.

Her response was involuntary. "No," she wailed, "honestly, no. It's true. I'm sorry. I didn't know it was my fault. I didn't... I couldn't... I thought you... I thought we were going... thought it wouldn't matter... thought you would be pleased."

"Pleased? Pleased?" His voice was rising to falsetto now. "Why the hell did you think I'd be *pleased*, you little fool? Pleased to be hitched up to the likes of you for the rest of my life? Pleased to be held accountable for your bastard?" – this last screamed at fever pitch. He was out of control. She herself wept uncontrollably, her hands in her face as she sat naked and shivering on the bed.

Quickly, he dragged on his trousers and shirt, forced his feet into his shoes and stormed out of the room. The walls shook as the door slammed behind him. Moments later, she heard the ground floor door slam as well, and she knew he would be out in the street. She was, at least, safe for the moment. And in her safety, the floodgates opened. She wailed and sobbed, urinating involuntarily and shaking uncontrollably as she sat, legs unmoving, as if frozen to the bed. She was 13 again.

Friday 8ᵗʰ July 1988 9.05 pm BST

Slowly, 13 had become 14, then dragged itself through 15 and 16, and all the way up to 19. But 19 didn't feel very different from 13. It just carried more responsibility. The crying had finally subsided. Paula had washed and dressed herself, leaving the room and her dreams for the last time. Walking down the stairs and through the front door, she had been confronted with the question of where to go. Not home. Home wouldn't be home anymore; not if you were the daughter of a socially sensitive Pentecostal minister and you were 19 and pregnant with no partner.

Without much thought, she had wandered aimlessly, finally ending up at the railway station. From there, the music coming from the Liverpool Pub had offered the possibility of, if not solace, then, an opportunity to forget her problems for a spell.

She really had not planned to talk to anyone.

She really had not considered the possibility of anyone spiking her shandy and leading her round to the alley at the back of the pub.

She really had not considered the possibility of three determined young men intent on forcibly removing her clothes as an enjoyable prerequisite to gang rape.

Nor, however, when forced to confront such matters by the very fact that they were happening, had she considered the possibility of two young Irish men responding to the sound of her piercing screams. And she had certainly not considered the capability of a heavily built six-foot-two Irish man's ability to snap the fingers of one of her assailants, whilst simultaneously delivering a well-aimed kick to the groin of a second, and this at the same time as his rather less-well-built younger brother dispatched a third with a trained left hook.

The Irishmen's defence of the honour of the young lady had been entirely unexpected and it was only a matter of seconds before the would-be rapists fled. With the festivities over, Denny stood, looking at the scene in some confusion.

"Sure, an' don't ya' know it's impolite to watch a young lady while she's gettin' herself dressed, Denny?" came Sean's somehow comforting comment. And in an act of almost anachronistic chivalry, the two Irishmen turned their backs on the shocked young woman, who replaced her blouse and pulled down her skirt, rendering herself almost comfortable once more. And of course, when she was done, it was once again Sean, with his gift of sunny good humour and gentle flowing words, that suggested they all find somewhere for a nice quiet drink. And that was how they came to find themselves on the night train to London. Quite how it was that Paula found herself seated next to the almost silent Denny rather than the eloquent Sean, she could not later say. And how it was that they arrived the next morning at Euston with her sleeping head upon his shoulder and her hand cradling his hand in her lap will always remain one of the great unsolved mysteries of the universe.

Monday 7ᵗʰ February 1994 9.10 am GMT

Laura crawled into the cupboard next to the kitchen sink. She didn't mind playing on her own even if it was her birthday. She had tried to make friends, but Mummy and Da and Laura and Jamie moved house so often for Da to find work that she was never around new friends for long. Now, she sometimes wished she could have a friend who moved with her. Of course, Jamie moved with them, but he was too little to play. And anyway, he was having his nap right then. Mummy was napping too, so Laura had to play on her own. She had already played birthdays with an enormous cake pretended from the big round washing up bowl, except the tea spoons she pretended were candles wouldn't stand up properly in the Playdoh and the chairs where the guests would have sat looked a bit empty.

Laura thought hide and seek would probably be more fun. And that meant sitting in the cupboard in the darkness and counting to a hundred, then getting out and looking for yourself. Only, because you knew where you hid, you didn't take very long to find the spot.

So, in Laura got, and squeezed into the end where there were no pipes and she could see out through the little round screw hole that went right through into the living room and started counting. "1… 2…3…"

"Hi Babe," said the voice.

"What are you doing in my cupboard?" asked Laura.

"Waiting for you, Babe" said the voice.

"Shall we play hide and seek, then?" said Laura.

"That's my favourite game," said Gabe.

Tuesday 1ˢᵗ March 1994 7.15 pm GMT

With Laura and Jamie finally asleep, Paula settled down to dinner with Denny in front of the TV. Denny had insisted they stop watching Brookside back in January when they showed that disgusting Lesbian kiss. But Paula didn't mind too much because now EastEnders was on three times a week and it was much better.

"Den, I'm worried about Laura," she said when the rapid drum beat initiated the final credits.

"An' why would that be?" he replied in his Galway brogue, undiluted since his arrival in England six years before. Paula thought privately that his accent was part of the reason he'd found it so hard to find work. She reckoned that employers preferred to understand what their workers were saying. Not that she was a whole lot better with her Liverpudlian accent, now they had moved to Southampton. She had worked on it, of course, trying to better herself, as she saw it. But between the children, looking after a home and juggling health care assistant work in Southampton General, there was little time left for self-improvement.

She looked closely at him. Six years of labouring, of railway work, of dock work, of any kind of work at all must have started to make an impact, she thought. But there was nothing outwardly to show for it. And now he had given up smoking, his cough had disappeared and he had more energy. She though for the ten thousandth time, how fortunate she was to have a husband like Denny, particularly given the circumstances in which they had met. Her only real gripe was his unshakable insistence that the children be brought up Catholic. So, there had been christenings and family gatherings (the Ryans were dispersed worldwide but committed to reuniting when there was something to celebrate) and there had been visits from the priest and Sunday school every week for Laura since she was four. Paula considered it was a small enough price to pay in exchange for a man who unfailingly handed a pay packet over every Friday and had never once, so far as Paula knew, so much as glanced at another woman.

"She's got an imaginary friend."

"Aw, sure they all have that at her age."

"Mm. But this one has an American accent and calls her 'Babe'. He also tells her to read books I've never heard of and says she has to get ready."

"Get ready for what?"

"Apparently, he won't say. Just that she has to get ready."

"So, how's she s'posed to get ready when she doesn't know what for?"

"She told me he says he'll tell her when it's time. I could put up with all that, but he is now apparently accompanying her to school and she's insisting on sitting next to an empty chair, so that there's room for 'Gabe' to sit down. Mrs. Jackson put her foot down on that one. But it appears Gabe was not best pleased to have to stand at the back of the class. Apparently, it's bad for his wings to have to stand up too long."

"His wings." Denny turned to look at her, his beautiful wife who he was still proud of after six years and still told everyone about. "So, he's a fairy?"

"I guess he must be."

"Ah, I wouldn't worry about it. We were full o' stories of little people growing up back home. And sure, isn't an imagination a good thing in a child? She'll grow up the better for it. It's just a phase. It'll be over in six months. You'll see."

Only it wasn't.

Thursday 7th April 1994 6.10 pm BST

"Gabe is sad today, Mummy."

"Why, Queen?" replied Paula, glancing down at her daughter's plate to see if she'd eaten all her supper.

"His Tootsies are dead."

"Oh, he must have been sitting on them, Sweetheart. Tell him to give them a bit of a rub and they'll soon come back to life."

Paula had quite forgotten the brief exchange when reports of the Rwandan genocide started to filter onto the six o'clock news.

Tuesday 26th April 1994 5.10 pm BST

"Gabe says the China plane got broke, Mummy."

"Well, it was very careless of him to drop it, Darling. Tell him to hold it tighter next time."

"He says he held it as tight as he could. But he just wasn't strong enough. And now, all the people inside are dead."

"Oh, Sweetheart, you don't want to think about things like that. It was only a pretend plane. There weren't any real people on it, Sweetheart. And after dinner, Da will get some glue and mend it."

"There were real people on it, Mummy. There were 264 of them. And now, they're all dead. And Gabe is sad 'cos it wasn't their time to die."

Paula looked at her daughter quizzically. And when the six o'clock news came with news of 264 people dying in an airplane crash in China, she remembered the conversation.

Thursday 21st July 1994 7.00 pm BST

"Gabe made the Shoemaker hit Jupiter, Da."

"Sure, an' why was that, Milish'? Was Jupiter one of the elves who stole the Shoemaker's thread?"

"Noooo, Da. Not the shoemaker in the *book*, the Shoemaker in the *sky*. Gabe said he had to make it hit Jupiter or it would have hit Earth."

"Hush and snuggle down, Creena, or you'll be wakin' Jamie."

Denny didn't follow the news very closely, certainly nothing to do with astronomy.

Saturday 6th August 1994 8.04 pm BST

"Gabe says I have to get ready, Da."

"Really Milish? And what would that be for?"

"To help Mummy."

"Well that's an excellent idea, Sweetheart. Tell Gabe from me that he's a truly admirable fairy."

"He says I'll be sad when you're gone, but not as sad as Mummy will be and that's why I have to be especially helpful and make you proud of me."

"I'll always be proud a' ya, Darlin', you can be sure of that. But where does your Gabe think I'm goin' when I don't even know meself?"

Monday 8th August 1994 8.47 am BST

What put the matter beyond question was that the car had just passed its MOT. The certificate was dated four days earlier, and at first the garage's insurance company argued driver error. But the post mortem revealed no trace of alcohol or medical cause, and there hadn't been another car in motion in the street when the Ford Focus veered off the road. The brick wall it collided with collapsed onto the car, instantly killing the single occupant. The mechanical investigation confirmed that the brake pipe was badly corroded and a substantial amount of hydraulic fluid had drained out, as the residue on the road outside the house confirmed. The cause of the accident was, therefore, beyond dispute and the settlement was substantial.

Almost a year later, Paula spent it on a semi-detached house in Deacon Road, Southampton. Nothing would bring Denny back, but at least her children would have the permanent home that their father had always dreamed of providing for them.

Saturday 6th November 1994 2.23 am GMT

"Don't cry, Sweetheart."

"I'm so sorry, Gabe. And now, Mummy has to change the wet bed and my 'jamas too."

"She understands, Sweetheart. She really doesn't mind."

"I miss my Da, Gabe."

"He misses you too, Sweetheart. He says to tell you how much he loves you."

"Tell him how much I love him, Gabe."

"Sure thing, Sweetheart. Now, call Mummy to help with the bed."

Monday 26th December 1994 1.35 am GMT

"I miss him so much, Gabe."

"I know you do, Sweetheart."

"I tried to make Christmas nice for Mummy and Jamie. But it just wasn't the same. We had presents and turkey, but Da's place was empty and all we had to put there was just this photo. And we were all quiet. Then, Jamie started crying and I started crying and Mummy cried, too."

"Can I teach you a song to sing when you feel sad, Babe?"

"Yes."

When I find myself in times of trouble,
Mother Mary comes to me
Speaking words of wisdom, let it be
And in my hour of darkness
She is standing right in front of me
Speaking words of wisdom, let it be.

Tuesday 8th August 1995 10.00 am BST

"Mummy's going to need some special help today, Babe."

"Why, Gabe?"

"Because it's the anniversary of Da's death."

"OK. I'll draw her a picture of Da. What's an anniversary, Gabe?"

Thursday 8ᵗʰ August 1996 10.00 am BST

"Mummy's going to need some special help today, Babe."

"Why, Gabe?"

"Because it's the anniversary of Da's death."

"OK. I'll pick her some flowers. We can put them on Da's grave."

Friday 8ᵗʰ August 1997 10.00 am BST

"Mummy's going to need some special help today, Babe."

"I know, Gabe. It's because it's the anniversary of Da's death, isn't it?"

"Yes, Laura."

"Jamie and I will take her to Da's grave, then afterwards, we'll go to the McDonald's Da used to take us all to on a Saturday."

Saturday 8ᵗʰ August 1998 10.00 am BST

"Mummy's going to need some special help today, Gabe. It's the anniversary of Da's death."

He does not answer at first. He merely spreads his wings and wraps them gently around the little girl. Laura snuggles down deep. She cannot see him but she enjoys the softness and the scent of him.

"Laura?"

"Yes, Gabe?"

"Da says to tell you, he's so proud of you, he's fit to burst."

Philemon

Rule Eight:

Players will undertake play through Nominated Proxies and other Tangibles only. Any player who compromises this rule will account to the Game Maker for their conduct.

Saturday 18th December 1999 10.00 am GMT

At five foot two and three-quarter inches tall exactly, to say Philemon Littlemann lived up to his name would be something of a contradiction in terms. He had always been on the short side for his age – a consequence of being born in the era of ration books, his mother said. He had, perhaps understandably, developed a considerable need to compensate. If he hadn't chosen the Saviour's own trade and become a carpenter on leaving school, one might almost say he had a chip on his shoulder. But no one in the Church of the Body of Christ would be crass enough to make that joke. When some subtle reference was made to his stature within his hearing, Philemon would simply look at the guilty party with that superior look of his and say, "Matthew 6:27, brother. I assume you have read it?" If the adversary was biblically literate, the point would be adequately made without further comment. If not, Philemon would put his head back a little so as to be able to look down his nose at him despite their difference in height and suggest his tormentor would probably serve the Lord better by studying the scripture than by persecuting other brethren. Thus, Philemon's peers in the Church of the Body of Christ learned to treat him with a degree of circumspection and Philemon himself began to learn the rudiments of controlling others by guilt and manipulation – a facility he would employ with increasing expert precision as his adult years passed. As regards any Heathen that taunted him for his height, or simply expressed a gentle witticism on the subject, he simply told them to fuck off. Nothing meant less to Philemon than the opinion of the Ungodly.

Nevertheless, despite the admonition of Matthew 6:27 that he was so fond of quoting, he had prayed secretly and unceasingly that 'if it were possible, this cup might pass from him'. Each morning, when he rose and drew himself up to full height next to the tape measure stapled to the door frame, he found his condition unchanged and his prayers unanswered. It was only later that it occurred to him that, when he had prayed for God to add to his height, he had not specified whether he meant physically or spiritually.

Perhaps, it was this that resulted in Philemon becoming at first a spiritually focussed, but driven child and then, later, a spiritually manipulative but driven man. Whatever the task, Philemon needed to do it better, faster, more efficiently, more profitably than anyone else in the church. Perhaps, it also had some impact on the decision he was to make in adulthood to work with young people. Among them, at least, he was not perpetually reminded of his diminutive stature by a neck pain induced from looking upwards during every conversation. It was in this context that Philemon had discovered he carried a profound burden for the salvation of the children of Southampton.

It had first been in 1992 that the Spirit had laid upon him a deep and enduring word that he was to start a work amongst the young people of the town. This work was to be named '*The Sons of the Body of Christ*', and drew children from the age of 12 years and upwards. A year later, Philemon was satisfied with the progress being made by '*The Sons*', and started '*The Sisters of the Sons of the Body of Christ*'. As one of the elders of the church had observed in a closed meeting, Philemon had better not start any further subcategories of his work, or he might end up with a group called '*The Pet Hamsters of the Second Cousins of the Grandparents of the Sisters of the Sons of the Body of Christ*', and then he would run out of space on his headed notepaper. The roar of laughter the comment drew from all three elders present at the meeting summed up the attitude of the church and eldership to Philemon's work. They could hardly criticise it openly, since it was evidently leading young people in the direction of the Church. Nevertheless, they found it as difficult to take seriously as they found Philemon himself. Ever since his return from the mission field in 1991, he had simply failed to reintegrate back into the church. Of course, after all that time away with infrequent furlough visits back, many of the people he had originally known there were gone. Nevertheless, his dedication to the Lord, The Lord's work and the Church was, as all had to admit, exemplary. Hence, they found themselves simultaneously admiring the Work and quietly wishing that it had been someone else in the church who had started the young people's mission; someone not quite so problematic; someone a little more... well... taller.

Operating from a hired hall opposite the Veracity Recreation Ground in Bitterne, the *Work* settled into a pattern. A mid-week evening (Wednesdays for *The Sons*, Thursdays for *The Sisters of The Sons*) would commence at 7.00 pm with organised games – in the hall during the winter and on the recreation ground in the summer. When the young people had burned off enough energy, there would be eats – a glass of juice and a bun, all provided by Philemon personally, free of charge. Philemon would then bring the word of the Lord for that evening. He was always careful not to overdo it with the young people. Fifteen minutes was quite enough on a biblical topic chosen for its relevance to the age group and sex concerned. Finally, to the considerable comfort and gratitude of the parents of the young people, he would drive each member of his little congregation home in his minibus. which in the daytime found employment in his carpentry trade.

It was at this time, Philemon discovered the strangest of phenomena. He had cut his elocutory teeth on the mission field, of course. But out there, it was easy to get people to listen to you by virtue of the colour of your skin. Winning the attention of bored teenagers in Southampton was a quite different matter. Accordingly, he was somewhat surprised to find he was rather good at speaking to the young. You might even say he had a gift. You might even say he was a natural, since to his considerable pleasure, his young congregations seemed to find him completely mesmerising.

Whatever the reason why, within a year of the opening of *The Sons,* one of the teenage boys approached him with a question of how he might devote his life to Christ and be freed from the awful burden of sin he had been carrying ever since hearing of its existence during the very first of Philemon's sermons. That night, Philemon made a point of driving all the other young people home first, leaving Frank Gentleman until last. Then, when they were alone, he put his arm round the 14-year-old and led him, weeping, to the Saviour. Philemon was truly elated at the privilege of leading the boy to Christ. It would be wholly uncharitable to suggest that he might have derived any improper pleasure from the placement of his left arm around Frank's shoulder; or his right hand, throughout their shared moment of prayer, upon his knee.

Today, though, was a day for both looking back and looking forward, since it was Philemon's birthday. Indeed, at age 40, it was something of a watershed birthday – a day for reassessing the direction his life was taking. It was not a day for 'celebration' within the heathen meaning of the term, of course. Such practices as the sending of cards and the giving of gifts were spurned by Church members, be they for Christmas, or birthdays or any similar occasions. Such anniversaries, public or purely private, were opportunities for prayerful reflection. At Christmas, the Church would pray and reflect en masse on the coming of the Saviour and the response of the world. And it was common to spend birthdays in family or solitary reflection. Having no family, Philemon was apt to spend the day alone quietly. There had been a family once, of course; a family of origin, that is. But both his parents had died, and for Philemon himself, the much prayed for gift of marriage and a family had not materialised.

There had been a woman: long ago, one very special young woman with the light of heaven in her eyes and a smile that could melt the snow on the mountains of Arabah. That was back when he was 22. For a season, they had drawn close. And for the first time, in his happiness, he had let down his spiritual guard. Philemon had felt the onslaught of unfamiliar emotional urges... then the physical urges he had learned to subdue years before. He had found himself wanting more than was proper for him to want. He had spent whole nights on his knees in agony, praying one moment for delivery from this Satanic grip and the next moment that the Lord would grant him permission to marry this precious child of Heaven with her flowing golden hair and her laughing blue eyes. However, as it turned out, all the agony and all the praying proved to be superfluous. Laura had come to him and told him gently that she had decided it was impossible for her to be with someone so much shorter than herself.

Philemon's pain was indescribable. She could have hurt him no more if she had nailed his hands and his feet to a cross and raised him high for the members of the church to pelt in mockery. Yet, it was in this agony that he came to understand that the suffering itself had been the Lord's purpose in allowing the relationship to develop as far as it had. For now, he was able to understand and relate to the Christ's own suffering in a way he would never otherwise have been able. Few, he surmised, if any, had been called to tread this path before. He was greatly blessed, perhaps even uniquely blessed, set apart from the calling of other men, summoned to live by a different standard for a different purpose. Whatever the work was for which the Lord was preparing him, it was better done without the aid of a helpmeet. The road would be lonely, but unquestionably, the Spirit of God would enable him to bear the solitude. And there would be compensation. There would be allowances. Philemon was quite certain that his God fully understood his needs.

Within a year, Laura had married a man from another church: a man that stood over six-foot tall amongst the flowers and bridesmaids and smiling faces, as before the altar he slipped a golden ring on her finger.

Philemon watched, uninvited, from the doorway.

Within a month, he had committed to the mission field and flown to a remote corner of tropical Cameroon where he was to spend the next nine years.

With the energy of the spurned, he had thrown himself into that *Work*. The mission was in desperate need of people with practical skills and his carpentry easily kept him busy six days a week, with evenings and Sundays largely taken up with devotions. Only the nights were difficult. Only in the darkness of the small hours when the compound was silent and the monkeys were calling from the rainforest beyond, did Satan come to him. Then, Philemon would writhe upon his bed, his hands burning with the temptation, as he hungered in his deep places for what the Church had always forbidden, only eventually, to yield and then, repent in sweat and shame as the first light of the coming dawn cast condemnation across his window. Night after night, in a personal Gethsemane and Calvary of agony and repentance, inside him, his dove struggled with his raven for almost nine years.

Then came Jonathan. And Philemon knew he would struggle with sin no more.

Of course, it took time and much prayer and study for Philemon to be persuaded of the inescapable message emanating from his body, and acknowledge that Jonathan was not Satan's temptation, but rather was the Lord's gift. And this only came to him when he was ready to accept a new learning, a new Truth, a different Truth from the Truth taught by the Church of the Body of Christ. Only when Philemon's years of struggle had at last brought him to the end of himself, to a final acknowledgement that God had created him exactly as He intended him to be, was he ready to accept God's true grace and acknowledge the Lord's hand was on him in an utterly different way from other men. What to others might be sin, was to Philemon fundamental to his calling. It was so obvious to him now that he wondered why he had never seen it before. He was summoned to live by different commandments, to a different standard, with different allowances.

The arrival of this young man, this Gift of Jehovah, in the Sunday afternoon teenagers' bible class with his adoring eyes that never left the diminutive Englishman as he spoke, was the final confirmation Philemon needed that he was exempt from the simplistic moral code that had been created for other men. He was, quite simply, the *Lord s Anointed*.

And when he had finally accepted this clear and obvious Truth, in secret, the soul of Jonathan was knit with the soul of Philemon and Jonathan loved Philemon as his own soul. Then, having had him once, Philemon took him again and again and again. And the love of Jonathan was wonderful to Philemon, passing the love of women. And there was no condemnation, for how could there be any condemnation of the *Lord s Anointed* in Christ Jesus? For Philemon now knew with the conviction of Heaven itself that the Lord's Anointed was beyond the commitment of sin and was in need of no forgiveness.

But when Philemon had loved Jonathan, so that love was no longer as new to him as the dew upon the mountain, Philemon once more decided that he had heard the voice of the Lord that spake unto his *Anointed* and it did tell him it was time for Jonathan to be cut off from fellowship with the *Lord s Anointed*. So, in secret did Philemon take Jonathan into the Forest. And under a cascading waterfall he took to him the knife of Abraham and in blood did he sever Jonathan from fellowship. And Philemon convinced himself that the blood of the sacrifice was a sweet, smelling savour in the nostrils of his god.

Then, seeing the blood upon the knife and upon the hands of the

Lord s Anointed, Philemon awoke as it were from a deep sleep. And Philemon knew what he had done. And he knew it would take time to re-convince himself he had not sinned after all.

The Southampton of 1991 to which Philemon returned was very different from the one he had left in 1982. There was a buoyancy, a confidence about England that had barely been stirring when he had departed. Something to do with winning a war? Something to do with the making of money? All such concerns were as nothing to Philemon. He looked around at the trappings of wealth that he saw – the new shopping centres, the new cars, the new selfishness and automatically thought of Luke 12 and the parable of the rich man who said, *"This will I do: I will pull down my barns, and build greater; and there will I bestow all my fruits and my goods. And I will say to my soul, Soul, thou hast much goods laid up for many years; take thine ease, eat, drink, and be merry."*

Philemon saw much ease taking about him, much merriment and much laying up of this world's goods. And he remembered how God said to that rich man: *"Thou fool, this night thy soul shall be required of thee: then, whose shall those things be, which thou hast provided?"*

What was most difficult for Philemon to understand, was the way the Church of the Body of Christ had embraced the changed orthodoxy of the world about it. In his absence, it had profited materially. A considerable wealth had been amassed from the sale of long-owned pieces of land that turned out to be suitable for development. And the sums so realised had been substantially enhanced by judicious (or was that lucky?) stock market investment.

Philemon had nothing, and he knew the Lord had nothing, against material wealth. But this was a question of how it was being used. Though the growth in the congregation that Philemon had worked and prayed for had stalled, the amassed material resources of the church were being squandered. Vehicles had been acquired where there was, to Philemon's thinking, no clear need. Elders were funded to attend international conferences in exotic locations. And though there could, of course, be no suggestion of impropriety, the elders were now living in homes far more valuable than they had previously occupied, with no obvious source of income to pay for them.

Philemon kept his counsel. For as much as five years, the growing work amongst the young people of Southampton kept him sufficiently absorbed that he was able to remain silent regarding his concerns about the direction of the church, just as he was able to suppress his own memories about the events that had taken place in Cameroon.

But as the young people's work grew, his vision for a greater adult work grew with it. Upon his knees, aching in prayer for the glory of the Lord to be revealed, he visualised a large new church building, a powerful pastor in leadership, intercessory missions to the heathen, a huge auditorium filled with worshipers, healings, conversions by the thousand. Sometimes, he would pray and visualise for hours on end. Philemon could see the rows of sinners desperate for forgiveness. He could see their arms reaching forward, the tears of repentance upon their pleading faces. He could hear the organ playing softly as the call to repentance was given, the old, old hymn playing:

Just as I am, without one plea,
But that thy blood was shed for me.

He could see them forming a line to be prayed for. He could see them dropping vast wealth into his collection plates. He could see them waiting hours merely for the chance to see him, to touch the gold ring upon his finger. And as he prayed so very fervently that this vision might be made real, and he asked how he himself might make it real at any cost, it seemed to Philemon that a word formed in letters of holy fire in the air before him. And the light of that word burned so brightly that it left an imprint on the retinas of his eyes, so that, open or closed, waking or sleeping, always did he see this word before him.

And that word was 'Power'.

And Philemon knew in his heart that the god Power awaited only the coming of the goddess Opportunity to spawn the progeny Domination.

It had started with a weakening of the doctrine of the role of women in the Church. Philemon had left behind a body of believers in which women were entirely silent except for the singing of hymns. He had returned to one in which in the very first service he attended, a woman deigned to give the notices *without wearing a headscarf*. He was speechless. But when the next Sunday, a woman stood to deliver a sermon, it was more than he could bear and he walked out of the church, moments after she started speaking. He knew where his interests lay, however, and he knew that he was as yet in no position to influence church policy. But he was also not alone in his hatred of the abomination of a woman's voice being heard in the House of the Lord. For there were others that acknowledged as he did that Eve had sinned first and tempted Adam into sin; that as a result, the curse of women had been visited upon Eve that she and her daughters would forever bear this reminder of original sin.

Others, too, were less than comfortable with the financial excesses that were now becoming more openly practised by the eldership. Philemon maintained his strategic silence as he steadily noted more and more members of the congregation on whom he would be able to rely when he made his move.

The goddess Opportunity arrived from a quite unexpected source on Saturday 26th February 1995. Knowledge of the collapse of Barings, the bank in which the eldership had invested some 60% of the resources of the church, entered the public domain. By Sunday morning, with the news just breaking and the consequences far from clear, Philemon decided there was no rush to take action. And that gave him eight days to determine precisely how the goddess Opportunity would be introduced to the god Power to be fucked to his considerable advantage.

By Sunday 5th March, he had met with the most reliable members of the congregation and agreed the matter in principle. By the same date, he had fully researched the Trust Deed under which the trustees were appointed to run the financial affairs of the church. So much for matters financial. However, there was no written constitution that specified the method of governance of the church in non-financial affairs, for no one had ever conceived of a situation in which there would be a need for anything more than careful, prayerful consideration of the will of God.

So, at 11.39 am, precisely, on Sunday 5th March, immediately following the breaking of bread, Philemon rose to speak. If the eldership had hoped to keep knowledge of the decimation of the church's funds from the congregation, they were to be disappointed. In precise language, more reminiscent of a lawyer's office than a church pulpit, he systematically revealed the full catalogue of the Elderships' failings, both financial and spiritual. By the time he finished, eighty-seven minutes later, without making any libelous accusations, Philemon had sewn sufficient seeds of doubt in the minds of his listeners that they would never again trust their triumvirate of elders. And having completely undermined the confidence of the congregation in the existing method of governance and financial control, in the great tradition of the would-be dictators of history before him, he left it to others to propose the new route forward: others, of course, who had already been comprehensively instructed in what was required of them.

Thus, well after the normal time for the ending of the service, speaker after speaker rose, condemning the individuals and the system that had today brought the church to its financial and spiritual knees. All called for the removal of the triumvirate as eldership and as board of trustees and their immediate replacement with a single point of control – a Pastor. As a wave of murmured approval rotated clockwise around the church, Philemon sat silently, knowing that the Trust Deed called only for a majority of votes of the congregation to change the church's financial governance. As the disgraced elders left their elevated seats and slunk away with angry looks, the question was expressed by several, "Who shall lead us? Who shall be our Pastor?"

A lone, unidentified voice emanated from the back of the hall: a young male voice, and with the speaker being invisible to most, a voice crying in the wilderness, representing as it were, the future of the church. "Let it be Philemon." Following a moment's silence, the echoes were universal in their consensus.

Philemon made as if to deny the request. "No, let it be the most spiritual amongst us," he replied – but not so loud as to risk being listened to. And the voices of the congregation rose above Philemon's voice until, as if spontaneously, two members of the congregation who had been most vociferous on the matter of the doctrine of women in the church, rose and led Philemon to the pulpit, beseeching him to accept the appointment.

Philemon's acceptance speech lived on in the church's collective memory for years after that day. He spoke of piety and repentance, of freedom and submission, of his vision for a church that called out a single message resonating like a hymn of grace. And the Church of the Body of Christ wept in united repentance that such proud rebelliousness could ever have arisen among them. And when the weeping was done and repentance complete and when they had assured one another of the Lord's grace and forgiveness, Philemon shook every hand and looked into every eye as they filed out. Then, he stood watching, a smile of considerable satisfaction on his lips, as they drove home in their Mercedes and their BMWs to their, by now, rather overcooked roast Sunday lunches.

When all had left, he returned to the church and locked the entrance door. Glancing ironically at the trestle tables in the foyer laden with hymn books and church magazines and tracts of John 3 on New Birth, he pushed the swing door open and entered the main hall of the church.

Frank stood. Without speaking, Philemon took him in his arms and kissed him, a long slow kiss. Then, breaking from the embrace, he stood back, and smiling, struck him across the cheek with his right palm so as to draw blood. And then, they both collapsed in laughter.

On the Monday, Philemon met the Triumvirate and handed over sample documentation evidencing prima facie fraud upon the Trust. His price for not forwarding this to the police was their signed agreement to the transfer of all Trustee rights and responsibilities to himself, together with their individual letters of congratulatory approval to him on his appointment as Pastor, which he had already drafted for their signature. They all considered this an acceptable price. Rather less acceptable was the requirement that they hand back the keys to their Trust-supplied executive cars. Hardest of all was the replacement of their subsidised interest rates on their Trust-provided, interest-only mortgages with market-rate commercial loans, including a clause requiring repayment of all capital within twelve months. But in practice, none of them preferred the prospect of a highly public fraud investigation. And Philemon saw that it was good. And the evening and the morning were the first day.

On Tuesday, Philemon spent the day collecting the cars and

driving them to auction. And he thought the reserve prices for the cars pretty encouraging. And the evening and the morning were the second day.

On the Wednesday, he passed the incriminating file anonymously to the Police. And the police took a considerable interest. And the evening and the morning were the third day.

On the Thursday, he held the meeting of *The Sisters* as normal. No one was saved. But later that night, the three elders were taken in for questioning under caution. And Philemon saw that it was promising. And the evening and the morning were the fourth day.

On the Friday, the car auction yielded £37,210.87 net of auction costs from the disposal of the cars. And Philemon saw that it was good. And the evening and the morning were the fifth day.

On the Saturday, he placed the cash in a safety deposit box at a franchise operation on Southampton High Street. And Philemon saw that it was most satisfactory. And the evening and the morning were the sixth day.

On the Sunday, he sent word to the Church that the Lord had called him to spend the day in fasting and deep prayer and that he would, therefore, not be attending the service.

And on the seventh day, Philemon ended his work which he had made; and he rested on the seventh day from all his work which he had made. And he sat up in bed in his little two-bedroomed flat in Shirley, cradling an excellent single malt whisky, and looked upon the work that he had made. And seeing the work that he had made, he saw that it was good and smiled said unto no one except himself, "Fuck, am I good *or what*?!" And the evening and the morning were the seventh day.

However, Philemon was not a man to become caught up in his accomplishments. He knew that the support he had engendered would usher in something of a honeymoon period that could not be relied upon to sustain itself indefinitely. He had had plenty of time to devise his strategy following his return from the mission field three years earlier and was ready to proceed without delay.

A second wave of emotional commitment was required to achieve the consolidation. Alienation, and then excommunication, of the few revisionist elements that remained after his spiritual coup, as he liked to think of it, was really not too difficult. A pornographic magazine planted in a raincoat in the cloakroom on a wet Sunday when his sermon was on the subject of sexual purity; the proceeds of the collection plate turning up in a handbag on the day he spoke on the parable of the rich young ruler; a video recording (genuine, as it happened) of the excessive chastisement of a child at her own home when Philemon's subject was 'Suffer little children to come unto me'. All this laid more than enough foundation to ensure that he never needed to voice the denouncements personally. The departure of each problematic member of the congregation, though an end in itself, also had a tangential impact: that of drawing all who remained into closer unity behind a Pastor who was as quick to tell his flock what to believe and do as they were to be told. Within the year, the church sang and spoke with one voice – whatever and whenever the Pastor told them to.

The third phase of Philemon's strategy to cement control and direction of the church was doctrinal and was due to be initiated on 31st August 1997. He had intended to announce from the pulpit that he had been instructed by the Lord to follow in the footsteps of the Christ and depart into a high and remote place to fast and pray. Inconveniently, the Princess of Wales chose the very same day to die. Philemon would not normally have let such an insignificant worldly event influence his timetable. However, he correctly predicted that a national if not international outpouring of grief would take place in the wake of the death. He would be able to surf this unplanned wave rapidly forward if he got his timing right. Judiciously, he chose as his text that day, Luke 1:28 and preached on 'Blessed art thou among women', hitting the emotional note perfectly.

It was not until after the young woman's funeral on September 6th that he was able to return congruently to his planned fast. For biblical conformity, he considered saying it was to be for forty days, but decided, finally, he couldn't rely on Frank and his other Deacons to hold things together for that long just yet. They were, in fairness, all young and new appointees drawn from the ranks of *The Sons* and *The Sisters*. So, in order to avoid putting them under too much strain, Philemon decided God had summoned him to fast and pray for just three weeks. Nevertheless, he reckoned it would be long enough for a pretty good long-haul winter sun holiday. Eventually, settling on Miami Beach, he booked an Upper Class return on Virgin Atlantic and an all-inclusive at the Loews Miami Beach Hotel through a travel agent in Portsmouth. The necessary cash was drawn from the safety deposit box on Southampton High Street. Philemon toyed with the idea of taking one or two of the young people with him as a reward for their personal devotion and rather intimate services to him. In the end, though, he concluded they weren't quite ready for such an arduous spiritual battle and decided against it.

The first night following his arrival, he sat in his suite overlooking the beach. Philemon watched as a hotel employee piloted a small rolling machine up and down, flattening the sand, almost as if he were ironing it, as the waves lapped gently against the shoreline. Dinner arrived within seconds of the arranged time, courtesy of Room Service. A tall, powerfully built Afro-American waiter of perhaps 20, impeccably dressed in white, wheeled in a large trolley. The New York strip steak was nothing short of perfect.

Later, after Gus had returned at the end of his shift, condensation ran down the neck of the upturned Napa Valley Chardonnay bottle as it stood in the remains of the iced water in the cooler on the bedside table. The white uniform lay crumpled on the floor.

The first Sunday following his return, Philemon announced the results of his three weeks of prayer and fasting from the pulpit with due emotion. The Lord had revealed to him, he said with shaking voice, a new Truth for the coming new century. And this was a Truth of such enormity, said Philemon, that he had hesitated over whether the Church of the Body of Christ was yet ready, was yet mature enough, to understand it and cope with its implications. And he had said to the Lord, "No, Lord, for this is more than your people can take at this time. This Truth is too great, too powerful, too deep for any to hear yet." But the Lord had said to Philemon, "Let my people hear my word." And Philemon had begged the Lord not to lay such a burden on his people for a season more; to let them enjoy their spiritual childhood a little longer. But as Philemon said, leaning tearfully forward over the pulpit, the Lord had again said, "No, for My people are ready and there is so little time for them to prepare themselves." So, Philemon spoke the *Truth* to the Lord's People and prayed they would prove strong enough, mature enough to bear it, for this was the doctrine of *SecondCome*.

Philemon was particularly fond of the mid-word capitalisation – he reckoned it would make the doctrine all the more memorable and particularly noticeable in the press release. The substance of *SecondCome* was that the Messiah of FirstCome had, as everyone knew, promised to return. This much was non-controversial, unless you happened to be big on a-millennialism, or pre-millennialism or any of that crap floating round the bible schools. Philemon didn't give a toss about any of it. What mattered much more was that it really wasn't such a large step to persuade the congregation that

SecondCome would occur in the fast-approaching Millennium year. He reckoned he was sticking his neck out a bit, given he had only three years to consolidate his position before having to come up with the goods or an excellent excuse, but in reality, this artificial Augustinian construct was far too good an opportunity to miss. He was confident he would find a means of satisfying expectations one way or another by the end of the year 2000.

Of course, what the doctrine of *SecondCome* gave him was a perfect opportunity of sharing his vision of the future with the church and his expanding audience beyond it. That vision of a holy crusade, an endless campaign to bring sinners to Christ, healings, miracles, mass conversions and so on, would take resources – far more resources than the Church of the Body of Christ presently had available. But this was nothing, said Philemon, to a God who owned the cattle on a thousand hills. The Lord would provide – so long as the church was ready to share in the burden. Philemon was particularly proud of his emotional appeal for funds that morning. Would they, the Lord's people, rise to the task of gathering in the harvest? Would they forsake everything of this world for God's declared purpose? Would they ready themselves for *SecondCome*? Would they, in particular, open their bank accounts unreservedly, as the Spirit of God moved their hearts, now, this very day? Would they show their commitment by taking up a second collection that morning, cheques only please, and would those cheques all please have at least two zeros on them? As the organ started the old, old hymn:

Just as I am, without one plea...

which in Philemon's eyes had never been bettered for this purpose, the young Deacons moved quietly forward from the back of the church. As they passed the offering plates up and down the well-filled rows, there was a rustling of paper and the whisper of conversation as requests to borrow pens were made by the deeply spiritually moved. The sound of nibs signing cheques was pleasingly audible to the Pastor as he stood, weeping, in the pulpit. Were his tears for the spilled Blood of the Lamb or for the leading of lambs to the slaughter? Who gave a damn? For surely the Spirit was in this place.

After the service, Philemon counted the cheques and smiled. The sum raised in this one collection exceeded the proceeds of the sale of the elders' cars. And, oh dear, some of the cheques were made personally to Philemon Littlemann and others to cash. But not to worry. Philemon was certain the Lord would reveal a solution to that problem quite promptly.

But there was something else that had arisen whilst in Florida. In one of those events in which the religious would see God's hand and the non-religious would consider serendipitous, his visit to the USA revealed to him the power of the Internet before most Europeans had even heard of it. Accordingly, even before he had implemented the third phase of his strategy with the announcement of *SecondCome*, Philemon had planned the fourth phase. He would become one of the first (and, as it turned out, the most successful) European Internet Christian broadcasters. And the establishment of www.thechurchofthebodyofchrist.co.uk would be funded by a strategic acquisition of domain names of European companies that they themselves would not yet even be aware they would need to survive in the twenty-first century. He was not alone in holding such organisations to ransom over the use of their own names. But not to worry. Philemon was not a greedy man. He didn't mind sharing wealth.

And thus it was that by 18th December 1999, Philemon's fortieth birthday, when he was conducting his review of the past and his plans for the future, Pastor Littlemann had a considerable amount to thank God for – except that he had long since ceased believing in the God of his youth. He did, however, have one problem. It was thirteen days until the Millennium year and he didn't have a clue how to initiate *SecondCome* to the satisfaction of his now very large and rather credulous congregation of followers. Not to worry. The Lord would provide. Or failing that, he'd improvise.

Sister Serenity

Rule Twelve:

The free will of Nominated Proxies may be influenced but never withdrawn.

Saturday 22nd August 1998 11.17 am BST

"What's a date, Gabe?"

"It's when two people spend some time together to get to know each other a bit better, Babe. But... you knew that already, didn't you?"

"...Kinda."

"So... maybe, there's something else you want to ask about it, Babe?"

"...Kinda."

"And that would be?"

"Well... if Mummy's going on a date tonight... does that mean that Da isn't going to be my Da any more?"

"Would you like me to ask him for you, Babe?"

"Uh huh."

"Your Da says there's about as much chance of him stopping being your Da as there is of me turning into a pony."

"You're not going to turn into a pony are you, Gabe?"

"I've got two great big wings ready to wrap round you that say no, Babe. Want a snuggle?"

"Uh huh. And tell my Da, I love him, will you?"

"He says 'Love you back', Babe and that it's ok to love him too."

"Who?"

"Haddon Spurgeon."

"Who's Haddon Spurgeon?"

"He's the man your Mummy's going to marry."

"On their date, tonight?"

"No, in about a year, Babe. But don't tell Mummy 'cos she's not fallen in love with him yet."

"Haddon's a funny name, isn't it?"

"It's an old name. He's named for a famous ancestor of his, Charles Haddon Spurgeon, who lived about a hundred and fifty years ago. Charles is a great mate of mine actually, a bit fuddy-duddy and still refuses to shave off his handlebar moustache. But I love him to bits."

"Can I be bridesmaid, Gabe?"

"Now, that's one you're going to have to ask Mummy, Babe. But not this year, ok?"

Saturday 18th December 1999 4.24 pm GMT

"Don't you think it's odd that Mummy's getting married on a Friday, Gabe?"

"Why so, Babe?"

"Cos *everybody* gets married on a Saturday. I'm going to get married on a Saturday when I get married."

"Actually, Babe, you're not going to get married on a Saturday."

"But Mummy and Haddon are getting married on the last day of the year 'cos Haddon says he wants their wedding to last for two centuries! So, the wedding is at four o'clock and the reception is at eight o'clock and it's going on til after midnight and I'm allowed to stay up and I'm going to change my name to Spurgeon, so it's the same as Mummy's new name and I'm going to be a bridesmaid and my dress is turquoise which is a colour like green but really like blue and there's going to be wedding cake and a band and fireworks and *everything*!"

"Is there, Babe? Actually, I can see quite a few fireworks coming up for you in the new century, but let's not worry too much about that now."

Sunday 7th February 2000 10.10 pm GMT

"Hi, Gabe. It's past bedtime. I thought you weren't coming today."

"Happy Birthday, Babe."

"You remembered!"

"Of course, I always remember. And it's another anniversary too."

"How do you mean?"

"It's exactly eight years since we met in the cupboard."

"Oh yes! How clever of you to remember. I'd quite forgotten."

"How old are you now, Sweetheart?"

"Oh, Gabe! You know. You know, I'm twelve. I'm nearly grown up!"

"Yes, I know, Sweetheart. A new century and you are indeed nearly grown up. So… there's something we need to talk about, Babe."

"Oh, Gabe! You look just like Mummy does when she wants to '*discuss something important*'."

"This is important, Sweetheart."

"Hey, I hope you're not going to tell me about sex. We did sex in school last term."

"I sincerely hope you didn't!"

"You know what I mean. But when grown-ups get serious and want to '*discuss something important*' it usually means something horrid is going to happen."

"Not horrid, but maybe a little bit difficult at first."

"What, Gabe? You're upsetting me now. I'm frightened."

"Don't be, Sweetheart. Whatever happens you know I'll always love you and I'll never, ever, let anyone hurt you. OK?"

"Hm. I suppose so. So, what is it that's so important we have to discuss it on my birthday?"

"Laura, How many other 12-year-olds do you know who have imaginary friends?"

"Don't be silly, Gabe. You're not imaginary. You're just invisible. You're my best friend."

"Sweetheart, I'm as real to you as you are to me. But other people won't see it that way as you get older."

"But I've promised you, Gabe, I'll never tell! And I've never mentioned you to anyone since Da died."

"I know. You've done really, really well, Laura. But one day, you'll make a mistake and let slip that you talk to me. And then, they'll come down hard on you. You're nearly a teenager. The kids will tease you mercilessly and the grown-ups will start mumbling about Psychologists."

"That's what I want to be when I grow up, Gabe."

"I know you do, Babe. But for now, we have to get you concentrating on growing up through what are going to be some pretty eventful teenage years. And if you're going to do that, well…"

"So… you're leaving me, Gabe?"

"Not in the way you're thinking, Babe."

"Don't leave me, Gabe. I love you."

"Sweetheart, I give you my absolute promise, I will always be there looking out for you. But you don't need me now – not like you did when we first met. And we do have to make space for you to do the things that other teenagers do."

"Bye, Gabe."

"Don't be huffy, Sweetheart. You know I'm right, don't you?"

"Oh, Gabe! I'm gonna miss you, *so much*!"

"Don't cry, Babe. I hate it when you cry."

"Wrap me up in your wings like you used to do, when I was little."

"Like this? Please don't cry any more, Sweetheart."

"Shut up and hold me, til I go to sleep."

"You'll remember me whenever you see feathers."

Henry

Rule Fifteen:

Should a player question the objectivity of the Arbiter an appeal will be made directly to the Game Maker.

Thursday 17ᵗʰ April 2008 9.04 am BST

Although I had so far spent only two nights in Oxford, I had been deeply distressed by the previous afternoon's events. Talis had now got me into serious trouble with two women and I was concerned that there was a pattern beginning to emerge, both in terms of the unintended consequences of his actions and also my attitude towards him. I was, and am, sufficiently psychologically aware to realise that there was nothing other than myself stopping me from getting rid of him. The problem was that I just could not bring myself to do so. I had, quite simply, become attached to him very, very quickly. By the time I arrived home, I had made a decision.

It was now only a week before the university term began that led up to my final exams. I tried to concentrate on my books. I was reading for my exam in epistemology. *Philosophers after the Renaissance saw epistemology differently*, I read. *Some regarded knowledge as the product of the senses and therefore, only as reliable as those senses, whilst others considered it to be the product of rational reflection. Several current philosophers consider that though knowledge has to be developed by observation, it is still absolute. In the end, all have to acknowledge that there is no entirely reliable means of proving that knowledge or information is consistent, any more than there are means of demonstrating one s actions are entirely free and of one s own choice.*

I looked down at Talis snoozing beside me on the bed, his chest rising and falling in contented slumber. I faced an incredibly difficult decision. I knew that if I did not give myself maximum opportunity to devote myself to my studies, then my results, and the whole of my future career, would suffer – and all because of some strange creature I had known for only days and which was apparently invisible to everyone else. I couldn't let it go on. I knew I had to get rid of Talis before he damaged me fundamentally. But before I could bring myself to do so, I would have to do something about myself – something about my attachment to the little creature. As he snored peacefully on my bed, I reached for my laptop and Googled: Psychologist+Specialist+Attachment+Talisman+Oxford. In a second or so, Google had returned over eleven thousand suggested entries, but only the one at the top of the list contained all the search criteria. Eagerly, I clicked onto the site of Dr Hans Schmetterling.

Schmetterling's website was an amalgam of unintelligible psychobabble combined with empathic sounding phrases evidently designed to make me feel I would be listened to with sympathy, whatever my problem. I looked in vain for some reference on the site to his experience in dealing with Talis as Google had apparently indicated, but could find none until I was just about to e-mail him. It was then that I noticed that his website and e-mail were hosted by Talisman.net. "So much for experience with my problem," I thought wistfully. I decided to phone instead. I got a polished secretarial kind of voice at the other end. Yes, Dr Schmetterling was indeed taking new clients at the moment. And yes, fortunately for me he had a cancellation the very next day. I could see him tomorrow at 11.00 am. The time couldn't go fast enough as I was concerned. For the rest of the day until suppertime, I busied myself with Internet trivia, Talis apparently content to sit on my bed gazing up at me lovingly. We both slept soundly that night. I woke the next morning with sadness and hope in my heart in equal measure.

Friday 18th April 2008 10.37 am BST

I walked into an anonymous looking building that stood down a small lane just off Turl Street. Inside the front door, the wall of the empty entrance area held perhaps a dozen polished brass plaques, displaying the credentials of a boggling range of therapists. Having found Schmetterling's, I headed straight for the first floor, with Talis snoozing peacefully in his carrier bag. Once inside the front door of the office, I was greeted with a smile by an attractive receptionist just a year or two older than me who quite definitely did not sport a Mohican haircut. Her pretty brown eyes and carefully styled, black shoulder-length hair were evidently more than enough to attract all the male attention she would wish. Under other circumstances, I might well have sought to explore the possibilities, but I was distracted almost immediately.

"Are you the Talisman?" she enquired. I stopped in my tracks.

"Come again?" I responded.

She looked a little perturbed. "I asked if you were Mr. Tallison. Mr Tallison who has an appointment with Dr Schmetterling in five minutes?"

"Oh… yes," I responded, "I'm Harry Tallison."

Surely, surely, I had simply misheard her. It was a perfectly reasonable mistake given the stress I'd been under; perfectly reasonable; nothing to worry about at all. I shook the carrier bag gently to reassure myself of the continuing presence of my new-found friend.

"Please take a seat," she continued in a well-oiled professional ritual, motioning to the seating behind me. Dr Schmetterling will be with you shortly.

After a few moments, there was a buzz from a small box on the secretary's desk. She looked up and caught my eye. "Please go in now, Talisman," she said, motioning towards a door.

"I am *not* going to react," I thought as I got up. "I know I'm hearing things, and it's all part of the stress I'm under." I entered the door, apprehensive as to what Schmetterling would be like and how I would explain my problem. "Still," I reassured myself, "I'm certain he'll understand and the solution will be obvious to him."

Schmetterling's office was large and comfortably furnished, if a little shabby. Bookcases lined two of the walls opposite each other, filled with a kaleidoscope of coloured books and magazines that seemed to spill over to the various coffee tables and bureaux scattered around the room in a cliché of the archetypal absent-minded professor's study. On the third wall was a Victorian fireplace, with two large armchairs in front of it. On the fourth wall behind the desk, hung two photographs. Large name plates underneath confirmed the one as Sigmund Freud (1856–1939) and the other as Carl Jung (1875–1961). But the biggest cliché of all was reserved for Schmetterling himself. If I'd been asked to create a caricature of an odd psychologist, I'd likely have started by giving him a strong German accent. I'd have followed that by making him around 60, giving him a full head of grey hair that stuck out, Einstein-like, in all directions and dressing him in a worn, shiny brown suit with an equally ancient sleeveless green pullover underneath. He'd have had horn-rimmed spectacles pushed up onto his forehead which he'd forget were there and he'd have started the conversation by saying "Gutten tag."

Well, I have to admit, I was wrong. The horn-rimmed specs were actually on his nose and the sleeveless pullover was bright red.

"Guten Tag," said Dr Schmetterling as he rose to meet me, leaning across the desk to shake my hand, "Schmetterling."

"Talisman," I answered, trying to sound confident. "Er… sorry… I mean Tallison," as I took his hand. The archetypal absent-minded professor motioned towards two armchairs by the empty fireplace. I followed the gesture and we each settled into a chair.

Schmetterling watched me get comfortable and said nothing. After a few moments, I look at him, waiting for him to start. He placed his elbows on the arms of his chair, laced his fingers together and looked at me expectantly through the horn-rimmed spectacles. Schmetterling was a man of few words.

"Well… I'm not sure where to start," I said, looking to him for guidance. His head moved slightly to the right and he continued to look at me enquiringly. "Well… I've… got a problem." No response. "I don't know if you've ever treated it before or even if you've ever seen it before. But I've... become rather attached to something unusual. And I'm finding it... difficult... difficult to rid myself of it. Completely irrational, I know, but that's how it is."

His eyebrows rose slightly. I swallowed hard.

"I have a Talis." There. I'd said it. The worst was over. Schmetterling would start asking questions now and then offer a complete solution.

His eyebrows rose slightly further. I swallowed slightly harder.

"That is, I have a talisman and it's come to life and now it's a Talis-man and I call him Talis and he's growing and he gets up to mischief and he's interfering with my love life and he's causing trouble on trains."

There were three sounds simultaneously that attracted my attention. Firstly, Schmettering coughed and shifted slightly in his chair. Was the timing of the cough significant? Was there meaning in his bodily repositioning? He said nothing. At my feet, Talis began to move in his carrier bag. That old familiar sinking feeling started again like a lump of lead dropping from my throat to my stomach. The third sound was a kind of rustling from behind the desk. I glanced up. Both Jung and Freud were leaning forward in their frames, looking at me intently. Talis pushed his way out of the carrier bag and climbed up onto my knee. He looked first at Schmetterling. Schmetterling looked back at him, his face devoid of emotion. Then, Talis looked at Freud and Jung on the wall.

"Guten Tag, Herr Talisman," said Jung. "Vie gehts es?" Talis stood on my lap, waved enthusiastically at Jung, and gave him a big smile and a thumbs-up sign.

I looked at Schmetterling expecting a comment, if not an intervention.

"Warum sprechts du mit das?" said Freud in a disdainful tone to Jung. "Is only sex-symbol."

Talis looked at Freud with an expression of considerable malice.

Schmetterling continued to look back at me questioningly. I couldn't be sure if he could see Talis, or hear the voices coming from the picture.

"Ist nicht sex-symbol. Ist archetype," Jung replied, tossing his head slightly.

Talis continued to look intently at both pictures, nodded his head rapidly and shook his finger critically at Freud. Showing no response, Freud took out his pipe, filled it from a little leather pouch in a ritualistic, psychiatric kind of way, and lit it with a silver lighter. Then, he sat back in his frame, supported his right elbow in his left hand, and puffed thoughtfully on the pipe.

"Nein. Ist sex symbol," he finally said. "Herr Tallison vonts sex viz hiz mutter. Der Talisman ist *phallic symbol*."

He nodded once decisively at Jung, confident he had won the argument.

Schmetterling still said nothing, his eyes never leaving me.

Talis squealed in objection and leapt up and down on my lap.

"Nein!" said Jung, his voice raised considerably. "Herr Talis-man ist *real*. Ve all see him und hear him, nein? Er is Herr Tallison's expression of archetype from collective unconscious. All ve need to do is understand vitch archetype he is."

Now, it was Jung's turn to look disdainful.

Talis nodded vigorously throughout Jung's statement.

My eyes returned to Schmetterling. He of course stared right back at me. Finally, I summoned sufficient courage to ask, "You can hear them, can't you?"

He looked at me for several seconds before answering, his head leaning slightly to one side in a confident, professional kind of way.

"Hear who?" he finally answered.

"Well, Freud and Jung, of course. Their argument."

"Oh, ya," replied Schmetterling. "I hear their arguments all the time."

"So… which of them is right?"

He looked at me for several more seconds, then said,

"Why does it matter to you which is right?"

"Well… it's pretty important to Talis. He wants to know if he's real or not. And come to think of it. That's rather important to me as well."

Schmetterling looked back intently, his elbows not having moved once from the arms of his chair, his fingers still laced together. I found myself wondering if he mustn't suffer intense pins and needles after every counselling session. Finally, he moved. At least his torso moved, as he leaned forward, his elbows still welded to their position. He looked intensely at Talis then intensely at me.

"Do you see him, Herr Professor? Do you see Talis?"

"Young man," he finally replied. "I do not think it is important whether Freud is right or whether Jung is right. Und I do not sink it is important what I see. What I think is important is what you see and why you see it."

From Jung's photo frames there was a loud call of "Ya, richtig!" and applause. I looked at Freud. He nodded once, rather grudgingly.

"Our time is up," said Schmetterling. "If you wish, please made another appointment on you way out."

I was being dismissed. As I placed Talis back in the carrier bag, he waved once more to Jung with a wide smile. I walked out into the receptionist's office and was in the process of deciding whether to make another appointment or ask for a date when my phone buzzed.

It was a text message. And it was from Laura. I excused myself momentarily from the captivating secretary and looked at the message.

'Henry, I know you don t love me anymore and I can live with that. But I m in terrible, terrible danger and I have no one but you to turn to. Please, please help me.'

Philemon

Rule Eight:

Players will undertake play through Nominated Proxies and other Tangibles only. Any player who compromises this rule will account to the Game Maker for their conduct.

Sunday 31ˢᵗ December 2000 10.30 am GMT

"Do not be deceived. This is no fairy tale."

He is standing at the front of the main church hall. The official capacity is 275 but the congregation is well in excess of 300, and there are over twice as many more in the overflow rooms, watching on the remote video links. The Internet link is broadcasting from www.thechurchofthebodyofchrist.org to an additional congregation that he can only guess at, but believes numbers into the thousands, perhaps tens of thousands. The ceiling of the room is not as high as he would like it to be. It cannot create those cathedral echoes so beloved of the preachers of old – Wesley, Whitfield, Spurgeon – those that he might, in a different incarnation, call his heroes. As yet, he merely dreams of his own Tabernacle, where the Word of God will reverberate to the ceiling and back. Behind the lectern, the podium on which he stands is reached by an additional step and is some 30 centimetres (or a foot, as Philemon Littlemann specified it) above the stage. His diminutive stature, as a result, is soon forgotten when he begins speaking, for all fall under the spell of that mesmerising voice.

His shoulders are hunched as if he is poised to leap. He holds his hands closely together in a gesture of intense supplication. His eyes close momentarily, his expression intense, almost as if he is in pain. The words come slowly, emphatically, each carefully weighed. Leaning slightly forward now, his mouth almost touches the microphone. Eyes still closed and brow deeply furrowed, those hypnotic hands swing gently forward and back in time, emphasising each word.

"Do not be deceived, for the fault does not lie, and never did lie, with God. You do not need me to tell you that it is the last day of the last year of the Millennium. And some of you have been talking. Do I say talking? Let me rather say murmuring, as the Children of Israel murmured against the Lord in the wilderness.

Yes, Beloved. They murmured and they complained against the manna that the Lord sent to sustain them. And they cried out to be returned to Egypt and slavery as they wandered round in a circle for 40 years."

He looks slowly round the church. He is silent for three seconds, four, five. They are on the point of wondering if he has finished already.

He continues, the silence emphasising his words. "Yet God had made them a promise, had He not, Beloved? Had He not told them they were to enter the Promised Land? So, you say to me, 'Pastor, why did God lie? Why did God break his promise to lead them into the Promised Land?' And I tell you this."

His voice is rising in volume, increasing in speed, though not in pitch, until he is all but shouting. *God is not a man, that he should lie. Neither the son of man that he should repent.*

He continues almost in a whisper now, so that in unison the congregation in the hall, and in the overflow, leans forward unconsciously, attempting to hear better. He visualises countless others at home, leaning closer to their computers. "But I say to you this, Beloved. God did not lie. He simply delayed fulfilling his promise for 40 years until every last Israelite who had left Egypt had died. Not one of that generation entered the land that the Lord had promised. And why? You ask me why? I tell you this."

And with all the breath he can muster, he throws his head back and roars a single word: "UNBELIEF."

They fall back in their seats involuntarily at the blast of sound over the speakers. He wishes the camera were on them so as to record the moment. He makes a mental note that their broadcast facilities and expertise in using them must both improve rapidly. "Unbelief, brethren; *the same unbelief that I witness in this church, here today.*"

He turns his back on them and lifts his arms to the cross hanging behind him on the wall. Some two metres wide, three metres high, and made of polished steel, it shines in the beam of the spotlight trained on it from the ceiling.

"Oh, Lord! Oh, my God! When will these stony hearts melt, Lord? When will your children believe you, Lord, such that you can deliver on your promise? For Lord, I know your promise of SecondCome will not appear amongst us until we have banished unbelief."

In silence, he falls to the floor, kneeling in front of the cross, his back still to the congregation, his arms raised high, as if beseeching. His lapel microphone picks up the sound of his breathing; his weeping. Sotto voce, he whispers, "Oh, Je-sussss. Oh, Loooord. Oh, my Father, God. I am so sorry. With all my heart, I repent. These children cannot repent, Lord. They do not know the sin they have committed, and they do not understand how needful is their repentance. So, I shall repent for them, oh, my God." And he falls weeping, prostrate, beating the floor with his fists.

They do not know what to do. They have never seen him like this before. They shuffle uneasily in their seats wanting direction, wanting instruction, wanting to be told what to do; until, that is, a voice emanates from the rear of the hall through a microphone that just happens to have been placed there and is now switched on.

"No, Pastor. No! This cannot be. The sin is not yours, Pastor. The unbelief is not yours. You are blameless, Pastor."

They look around to see who is talking, but cannot identify him.

"The sin is mine, Pastor. I am the unbeliever in this congregation, for I have doubted *SecondCome*."

Then, apparently quite spontaneously, an unamplified voice calls out from the left midsection of the congregation. "I am the unbeliever. The sin is mine." There is a shuffling and scraping of chairs. The speaker moves forward and falls to her knees in front of the pulpit – a woman perhaps in her late 20s, yet dressed in twinset, pearls and tweed skirt as if she were in her 50s, a long headscarf loosely about her shoulders. "Lord, Pastor, I am so sorry for my sin. I am the unbeliever. The sin is mine."

Then, the statement is repeated by a tearful male voice from somewhere in the rear right of the congregation. "I am the unbeliever. The sin is mine."

And now, the congregation takes up the words as a chant, weeping and repeating in unison, "I am the unbeliever. The sin is mine." Louder and louder the chant rises, now accompanied by a stamping of feet. Minute after minute it continues until the building is shaking. Philemon has risen as they chant. He is back on the podium. He makes no attempt to stop them. He knows that he could not while they are in this frenzy. So, he waits, surveying them, until tiredness slowly sets in and the volume begins to drop.

"Beloved."

It is a single word, and delivered sotto voce once again.

"The Lord has heard you. Your sin has been washed in the Blood of the Lamb."

At first, they do not hear. So, he waits, repeats a little louder. And now, they begin to take notice. All over the hall, they are dropping spontaneously to their knees, weeping uncontrollably for their sin and pleading, from their misery of divine separation, for forgiveness.

Philemon Littlemann descends from the podium now and walks among them. He reaches his hands towards them, messiah-like. He wears on the third finger of his left hand a gold wedding ring with a cross set upon it. The message of marriage to the Lord, of the Bride of Christ, is almost vocal. Some now reach out to touch the ring, and some draw his hand to their faces to kiss it. Others seek merely to touch his long black academic cloak (though none could say when the doctorate was conferred, or which authorised institution has issued the certificate on the wall of his study) as it glides past them. Surely, God is in this place.

Sunday 9th December 2001 12.30 am EST

"I must say, I've grown rather fond of Miami."

He is sitting up in bed. The remnants of a room service brunch are strewn in various locations around the tenth-floor suite. The sliding door to one of the balconies stands open and if they pay attention, they can hear the waves rolling in onto the sunlit beach below. In the corner the TV is playing a 1989 movie, Field of Dreams. Kevin Costner is looking confused, having just seen a vision of a baseball field and heard a message from a disembodied voice.

"It doesn't seem much like a three-week fast to me, *Pastor*." Frank's voice came to him from his left with a hint of humour.

Philemon studies the tall, slim glass of Bollinger that he holds by the stem between two fingers of his right hand as he considers his answer. The tiny bubbles rise rapidly to the surface of the pale, yellow liquid, as if intent upon emancipation. Then, without turning, he says, "I find there is much in the ways of the Spirit that is not what it first seems, brother Frank. Surely, the soul of the spiritual man communes with the Holy Ghost at all times."

Frank smiles at the irony. "Even now, Pastor?"

With his eyes on the movie, Philemon slides his left hand down under the covers, feeling for Frank's cock. Frank inclines towards him.

"Even now."

Then, seemingly, Philemon changes his mind and turns instead to his right, where the sleeping form of Gus does not stir until he pours the champagne like a waterfall over his belly and leans forward to press his lips to it. Then, he looks up at Frank who is repositioning his body so as to get in on the action. "Besides, God has just told me what He is going to say on Christmas Eve."

Shoeless Joe hits a home run.

Sunday 23rd December 2001 10.30 am GMT

There is silence as he ascends the steps to the stage and on up to the podium. It has been years since any hint of humour has been heard in this church building connected in any way to his height. In fact, this building has heard very little laughter on any topic for quite a few years now. He adjusts the microphone on the lectern and begins.

"Three weeks, Beloved. Three weeks of prayer and fasting in a high and lonely place. Were you there with me as I beseeched the Lord, Beloved? Did you listen as I prayed and wept on your behalf, calling upon His Holy Name to deliver the promise of *SecondCome*?"

There are whispers around the church of 'Hallelujah', and 'Praise be to His Holy Name', and a dozen other similar aphorisms.

"For twenty days, the Lord was silent. For twenty days, I called upon His Name and He did not answer me. But here is the lesson in faith, Beloved. For it was on the twenty-first day that God spoke. And you will ask me, 'Pastor, in what words of scripture did the Lord speak to you?' And I will refer you to 1 Kings 19, when Elijah stood upon the mount before the Lord. And I will ask you, Beloved, when the strong wind came, was the Lord in the strong wind? I tell you, He was not. And when the earthquake followed, was He in the earthquake? I say unto you, again, He was not. And was the Lord in the fire that came after the earthquake? I say to you a third time, NO! The Lord was in none of these things."

He leans forward now and whispers into the microphone, causing that involuntary forward movement as they lean towards him to hear.

"Beloved, I ask you, what would have happened if this servant of the Lord had become disheartened on the tenth day? What would have happened if, on the eleventh day or the twelfth day, the Lord's servant had said, 'It's no use. God is not here. God is not coming?' I tell you, Beloved, there would have been *no word from the Lord, for the Lord abhors unbelief.* So, I say to you, just as I had to wait until the twenty-first day, and to go on believing through twenty days of silence that the Lord would speak, so, God has made us wait upon his word until the twenty-first century, *because of your unbelief.*"

He raises his arm in his trademark point and turns deliberately around the room, seemingly singling out every member of the congregation. His gesture lingers on the camera for the benefit of those watching on CCTV.

"Beloved, I have a question for you."

There is a shuffling, a squirming in seats.

"Are you ready?"

He is silent for three, four, five seconds, the unspoken question hanging above them in the air so that they can almost breath it in.

"It is the twenty-first century. *Will... you... believe... he... is... coming?*"

Then, a voice from the front row. "Yes, Pastor, I *will* believe." Rapidly, the statement is taken up and repeated from all parts of the hall until it solidifies into another chant. "I *will* believe. I *will* believe. I *will* believe."

And with this, he joins in from the podium, thrusting his fist into the air on the word '*will*' and screaming into the microphone "I *will* believe. I *will* believe." For perhaps six or seven minutes the building reverberates to the chant – we cannot be sure exactly how long for no one is timing it. Following the usual pattern, as the chant dies away, he leans forward to the microphone once more.

"Then, if you truly will believe, Beloved, I say this to you:

If you build it, He will come."

Monday 1st April 2002 11.42 am BST

"She's asked me if she can go to something called *Sisters*".

Haddon Spurgeon is sitting at the kitchen table reading the

remnants of Easter Day's Sunday Times, the dishwasher murmuring in the background. "Whose sister's?"

"Not whose, it's *Sisters* with a capital 'S'. It seems to be some church youth club thingy," replied Paula.

"What, at St. Andrew's?"

"No, she stopped going there, ages ago."

"So, what's wrong with the youth club at St. Andrew's?"

"That's what I asked. She said Jodie and all her friends go to *Sisters* on a Thursday evening in Bitterne."

"Bit of a trek, isn't it? How will she get home? Bus?"

"She says that someone brings them all home in a minibus?"

"That's something to be thankful for. I suppose it's ok, so long as Jodie goes with her. Tell her she has to be home by ten."

Saturday 4th January 2003 10.30 am GMT

They meet in one of the break-out rooms. It's cheaper than heating the big hall for one small meeting. Indeed, this morning, Philemon has decreed that it is not cold enough to turn the electric heater on, anyway. So, they sit without removing coats and gloves. For over a year now, the Church of the Body of Christ has been preoccupied (some would say fixated) on the making and saving of money. All Sunday collections have been reserved. All unnecessary expenditure (missionary donations, after service refreshments, purchase of tracts for distribution and so on) has been eliminated in the pursuit of the goal of raising £1,500,000 by the end of 2003. If the target is not achieved by that date, the whole exercise will have been pointless.

Philemon had walked from the podium on the Sunday before Christmas 2001, after making his closing statement. Without a word to anyone, he had proceeded straight out of the church and driven home. Behind him, puzzled members of the congregation turned to one another in confusion, seeking confirmation of what he had just said. The consensus was that they had heard right. The statement had been, *"If you build it, He will come."* Some managed to infer that by *"He will come"*, Pastor was referring to *SecondCome*. But no one had the slightest idea of what they were to build.

While the greater part of the congregation had simply headed home in their confusion, a few who liked to consider themselves leading members of the church stood in the car park discussing the Pastor's enigmatic statement. A decision was arrived at that three of them, Harold Jowlett (Planning Officer with Hampshire County Council, 44 years of age, short, prematurely balding, married for nineteen years with twin teenage daughters, rather too attached to fine wine for the good of his waistline), Jonny Ropen (self-employed painter and decorator, 37 years old, tall, athletic and toned from regular attendance at David Lloyd, married, unblessed with children despite much prayer and fasting by himself and his wife) and Adrian Pride (owner of three men's outfitters, 48 years, unhappily married for 29 years, happily childless and secretly prone to serial adultery, Internet pornography and lusting after prepubescent girls, but only from a distance so far) would take the unusual step of visiting Pastor Littlemann uninvited, at home that afternoon to enquire further as to the meaning of his closing remark.

Arriving in one car at the 1970s block in Shirley, they had parked in the only empty parking space, next to an ancient Austin Allegro that had been left at a 45-degree angle over two spaces. They took the lift to the second floor of the block, and made their way quickly past the open door of an apartment from which 1980s punk rock music (if it can be called music) was emanating, accompanied by a drunken female voice. It was beyond the understanding of anyone why Pastor Littlemann had chosen to continue living here all that time, despite having formerly run a successful carpentry business and now being paid a rather generous salary by the church. They did not know, of course, of the various other properties that Pastor

Littlemann had acquired over the preceding eight years at advantageous recessionary prices, or the source of the funds with which he had made his acquisitions. Nor did they know that he rarely returned to the flat in Shirley, having numerous alternative places to sleep (alone or accompanied) when it suited him to do so.

But on this occasion, he had correctly predicted that some of the bolder elements of the congregation would summon sufficient temerity to visit him uninvited – and that suited his purposes just fine. So, Philemon's afternoon had been spent engendering a sense of exclusivity amongst this little group of Believers, by the sharing of his vision for the erection (the choice of word being duly noted by Adrian Pride) of the Southampton Tabernacle. The group had been surprised and impressed that the Lord had already led Philemon to a long disused brownfield site of some 4.5 acres and that he had already bought an option to purchase from the elderly owner who, despite having no progeny to whom he could leave his not inconsiderable fortune, still required a price of £1,500,000. Philemon did not, of course, mention the 20% discount that would be returnable to him personally from this sum in the event that purchase took place before 31st December 2003. It was a very small step for this little group to form itself into a self-appointed financial steering committee for the raising of the required funds. And when, the following Sunday morning, Pastor Littlemann had finally disclosed to the congregation the meaning of his closing statement the preceding Sunday, and had personally opened the fund with a donation of £10,000, the special look he gave to each member of this elevated and privileged group left them with little option other than to match his personal donation pound for pound. And since all was closely observed by the congregation and the CCTV as well as being Internet broadcast, it was not particularly surprising that the Southampton Tabernacle Building Fund had opened 2002 with a bank balance just in excess of £214,000. When it was later noticed by the Treasurer, that Pastor Littlemann had inadvertently signed his cheque on the Mission Fund instead of his personal account, Philemon promised to reimburse the Mission Fund expeditiously. The Treasurer didn't know what 'expeditiously' meant, but he was sure it was *Of The Spirit* and sought no further information.

So now, at the beginning of 2003, the steering committee found itself in the rather ironic position of being responsible for a bank balance that had grown to over £700,000, yet feeling it could not afford to heat a small room for its meetings, lest they risk the ignominious failure of not reaching the target sum by the due date.

Sunday 7ᵗʰ December 2003 10.30 am GMT

As he ascends the steps to the podium, not all eyes are upon him. For the last year, on the front wall, to the left of the steel cross, has hung a large poster drawn up by the Sunday School and headed with the words 'The Lord's Cash Barometer'. It is calibrated all the way up to £1,500,000. The barometer is coloured red just past the £1,000,000 mark. With 24 days left to the deadline, the Church of the Body of Christ is still almost half a million pounds short of its target.

They are wondering what he will say today. More admonition for their unbelief, perhaps? (Last Sunday's sermon was on Mark 9:24 – 'I believe. Help Thou mine unbelief.') Another appeal for money? Most of them have already given so much that they are having difficulty paying their heating bills. Foreign holidays are a distant memory.

He switches on the microphone and says, without emotion, "Good morning, Beloved. My text for today is Matthew Chapter 10, verse 8. Brother Harold Jowlett, please read the verse."

With the swaying gait of the clinically obese, Harold slowly mounts the stage, the jacket of his Marks & Spencer blue pinstripe suit sliding slightly from left to right and back again with each step he takes. He stands below the podium to Philemon's right, facing the congregation, his expression seemingly alternating between fear of error and self-importance for his temporary elevation. Philemon's head remains a full 30 centimetres above Harold's, even given their differences in height. The camera operator has already been instructed to zoom in on Harold's face as he opens his black, leather-bound Scofield bible. As it picks up the drops of perspiration on his forehead, he reads, "Freely ye have received, freely give." He stops and looks up, first at the congregation, then at Philemon.

Philemon follows quickly with "Thank you, brother." Harolds's ten seconds of fame are over and he dismounts the stage, wiping a large paper tissue across his sweating face as he goes. The camera reverts immediately to its normal focus on Philemon. Harold is immediately forgotten, reconsigned to the ranks of the irrelevant, as the congregation now awaits the Pastor's words. All have but one thought in their mind. How will Pastor Littlemann resolve for them the shortfall of £500,000, yet to be raised, with only 24 days in which to do it. No one stands ready to be accused of unbelief – not after the last time. But many are resigned to failure and to ridicule, since the Southampton Echo has already run two patronising articles on the subject and at least one person has made an unconfirmed claim to have been telephoned by a researcher from the BBC's 'Rogue Traders' programme.

Philemon looks slowly round the hall, then focuses his gaze on the camera for the benefit of those viewing on the remote links which now number more than a dozen and rising. Without uttering a word, he reaches into his pocket and takes out a bunch of keys. The camera pans in to focus on his hands as he detaches a vehicle remote control and ignition key. Wordlessly, still alternating his gaze out across the congregation and then back on the camera, he descends the podium and stage steps to the floor of the hall. Then, striding so rapidly down the central aisle that his academic robes billow out behind him, he walks directly to the door, dropping the key and the remote into the collection plate as he passes. He walks to the bus stop where he can catch the bus to Shirley and his little-used flat.

Back in the bare, drab hall, the congregation looks around confused. Some have got the point, others not. There is at first merely a ripple of murmuring. Low conversations gradually rising in volume. Then, several voices rise above the melee, some nervous, at least one angry and another approaching hysteria.

"He can't mean that."

"I'm disabled – I can't manage without mine."

"I need mine for work."

"How will I get the kids to school?"

But despite the protestations, by the time Frank locks the hall some 40 minutes later, the collection plate is full of keys.

Sunday 7th December 2003 7.30 pm GMT

Frank has cycled to Ocean Village, removed his bicycle lamps and secured his bicycle to a rack with a U-lock. He presses the entry phone on apartment 907 of a luxury block. The buzzer sounds and he enters, taking the lift, predictably, to the ninth floor. The door to the apartment is already open. The occupant can be seen standing in front of the plate-glass sliding door which in summer would be open onto the balcony. He is holding a champagne glass and looking out over the marina towards Cowes. Frank hands him a package that moves and clinks slightly as he passes it over. He and Philemon had estimated between the hall and the CCTV links there would be over 200 car drivers on site today. The deacons had counted over 170 cars in the car park, many double-parked, as had become normal.

Frank is pleased to confirm that the package contains over a hundred sets of keys. The drama of the morning's events is somewhat overshadowed by the practicality of having to sort out which set belonged to which owner and which car. But the inconvenience will be a minor one. For several weeks, preceding Philemon's spontaneous gesture, note has been taken by trusted members of *The Sons* of who arrived at church in which vehicle with which registration number. Particular attention has been paid to those who preferred to park in the local side streets in order to avoid having to negotiate the car park. Tomorrow, several members of *The Sons* will report in sick to school. For some, their day will be spent matching keys to vehicles. Others will man the phones in shifts until all owners have been contacted and asked to send in their signed ownership certificates. Conversations have already been held with British Car Auctions in Camberley, Enfield and Paddock Wood. The transporters are booked for Tuesday and Wednesday.

Some donors, no doubt, will think better of the gesture as they face having to walk to work and school over the next day or so. They will likely demand their keys back, probably leaving the church, never to be seen again. Philemon does not mind. He knows that these will be more than offset by other sets of keys yet to come in from the remote CCTV links and, of course, the donations. There will be many donations due to God's amazing gift of the Internet.

Those that must go, will go. Those that should stay, will stay. For Philemon is adamant and utterly sincere upon this particular point: *"No man can serve two masters, for either he will hate the one and love the other; or else he will hold to the one and despise the other. Ye cannot serve God and mammon."*

Wednesday 31ˢᵗ December 2003 11.00 am GMT

There are privileges that attend the rank of Senior Partner in the third largest firm of solicitors in Southampton. One of them, in the opinion of Moss Goldlock (universally referred to out of his earshot, due to his almost complete absence of hair, as Goldilocks), is not having to attend the office on New Year's Eve. Nevertheless, in order to facilitate the transfer of four and a half acres of land abutting the Itchen River that belong to his oldest client, Saul Brinberg, that is exactly what he is doing. Goldlock's billable hours have failed to hit target for the second year running and some of his partners are beginning to mumble the 'R' word. At a mere 67 years of age and with the prospect of spending his days with a wife he has not spoken to kindly in twenty years, Moss finds the idea of retirement unappealing. And for another thing, with Brinberg now having surpassed the grand age of 90, Goldilocks isn't about to risk losing the account through laziness just before the largest estate ever to come the firm's way finally drops into his lap.

So, on this last day of 2003, he has opened the office and waited in the hallway for his client. Though Brinberg arrives chauffeur-driven (he has not driven since his doctor diagnosed a heart murmur three years earlier), the vehicle is a modest Skoda Superb. Goldilocks notes that Brinberg did not accumulate his fortune by frittering it on unnecessary frivolities. He shows the elderly gentleman into the lift and they rise to the fourth floor. Exiting, he reaches to open the door and usher him into the large, book-lined meeting room (naturally, one would never show a client like Saul Brinberg into the small meeting room). Brinberg flicks the gesture away and strides ahead of the bald lawyer at a pace more appropriate to a man twenty years his junior. Goldilocks reassesses the anticipated date for that much-anticipated probate instruction.

Flasks of coffee stand ready on the table. Goldilocks proffers. Brinberg flicks. When he is sure the old man is comfortably seated, he opens a door at the far end of the room. Philemon Littlemann has chosen a Hong Kong-tailored, narrow pinstripe for the occasion, cut in such a way as to add a good half inch to most people's perception of his height. It is offset with a Hilditch & Key monogrammed white shirt and Brunswick 2 shoes by Crockett &

Jones. The latter have been selected from the Handmade Collection due to their being capable of having a slight platform invisibly inserted that gives him a further half-inch of height. He carries a briefcase containing a banker's draft for £1,200,000 that is lying on top of six thousand fifty-pound notes. He sits directly opposite Brinberg, the early morning light that illuminates him from behind lending him an almost angelic appearance. Sitting next to his client, Goldilocks winces at the sound of scraping as the laughably short man slides the briefcase across the width of the walnut table (even if it is only veneer, it still cost a fortune) to his client. He makes to intercept it, but Saul flicks a third time and he pulls back his hand quickly. The old man spins the case around, opens it and takes out the draft, barely looking at it. He pushes it to the lawyer on his right without looking at him. Goldilocks winces again as Brinberg closes the briefcase and slides it back over the width of the walnut veneer table to Littlemann.

"Sign it over." The instruction is to Goldilocks but Brinberg's eyes have never left Littlemann's.

Goldilocks is still explaining Land Registry formalities as the old man and the short man rise simultaneously and leave the room together. Philemon presses the lift button and stands back in deference to age and nothing more. When the car door opens, he steps in behind Brinberg. Just as the doors are closing he looks up at the old man out of the corner of his eye and says, "Ever considered changing religion?" The doors close and the two of them break into helpless laughter. By the time the car reaches the ground floor, Brinberg has died of a heart attack. On the fourth floor, Goldilocks is still dreaming of a probate instruction.

Saturday 7ᵗʰ February 2004 11.00 am GMT
"Happy birthday, sweet sixteen."
He hands Laura a flexible gift-wrapped package. Shortly, she will

open it to find the pair of the Elle denim jeans she has been eying wishfully in the magazine ad for some weeks. He had won her heart quickly with the interest he took in her after marrying her mother, and nothing has changed in the meantime.

"Oh, Haddon! Don't embarrass the girl!" Paula is being protective.

"Embarrass? That's not embarrassing. Now, if I'd started humming '*Sweet sixteen and never been kissed*', now, *that* would have been embarrassing."

Laura pokes her tongue out and throws a cushion at him. A single feather escapes and rises, though there is no window open, no breeze. She stops momentarily, her mind elsewhere.

"I have a gift for you too, darling."

Paula reaches her hand towards her daughter, palm upwards. On it is a ring box. Laura's mind slips back into the room.

"Oh, Mummy! That looks exciting. What is it?

"Something my grandmother gave my mother on her sixteenth birthday and that she gave to me on mine. Now you're sixteen, it's yours. But look after it very carefully. It's very old – definitely a family heirloom."

Laura opens the box. It contains a gold wedding ring. Inside the ring is an inscription that is becoming worn and harder to read. Laura can just make it out. 'Let him kiss me with the kisses of his mouth.'

Saturday 7th February 2004 11.10 am GMT

They meet in one of the break-out rooms. It's cheaper than heating the big hall for one small meeting. Mercifully, Pastor Littlemann has permitted them to heat the room this winter. Harold suspects it's only temporary though. Once the Pastor really focusses on building the Southampton Tabernacle, once he realises how much money needs to be raised, Henry is sure the heating will be deemed unaffordable once again.

Jowlett, Ropen and Pride (Jonny always thinks it makes them sound like a firm of estate agents when people say it like that) are standing, waiting. It is rare for Pastor to be late for a meeting. At that moment, Philemon pushes open the door and strides in followed by two rather taller, suited men.

"Gentlemen, meet Messrs Thomas and Wharlow from TW Church Design, universally known in the profession as Mr T and Mr W. You will know them, I am sure, by reputation, TW being the acknowledged leading church designers in the UK." Harold, of course, does know this, having received planning applications from them before. The others say nothing, not wishing to draw attention to their ignorance.

The statutory greetings are undertaken. Philemon then holds out his hand to Mr T who passes him a set of rolled architectural plans. With some drama, he flattens them out on the table in front of him: plans, elevations, and, most important to all but Harold Jowlett, computer-generated visuals. To say that the building is impressive would fall way short of the truth. It stands four storeys high under an illuminated needle-like spire that rises a further 35 metres into the air. At almost 70,000 square metres, its footprint is the equivalent of a dozen houses. Entrance halls, break-out rooms, prayer rooms, technology centre, kitchens & WCs on every floor, and all built around a hall with a seating capacity of 5,500. It has no ceiling, its walls rise through the centre of the building to a fully glazed roof, augmented by strategically placed sounding boards designed to create a cathedral-like reverberation to speech. Surely, God will be in this place. Behind the Tabernacle stands a waterside development of some forty luxury flats.

Philemon allows them several minutes of silence to take it in.

"Pastor... how much will this cost to build?" The question is not Harold's, but Adrian Pride's. As a planner, Harold Jowlett already knew the answer as soon as the number '70,000' was mentioned, and never mind the flats. He also knew the probable reaction of the County Council Planning Department to the proposal to construct such a building. And now, he is beginning to realise how difficult a position he is going to be in with the likely conflict arising between work policies and his commitment to the church.

"About £9.5 million, depending on the quality of finishes." Littlemann's answer is matter of fact, almost nonchalant. "Oh, and Harold?"

"Yes, Pastor?"

"Turn the heating off, would you?"

Thursday 8th April 2004 9.10 am BST

In a week in which a bank holiday falls, it's normal for colleagues to save up their flexi-hours to enable them to take another day and a half off. That means they have to use only a further two and a half days from their annual leave allocation of 35 days (with more for long service and seniority) to get a full week off work. Though it's bending the rules a bit, most departments allow the whole process to be doubled up over Easter, given that there are bank holidays in two consecutive weeks. Most colleagues can, therefore, take two full weeks' break, whilst dipping into that all-important leave allowance by only one complete week's leave. Of course, the tricky bit is that the Department can't officially be closed. So, there has to be at least one person who doesn't get to do this.

When Harold Jowlett, Senior Planning Officer, volunteered to attend the office for not just one of the two weeks concerned but both of them, no one else objected. That's why, on the Thursday before Good Friday, Harold finds himself in an office as silent as…
. as silent as what? The grave? The Lord's people never see the grave – they go directly to be with him in paradise. The Marie Celeste? He's not a nautical man. As silent as… well, not to worry. It's quiet, anyway.

Planning Officers have a certain degree of latitude in deciding whether any given planning application can be determined within the department under *Delegated Powers* or whether it needs to be referred to the full Planning Committee of the Authority. Senior Planning Officers have rather more latitude in making such judgements. Harold Jowlett, after some 23 years in the same department, regards himself as nothing if not senior, even if he feels his pay grade suggests otherwise. He looks at the application on the desk before him, submitted by TW Church Design. It is correctly completed and signed. It has been accompanied by the correct fee, which has been banked. *Highways* has no objection. There are no known conservation issues. No other Department really counts in the pecking order of Planning Permissions. So... there's no real reason why he, as Senior Planning Officer, and sole representative of the department for this week and the next, should not approve the application under *Delegated Powers*, is there? Of course, he could delay until everyone else returns the week after next and a second signatory is available to sign off. But *Internal Audit* is forever admonishing them for the backlog of large applications. And a quick decision would be in everyone's interests, wouldn't it? So, it's ok to sign off and issue the Certificate himself, isn't it? He glances up, and around the office. Still seeing no one, he holds his hovering pen over the signature box. So, why is that little voice nagging away inside his head?

"Er, Harold? This building: it's enormous, isn't it? And er, luxury flats, Harold? Harold, what do those etched lines on that plan up there on the wall mean? Yes, the plan headed *City Development Plan 2003–2008*. Oh, it means Mixed Retail Development, does it? Then... shouldn't that mean everything in this location ought to be... well... shops? Lots of different shops? I don't think they mean selling religion either, Harold. Not unless people are paying money for it. Well, maybe on second thoughts, it is retail, then. But those luxury apartments, Harold? How do they fit in with the City Development Plan?"

He withdraws his hovering pen. He withdraws, that is, until he hears Pastor's voice from the pulpit last Sunday speaking on Psalm 24:1, 'The Earth is the Lord's and the fullness thereof...' And hadn't Pastor looked directly at him when he talked about God owning the whole Earth, and how, therefore, man's laws upon the earth should always remain subservient to the need of the Lord's work and the Lord's people? Harold's hand drifts over the signature box again. The heating is not on and it is not a particularly warm day for the time of year. Yet, his brow is sweating copiously and drops of perspiration are falling onto the desk, perilously close to the application. He prays hard, drops his pen to the paper, signs.

Three things have happened simultaneously. God's will has been done (in Harold's opinion, at least). The value of the assets that belong to the Trust of the Church of the Body of Christ (Sole Trustee, Philemon Littlemann) have risen in value five-fold. Harold Jowlett has committed an act of gross misconduct.

Sister Serenity

Rule Five:

Players will not commence play until the Arbiter has made physical contact with a Nominated Proxy of each player's choice. The Arbiter will then declare the Game open. Prior to this point, players may initiate contact with their Nominated Proxies ONLY in non-incarnate form. Any physical manifestation before the Arbiter declares the Game open will result in immediate forfeiture of the Game by the offending party.

Thursday 8th April 2004 5.22 pm BST

"Paula! There's a woman on the phone asking if serenity lives in this house. Sounds like she might be a Mormon or something. D'you want to talk to her?"

"She means Laura."

"Laura? Well, why doesn't she say so, then?"

Laura runs down the stairs and grabs the landline phone from Haddon, throws him a passing glare and heads back up to her room. Haddon thinks that someday, she'll be able to kill men at 60 paces with that look, but knows the peace of the house is not worth the risk of making the comment audibly. He wanders back into the kitchen, where Paula hands him a mug of freshly ground coffee.

"No one ever told me being stepfather to a teenage girl was going to be so difficult. Whatever happened to 'Hello Kitty' and McDonald's breakfasts?"

Paula cups her hand around his unshaven chin and turns his face towards her. She puckers up her lips and kisses him quickly on his.

"Do I take that as a declaration of hostilities for the long weekend, sweet husband?"

"Nah, course not. Don't you recognise a white flag when you see it waving? So, what's with the 'Serenity' business?"

"It's a *Sisters* thing. They've all decided to take a spiritual name. Don't worry. She'll have forgotten it by next week."

"So, what comes next? Ritual sacrifice of the hamster?"

"Don't be horrible, Had! She might be religious, but a lot of girls her age go round looking like the Rocky Horror Show, or taking drugs and sleeping with their boyfriends."

"How d'you know she isn't?"

"What, sleeping with her boyfriend? Well, for one thing, to the best of my knowledge, she hasn't got one and for another, she says she'll never so much as kiss a man unless she's going to marry him."

VICIOUS

"What she says and what she does might be two completely different things."

"True, but how many girls do you know that go out for an evening of sex carrying a headscarf and a black leather bible?"

"You have a point, sweet wife. I'll zip my lip."

"Good decision."

Thursday 8th April 2004 6.50 pm BST

She does her best to slip out of the house unnoticed, but rarely makes it without at least a shout from the kitchen of *"What time will you be home?"* Stepping onto the bus, she thinks about it. She knows it's only because they care about her. It's just that she wishes... she wishes... well, what does she wish? She gets so frustrated when she tries to put this into words. She loves them, she really does, but they don't understand how the world really works. Their eyes have been blinded by sin. They're *covered* by the Blood of the Lamb, of course. She has seen to that herself by her own intercession on their behalf and by her unfailing attendance at *Sisters*. Deacon Frank has confirmed as much to her himself. But they're not *washed* in the Blood, that's the problem. She sighs in some frustration when she thinks about the difference. At *Sisters*, they've all been *washed* in the Blood, they're all the Bride of Christ. And that means they can see the world the way it really is, with all its sin and evilness and the unbelief that is preventing *SecondCome* from happening even now. Why, oh why, can't the whole world believe as she and her sisters do? Because then, the Mother of God could arise and give birth to *SecondCome* and the Returned Messiah would spread love and joy and peace around the world and everyone would be happy.

Her train of thought is broken as the bus she is riding slows towards her destination. She picks up her bible and headscarf, scatters a few John 3:16 tracts on the empty seats and alights a few yards from the hall at Bitterne. In the Veracity Recreation Ground, the Goths are passing round a spliff. Later, they will meet up with their boyfriends and find somewhere quiet to make love.

Philemon

Rule Twelve:

The free will of Nominated Proxies may be influenced but never withdrawn.

Friday 30ᵗʰ April 2004 1.39 pm BST

Under other circumstances, Charles Macintosh would probably have taken the view that the most irritating feature of English planning law was the attendant publicity. *Permissions Granted* regularly feature in the Southampton Echo; interesting or controversial permissions frequently engender detailed press interest. But since the arrival of journalist Jennifer Gentleman at said newspaper, it rather appeared that Mr. Macintosh had refiled the whole matter from *'Irritating Necessities* to *'Enjoyable Distractions* . Despite their considerable difference in ages (he being somewhat closer to retirement than he permitted most around him to know, she being clearly more recently out of university than she would like to admit), the young lady appeared to have taken rather a shine to him, judging by her mode of dress and the attention she positively lavished upon him when they met. Entirely coincidentally, of course, his role as Director of Planning had already conferred a necessity of three lunch meetings between the two of them over the preceding month, a pattern which his rather overworked secretary, Madge Arnold, had noticed immediately. So, when Mr. Macintosh had asked her to book a table for 1.00 pm that afternoon in Quay Fifteen and to clear his diary for the rest of the afternoon, she had a pretty good idea who he'd be meeting. Madge's own lunch breaks (kept strictly to the 30 minutes between 1.00 pm and 1.30 pm for flexi-time reasons) were generally spent at her desk with a foil-wrapped crispbread sandwich in one hand and the telephone in the other. Today, she is speaking to her best friend and oppo at Matthis & Son, Babs Smith. She's known Babs *forever*, and they reckon they're joined at the hip (at parties, they bump their size 18 hips at that point and laugh helplessly). She's just been giving Babs the lowdown on this *Gentleman* woman and how she was dressed in a tight miniskirt and a blouse cut so low, the girl was bursting out of her Wonderbra, and "I mean *bursting*,

Darling" (not that Madge has actually seen her of course, but Babs doesn't need to know that, does she?) and they've just finished giggling about it and she's completely forgotten about the time (but not to worry, no one minds about a couple of minutes over, do they?) when Mr. Macintosh himself bursts through the door and without so much as a "Hi, Madge, how are you," he's into his office, yelling at her to get the Director of HR on the phone *immediately* and then slamming the door so as to make the opaque glass panel rattle. Then, it's "Ooh Babs, you'll never guess... sorry gotta go... call you tonight."

Thursday 24th June 2004 9.30 am BST
The British (or rather European Union) system of employment law prioritises punctiliousness over expeditiousness. All employers are theoretically bound by its requirements. Public sector employers adhere to them scrupulously, regardless of cost.

A preliminary meeting was held between Director of Planning and Director of HR on the afternoon of 30th April to review an apparent serious breach of discipline by a middle-ranking employee of the Planning Department. However, the letter to the accused confirming the Discovery Meeting at which that alleged breach would be discussed was not issued for over a week. Accordingly, Harold Jowlett remained active in post until 4.00 pm, Tuesday, 10th May. Of course, that meant Madge had plenty of time to report on events as they developed over the intervening week. And that, in turn, meant that Babs Smith at Matthis, Juli Harlworth in Admin and Rosie Turner in Rosie's Station Flower Shop could be kept fully up to date with the circumstances as they emerged moment by moment. So, who could blame Rosie for discussing it with her daughter, who, though only 16, was a very mature 16-year-old and could relate to such things? And who would blame Kylie Turner for sharing a matter with such profoundly spiritual implications with her dear friends at *Sisters* (purely so that they could pray about it, of course)? This was acknowledged to be a rather unfortunate way for the Jowlett twins to hear the news of their father's impending suspension for alleged wrongdoing on Thursday, 6th May at the weekly *Sisters'* prayer meeting. Nevertheless, their red-eyed arrival home that evening meant an inevitable conversation with their mother, who lived in perpetual fear of one or both of them returning bruised or pregnant or both after an evening out. It took Maureen Jowlett almost 24 hours to extract the complete story from them, whereupon she was initially visibly relieved to discover that her first fears had not been realised.

It was only over that weekend in full conversation with her husband that the true seriousness of the situation began to dawn on her. Then, her worst fear turned from pregnancy to loss of reputation and potential loss of pension rights.

Harold Jowlett was, therefore, unusually, if painfully, well prepared for the arrival of the letter announcing the Discovery Meeting that Monday, and for the meeting itself the following day. Not, of course, that any of that helped very much, since the matter, though extremely serious, was factually unambiguous. Nevertheless, as protocol required, the official letter he was handed on that day specified that his suspension was paid, and in no way should be taken to imply guilt.

It was, therefore, on 24th June that Harold found himself accompanied by his UNISON rep to a meeting in conference room 4 of the Planning Department's floor in one of Hampshire County Council's buildings in central Southampton. The meeting lasted precisely 9 minutes and 47 seconds. Once the Chairman opened the meeting, Harold was asked if he wanted to add anything to his statement. He did rather regret the somewhat blatant reference in the statement to the Holy Ghost having personally instructed him to approve the planning application for what was now being referred to as the Itchen River Development, but even Harold could not dispute the fact that he had done so. He therefore had nothing to add or to change. That exchange took 4 minutes and 49 seconds. The remaining 4 minutes and 58 seconds until the chairman closed the meeting were largely taken up with the movement of paper and coughing. The carefully timed, legally phrased termination letter that arrived the following Monday at Harold's home invited him to appeal within ten working days against instant dismissal without notice and with loss of pension rights. Despite advice from UNISON to the contrary, Harold saw no point in lodging such an appeal.

Friday 2nd July 2004 8.57 am BST

"Frank, I need to see Pastor."

"Hi, Harold. Let me just fire up the comp and check his diary for you… It's a busy month, I'm afraid. I can give you a ten-minute slot at 8.50 am on 30th July?"

"Frank, it's more serious than that. I need to see him now."

Harold's one hell of a moaner. But Frank can tell from his tone that his concern is genuine.

"OK, Next Thursday. 8th July. 9.10 am in the counselling room at the church. Best I can do."

Frank replaces the receiver and looks at Philemon enquiringly. The older man returns a wistful look and shakes his head. 8th July will pass without a meeting. Pastor Littlemann cannot be seen to be connected with this matter, now that the nationals have got hold of it. After all, the Church of the Body of Christ has a reputation to protect.

Wednesday 25th August 2004 11.47 am BST

"Man that is born of a woman hath but a short time to live, and is full of misery."

He's always loved that line. Mostly because of the word 'misery'. It so aptly sums up the attitude of nearly everyone he meets. And truth to tell, he has dined out on that misery for the best part of thirteen years, ever since his own faith finally died.

"He cometh up and is cut down like a flower; he flieth as it were a shadow, and never continueth in one stay."

So, he has, for most of that time, chosen to use the beautiful language of the 1559 Church of England burial service whenever there has been a death in the church.

"In the midst of life, we be in death: of whom may we seek for succor but of thee, O Lord, which for our sins justly art displeased."

He knows it by heart now. As he recites it, his mind wanders to the dear departed himself. Philemon does so admire a decisive man. And what more decisive act is open to a man than deliberately, to end his own life – particularly, when to do so is so conveniently in the interests of the Church of the Body of Christ?

"Yet, O Lord God most holy, O Lord most mighty, O holy and most merciful saviour, deliver us not into the bitter pains of eternal death."

By tradition, the widow is first to drop earth into the grave; then, the teenage twin daughters who are blubbering their little hearts out, bless 'em. Then, for some reason, it's that blonde girl from *Sisters*. He's noticed that pretty little creature from the get-go. Tried to think why she, out of all of them, has caught his attention, then realised it was the long, straight blonde hair – cut just like that bitch who'd pissed on him from her superior height all those years ago, when he still had feelings that could be hurt. What was her name? Lisa? Lorna? He can't remember now, it was so long ago. The cunt wouldn't marry him because he was too short. Mind, he'd had a quiet giggle when he heard the news about the bitch. But that was after he had returned from the Cameroon, years later. Her little sprog had gone down with leukaemia; died of it, aged four, apparently. Philemon might be short, but at least he didn't have her husband's defective genes.

"Thou knowest, Lord, the secrets of our hearts, shut not up thy merciful eyes to our prayers."

And what a way Harold had chosen to go out. That '76 Fixin! A queen among Pinot Noirs. What a choice to take with the tablets that was! He admires elegance almost as much as he admires decisiveness.

"But spare us, Lord most holy, O God most mighty, O holy and merciful saviour, thou most worthy judge eternal, suffer us not at our last hour for any pains of death to fall from thee."

But wherever did Harold manage to find it? Even the vineyard couldn't supply that particular vintage when Philemon had been looking himself a couple of years back. Hey, maybe Harold had some more at home! A little impromptu visit to comfort the grieving widow and orphans is definitely called for.

Saturday 4ᵗʰ September 2004 10.07 am BST

"This has been left for longer than it should, in my opinion."

"But Pastor, we couldn't simply press on with fundraising without acknowledging Harold's sad passing." It is the normally quiet Jonny Ropen who is speaking.

"Be that as it may, we have a £9.5 million development to undertake, and virtually no cash in hand. Whilst I am quite certain that God will provide, He does expect his children to help themselves, you know. This is why I am pleased to introduce onto this committee, Brother Able Matthis, son of the founder of Matthis & Son, of which you will of course all be aware, sole remaining family member of its board and its Finance Director. Welcome, Able. I know you will add considerable spiritual gravitas to our committee."

"Thank you, Pastor. My first observations may, I fear, not be entirely what you would like to hear. Firstly, I must remind the committee that we now have slightly less than three years within which to commence this development before the expiration of the planning permission. As we are all aware, it was granted under circumstances which have caused the County Council considerable embarrassment and we can be confident that there would be no possibility of its renewal if we did not commence work within that time. Secondly, and this is again in my opinion only, the most obvious way to fund the commencement of the building of the Southampton Tabernacle is to sell the land on which we have permission to build the flats."

For once, Philemon is unable to think of a response. He looks at Matthis, all but open mouthed, wishing already that he had considered more carefully the appointment to the finance committee of someone who clearly has his own opinions.

He wants to say, "Let a £3 million building site slip between my fingers? Over my dead body." What actually comes out is, "Thank you, brother. This is a matter that I shall consider prayerfully before the Lord."

Saturday 4ᵗʰ September 2004 10.07 pm BST

"Fuck!"

Philemon Littlemann is considering Brother Matthis' suggestion most prayerfully before the Lord.

"Fuck! Fuck! Fuck!"

"What's the problem, Phi?"

"Don't fucking call me Phi! You know I hate it."

"Sorry, *Phi-le-mon*." Frank edges away towards the far end of the bed. He has seen his lover become quite physical at times of intense anger before and isn't one to pummel his body daily.

"The problem, *Beloved*," Philemon replies, his tone laced with considerable sarcasm, "is money; fucking money; a commodity of which I do not have enough."

"You've got more of it than anyone I've ever met."

It's a risky comment, but one Frank can't resist making – quite apart from its being true.

"Well, it seems I haven't got enough to build a bloody church!"

Frank resists the temptation to comment on the somewhat ironic juxtaposition of the last two words of Philemon's sentence.

Instead, he says, "Oh, come here, man. Let me kiss you with the kisses of my mouth."

Philemon adheres to the scriptural exhortation.

Saturday 20th November 2004 11.45 am GMT

"It's no good, you know. There is no way you're going to get these people to part with enough cash to get this building underway within the next three years. You've raised less than £200,000 since you shelled out for the land and most of them have given you so much they can't afford to pay their gas bills."

Philemon would rather not have to admit it, but he knows Frank is right. Nevertheless, he has long regarded himself as a pragmatist. On Monday, T&W will be instructed to take tenders for the sale of the apartment land. Though the process is necessary, it's all rather tedious. He knows the market value of the land. He knows how much he will get from its sale. He knows he won't see the cash this side of the year end.

In order to buoy his flagging spirit, he will announce tomorrow that the Lord has called for yet another fortnight of prayer and fasting. When he returns, he will be able to announce the Lord's instructions to sell the apartment land. Two weeks' prayer and fasting won't be so bad. It will be the Trump Sonesta this time. It's got much better views of the ocean than the Loews and besides, he and Frank haven't visited Gus all year.

Tuesday 7th February 2006 7.00 pm GMT

"Look, I can accept her not wanting an eighteenth-birthday party. Not everyone is a party animal, even at that age. But why can't she be here for a birthday supper with her family, Paula?"

"She says it's the most important day of her life so far and she has to offer it to the Lord. She took the day off school. No sickness excuse, or anything. Just told them she wasn't coming in. Goodness knows what they thought of that. Then, she went out first thing. Bible and headscarf in hand as usual. Said she was going to pray with her sisters, so not to wait up for her. Then, she said she and her sisters are the Brides of Christ now. And that wedding ring of Nanna's I gave her two years back – she's transferred it onto her left hand. Had, I'm getting seriously concerned about this."

"We're losing that girl, Paula. I used to think we'd be lucky to get through the teens without pregnancy or drug addiction. Now, it seems like she's come up with a different kind of addiction. It's a cult. You do know that, don't you? It doesn't matter how mainstream they pretend to be, I'm telling you this is not like St. Andrew's. She's tied up in something that's got a hold on her and she can't see it. And I'm actually not convinced anyone else can see it either. But I'm telling you, this is dangerous. It's not going to end well."

"So... what do we do? Go to the police?"

"I don't think there's anything we can do. She's 18 and no one's broken the law. We just have to tough it out."

Tuesday 1st May 2006 9.05 pm BST

He had wanted to do this alone. And for some reason he cannot quite explain, it had to be today. So now, he stands on the balcony of a spacious penthouse overlooking the Itchen River. It is one of four on the development, designer furnished of course. Registered in his own name, it is the sweetener in a deal he bitterly regrets: the one compensation for having let something as precious as land slip through his fingers. Some things, he thinks, even a spiritual man might allow himself to feel sad about: the rejection of repentance by the lost; the hard hearts of the Lord's people; missing out on a good fuck. And now, the sale of real estate. Philemon feels he's been fucked pretty good himself – by all those bastards who tune in to his Internet broadcast free of charge, yet are too tight-fisted to send him their money. He really, really wanted to build these apartments himself and keep as many as possible for rental. They're shooting up in value in this market, too. Others have bought three, four, even five of them for speculation. He has just this one. He will not live in it for long, of course. The views aren't nearly as good as his place at Ocean Quay. He will establish residency for tax purposes, and thus pay no Capital Gains Tax on the gain when he sells. Render unto Caesar only that which you haven't been able to hide in a safety deposit box or move to a tax haven. Then, he will move quietly back. The spiritual man must be prepared to inconvenience himself in the service of the Lord.

Monday 14ᵗʰ August 2006 9.25 pm BST
"English – A, French – A, Spanish – A. My God! She must be over the moon. Where is she?"

"Actually, Had, she doesn't know yet. She went out early to a prayer meeting in Bitterne."

Haddon Spurgeon groans inwardly. His dilemma is always the same. He loves this child to bits and wants everything to be wonderful for her. He has cared for her as he would his own for nine years. Yet, she is not his blood. And that means there is a limit to how far he can press her. Haddon is aware he consistently defers to Paula on questions relating to the children. Yet, he constantly questions whether he is doing the right thing when he does. Left to him, this *Sisters* thing would have been nailed to the floor years ago.

As it is, he watches the girl perpetually risking her long-term interests by prioritising beliefs she will have abandoned within two years. Yet, he feels himself powerless to break the pattern.

"And Had…"

"Yes?"

"I think it's time I told you, she's decided to take a gap year."

"Well, that may turn out to be a good thing. She can go travel the world, shake off this religious stuff. By the time she gets back, she'll have forgotten what a bible looks like."

"Well, that's the point, I'm afraid. She says she's taking a year out to do outreach work with the *Sisters* here in Southampton."

Monday 1ˢᵗ January 2007 9.00 pm GMT

"Turn that heating off! We can't afford it. Brother Able, financial report, please."

"We were doing well. £3.1 million on the sale of the apartment land, £200k that we had to start with and another £150k, raised last year. But it's virtually all been spent. We're roughly half way through the build programme. Not building the flats has reduced the total cost by £2.5 million. So, we're left with about another £3.5 million to find. I estimate we have enough to pay another two monthly surveyors' valuations before we run out."

"And then?" Philemon knows the answer, anyway.

"And then, the builders down tools. Possibly, even sue us under the contract."

"Your recommendation?"

Able is silent for a long time.

"There is no sustainable solution that leaps to mind. We were hoping donations would keep up with expenditure. But I'm afraid your Internet audience simply has not grown in line with expectations. The physical congregation is holding up well. We're running two Sunday morning services now, back to back. But they've all given just about everything they have. I'm rather afraid you may have killed the golden goose."

Philemon eyes the big man closely. He doesn't like him much. But then, he doesn't need to. Able is giving him what he most needs but least wants – honest advice. He is silent a long time. Then, he looks straight at Able and says,

"Silver and Gold have I none. But such as I have, give I thee. In the name of Jesus Christ of Nazareth, get up and walk."

All three members of the committee look at him in complete confusion.

"We need this church on its feet."

And with that, he rises to his own feet and walks out.

Sister Serenity

Rule Twelve:

The free will of Nominated Proxies may be influenced but never withdrawn.

Saturday 20th January 2007 11.14 am GMT

Two *Sons* are singing on Portland Terrace, just outside the main entrance to the West Quay shopping centre. Acoustic guitar music is competing for attention with a sub-zero wind that is literally whistling. The wind chill factor makes it feel even colder. If the Lamb they are singing about were actually present, the RSPCA would be prosecuting them for animal cruelty. Such shoppers as are about are not lingering. Eventually, the music makers come to the sensible decision to pack up and head home for an early lunch. All the *Sisters* who were with them, except one, have long since given up handing out tracts. Even in gloves, their fingers were threatening them with frostbite. Only one remains. Wrapped in a full-length coat and neck scarf, only her face and long blonde hair are visible, and that is covered by an emerald green chiffon headscarf. She carries on alone, pressing tracts into the hands of anyone willing to accept them.

A dark-haired young man, a little taller and probably a little older than Serenity, passes. She hands him a tract on salvation. As he accepts it, his hand brushes hers. He attempts to catch her eye, but her attention is focused on the passing shoppers, looking for the next lost soul to whom she can give the good news of salvation. He carries on into West Quay where he waits a minute or so before venturing back out again towards the blonde girl in the headscarf. He passes once more. This time, she hands him a copy of St. John's Gospel. Again, their hands touch. Again, he fails to make eye contact. This time, he walks a little way up Portland Terrace while the girl continues to concentrate intently on reaching the lost souls around her. He glances down and flicks through the booklet. He comes to a highlighted passage – chapter 3 verse 16 – and reads. Then, he walks back to the blonde girl. This time, he stands to the side to her. For a moment, she does not notice. Then, feeling his presence, she turns to him questioningly. He quotes what he has just read, "*For God so loved the world, that he gave his only begotten Son, that whosoever believeth in him should not perish, but have everlasting life.*"

She looks at him quizzically, not sure whether she is being mocked or supported.

"Can I buy you a coffee?" he asks.

She hesitates, evaluating. Then, she nods, packs up her bag of tracts and points towards Starbucks.

Sunday 11th February 2007 8.48 am GMT

She is deeply uneasy. Her disquiet has been growing for a year. She used to be edified by *Sisters*, sustained by it. Once, she virtually lived for Thursday evenings, keeping herself going through the rest of the week by rising early in the morning to pray, read her bible and sing to the Lord. But if she's honest about it, *Sisters* has lost something. No, that's not it. She, Serenity, has lost something. She has lost her serenity, she thinks ironically. A nagging awareness of the immaturity of *Sisters* has been growing in her heart all year long – a realization that what she once believed doesn't make quite the same obvious sense to her any longer. If she's honest with herself, she's known for some months it's time to leave it behind, to grow and move on. She's just not been willing to admit it to herself. But this is the last Sunday of her eighteenth year. Childhood is over. When she was a child she thought as a child, spake as a child, understood as a child. But now she is a woman, she must put away childish things. It's time to take hold of adult realities, adult responsibilities.

She has told no one of her decision. How could she look all those dear, young, enthusiastic believers in the face and tell them she no longer believes what they hold true? She simply could not face doing it. So, last Thursday evening, she slipped silently out of the prayer meeting a little early, crying. She walked one bus stop closer to home than usual, in case any of her dear friends should catch her at her normal stop and ask her what was wrong. She knows she would have broken down completely if that had happened. So, it's better this way. She will just disappear, let them carry on without her.

That is why she is now on her way to her first full Sunday morning service at the Church of the Body of Christ. She *is* the Bride. She has to meet her Bridegroom face to face.

Philemon

Rule Nine:

Players may choose more than one Proxy if they so wish.

Sunday 11ᵗʰ February 2007 10.00 am GMT

He mounts the pulpit in familiar fashion, adjusts the microphone, leans in; silence; three seconds, four, five. They are familiar with this routine. Ten seconds. But this is longer than normal. Fifteen. It's becoming uncomfortable. Thirty seconds. Now, they are squirming in their seats as he looks down at them. Sixty seconds pass before he opens his mouth. As he finally begins, sighs of relief are audible.

"My text today is taken from The Thoughts of the Apostles, Chapter 3, verse 6."

He stops and looks around the room. No one has yet realised the point he is making.

"Can anyone quote for me, without looking it up, 'The Thoughts of the Apostles, Chapter 3, verse 6'?"

Silence.

A lone voice from somewhere to the left of him starts, "Silver and Gold have I none..."

He interjects.

"No! no, no, No, No, NO! Beloved, are you all so unlearned in the words of Scripture? There is NO SUCH BOOK! There is no book anywhere in Scripture called 'The Thoughts of the Apostles'. Now, can someone please tell me the book that *is* in Scripture that I might be referring to?

A further silence. They all have the point now, but no one wants to risk speaking up lest he again contradict them.

"Is there no one in this who can tell me the name of the book? All right then, tell me this. Who is the youngest person in this congregation today?"

After a pause, a young female voice sounds quietly from the middle of the left side of the church. "Please, Pastor, I think it might be me." He turns to face the speaker.

"Stand, would you please, child."

Serenity rises uncertainly to her feet.

"Can *you* tell me the name of the book, child?"

"Pastor, I believe you mean the Acts of the Apostles."

"Yes, child! Yes. The Acts of the Apostles. Not the *Thoughts* of the Apostles. The *Acts* of the Apostles. And can you tell me what is in chapter 3 verse 6?"

Serenity hesitates a moment. But she has read the verse many times and can quote it verbatim.

"Silver and Gold have I none. But such as I have, give I thee. In the name of Jesus Christ..."

"Yes, child, yes! You are so right. You are so very right. For these are the ACTS of the Apostles. 'Silver and Gold have I none, but such as I have, give I thee.' Not, 'I'll think about giving it to thee.' Not, 'I'll leave it to thee in my will.' Brethren, who amongst us has silver or gold? Who has held back on their silver and gold when the Lord's work is waiting to be done? When souls are crying daily for salvation, who in this church is failing to *ACT*? When souls are dying daily, only to be thrown into Hell because they have not been washed in the Blood of the Lamb, who is not *ACTING*? Look, Beloved. I, too, am at fault. I, too, have gold. Deacon Frank, come forward."

Frank walks steadily down the central aisle from the back of the hall to the front, offering plate in hand. As he arrives and stands below the podium, Philemon pulls his gold ring overtly from his finger and holds it high for all to see, for the cameras to see, for those viewing the podcast over the Internet to see. The central spotlight catches the cross on the ring, making it flash. Holding it between his right thumb and forefinger, he places it theatrically into the offering plate.

"Pastor," responds Frank, in a voice loud enough for the microphones to pick up. "I, too, have gold." And with that, he removes a new ring from his own finger and an unfamiliar wristwatch from his wrist. He drops them very obviously into the offering plate, so that all can see. And now, the room is alive with voice and motion.

"I, too, have gold." At the front right of the hall a middle-aged woman removes her wedding ring. A deacon moves in with another offering plate. She deposits her ring. All over the hall, people are echoing the chant now. "I, too, have gold. I, too, have gold."

And now, they start another chant. "Such as I have, give I thee." Item after item is deposited in the plates as a hysteria of chant and divestment sweeps through the room.

In the break-out rooms and in the remote video transmissions rooms all over the country, he knows the same will be happening.

Still standing, Serenity looks down at her grandmother's wedding ring that she has now taken to wearing on her left hand in acknowledgement of her being the Bride of Christ. She thinks about the inscription inside, 'Let him kiss me with the kisses of his mouth'. She knows she cannot withhold what her Husband is calling her to give, regardless of how many generations it has been in the family. She drops it into the offering plate as it passes down her row.

Philemon stands on the podium looking round the hall in satisfaction. As he watches, in particular, the young blonde girl from *Sisters* remove a ring from her finger, he gives passing question to why she has been wearing it on her wedding ring finger anyway. Surely, she is not married. But there is definitely something about that girl; something he cannot get out of his mind.

Sunday 11th February 2007 7.04 pm GMT
Two morning services and an evening service in the main hall, three break-out rooms and over a dozen remote locations have yielded a considerable haul of jewellery. It will all be counted and valued in due course, together with what gets sent in to the appeal at the end of the Internet broadcast. Philemon realises this probably really is

the last substantial collection he can raise from the faithful flock for the foreseeable future. But he would rather take what they have now, than see them buried in it or bequeathing it to their undeserving progeny. The priority, however, is to retrieve his own ring with the cross on it. He rarely allows himself sentimentality, but this particular item does hold some personal value to him and he's far too attached to it to let it disappear. He empties the bag and sorts systematically through for the ring with the cross on it. Then, his eye is caught by something else. A ring with exquisite workmanship; a ring with a barely visible inscription inside it. He picks it up and studies intently. 'Let him kiss me with the kisses of his mouth.' He stiffens. A coincidence undoubtedly, but a spooky one, nevertheless.

"The Song of Songs that is Solomon's," he says to the empty flat, "Chapter 1, verse 2." He looks at it for a long, long time. Coincidence or not, he needs to know who this belonged to.

Thursday 15ᵗʰ March 2007 9.57 am GMT

As it turned out, the gesture had been more symbolic than lucrative. When all the jewellery had been accumulated (apart from the pastor's ring and the Song of Songs ring, of course) it was taken to a jeweller in Farringdon (they wouldn't come as far as Southampton) who offered less than £100,000. For once, Philemon Littlemann was genuinely surprised and disappointed. He knew, of course, it would be subjected to a substantial mark up. He never did discover, however, that over the following three months the jeweller progressively disposed of their purchases for something over £0.5 million in total. As it was, he had returned to Southampton with a cheque in his left breast pocket for £98,272 made out to him personally, of course. For once, money was as physically close to his heart as it was metaphorically. But the heart it covered was worried; worried to the tune of the £3.5 million he still needed to complete the building of the Tabernacle. However, even Philemon Littlemann was now aware he had, to all intents and purposes, lost the race against time. Offerings and the expanding ministry would eventually achieve the necessary sum but there was no telling how long it would take to do so. Philemon hated the idea of borrowing money. Or perhaps, more properly put, he hated the idea of having to pay it back, particularly with interest. But there again, this was 2007. Property values had been rising since '96 and positively booming since the Dot Com bubble in '02. The stock markets were soaring, he was being offered credit cards by banks he'd never heard of and the American banks were securitising the housing market. If there was ever a year in which he would be safe borrowing money, 2007 was surely that year, right? So, it was time to value the portfolio and borrow what was needed to complete the building, right? You had to speculate to accumulate, right?

But by the end of February, Philemon had established he had a problem. All the banks were quite happy with the amount of security he had to offer, since his property portfolio was now substantial. But none of them could see how he was going to pay back the loan with only the offering income the Church of the Body of Christ could rely on. So, that is why, on a chilly mid-March morning, he finds himself once again dressed in pinstripes and monogrammed shirt in a second-floor waiting room of a foreign bank that two weeks ago he'd never heard of, called 'Icebanki'. He has taken to alternating the wearing of the Song of Songs ring with his own. Today, it is on the third finger of his right hand.

Out of boredom, he is studying the grain on the polished yew table (solid wood, of course – this is a London investment bank, not some provincial solicitor's practice) as the door at the end of the room is opened by a tall, dark-haired young woman in white blouse and grey business skirt who introduces herself as Amelia Fotherington-Smyth. An austere hair arrangement and unfashionable glasses cannot hide the fact that she is unusually attractive. She takes his order for espresso deferentially and tells him that Sir Fredrick will be a few moments late. Then, in a hushed tone that is somewhere between confidential and conspiratorial, she whispers that Sir Fredrick has been suffering considerable pain from his war wound for several days, and if he needs to leave the room quickly, will Philemon please not show surprise. Shortly after she exits the room, the door opens again to the entry of a grey, balding man in his mid-fifties leaning heavily on a cane, followed once more by the dark-haired secretary carrying several box files. The next two hours are devoted to an exploration of Philemon's requirements and the business case for Icebanki to support him, with a liberal peppering of references to the Falklands War, Goose Green, Colonel Herbie Jones, and 2 Para, that leave Philemon quite certain that the speaker has been no closer to seeing military service than he has to the Falkland Islands themselves. Nevertheless, he refrains from making reference either to this or the adoring looks the young woman casts repeatedly at Sir Fredrick throughout the meeting. By the end, he is still unclear as to whether the stories have been for his benefit as prospective client or hers as prospective lover. Later, he realises the difference is immaterial. Before the day finishes, Sir Fredrick Dickinson will have fucked them both.

But Philemon is outcome orientated. He's a pragmatist. He knows what he needs and he knows this is the only show in town to offer it. As an avid 'Star Trek' fan, he also knows when resistance is futile. If in the process, he has to offer a little sycophantic deference to a pathetically inadequate, self-inflated, narcissistic knight of the realm, well, he can cope with that. So, when the usurious Icebanki interest rate and charges are spelt out, he puts up less resistance than the Argies did at Goose Green and probably no more than the dark-haired secretary will offer later that evening. Even though he is being knowingly screwed over, Philemon can smile almost as sweetly as she will. By noon, he has shaken hands on a loan for £3.5 million. Intriguingly, it is only upon shaking his hand that Sir Fredrick lets his guard drop – apparently, because he notices the ring. He has stopped mid-sentence to comment on it. Philemon, somehow, gains the impression that it had some meaning for him. But no matter. The moment passes.

Some requirements of the deal make him instinctively a little uneasy. It is to be concluded in the Isle of Man, with all the property deeds deposited in Douglas. The money is more overdraft than loan, repayable, as the paperwork states, on demand. The Trust's liquid funds are to be deposited in the Douglas branch of Icebanki from where its day-to-day banking will be conducted. None of this, ultimately, matters to Philemon, though. Within 48 hours, after a short flight from Southampton to Douglas, he will have access to the funds he needs to complete the Southampton Tabernacle. Flush with success, he takes the stairs two at a time on the way down, and strides confidently past the reception desk. If he had stopped to sign out, he might have noticed the calendar that reads 15th March. But even if he did, it might have meant nothing to him. To Philemon, Shakespeare is just another dead writer. And maybe even if he had known something of the soul of the Bard, he would have inclined less to the Soothsayer's *Beware the Ides of March*, and more to Mark Antony's *Ambition should be made of sterner stuff.* As it is, Philemon's literary awareness reaches no further than Rhett Butler's last words to Scarlett O'Hara. If it had, maybe things would have worked out differently.

With the loan secured and being freely drawn down, the construction of Philemon's great edifice continues smoothly throughout 2007, with completion set for October 2008 and an opening ceremony set for Christmas Day. However, all this is still somewhat in the future for now and Philemon has other matters to attend to. He has somewhat neglected the nurturing of his flock, not to mention the grooming of their donations, for too long. It is time to move the spiritual life of the Church of the Body of Christ up a gear. This will require some kind of focal event. But no matter, Philemon is more than adept at engineering those. What he does not count on, however, is the intervention of Fate or Chance, or, if he were a religious man, perhaps, he would call it the moving of the Holy Spirit. Whatever the interpretation of cause, a chain of events will be set in motion the following Sunday. For Philemon has decided it is high time to revert to the matter of *SecondCome*. And he has an uncanny sense that it will be best addressed if preceded by the establishment of the identity of the person to whom the Song of Songs ring had belonged.

Sister Serenity

Rule Eleven:

Players may make themselves visible to their Nominated Proxies but must not intervene directly in the chain of events.

Saturday 17th March 2007 11.50 am GMT

It's the fourth time. She has to give him full credit for tenacity, even if she is going to have to keep on disappointing him. She belongs to the Lord. She is the Bride of Christ, just as Pastor has said so many times. She'll never be able to give herself to a man and it's wrong to create an expectation in him that she cannot fulfil. Yet here he is once more.

After that first coffee, he had, of course, asked to see her again. She wanted to make clear the basis for doing so was purely spiritual, that she had no romantic interest in him. So, she said she would see him in two weeks. When she returned to West Quay delivering tracts again two weeks later (her last remaining commitment to *Sisters*), he was waiting for her. Though he caught her eye almost immediately this time and drew a smile from her, he watched her and her *Sisters*, and listened to the *Sons* music for perhaps an hour before he approached. All the while, she had been watching him, too, repeating to herself that this was a lost soul, that winning him for Jesus was her duty, that there was nothing personal involved whatsoever. No fewer tracts were delivered; no fewer John's Gospels were handed out. In fact, only by a close study of Serenity as she went about her familiar business would you have realised there was anything different about her. Yet, it had to be acknowledged that when he approached her, her smile came sooner than was absolutely necessary for courtesy and her eyes betrayed the existence of what she might have called a warm spot for him. A second coffee followed and a little more of each other's circumstances were disclosed. A further appointment was made, once again, for two weeks' hence, and on 17th February, a similar pattern was followed. Except that by the end of their time in Starbucks, Serenity was letting Henry call her Laura (he'd felt truly foolish sustaining the use of her chosen name for so long, but to give the boy his due, he'd stuck with it until she began to thaw). She was also rather hoping he would ask if he could see her again. Laura was truly disappointed (though succeeded in not showing it) when he said the soonest he could see her would be 17th March, but more than happy that this time, he suggested lunch. Somewhat to her surprise, Serenity found herself thinking about him rather more than she would have wished over the intervening month. Even more surprising, though, was that, after two weeks, she began to feel resentful at the delay and wondering who else he might be seeing in the meantime. By the end of the third week, she was truly regretting that she had refused his suggestion that they exchange phone numbers in order to text each other. So that, by the time 17th March finally arrived, she had convinced herself that he wasn't interested (though she never did clarify to herself whether she meant in the Lord or in herself) and she wouldn't see him again.

As it is, the *Sons* and the *Sisters* are not holding an outreach today. Nevertheless, Laura arrives at West Quay at the normal time of 10.00 am, just in case he might come after all. The biggest surprise of all should be the jolt her heart gives her when she sees him standing waiting. The reason it isn't, is that she is distracted by the spontaneous hug she gives him. Had she not checked her urges, it could easily have been rather more than just a hug that passes between them. But she remembers in time that she is betrothed to the Son of God, and that anything more than a hug of friendship would be unseemly.

Over coffee and then, later, lunch, when Henry explains that the reason for the long gap between visits has been his inability to afford the train fare from Oxford, she is relieved. When he confirms that term is now over and he has applied to work at Matthis & Son in Southampton for the next six weeks, she is positively elated (though she reminds herself that her purpose here is only the salvation of his soul). By the time they part, just before 4.00 pm, she has invited him to the following morning's Sunday service. He has hesitated, torn between wanting to see her again and, as a committed adherent to the philosophy of epistemology, emphatically not wanting to be drawn into religion. He counters with a suggestion that they take an afternoon walk in the New Forest after the service has finished. Mildly disappointed, she acquiesces.

Sunday 18th March 2007 11.00 am GMT

You have to be seated early now, if you want to be guaranteed entry. Serenity likes to sit on the far right of the church about half way down, and if you want to be that specific about your location you need to be in your seat a good hour before Pastor arrives. So here she has been waiting since 9.30 am, reading her bible, praying and speaking softly in tongues to herself. She doesn't like to admit publicly that the Spirit of God has given her this gift. It seems to Serenity that something so important must be kept secret, lest she appears to others as boastful. Nevertheless, the young woman whispering prayers in a strange language, adorned with an emerald green headscarf over her long blonde hair, cannot help but make an impact on all who see her as they file into the church for the morning's service. Serenity does not know it, but she has already been seen by many as someone noteworthy.

Philemon rises in his habitual way and mounts the podium, then stands gazing down on the hopeful below him. At this moment, they repeatedly remind him of a clutch of hungry chicks in the nest, beaks spread to maximum width in anticipation of the parent bird dropping predigested food. However, he resists the temptation to vocalise his cynicism. He begins.

"Good morning, Beloved. The Lord's word this morning is taken from Song of Songs, Chapter 1, verse 1-3. Deacon Frank, would you read, please?"

Frank opens his bible at the preselected place and reads, "The Song of Songs which is Solomon's. Let him kiss me with the kisses of his mouth: for thy love is better than wine. Because of the savour of thy good ointments, thy name is as ointment poured forth, therefore do the virgins love thee."

Frank sits.

Philemon goes on to preach an average sermon with an average appeal that generates an average number of emotional aphorisms and an average collection plate. By the time he drives home, he has all but forgotten what he said.

He has, however, obtained the information he wants before Frank has sat down. This he has done by no more demanding an act than scanning his eyes over the congregation to see who reacted when Frank reached the relevant part of the text. And as Frank had read *Let him kiss me with the kisses of his mouth*, only one person moved. Serenity, the young woman with an intriguing penchant for catching his attention, had sat up sharply and stared hard at Frank. Philemon now drives home on autopilot. The only thought on his mind is how to use this information most profitably. By the time he reaches Ocean Village, that first thought has been juxtaposed by a second. By Christmas next year, the Tabernacle will be open for business. And by then, God has to be seen to make good on that throwaway line of his from years before, *'If you build it, he will come*. How precisely he will do this, he does not yet know. But he does know that Serenity and the Song of Songs ring may well play a material part.

He also knows he has to come up with the answer soon. Time and banks wait for no man.

Sunday 18th March 2007 3.12 pm GMT
She is used to hearing the voice of God in so many different ways. Anything from the roar of thunder to the burbling of a brook, from reading Scripture to the Pastor's instructions from pulpit on a Sunday. All of these are ways in which the Spirit of God has made His will known to her for as long as she has had her faith.

When, at the 'Silver & Gold' service, as it had come to be known, Pastor had called for gold, she had willingly given up her mother's ring, despite knowing she would face anger and criticism at home. Indeed, that inevitable confrontation had even been useful in its own way, for she had taken it as an opportunity to announce she would take a further year at least before going to university. That in itself had resulted in the angry retort from Haddon that she was old enough to pay her own way in the world and could get a job. Later, they had all been thankful that he had stopped short of telling her to leave home.

But this morning's reference to the inscription inside her ring had her confused. It wasn't often that Pastor's sermons left her bored. But she had to face it. This was a less than average quality sermon that generated a less than average spiritual response in her. It had, however, given her mind time to drift, and in so doing, to dwell on the meaning of the quoted text. What did the Lord have in mind for her, as a betrothed bride of Christ?

Now, some forty minutes or so after Henry had collected her from home in his rickety old car, they have parked and are walking one of the innumerable little paths on the south-eastern side of the New Forest. She acknowledges to herself that the walk is a new development in their relationship. She has already recognised that she soon will have to accept that something is happening here that goes beyond an act of spiritual outreach. But not yet, dear Lord, please, not yet. She is not ready to face the dilemma of contradiction that will be implied by admitting to herself she has feelings for this man, despite her being the Bride of Christ. So, not yet, please, dear Lord, not yet.

"Why so quiet?"

Neither of them has spoken for some time. The sound of his voice comes to her from far away to a field of inner thoughts her mind is meandering through. Quickly, she finds her way back to this time and this place. As she does, she sees they are crossing a clearing where the ponies are standing in a close group, chewing on the gorse and waiting for the spring sunshine that will not arrive for some weeks yet. Before she has a chance to answer, the rain that has threatened since they left the car, now starts without warning. Equally devoid of warning is his act of taking her by the hand and running her towards the nearest large oak tree at the edge of the clearing where, she realises, he is hoping there will be some shelter from the downpour. As they arrive, a little breathless, huge drops of water begin to fall. She puts out her hands to the trunk of the tree to stop her forward motion. And now, she is as aware of him standing close behind her as she is of the presence of the Holy Spirit permanently around her. He places his hands on her shoulders and turns her, gently lifting her chin until she looks into her eyes. Then, comes the deluge. There is nowhere to shelter from this form of precipitation. The contradictions and dilemmas and conundrums are irrelevant as, *'Not yet, please, dear Lord, not yet,'* gives way to *'Let him kiss me with the kisses of his mouth'*.

Friday 27th April 2007 10.17 am BST

She has not moved from the yellow line for the last two minutes. But a silent voice calls to her from far away that her safety is at risk. She steps back two paces without really thinking about it, as the wind borne before the non-stop train drives through the station, followed, a moment later, by the huge engine itself.

Gradually, her consciousness returns to the here and now of platform 1 at Southampton Central and the prospect of eight empty weeks stretching forward to 29th June when his Trinity term will finish. Yes, he will be back at least once during that time. Yes, he has said she can visit him in College. Yes, they have the phone, text and e-mail. But no, she will not be with him. And no, she will not be able to put her head on his shoulder, or push his hand gently away as he tries to slip it between the buttons of her blouse. And no, she will not enjoy the sense of growing but forbidden desire rising from her solar plexus to arrive as a warmth on her heart and a flush on her face as he kisses her with the kisses of his mouth.

For now, she has to step into a reality she has been avoiding for these last six weeks that have been so different from anything she has ever experienced before. She can no longer ignore the dilemma that weighs like concrete on her soul. Her beliefs tell her she is the betrothed of the Son of God. Her feelings tell her she is in love with this man. Grateful, now that he has gone, that she has taken no irrevocable physical step, she nevertheless has to come to terms with the contradiction she confronts.

She has also to find a job. As she exits the station on the south side to collect his Ford Fiesta that he has lent her for the term, she passes the kiosk where that afternoon's Evening Standard is already on sale. Somewhere inside, buried deep towards the back is an article about an American company called New Century Finance filing for something called Chapter 11. Laura, of course, does not see this, nor would she understand it if she had. How often do those events that most profoundly influence our lives slide past our conscious minds unnoticed? How often do butterflies' flapping wings set off earthquakes? Chaos comes in many forms.

Laura looks up and over the four lanes of the Western Esplanade, to a coffee shop on the far side of the road. Being a Barista can't be that bad. Everyone does it, don't they? There are worse ways of spending your life than serving coffee all through the day and praying on your knees by your bed all through the night. It can't be that bad. Everyone does it, don't they?

Thursday 9th August 2007 11.00 am BST
The European Central Bank blows 95 billion Euros of your money 'improving liquidity' in the European Money Market. Over the next

two days it adds a further 108.7 billion Euros. The world turns once every 24 hours or so, just as it always does. How is Laura to know it has changed forever? How, indeed, is Philemon to know?

Friday 14th September 2007 6.11 pm BST

She got the job! Trainee barista, starting next Monday. She's upbeat when she tells her parents, but they find it hard to conceal their disappointment. Their daughter was capable of so much more. As she climbs the stairs to her room, her bible, and an evening on her knees, Haddon refocuses on the early evening news and the pictures of long queues forming outside the Northern Rock Bank. Down at the waterfront, Philemon's TV is tuned to the same station. He glances at the story feeling a little smug. He has no money in Northern Rock. This won't affect him. Losses, like taxes, are for the little people.

Wednesday 10th October 2007 11.14 am BST

"Freddie's little girlie's been on the blower about that ring again."

"I presume you are referring to Sir Fredrick Dickinson's secretary?"

"Uh huh."

"And you said?"

"Told her it wasn't for sale, just like you told me to."

Philemon looks down at the ring on the little finger of his left hand. He would dearly love to be able to wear it on his third finger, but he has been advised that enlarging it would compromise the design and severely reduce its value.

He enjoys owning something that someone else wants desperately, especially when that someone is the person who's forced him to deposit all the Trust's liquid funds in an offshore account on the Isle of Man.

Monday 24ᵗʰ December 2007 7.00 pm GMT

"She's absolutely genuine, boss; the real article. I can't tempt her, fault her or catch her out. Serenity is a genuine believer."

"Pity. It would have hurt her less if she was one of us."

Tuesday 25ᵗʰ December 2007 1.15 am GMT

Cain struggled with Abel. Genesis is clear on this.

The old nature in us struggles against the new. Pastor has preached it many times.

It had been fine meeting him for coffee, witnessing to him, looking for the conviction of the Holy Spirit in his eyes.

It had been perfectly ok having lunch with him, feeling strangely able to share the deeper truths of her inner self in a way she had been unable to even at *Sisters*, despite his still being, as yet, an unbeliever. It had even been nice to be kissed that afternoon in the clearing in the forest, for he had taken her by surprise and she had felt no sense of responsibility. But sometime after that – and Serenity couldn't pinpoint precisely when – contentment had changed into something less appealing to her betrothed spirit. She had been a while acknowledging the right term for it. Eventually, she realised there were two. Love? Yes, certainly, she was beginning to love him; but more than that, she found in herself a preoccupation with him that began to interfere with her habitual focus on the Lord. Eventually, though it was distasteful to her to do so, she could name it only as desire.

As the weeks passed, she oscillated between an irresistible urge to draw him to her and an equal and opposite reflex action to repel him. He had failed in his attempt to gain employment with Matthis and Son, being left with the option only of placing his name on the waiting list. On his advice, she had done the same. So, they had spent the next few weeks of his vacation workless and penniless. The car remained on the road at the generosity of his parents. Her only income came from hers, newly grateful at, and anxious to support their daughter's apparent homage to, normality, when she first announced the existence of a boyfriend and later, brought him to meet them. Given their daughter's strange religion, they would cheerfully have approved of virtually anything male that walked upright and could make three-word sentences that didn't involve 'hallelujah' or 'amen'. When they discovered he was an Oxford undergraduate, they were speechless. When it emerged that he had nothing to do with the Church of the Body of Christ, they were near ecstatic.

Weather had permitted the growing relationship to be pursued out of doors, mostly walking in the Forest. Here, Henry sought to advance the physical connection in all the normal ways, discovering that Laura would at first acquiesce just so far, until Serenity redrew the invisible limits.

Cain struggled with Abel.

Serenity struggled with Laura, forced into acknowledging that her old nature was not dead after all, merely sleeping until awakened by a kiss.

Enjoyment was thus interspersed with confusion seasoned liberally with irritation and argument. Then, there would be cross words and the angry slamming of car doors, tears, prayers by at least one of their bedsides, followed by late night texts of apology that morphed into mutual admissions of sexual desire expressed graphically but entirely safely, given the 28 miles that lay between Brockenhurst and Deacon Road, Southampton. In Brockenhurst, Henry would commonly lull himself to sleep in the time-honoured fashion of young men denied sexual expression by their inexperienced lovers. In Deacon Road, Laura would lie awake hungering equally for the same relief, denied it by the reminders of the sterner Sister Serenity as to her betrothed status and obligations to her Lord.

Cain struggled with Abel.

But that struggle came nowhere close to what Laura and Serenity experienced over that Easter university vacation.

She had stood on that station platform on 27th April 2007 and waved him off, deeply troubled by the prospect of six weeks of stomach-twisting contradiction inside herself. As the train pulled away for Oxford, Serenity's initial wave of relief that her commitment to the Lord was no longer at risk soon slid into Laura's profound fear that she would lose this man as a result of her inconsistent behaviour and anger at herself for not being able to let go with him.

By the time he returned for the summer vacation, Serenity had definitely decided she had no option but to end the relationship. She did so by text, signing it Serenity. A week later, when Henry had discovered which coffee shop she was working in and had stood outside all morning waiting for her shift to end, Laura had weakened sufficiently to invite him in for a free coffee during the early afternoon lull. Then came the acceptance of an offer of a lift at end of shift which somehow had ended up taking them in the opposite direction from home and out to the Forest where she had unwisely allowed herself to slip into his arms. Then came the kisses of his mouth and once again Laura knew she belonged to him just as certainly as Serenity knew she belonged to the Son of God.

And so the pattern had continued. Henry showed a rather unlikely patience for a man of 20 whilst waiting for this somewhat confused young lady to yield to her own passionate urges. Laura thought of little but Henry during her working days until the evening came and she could be with him once again. Then, at some point during the evening, Henry would test the boundaries of her resolve until her body was all but screaming out for him. But always, always, Serenity would forbid the crossing of that invisible line. He might well kiss her with the kisses of his mouth. But he was consistently to be denied the pleasure of lying all night betwixt her breasts.

So now, after some nine months of this excruciating oscillation, in the first moments of this Christmas morning, she is kneeling once again by her bedside. Her emerald scarf lies loose around her shoulders, her bible and the picture of her lovely and long-dead father are in front of her on the bed. She is weeping softly, beseeching her Saviour, her husband-to-be, for a sign of what she is to do. For at last, this evening, Henry has told her that he has reached the limit of his patience. He is willing that, if she wishes, they should announce their engagement, but has said so knowing she will turn even this down in her uncertainty. Either way, though, he cannot continue, he says, in this relationship without removal of the sexual boundaries she has imposed. She must have sex with him or end the relationship. He wants her very much. But he has to leave the decision with her.

So, Serenity does the only thing she knows how. She gets on her knees, prays, and seeks a sign from her God, just as the Magi had sought a sign in the sky two thousand years previously.

And as the darkness hours of Christmas morning slip silently by, she understands now that she has never properly characterised the nature of her inner conflict. For though she has thought of Cain and Able, now she sees her struggle is that of Jacob. She opens her Bible to Genesis 32 and reads.

And Jacob was left alone; and there wrestled a man with him until the breaking of the day. And when he saw that he prevailed not against him, he touched the hollow of his thigh; and the hollow of Jacob s thigh was out of joint, as he wrestled with him. And he said, Let me go, for the day breaketh. And he said, I will not let thee go, except thou bless me. And he said unto him, What is thy name? And he said, Jacob. And he said, Thy name shall be called no more Jacob, but Israel: for as a prince hast thou power with God and with men, and hast prevailed. And Jacob asked him, and said, Tell me, I pray thee, thy name. And he said, Wherefore is it that thou dost ask after my name? And he blessed him there. And Jacob called the name of the place Peniel: for I have seen God face to face, and my life is preserved.

A tenuous slice of daylight slides between the curtains to discover that sometime during the night, she has woken for long enough to undress and slip between the sheets. With dawn reaching to her through the widow, she rises through the layers of sleep, examining her soul at each stage, remembering sorrowfully, her dilemma of the night before. Now, reaching a full waking state, she stretches and is surprised to find herself more refreshed than she expected. She throws back the covers, rises and wishes her God happy birthday. She notices the slight, throbbing pain in her left thigh and wonder if God has touched her during the night. Shortly, she will look back at the bed and see blood. She will assume her period has started. She will be right and she will be glad. But her dilemma will not yet be resolved.

Tuesday 25th December 2007 11.00 am GMT

He stands at the podium keenly aware he will last in this role only as long as he can repeatedly bring to these people something new, something powerfully novel to grab them afresh. And he knows how close he is sailing to the wind (he hates clichés but can think of no more apt way of expressing this). There are those who have been asking difficult questions; questions concerning *SecondCome*; questions relating to the use of church and Trust resources. And though he has thus far deflected them successfully, he has begun to wake in the night. Listening to Frank's steady breathing next to him, he has been challenged by his own questions. These have mostly been of the 'what if' variety. He cannot admit them even to Frank, for reason of the weakness they would display. And Philemon Littlemann can never, never admit to weakness. So, he lies awake, soaking the bed clothes with his sweat until he falls asleep, only to wake to the chilly winter light and a bitter cold that has soaked through his skin and into his vital organs.

He is as good only as his last sermon. And he has yet to address the question of how long, how many weeks, months, years, he can continue to deliver what is required. He is what other men would call 'tired'.

But today is not a day on which Philemon can indulge his tiredness. Today is the anniversary of the Saviour's birth.

The Church of the Body of Christ has long been familiar with their pastor's traditional three-week fast that precedes this day. They know he has, for many years now, risen up to a high place, supported only by Deacon Frank, as the patriarchs of old would ascend into the high mountains, supported only by a single manservant. They know only that for this time, he enters into the passion of their Saviour, to return, as Moses returned from Mount Sinai, with the commandments of their God. They must know nothing, however, of a hotel called the Trump Sonesta, of a young man called Gus or of a bed wide enough for three. Nor can they be permitted to know that on this particular meditation, Philemon made a spontaneous decision to treat Frank and Gus to a short flight to Orlando in a twin propeller, twelve-seat aircraft and a two-day visit to Disney World. Yet, even if they were party to such confidential information, perhaps one or two of them would still see the Lord's hand at work. For it is here in the Disney Village, so sensitively prepared for Christmas, that Philemon had stopped to idle away a few minutes in front of the traditional nativity play. And, if you are inclined to do so, you may wish to praise God that he did. For now, he has the complete answer to the twin conundrums of both *SecondCome* and his financial challenges: an answer that will take precisely twelve months to enact, but will establish his position forever.

As the clock hand touches eleven, he begins reading from his huge zippered bible without specifying the text. Holding the book in his left hand, raised up over the congregation, he cannot see the words he is quoting. Each eye, each camera, is fixed upon him. *"And in the sixth month the angel Gabriel was sent from God unto a city of Galilee, named Nazareth to a virgin espoused to a man whose name was Joseph, of the house of David; and the virgin s name was Mary."*

In the congregation beneath him, the young blonde woman in the emerald green headscarf is momentarily distracted by a small feather wafting above her on an air current. She is trying to remember something just beyond the edge of conscious memory… some childhood game she used to play, a bit like Hide-and-seek; some meaning she attributed to feathers when she was little. Then she snaps her attention back to the Pastor's words, chiding herself for being so easily distracted.

"And the angel came in unto her, and said, Hail, thou that art highly favoured, the Lord is with thee: blessed art thou among women. And when she saw him, she was troubled at his saying, and cast in her mind what manner of salutation this should be. And the angel said unto her, Fear not, Mary: for thou hast found favour with God. And, behold, thou shalt conceive in thy womb, and bring forth a son, and shalt call his name JESUS."

He stops and looks around at the congregation. His trademark silence of five seconds, ten seconds, thirty seconds or more is well known to them. But it is no less disturbing for its familiarity, for they know a question will follow; or if not a question, an admonition, a challenge of some sort that will strike deeply into their hearts.

"Beloved, do you believe the Bible?" There are the small sounds of posteriors shifting in seats that confirms he has asked something that generates discomfort in some of them.

"It is a question each person in this room has asked of themselves many times. Some of you have answered openly, some inwardly. Some have answered honestly, some dishonestly. But remember. God knows the true answer each of you should be giving to this question. So, let me ask you this. Do you believe a virgin bore a child?"

He looks carefully around the room, achieving eye contact with many, seeming to achieve it with all. He continues to quote, the bible still held aloft.

"*Then said Mary unto the angel, How shall this be, seeing I know not a man? And the angel answered and said unto her, The Holy Ghost shall come upon thee, and the power of the Highest shall overshadow thee: therefore, also that holy thing which shall be born of thee shall be called the Son of God.* Brethren, let me tell you this: it is time to believe God."

The 'Amens' are starting now, quiet and unobtrusive at first but progressively seeking to reach his volume and pace.

"It is time to acknowledge that miracles *happen*, Beloved. It is time to believe that this is once again the *Age* of Miracles. For I tell you that two thousand years ago, God walked upon this earth only because a virgin said to an angel, *"Behold the handmaid of the Lord; be it unto me according to thy word."*

"Amen, Lord. Hallelujah, Jesus" comes louder and more urgently from the floor of the hall.

"Are you waiting for *SecondCome*, Brethren? Have you become bored, waiting for the Lord to deliver on his promise? Are you giving up on ever seeing your God's power? Then listen to me, for I tell you (his pace of delivery slows noticeably as he emphasises each word individually) that now is the time of *Fulfilment*, now is the time of *Promise*, now is the time of *Delivery*."

He speeds up his speech again, volume rising. And their heart rates are rising with him. This is what they want to hear. This is what thrills them. This is what wows them. This is what brings them back week after week, in ever-increasing numbers that fill the hall and the remote locations, time after time.

277

"And I tell you, Beloved, that *SecondCome* is *almost upon us.*" His head is thrown back, his arms extended towards Heaven. He is roaring it out now, and they are falling to their knees, chorusing 'Hallelujah', and 'Praise God', and 'Glory be to His Holy name'. He stands silent for a while, watching them vent their excitement. Then, continues almost inaudibly.

"Beloved, would you believe me… could you believe me… were I to say to you there is a virgin hearing the word of God *today*? You say, 'Yes, Pastor, there are many righteous young women in our midst.'" The volume begins to rise. "But I ask you again, could you believe that the Lord is telling his handmaiden at this very moment that she will conceive, such that her soul doth magnify the Lord, and her spirit doth rejoice in God her Saviour? And beloved, because of that belief of this one, single, handmaiden of the Lord, *she will conceive. And God will walk upon this earth again.*"

Now there are only two people in that place who are silent. One is standing on a podium raised to a height that has induced so many for so long to forget the diminutive stature of the man himself. He is observing wordlessly what can only be described as pandemonium in the hall below him. For here, all but one, it seems, have fallen on their faces, or risen to their feet, and they are praying and praising and singing in the Spirit and speaking in tongues of which none knows the meaning. If we were so inclined, we might almost believe that the Spirit of God is sweeping through this place.

The other is a young woman with long blonde hair covered by an emerald green headscarf, though as usual it has fallen to her shoulders. Her hair shines in a shaft of winter sunlight that has burned through the December clouds. She is watching a feather wafting high over the congregation, visible by virtue of being caught in the same sunlight that is illuminating her. There are tears running down both her cheeks and even the most generous would say that she does not look her best this morning. Her lips are moving but no sound is emerging. But even though we cannot hear, we know the words she is saying, for they have been passed down to us like a legacy by perhaps eighty generations, across two thousand years:

> *My soul doth magnify the Lord,*
> *And my spirit hath rejoiced in God my Saviour.*
> *For he hath regarded the low estate of his handmaiden: for, behold,*
> *from henceforth all generations shall call me blessed.*
> *For he that is mighty hath done to me great things; and holy is his*
> *name.*

He sees her. He alone, for all others in that place are too busy beseeching God to recreate the virgin birth of *FirstCome*. Then, slowly, her tear-filled eyes rise and meet his. Both of them know the beseeching is superfluous. God has already heard them.

Tuesday 25th December 2007 11.00 pm GMT

"Alright Phi, I'm impressed. But how the fuck are you going to deliver this time?"

"I suppose you're too young for 'The Boxer' to mean anything to you?"

"Which boxer?"

"I have squandered my resistance for a pocket full of mumbles –
such are promises.
All lies and jests.
Still, a man hears what he wants to hear
and disregards the rest,
"And don't call me Phi."

Tuesday 25th December 2007 11.00 pm GMT

She texts rapidly, as if she is afraid that any lull in her speed will weaken her resolve. "My darling Henry. I will love you all my life.

279

But though my heart is yours my body cannot be. I am to bring forth *SecondCome*. Yours, in spirit, if not in flesh, Serenity."

Tuesday 25th December 2007 11.03 pm GMT

He is almost asleep in front of the late-night movie. Mum and Dad went to bed half an hour ago. He likes the family traditions that have once again been enacted in his household. He smiled when his dad took a photo of him with his arms round his mother in front of the Christmas tree. She was so pleased with it she insisted that it was printed off immediately and placed on the noticeboard in the kitchen. She kept going out of the lounge, even during EastEnders, to look at it. He enjoys making her happy.

It's been an ok Christmas Day. He just wishes that Laura had been there too. That would have made it perfect. But he has to give her time. Maybe next Christmas, they will be together. Something inside seems to react to that thought. It feels right. Next Christmas, they will be together.

The phone buzzes with a text interrupting his doze. He assumes it's the usual 'Good night, darling' from Laura. He opens it; reads it; re-reads it. Then, without warning, he sits up straight, screams "Fuck," and throws the phone at the TV screen. Tomorrow, he will regard himself fortunate that it misses. But it does take a noticeable gouge out of the chrome stand and cracks the phone's own screen. And that will take some explaining.

Tuesday 1st January 2008 1.03 am GMT

"Oh Lord, what a fool I've been. I didn't think this through for long enough. It's only been a week and I miss him so much. And now, you show me this."

Her bible is open at Matthew, Chapter 1. She has read the passage so many times but not like she has read it this evening:

Now, the birth of Jesus Christ was on this wise: When as his mother, Mary was espoused to Joseph, before they came together, she was found with child of the Holy Ghost. Then, Joseph her husband, being a just man, and not willing to make her a public example, was minded to put her away privily. But while he thought on these things, behold, the angel of the LORD appeared unto him in a dream, saying, Joseph, thou son of David, fear not to take unto thee, Mary, thy wife: for that which is conceived in her is of the Holy Ghost. And she shall bring forth a son, and thou shalt call his name, JESUS: for he shall save his people from their sins. Now, all this was done, that it might be fulfilled which was spoken of the Lord by the prophet, saying, Behold, a virgin shall be with child, and shall bring forth a son, and they shall call his name Emmanuel, which being interpreted is, God with us. Then, Joseph being raised from sleep did as the angel of the Lord had bidden him, and took unto him his wife: And knew her not till she had brought forth her firstborn son: and he called his name JESUS.

"Oh, Father, you never did mean me to leave him, did you? You've asked me to bear the *SecondCome* Christ Child. But you didn't say anything about leaving the man I loved. You didn't ask Mary to do it and you didn't ask me to do it." Her prayer comes between sobs now. "Oh, Lord, how could I have got it so wrong? I need him too, Lord. I want to marry him. Oh, Father... I don't know what else to say. I wanted so much to do your will. I tried so hard to obey you and Pastor. All I ever wanted was to serve you; to love you. I have let you down, Father. Will you forgive me? Will you give me another chance? I promise, I will do better. Please, Father, give me a sign of your forgiveness... that you still love me... that you will let me try again."

Then, her phone buzzes. Spirituality? Serendipity? Synchronicity? Maybe, it all depends on who you are. Maybe, it depends on who you want to be. She knows without looking that the text is from him.

Tuesday 1ˢᵗ January 2008 8.53 am GMT

Except it wasn't. The text had read 'Southampton U*Phone*. 200 minutes for the price of 100.' Then, a number. She had looked at it in disbelief and then burst into a fit of sobs that had woken her mother who had sat with her by her bedside until her misery had subsided sufficiently for her to sleep. And that is what she is doing now, while her mother has phoned work to explain she will not be in today. Then, with much forethought, she phones Henry.

"Henry, dear? It's Paula. Can I talk to you for a minute, please?"

Within the specified minute, she has established that it is Laura who has ended the relationship. She has also, she thinks, understood why, if it's to be believed. She wanders slowly into the kitchen where her husband is eating buttered toast in front of a folded copy of the Daily Telegraph.

"Had, we need to talk. Henry says Laura's dumped him because she can't have sex with him."

He answers without looking up. "Well, it's not illegal. Can't you talk to her?"

"She says, she can't have sex with him because she is to bring forth *SecondCome*."

He glances at her. "What the hell's that supposed to mean?"

"She's mentioned the term to me before. It means the second coming of Jesus."

He's looked up properly from his paper now. "So, she won't have sex with her boyfriend because Jesus is coming again?"

"It's a little more complicated than that. If I've got it right. She won't have sex with her boyfriend because she has been chosen to give birth to Jesus Christ."

"Good God!"

"Well, yes. I suppose you could put it that way."

Wednesday 2nd January 2008 9.14 am GMT

She hadn't been able to sustain it. She had admitted to herself during that awful night on New Year's Eve that this was the real thing. Love. She knew she would not be able to keep away from him. She was as certain about that as she was about her calling to bear *SecondCome*. So, she had asked to borrow her father's car. He had agreed immediately to the tear-laden request. She had seen the worried looks on their faces as she left the house and managed a smile of encouragement for their sakes. Then, she had wept silently all the way to Brockenhurst, fortunate that there was so little traffic on the road on the day following New Year's Day. His mother had answered the door, taken one look at the poor distraught girl and angrily called Henry down from his bedroom immediately. He arrived bemused as to what he had done wrong, whereupon his mother had bundled them both out of the house suitably dressed for a winter walk. By the time the light began to fail, they had returned. As Laura drove away, Henry had opened the front door to confront his mother's enquiring look, shrugged his shoulders and simply said, "It's on again." Then, he had taken the stairs two at a time before she had a chance to question him further.

Laura has commenced the drive home weeping, but this time with relief. On the way, she prays again. But this time, she has had to think whether the prayer she is considering is Godly. She reckons that a billion or so Catholics worldwide can't all be wrong, so, even if Pastor had not specifically sanctioned it, it must be ok to do this.

"Was it this hard for you?"

First, there is nothing. Then, though she cannot take her eyes off the road in the dark, she has the uncanny feeling that someone is sitting in the rear passenger seat.

"I loved my fiancé as deeply as you love Henry."

Serenity shakes a little, more from surprise than fear. She was expecting a voice in her head, not a presence in the car and an audible response.

"How did you cope? With the sex thing, I mean? It must have been hard for both of you, too." It feels most odd to be asking this particular person about this particular subject.

"Yes, it was hard; harder on him than me, really. I had the baby to think about. But he was such a darling. He knew he had to wait and he did exactly that. I couldn't have asked for more from him in those early days. Everyone thought we'd sinned – jumped the gun, as you would say in this age. He never once denied it and that made me love him all the more."

The lights of Southampton are around her now and she feels safe to move the mirror just a little so that she can see who she is talking to. But she only has a moment to do so safely and with the streetlights streaming past, she gets only the briefest impression: a young woman, about her own age and build. But she does manage to see an emerald green headscarf around her neck.

And now, she is arriving at Deacon Road, slowing towards a halt in order to stop outside the house, thinking a trick of the light in the mirror was making her see her own reflection.

"You can talk to me any time you want to, you know. I've told Gabe I'll be here for you any time you need me."

Laura hits the brake hard and stops suddenly, two houses away from home. She turns to look directly at the young woman. But she has gone. Only a small feather wafts slowly down to settle silently on the back seat.

Friday 18ᵗʰ January 2008 10.17 am GMT
She has not moved from the yellow line for the last two minutes. But a silent voice calls to her from far away that her safety is at risk. She steps back two paces without really thinking about it, as the wind borne before the non-stop train drives through the station, followed a moment later, by the huge engine itself.

Gradually, her consciousness returns to the here and now of

platform 1 at Southampton Central and the prospect of eight empty weeks stretching forward to 15th March when his Hilary term will finish.

In the weeks after the New Year turned, they had established a reasonably satisfactory compromise. She had allowed him a little more intimacy with her body. He had acknowledged that nothing more would be permitted, unless, and until they were married. He had muttered something about old-fashioned values under his breath but had, nevertheless, accepted the arrangement. She had told him she loved him. Many times, she had told him. When she looked at him questioningly, hoping for a reciprocal response, he had merely kissed her. She decided he just needed more time.

And now, they would both have plenty of that. Eight weeks apart with a couple of brief visits thrown in was more time than she wanted to think about.

Tuesday 22nd January 2008 11.12 pm GMT

She is praying by her bedside just as she always does. Her meditations now are almost exclusively on the nativity story. She has read both biblical versions of it through more times than she can remember. She has looked up apocryphal versions and historical references through the centuries on Wikipedia until she knows almost to reciteable standard, everything she can find that has ever been written on the subject. She has examined her body mentally and physically in minute detail every morning in bed before waking fully, seeking some confirmation that her pregnancy has indeed started, having decided a pregnancy test would amount to disbelieving God and might be wrong anyway. She has prayed, prayed so hard for a sign. A movement inside her; an intimate physical change; even morning sickness would give her the confirmation she is so hungry to receive. Serenity rises from the bed, leaving her bible and the picture of her father on the dishevelled quilt cover and heads for the bathroom – the only kind of respite she will permit herself when she is praying. Yet, even here, as she locks the door and sits on the toilet, she is still praying, her body on autopilot. And, as her water begins to flow, she feels something deep inside. She concentrates, not even having time to ask herself or the Lord, if this is the confirmation she seeks. Then, she looks down and indeed discovers a sign as to the state of her body. Her flow is red. She turns her face to heaven and howls.

Sunday 17th February 2008 11.00 am GMT
Her Majesty's Government announces the nationalization of the Northern Rock Bank.

Saturday 23rd February 2008 6.12 pm GMT
More blood.

She is on her knees again, head buried in her arms, her bible and picture of her father in front of her on the bed. She is utterly confused, and all but past caring. Had she been wrong? Misinterpreted? Is God toying with her? Is he really there at all? Tomorrow, she will miss church for the first time in her adult life. She is close to giving up. The man she loves will be home in three weeks' time. What then? Can she honestly keep him waiting when God himself is mocking her?

"You're not the first, you know."

She is somewhere between wake and sleep. Is this just another dream?

"Everything you are feeling, I experienced in my time before you."

She lifts her head slightly to look at the young woman, so strangely like herself in appearance and age, and yet, somehow, not like her at all.

"But you were pregnant. I can't even claim that. I'm just being made a complete fool of. Somewhere, up there, the angels are having a good old roar of laughter at my expense."

The woman does not respond.

"Alright, maybe they're not. But I'm still not pregnant and you were. It was much easier for you."

The woman raises an eyebrow warily. "You think it was easy being unmarried and pregnant in my day? There were those who wanted to stone me to death and throw Joseph out of the synagogue. I lived in an extremely sexist world, Serenity."

A silence follows.

"What did Gabe tell you when he knew your Da was going to die?"

She casts her mind back through the years to her childhood fantasies of an invisible friend.

"He said, I had to get ready."

"Are you ready?"

"Are you ready, Laura?"

The voice has changed. She is coming up through that place between sleep and wakefulness.

"Are you ready yet, Laura?"

The voice is her mother's and they are due at Haddon's sister's house for dinner in fifteen minutes.

A feather has broken lose from her quilt and is sitting on her bible, looking at her.

Saturday 15th March 2008 7.15 pm GMT

She and his mother had been waiting for him all afternoon. He finally stumbled through the door just before 4.00 pm, after an eight-week absence, laden with rucksack, suitcase and carrier bags. His mother had constrained the maternal urge to press him into spending his first moments home with her and shooed them off up to his room with a knowing look at Laura, who had tried not to blush but had failed miserably. Now, they are lying in each other's arms on his single bed under the window. His head is on her breasts. She would have uncovered them for his pleasure, but he had fallen asleep as soon as they lay down. So, she holds him, listening to his breathing, thinking of the strange history of their relationship and looking round his room, which is dominated by music. On one side of the closed-off fireplace is his own CD collection, the largest she has ever seen. Then, there is the antique Bang & Olufsen stereo, vintage 1988, bought on eBay for his eighteenth birthday. On the other side of it stands the vinyl collection he inherited from his uncle, whose musical tastes, in their time, had evidently been as eclectic as Henry's own. The uncle had collected music from the 1970s until he was killed in a road accident in 1993 at the age of 37. Henry's own collection had started in 1998. Of course, she would have preferred he got rid of some of his uncle's records – the punk, for example. Mostly musically indifferent at best, they contained a language of aggression and confrontation, quite different from her own collection of inspirational music, founded on love. But Henry had been loath to break up so comprehensive a collection and even played some of it for her from time to time. On one occasion, he had taken out what he said was his uncle's pride and joy – a rare copy of the Sex Pistol's 'God Save the Queen'. 'Music' was barely an appropriate term for it of course, and she had insisted he switch it off almost as soon as it started. Then, they had giggled their way through this strange music of a mercifully passed era.

She loves the feeling of his sleeping body against her, her arms cradling him, his regular breathing pressing his chest against her. The rhythm lulls her gently into a warm and comfortable place of love where it would be so easy to open herself to him: to love him as he wants, as indeed, she wants. Why has she been so resistant? God has been playing with her. Or perhaps more correctly, she has completely misunderstood His will for her. So why not? Why not slip into bed with him and allow their union to happen? She changes position just a little in order to start removing her clothes. Then, he makes a small movement of his own; a sound. Then, as he comes awake, an "Oh fuck" and he farts loudly.

The magic is broken irreparably. She swings her legs off the bed and heads for the bathroom.

Thursday 27th March 2008 9.12pm GMT

Laura is in Starbucks screaming uncontrollably.

Friday 28th March 2008 9.02 am GMT

The planned trip to see Cloverfield last evening never did happen.

After the awful texts, Henry could do nothing to stop Laura's panic, so he simply drove her home and sat holding her in the car outside. Eventually, the tears subsided. She insisted on going in alone.

Having slept little, she recognises she is in no condition to go to work this morning and would far rather stay home praying and reading her bible. So, she phones in sick and takes the opportunity to correct Matthis' mistake over the spelling of her surname.

While she is upstairs praying, Haddon and Paula have taken the opportunity to call the police.

Sunday 6th April 2008 7.00 am BST

It's the day after his twenty-first. They had spent the earlier part of his birthday together but he'd asked if she minded if he went off for a celebratory drink with some old schoolmates in the evening. He wasn't to know that she had finally come to a decision. She'd given him lots of little gifts earlier in the day. But the really big gift she had been saving for the evening. She couldn't really grudge him a few hours with friends though, could she? Her gift would wait for today. So, here she lies, enjoying a rare luxury of a Sunday morning lie in. She will go to church as normal. She will return home for lunch as normal. Then, she will go to him and everything will change forever. She's too mature to think she'll suddenly cease to be a child and become a woman or any dross like that. But it's a huge step. And she wouldn't be contemplating it if things had worked out differently with *SecondCome*. But now, there's nothing to do but sadly acknowledge her mistake and forget her silly dreams; dreams born of exhaustion; dreams of visitations by spiritual beings and religious icons who never really existed beyond her own reflection in a car mirror.

It's time to get on with a proper life. So, yes, in a funny kind of a way, life starts for Laura today.

Monday 7th April 2008 6.05 am BST

"You're a useless cunt." The word is profoundly jarring to her. Her reflection blinks back at her in surprise, shocked that she has actually used it in vocal speech. "Your God doesn't want you to bear his son and your man doesn't want to make love to your heart or even to fuck your body. What good are you to anyone?" She glances at the reflection of the bed, the bedclothes drawn back. She notices the small red stain, the first vestige of her bodily state that bears away the last vestige of hope that even at this late stage she might have got it right after all. God might still have a use for her? It's a laughable fantasy that she will no longer permit herself.

For the first time, she notices the throbbing in her left hand. She looks down. There is blood in the centre of her palm.

Friday 11th April 2008 10.11 am BST

Staying at home's been all very well. And, truly, Laura's not felt like going out this week after so much pain from so many causes at once. Her phone has received nothing from Henry and she's not felt up to contacting him, so presumably, this is it. The end of her relationship. The end of her dreams. The end of love. And her hand hurts and won't stop bleeding.

Reading the bible offers little comfort and there have been no visitations from religious icons. She hasn't even seen a feather, she remarks wryly to herself. So, that presumably means the end of her beliefs as well.

Under the circumstances, it's rather a relief when the house phone rings. With everyone at work or at school there's no one but her in the house to answer it. She runs down the stairs to catch it before it stops.

She can think of people she'd rather have call her than the odd union shop steward from work, but Tracey honestly sounds so nice over the phone that Laura is glad of a few minutes' chat. And actually, yes, a wage packet in cash would come in really useful right now.

Friday 11th April 2008 12.00 noon BST

So, here's Tracey arriving outside the house in Deacon Road.

And here's Laura opening the door, smiling.

And here's Laura going out to the car with Tracey to collect her P45 and pay.

And here's Laura sitting in the passenger seat for a moment to sign the receipt.

And here's Tracey getting in beside her.

And here's Tracey stabbing a hypodermic into Laura's upper arm.

And here's Laura with a look of horror on her face as she falls unconscious.

Friday 11th April 2008 9.14 pm BST

She's not sure where she is. At home? At Henry's? It's dark. She's drifting in and out of trance...delirium... sleep... whatever. She can't wake up properly and there are nightmare images passing in front of her face. A huge fat woman with a knife and purple hair. She looks familiar. Punk rock music somewhere. A wispy shimmering creature floating in the corner of the room, its face leering at her. Ropes holding her to a bed. She's wet and she's cold. She thinks she might have wet the bed just like back when she was small. She's not sure how old she is. 4? 20? She can't tell. She wants to get up to change the sheets. But when she tries to rise from the bed, she can't. Are the ropes real? Is she sick? Very, very sick? Has she taken something that's making her like this? She can't quite get it all into focus? And when she tries to call for help, she can't move her lips. It's almost like something's stuck on them.

Friday 11th April 2008 2.37 am BST

It's insane. She has to be hallucinating. None of this can possibly be real. Tracey from Matthis. A big knife scraping up and down her tummy like she was in an Edgar Allan Poe story. Tracey… no… Tolly jamming the knife into the pillow by her face. Herself screaming. That sickening wispy creature hovering over them, leering, excited.

Then, it all changed. Tracey… Tolly left the room. The wispy thing followed her. Alone; then music; but not punk rock. A tune she half recognises from… when? Floating upwards, eyes closed; to heaven? Is she dead? The music isn't quite… music. Someone is humming. The memory of the tune is coming back. And now, the words start to form in her mind… "Cloudy night… shining light… shine on til tomorrow."

She dares not open her eyes yet. Her heavenly hallucination must be with her again. She knows now her conversations with Mary, Mother of God have not been real, but there is some comfort in them nonetheless, some respite from this terror-filled dream from which she seems unable to escape. A few words with a fictitious

Mary would indeed be comforting right now. So, she opens her eyes; and sees. She is indeed floating. Just below the ceiling. The humming is coming from beneath her. She looks down, a little vertiginously. Below her on the bed is her own semi-naked body, tied spreadeagled to the bedposts. At any other time, she would be embarrassed by the immodesty. But it's hardly a priority now.

She becomes aware that the humming has changed to soft, almost whispered singing. And the words are unambiguous now.

And when the broken-hearted people
Living in the world agree
There will be an answer, let it be
For though they may be parted
There is still a chance that they will see
There will be an answer, let it be

There are feathers floating all around the room. They must have been released from the pillow when Tolly stabbed through it.

Sitting casually on the chest of drawers, arms folded, legs stretched out in front of him, ankles crossed, is the singer. He stops. He looks up at her with a raised eyebrow. He is enormous. Even at this angle she can see he must be over two and a half metres tall. But that's not what impresses her most. She would never have guessed when she was little that they were so big. But he is holding them fully extended and the tips are touching both walls. His wing span is a little short of four metres. He stops singing and looks up at her. He smiles.

"Hey, Babe."

Friday 11th April 2008 2.48 am BST
"Wake up, Babe."

She opens her eyes. She is still floating near the ceiling, but vertically now and he is with her. They are floating, not flying. His wings are folded onto his back.

"Oh, Gabe!" she whispers. "You came back."

She throws her arms around and wants to hug him forever.

When she finally does release him, she says, "But Gabe... how come I can see you? You're supposed to be invisible."

"Same reason you can see yourself down there, Babe. You're out of body. Astral Plane-ing, your people call it.

"Pastor says that's of the Devil."

"Yeah? Well, he's not the only one who can do it, believe you me."

"And Gabe, you're enormous! However did you fit in my little cupboard?"

"Same way your soul fits into your body, Babe. But listen, we don't have long, so it's really, really important you listen closely to me, ok? In a moment, you're going to have to get back in your body. And Laura, that's going to be scary and it's going to hurt. And it's going to be hard for you to believe I'm still here, because once you're back in your body, you won't be able to see me again, OK?"

She is aware, for the first time, of the absence of pain in her present state. "Can't we just stay like this, Gabe?"

"You have work to do, Babe."

"What work?"

He looks at her quizzically. "I thought you knew. I heard Him say it to you."

"What?"

"*Thou hast found favour with God. And, behold, thou shalt conceive in thy womb.*"

"Oh, Gabe. Don't make a fool of me. I've been through this already. I thought it was me. I thought God had chosen me to bear *SecondCome*. But I've never had sex and I'm not pregnant."

He looks back at her reproachfully.

"I bled, Gabe," she continues emphatically. "On Monday. That's four days ago. I'm not pregnant."

"Where did you bleed from, Babe?

She thinks first that the question is unusually personal, particularly coming from him. Then her attention shifts to the throbbing in her hand and the blood on her palm.

"Babe, didn't you ever read, *'The Holy Ghost has come upon thee, and the power of the Highest has overshadowed thee: therefore*, also that *holy thing which shall be born of thee shall be called the Son of God.* "

And now, she begins to see it; begins to see how little she is in the world and how great her God is; how long He spends planning for and how short her life is. She thinks back over the hope and the belief and the uncertainty and the devastation. Immediately, she is sorry for doubting him. But that doubt is now in the past forever. She hesitates.

"Is there something else, Babe?"

"There's something I want to ask. I think I know the answer. But I need to ask it anyway."

"Ask anything, Babe."

"Gabe, who are you? Who are you really?"

He takes her by the hands and floats her slowly down towards the floor and her waiting body. At floor level, as they stand hand in hand facing each other, she struggles to look up into his face, being perhaps only two-thirds of his height. She watches in awe as slowly once again, his wings unfold to their full span. Then, the light begins. From the level of his solar plexus, it starts by offering no more illumination than a weak light bulb would. Steadily, it brightens, almost as if he is warming up or progressively removing layers of covering. And now, he shines so brightly, she is forced to shield her eyes. And yet, the brightening continues, until even in this out-of-body state that is so new to her, she is obliged to glide back, away from him. Finally, the room is brighter than a mid-summer day. And the light is throbbing, pulsing, reverberating through him, and now through her too.

He has not spoken, but she knows his answer anyway. She replies.

"Be it unto me according to thy word."

Through closed eyes, she is aware of an easing of the brightening and those oh-so- familiar wings wrap gently around her until once again, she feels safe.

"We don't have long, Babe. You've got to get back into that body very soon. And when you're there, this is what you must do."

Saturday 12th April 2008 3.48 am BST

Laura can't quite believe that she had it in her to be this confrontational. But then, with Gabe back at her side, maybe anything's possible. That movement she had made from under the sink to kick Tolly in the stomach – it was straight out of a movie. Immediately afterwards, she was afraid that she might really have hurt her... maybe even killed her. She was too frightened to get too close, so she pushed her with her foot. Tolly hadn't moved. Then Gabe had spoken to her, audibly, she thinks, in that strange American accent she remembers from childhood. "There's no more time," he had said to her. "Let's get this fixed." She'd picked up the knife from the bathroom floor and taken it into the bedroom to cut the ropes. Then, she had grabbed her clothes and her shoes and her bag and fled from the cottage in her underwear.

Sunday 13th April 2008 4.14 pm BST

She had fled from the cottage and into the darkness with no sense of who she was, or where she was, or the direction in which she was running. When she felt instinctively that she had put a semi-safe distance between herself and her assailant, she stopped, her heart beating so much, it hurt, her lungs fighting for air. Eventually, she had normalised sufficiently for speech. "Where now, Gabe?" she had asked. To her panic-stricken shock, her question had gone unanswered. She had asked again, calling his name out as loudly as she dared into the darkness, yet knowing already that she was alone. Then, without conscious decision, she had walked, not knowing what to do or where to go next, until finally, she found herself at a beach with beach huts on a raised concrete walkway. Squeezing herself between the two nearest, she made her way behind the row, oblivious to the sounds of flight that emanated from the small, scurrying creatures whose sleep she was disturbing. She had just long enough to put her outer clothes back on before falling, exhausted, into a shallow sleep where her confused dreams were populated by hunting knives and leering wispy faces.

She had awoken to full daylight. Unable to guess at how long she had slept, and with no watch to give her the time, something in the air suggested morning, perhaps late morning. She had emerged from behind the beach huts with hair dishevelled and shirt torn, looking uncomfortably like the bag ladies in the Southampton parks that she and her *Sisters* had sought to save from their sins, in what now seemed an earlier lifetime.

She had made her way as unobtrusively as possible, nevertheless drawing stares from ice cream stands and cafés, until she finally reached some public lavatories that were open and, mercifully, unattended. Here, she had tidied herself as best she was able and redressed her hand with a piece of cloth torn from her shirt, checking perpetually in the mirror to ensure the mad woman had not somehow followed her. Then, it was a matter of locating a phone kiosk, a tearful reverse-charge call home, and a delay while she asked a surprised middle- aged lady walking a Shih Tzu where she was, in order to give her family her location. Even armed with the correct information, it still took Haddon, Paula and Jamie over two hours to find her. When finally, they did arrive, she collapsed, sobbing into her mother's arms, to be led gently back to the car and a sleep-filled journey home, with Jamie observing silently in fear and confusion.

Now, as they round the corner into Deacon Road, Paula and Haddon are confronted with a trio of police cars, their blue lights turning nonchalantly on their roofs. Within seconds, the police have identified Haddon's Ford Mondeo, surrounding it with perhaps eight or nine officers in black uniforms and utility vests who stare at the sleeping figure in the back.

Without hesitation, one steps forward and opens the nearside rear door. Laura wakes from the sudden gust of air to find herself staring up into the confrontational expression of an officer whose body language all but screams 'Make my Day'. Before she is fully awake, he has instructed her to get out of the car. Many in the considerable crowd of onlookers watch the remaining officers stiffen as if poised for attack or pursuit or domination should any such response be required.

Disorientated, Laura stands to the sound of the voice that seems to be calling to her from somewhere far away. Later, she will remember that she has been turned around and manacled as the voice continues, "Laura Nichola Spurgeon. I am arresting you on suspicion of the unlawful kidnapping and false imprisonment of Tracey Boudicca Tolpuddle Jones. You do not have to say anything, but it may harm your defence if you do not mention, when questioned, something you later rely on in court. Anything you do say may be given in evidence."

Hands that belong to the voice take her by the shoulders and turn her around again, then lead her by the arm to one of the waiting police cars, its rear door open and its engine running. The rest of the family is ushered, a little less aggressively, into the remaining cars and driven away. Then, in seconds, there is silence. Though the crowd of onlookers is still present, no one is speaking. The police have disappeared as quickly as they arrived, leaving a lingering atmosphere of disbelief, almost as if they have been there to enact a scene from some early evening TV drama.

In the Veracity Recreation Ground, the last of the bluebells are swaying under the trees.

In the back of the police car, the radio chatter is interrupted by Paula's steady sobs.

In Deacon Road, nothing breaks the late Sunday afternoon silence.

Tolly

Rule Twelve:

The free will of Nominated Proxies may be influenced but never withdrawn. Players must work through the inherent characteristics of their chosen Proxies.

Sunday 13th April 2008 11.50 am BST

I can tell you for a fact that Detective Inspector Lewis Hathaway would definitely, definitely, not have joined the force if he had known. On several occasions over the last year, he has even considered resigning, so relentless has the teasing become. But in 2006, when the fictional detective had been given his own series for the first time, thus conferring a significance upon Hathaway's own surname of which he could never previously have conceived, he was turning 45 years of age. That was two years ago. At 47, there is a surreptitiously immobilising indolence that anchors a man to his career. In just five more years, he will have accumulated 30 years of continuous service, bestowing, at the still relatively young age of 52, a pension entitlement of around £30,000. A man can put up with a lot of peer mockery for the prospect of £30,000, especially if he doesn't have to get out of bed for it. And that's £30,000 this year, next year and every year until... well, until forever if you're still only 47, you have a pretty second wife of 36, and neither of you has yet to come to understand properly the concept of your own mortality. Hathaway will never live to draw his prized pension, because in 2014, he will die in a collision with a motorcycle on the A3. Still, we don't need to dwell on that now, do we, because what matters is that the pension, the delicious, inflation-proofed pension of £30,000 a year, every year for ever and ever is almost close enough to smell and entirely close enough to motivate Inspector Hathaway into seeing out his remaining years in the job. And sitting out a quiet Sunday morning shift in Chatsworth Road Police Station, with the air of a spring tide wafting in through the window, well, there's not much demanding that can happen is there? Maybe, he can even get away early and he and Anne can take the dinghy out and... well, let's just say, the day could well end pleasantly.

So, he's finishing his second cup of ground coffee (rank has its privileges, they tell me) when he hears the commotion outside in the main office and, irritated, goes out to investigate. Tolly's usual presenting image of physical volume, purple Mohican haircut and black Goth clothing is today supplemented by mascara tear streaks down her cheeks, smeared lipstick across her lower lip and chin and a high-pitched hysterical voice shrieking at a pace and pitch that renders it completely unintelligible.

But let's rewind a bit to see how Tolly got here.

Laura's kick, at just after 4.00 am today, had been perfectly aimed. It caught Tolly right in the gut and completely winded her. I have to congratulate that girl, you can almost believe that Gabe has been teaching her Kung Fu. Fortunately, I was able to tune Tolly into his speech, so when my star middle-aged punk rocker heard his voice, she just used it to reinforce her existing beliefs. '*Still, a man hears what he wants to hear and disregards the rest*,' as someone said.

When Tolly regained consciousness, Laura, of course, had disappeared. Tolly knew she had to act before the Yankee witchbitch did, or all she had worked for all her life would be lost and she'd likely find herself in gaol. Well, it took a little prompting from me, but she was soon working herself up into a fit state to play a convincing victim when she arrived at the police station. So, that's when she burst in on Hathaway's hopes of a quiet Sunday morning, followed by a nice little dinghy trip and who knows what.

By 12.30, Hathaway has got her talking coherently enough to realise that, though she's a bit unusual, she's mentally lucid and she's been abducted by some vicious little bully from work who has evidently been acting out her playground fantasies of the pretty girl beating up on the ugly girl.

By 13.00 hours, he's got the Southampton force out looking out for one Laura Spurgeon at her home address in Deacon Road.

By 14.00, he's had the cottage cordoned off as a crime scene and Forensic have had their Sunday afternoon snoozes interrupted.

By 15.00, his officers are taking reports from the public who saw the little bitch on the sea front that morning. They've been informed that a man, woman and boy came and took her away in a Ford Mondeo less than an hour before.

By 16.00, he's briefed Southampton to expect the imminent return of the Spurgeon family to Deacon Road.

By 16.30, the radio has told him the Spurgeon girl is in transit back to Worthing and he has arranged a car to take the victim home.

By 18.00, Spurgeon is in the interview room.

By 19.00, he's been told a story that is a little different from the one he heard from Tolly. It's left him completely confused as to which of these nutcases is telling the truth – the one who says she's pregnant with Jesus Christ's second coming, or the one who thinks the Spurgeon girl is the reincarnation of Sid Vicious' girlfriend and is hell-bent on killing Tolly Jones at all costs. Laura Spurgeon has lodged a counter claim of kidnapping and for the first time in his career that he can remember, Inspector Lewis (as the buggers in the main office insist on calling him) thinks they're both completely bonkers and entirely deserve each other. He has a point.

By 20.00, the tide has long since turned, the dinghy is still on the trailer behind the car in the drive, as dry as the Sunday dinner that was left in the oven at 2.00 pm. and Mrs. Anne Hathaway is in no mood to respond enthusiastically to the cellophane-wrapped flowers from the fuel station.

Sunday 13ᵗʰ April 2008 6.30 pm BST

Tolly is angry. Earlier, her face matched the colour of her hair quite closely. Now, she's a little calmer, but still very, very cross. Having done a near perfect job on the gullible copper in Worthing, she's managed to blag herself a lift home in a police car. That's no more than her taxes justify as far as Tolly's concerned, but the spotty little teenage officer driving her won't stop to let her do some shopping on the way. So now, she's home at well past Asda's closing time and there's no food in the flat. What's worse is that along with her carved hunting knife (hunting knife officer? No, not mine. My kidnapper must have brought it to do me harm), the Fuzz has impounded her car as evidence. She's got nothing in the flat to smoke or eat. It would be inconceivable to Tolly to walk the quarter mile to the Londis on Shirley Road and anyway, they don't have permanently low prices there. But what she does have, is her Marjory's mobile phone (her own was also taken from the cottage by the police as potential evidence) and a whole pile of flyers for fast food delivery stacked up in a corner by the door. So, she phones out for pizza. Unfortunately, neither Domino's nor Papa John's are willing to stop off for Old Holborn on the way to her. Tolly's all set to do her Yeti impersonation on the delivery boy if he's willing to go to the corner store for her, but unfortunately, 'he' turns out to be a 'she' with a badge that declared her name to be Jodi and that she was happy to help. Jodi is sufficiently young and sufficiently straight that she turns and runs when Tolly starts to unzip her jeans. Later, Papa John's will send a well-built man, 2.2 metres tall, round to the flat, who will be impervious to Tolly's charms (I can't think why, can you?). He will stand with his foot in the door and his arms folded until, muttering, she retreats to raid the union subs box once again and pays him in 50p coins.

All that, though, is a little way in the future and just now, life is not without its compensations for Tolly. There's a twelve-pack of 4X in the fridge and she's finally got the Yankee witchbitch banged up, which is going to give her an unencumbered chance with Sid. Later, it will occur to her that Nancy's incarcerated status also prevents Tolly from doing her further harm. But not tonight. Tonight is about preparation for tomorrow when finally, she is certain, she and darling, darling Sid will finally, finally, consummate their blissful, eternal union. Tomorrow, oh tomorrow, why do you take so long to come? Tolly knows why. They learned it her in school. It's 'cos "Tomorrow and Tomorrow and Tomorrow creeps to the last silly bell of recorded time." So, they taught you Shakespeare, Tolly. But, did they teach you Charles William Day? No? Then, perhaps, you are yet to learn that "Tomorrow, chased by time, flies before us to eternity."

Monday 14th April 2008 6.30 pm BST

"It's your fuckin fault. Can you 'ear me dad? You never fuckin taught me fuckin proper about men. It's your fault I didn't say all them right things. It's your fault he ran away. It's your fault I'm on my funckin own again.

By now, I'm sure you don't need me to tell you who's talking, which room she's in in the flat and what she has in each hand while she's verbally abusing the mirror.

Something tells me not everything went according to plan in your reunion with darling Sid today, Tolly. Would you like to tell us about it?

"He was too timid, Dad. I fuckin scared 'im off after 'e fucked me. An I'm fuckin 'allucinated dad. I thought his prick had teeth an it smiled at me."

Oh, call back yesterday, Tolly, Let time return. But it won't, will it? 'Cos now, he's gone/ There's only pain.../ And you don't want to live this life/ If you can't live for him. And what's more, Tolly, you can't even get at the Yankee witchbitch, can you, 'cos you've had her banged up, haven't you? Well, don't worry too much about that, Doll. We can work together on that one in the morning. Go put your second-best copy of 'Sid Sings' on ('cos the Pigs are holding the best one along with the other evidence from the cottage) and get the 4X out. Roll a few smokes and just relax, Doll. We'll make it all better in the morning.

Hathaway is growing more uneasy by the minute. He's advanced his enquires considerably today, in particular, with the cottage owner, with Tolly and Laura's work place, with Laura's family. A small matter of a boyfriend has emerged to complicate things. But what's playing most on his mind is that Tolly's story isn't fitting the facts too well at all. The cottage owner says no, he never met the mother and daughter, but he thought it was the mother that made the booking, not the daughter. And there was that odd order for chocolate cake and Old Holborn rolling tobacco for the welcome pack. Somehow, Laura didn't look to him like a chocolate cake and Old Holborn kind of girl. In fact, the more he's talked to her, the more innocent and nice she seems to be. There again, there's the awkward matter of her religious persuasion. Hathaway's known a good few religious nutcases over the years – mostly harmless, but sometimes you can't be sure. But eventually, that well-honed policeman's instinct for the bleedin' obvious cuts in and it dawns on him that maybe, just maybe, Tolly is lying.

Finally, he concludes that, at the very minimum, they're one as bad as the other. And, at the maximum, Laura's the victim she claims to be and Tolly's the law breaker.

It's the knife that makes it difficult, of course. If it weren't for the knife, he could slap them both on the wrist and tell the pair of them to stop being so stupid. But the knife, well, that makes it more serious. And both their fingerprints on it too. Bloody awkward, that.

Thursday 15th April 2008 9.22 am BST

"Yes, this is Hathaway. Ah, Miss Jones... Tolly. I'm glad you've phoned. I was going to call you anyway. How can I help you? Withdraw the charges? Why would you want to do that? Well, yes, she is a nice girl... and yes, you could say she's just a bit misguided. How about you come down to the station and we talk it through a little further. The knife? Oh, yes, it's still here in the evidence room.

You'd like it back? So, you're now saying it's yours? Well, come down to the station and we'll have a talk about it."

He puts the phone down. Now, he's sure. Her wanting the knife has helped convinced him. They probably are both nutcases. But being a nutcase isn't enough to get you locked up on its own, he muses, now regretting being so hasty as to charge the girl. But what would be enough would be that the nutcase has carefully prepared a quiet location, taken her favourite music, food and smokes, injected the victim with a hypodermic and assaulted her with a hunting knife and, possibly, sexually.

And that is why, within the hour, he has re-examined Laura's statement, dismissed the charges and let her go.

What's finally convinced him, though, is the phone call and the text. A call, even a short one to a pizza joint, is automatically reported, if it's been made from a stolen phone. And a series of text messages overnight from the same phone to the phone of a suspect that you are holding that repeats the same message, "GONNAGETYAFUCKINYANKEE-WITCHBITCH". Now that, in Hathaway's book, is more than enough to secure a conviction.

Thursday 15th April 2008 11.44 pm BST

'Tracey Boudicca Tolpuddle Jones. I am arresting you for the kidnapping and assault of Laura Nichola Spurgeon. You do not have to…"

Oh, Tolly, Tolly, Tolly! Just when we were doing so well! If you'd simply have listened to me, this never would have happened. We could have had the job finished in days, if it weren't for your obsession with that knife. Still, not to worry. There will be a grand finale. A final round of the game. I promise you, you'll be there for it – and with the knife you love so much too. And maybe there will be an opportunity to hold the final somewhere and somewhen a little more appropriate to the occasion. I can promise you, Babe, that what Lu wants, Lu gets. And until then, don't worry about the little Yankee witchbitch. I will have other eyes on her. Don't you worry your pretty little shaven head about it at all.

Sister Serenity

Rule Six:

Players are free to invite Tangibles to observe play. Observers will not interfere with the chain of events.

Thursday 15ᵗʰ April 2008 6.15 pm BST

"Mummy, don't you understand, I can't stay here? She knows where I live. She could come back here any time."

"But Sweetheart, she's locked up now. She can't hurt you anymore."

"Mummy, you don't UNDERSTAND!" There is panic in her voice, real panic. "I'm pregnant, Mummy. Pregnant with the Saviour. I can't risk her hurting this baby, Mummy. He's too important."

Paula looks to her husband for support. But Haddon simply looks on, too dumbfounded to contribute to this utterly surreal conversation. He and Paula had both known it would be impossible to talk her out of this *SecondCome* thing. It's obvious in retrospect, she's been working herself up to it for months, if not years. And they can't be sure whether she's pregnant or not. She was certainly keen enough on that boyfriend, Henry, before their row. So that otherwise obvious part of the conversation, which would otherwise be obvious, is forgone.

"So, where will you go, darling?"

"I've spoken to people at the church. They said to ask Henry if he will help me. I've already texted him."

"And?"

"He's texted back. Says it doesn't matter what's wrong, he'll always be there to help me. He's asked if I can get to Oxford. Haddon, will you help me get to Oxford?"

The man can find no words capable of expressing his feelings. And he doesn't want to weep openly in front of the women. He simply nods.

Friday 16ᵗʰ April 2008 7.32 am BST

The Mondeo pulls away from Deacon Road containing a husband, a daughter and a hastily packed suitcase. It leaves a woman standing at the side of the road with tears in her eyes. She has never been religious. But Christmas visits to church with Denny and the children have been enough to plant the embryonic thoughts in her mind that return to her now, thoughts of a holy child, a dash to safety from an affronted king, hell-bent on destroying two thousand years of history and culture before it begins. She stands and wonders who the mother of Mary was, and what she had felt when her daughter had told her she was pregnant and unmarried. She stands and wonders whether her daughter's ravings are as nonsensical as it seems at first sight. She stands and wonders if history really does repeat itself. She stands and wonders.

Philemon

Rule Nine:

Players may choose more than one Proxy if they so wish.

Thursday 15ᵗʰ April 2008 1.30 pm BST

"Yes, she's just surfaced. Been in prison, it turns out. Something to do with a stalker, it seems. But it's sorted. She's out and still completely on message. She's now convinced she's pregnant and still a virgin… Well, I don't know. She was hardly about to let me verify it, was she! But Phi, she's in a panic. Says the stalker's coming after her with a hunting knife. Asked if we can hide her somewhere… I said no. Told her to go to her boyfriend… Oxford… OK. Well, I wasn't to know what you'd want, was I? I'll phone her and tell her she can have your flat in Shirley… OK, don't panic, Phi. I've got it all under control."

Maybe, he really does have it all under control. But would he be worried or reassured if he were to notice Lu's wispy presence hovering a metre up from the floor by the curtains that are blowing in the April breeze?

Saturday 1ˢᵗ May 2008 11.22 am BST

He makes a habit of reading the weekend broadsheets, well, the financial sections at least. The 24-point headline reads '*First drop in house prices in 12 years*'. The article beneath it tells of a report by the Nationwide yesterday of a steep decline in home buying over the preceding six months, which has now resulted in the stated reduction. He reassures himself, thinking, "It's only 1%. 1% is nothing." Anyway, he has his loans for the completion of the Tabernacle sewn up legally now. Nothing can go wrong. It can't last long. He can ride it out.

So, why doesn't he feel reassured?

Henry

Rule Ten:

Interaction between Proxies is a matter of free will. Players will do nothing to stimulate or retard it.

Friday 16th April 2008 4.45 pm BST

"I feel awkward."

"There's no need." I said it, but I felt just as awkward as she did. We hadn't parted on exactly the best of terms, though, and there was still a barrier between us. Her step-dad had dropped her off and hugged her. Then she had shooed him off back to Southampton. I'd taken her through college, where, thankfully, there were no prying eyes to look disapprovingly at her suitcase, and up into my room. Now she was sitting opposite me, hugging a cup of tea, her face blotchy and her eyes red. Talis sat quietly on my lap. Laura showed no signs of recognising him.

"Henry, I don't know how to tell you this, but I'm in a lot of trouble. A lot of danger." She looked down as she spoke. I knew she couldn't mean she was pregnant. We'd never got that far.

"Firstly, I'm pregnant."

I looked at her completely and absolutely flummoxed. She looked back, waiting for my reply. Eventually, I found my voice.

"Whose?" It was the only possible question.

"Well, not yours, anyway." I have to admit to a certain sense of relief when she actually uttered the words. "But I need you to listen to a story to explain. And Henry, I really, really, need you to believe me. Do you think you can do that?"

So, for the next hour, I sat silently listening to her story of a church and a pastor and a prophecy and an angel that seemed to suit himself as to when he helped her and when he didn't. And then, of course, there was Tolly, whom I had experienced quite sufficiently myself. It was all perfectly straightforward, logical and intelligible. All it required was that I believe that my girlfriend (or was that ex-girlfriend? – I really wasn't quite sure at that moment) had fallen pregnant by the Holy Spirit and would, in about nine months' time, give birth to the second coming of Jesus Christ: all perfectly reasonable, average everyday stuff.

Just as she was finishing, Talis shifted on my lap. I'd all but forgotten he was there. He stretched and yawned, then looked up at me, looked over at Laura, and gave me a big wink and a thumbs-up. He seemed pleased to see us back together again. Finally, she stopped speaking and looked at me.

"If it's all too much… if you don't believe me… if you're not willing to help me, just tell me and I'll go."

"Woh, slow down a little, will you. It's a lot to take in." I felt a sharp pain in my abdomen and let out an involuntary "Ouch". I looked down. Talis had prodded me with his spear and was frowning at me. He, at least, had no trouble believing her story and evidently felt I ought to as well. But if we were to move forward together in any way at all, the faith she was asking me for had to work both ways. I needed to know how she was going to deal with my own experiences of the supernatural.

"Laura," I answered a little formally, "It's a day for stretching our beliefs, it seems. Before I answer your question, I want to ask you what you can see sitting on my lap. Tell me, Laura, what do you see?"

She looked at Talis, then at me, seemingly confused. Then she looked at my lap again much more intently.

"I was going to say a cushion. But if that's what you meant, you'd not have asked. I'm hoping you're not just making a philosophical point. You know I don't understand all that stuff. But when I look really closely, I'm not absolutely certain of what I do see. It seems to shimmer when I concentrate on it. Perhaps you need to tell me about it?"

So, I did: in every detail, including what had happened that day in the Forest when she had set out with the intention of making love to me. Though she winced at that point, I continued, through the encounter with Tracey where she looked at me fearfully, through the story of the train ticket at which she laughed. Finally,

I told her of my encounter in Schmetterling's office and his final comment that what really mattered here was not what others saw, but what I saw, and why. She nodded vigorously in approval. So did Talis.

Without hesitation, she spoke. "Henry, if you had told me all this six months ago, I would likely have thought you bonkers. But having had so many of my own strange experiences lately, I'm entirely in agreement with your counsellor. What matters is not what I think I see, but what you see. And I'm going to tell you right now that I love you, and that I'm prepared to ignore what seems obvious to me and try to remember you're seeing the world from where you're looking at it, not where I'm looking at it. I can only hope you're willing to do the same for me. Because, Henry, not only do I love you, right now, I need you more than I've ever needed anybody.

My answer was without words. I stood up, setting Talis gently onto the floor, and took the two paces over to her chair, where I sat down on the floor in front of her. Then, I put my head in her lap and my right hand on her abdomen while I held her own right hand in my left. There was nothing to say. I, too, had found a way to step over the dividing wall of credulity that separates us one from another. Though I could not objectively verify her reality at that moment, and everything she said was outside my experience, I believed her because I chose to believe her. I chose to take on trust the experience of another human being for the sake of the love I held for her.

Unobtrusively, Talis made his way over to us and sat in my lap. And there, we four stayed, until the sun went down and the streetlamps flickered their sodium yellow light in through the window.

Sister Serenity

Rule Nine:

Players may choose more than one Proxy if they so wish.

Friday 13th June 2008 2.14 pm BST

How many of us ever discover what true happiness is? It's a corny old cliché to say that happiness is love and love is happiness. But old clichés are sometimes old clichés simply because they are true. Most of us spend our lives looking for that elusive state of happiness, overinvesting in one dream after another, only to see our hopes pillaged by the Furies, time after time. But Laura can tell you now, she is one of life's lucky ones. Despite all her problems and fears and the momentous task her God has asked her to undertake, she will tell you that the old cliché is true. For the last eight weeks, she could have been living through a nightmare constructed of her own fears and the threats of the insane world around her. But the sun has shone through an Oxford Trinity Term, she has been living with the man she loves and inside her body, she can feel the child she already loves growing daily. She knows there is no better recipe for happiness. She is determined to grab it and hold onto it for as long as she can possibly make it last. Who can argue with that?

Laura has, of course, wanted to make love to Henry, but she reminds herself of that conversation in the car (real or fictitious? With Mary or with herself? She doesn't really know now, or, for that matter, care). She knows she mustn't have him, mustn't give herself to him until the baby is born because there must be no ambiguity as to this child's parentage. Henry, like his longsuffering predecessor two thousand years before, has been more than understanding about it. Admittedly, it took him some time to get used to the idea that this pregnancy was genuine. But there was enough morning sickness and strange cravings ("Coal?" he had said to her incredulously. "Where am I supposed to get coal at this time of the morning in the middle of Oxford. I bet Joseph didn't have to go out looking for bloody coal at 2.00 am on the Sabbath morning.") to convince him pretty quickly. Adjusting to the idea of a nine-month wait for sex was harder. But then, as he later said to

326

her, he'd waited the better part of a year for her already, so what was another nine months? Some nights he has slept in the armchair while she lay in his bed. Sometimes, the desire for closeness has become too much and he has got in beside her. She had expected to have to fend his advances off as gently as possible. But to give him his due, all he had sought to do was hold her while they slept. If ever a girl needed convincing that a man loved her, she had thought, this was evidence enough.

But there again, the situation has been eased by his studies. He's been poring over books through most of each day and has been exhausted by the evening. Occasionally, they've been out to take in some inexpensive entertainment or other. Like most other colleges, St Joseph's Junior Common Room has rented punts on the river for the students to use, so they have managed some lazy summer evenings gliding up and down the Cherwell for a couple of hours, watching the grassy banks drift by. It's easy to forget your worries on the river. Was it Ratty who said that or someone else? She can't remember. Sometimes, you can even forget you're hungry. Because the reality is that there's virtually no money. So, Henry's been smuggling food out to her from the college kitchens where one of the chefs is a mate of his.

Henry is stressed of course. Who wouldn't be? Laura's been wondering whether this whole Talisman thing has been conjured up by his overwrought subconscious. But then she'll catch some apparently self-induced movement of that mustard-coloured cushion out of the corner of her eye and she will remember just what an act of faith she is asking him to undertake in believing her in what she knows to be certain. Reciprocally, she might not be able to see a Talis-man but she can damn well show enough confidence in her lover to believe he sees it. And now, he says it's getting smaller anyway. By the time he sits Schools, he's saying it's the size of an egg again. When he shows it to Laura, she at first sees just that –

an egg-shaped crystal, like the ones people sometimes display on coffee tables. What's more, all the intrusive behaviours Henry told her about seem to have stopped. He says the creature mostly sleeps now. He was quite content to take it into the Exam Schools in his pocket without worrying it might make a mess of things for him.

So, the summer term has passed with a genuine carefree happiness for Laura right up until this week. Eights Week, they call it. Boat crews bumping each other on the river (well, not really 'bumping'. As Henry explained to her, it means overtaking), weaving through the crowds with Pimms and strawberries & cream, an unjustifiable but oh, so divine treat paid for on a maxed-out credit card. Definitely an experience not to be missed if offered, and one once experienced, never to be forgotten. Trinity Term in Oxford is an eternal memory.

Now, they have packed to leave. Haddon will be here in the morning. Henry will lock the door to his room and hand in his key to a porter in the lodge who will look suspiciously, if belatedly, at Laura and her suitcase. She doesn't know if she will ever see Oxford again. But she will always think of it in Tom Hanks' words from one of her favourite old movies, 'Sleepless in Seattle', "For a little while there, we had it just perfect."

Saturday 14th June 2008 9.47 am BST

So, now they're pulling up Heddington Hill out towards the Ring Road and the M40. Her hand, which has been almost pain and blood free since she arrived in Oxford, is starting to throb again and the first signs of blood are beginning to appear on her palm. She wraps it in tissue paper and tries to ignore it. As she focusses on the future, her thoughts are already turning from Oxford to the little flat that Pastor Littlemann has made available to them in Shirley, Southampton. She couldn't believe his generosity when Frank called with the offer that they could live there at least until the baby was born. Henry's sitting in the front next to Haddon. Laura's been trying to stimulate some bonding, or at the very least some sort of conversation, between the two of them. It's not working. Had's concentrating on the traffic. Henry's listening to the sport on Radio 5. Laura's relieved Henry's not pulled the Talis-man out to ask for another opinion on it from Haddon. She can probably live with her father not making friends with her future husband. She's not sure she can live with him thinking his future son-in-law is totally bonkers. But there again, if you have a daughter who tells you she's going to give birth to the Saviour of the world, you can probably take most announcements in your stride.

Saturday 28th June 2008 9.47 am BST

It's been a breathless two weeks. A free-of-charge flat is a fantastic favour, of course, even if it's not in the most salubrious of blocks and the kitchen and bathroom are original 1970s vintage. But a bed to sleep in and a bowed sofa to sit on isn't the same as food on the table. Both she and Henry have been out looking for work. Her bump isn't showing yet, so she at least hasn't had to deal with employer prejudice against being pregnant. But work is not easy to be had at the moment, especially if you're trying to work close to home in Shirley. However, today is a day for celebration. After much foot slogging, she decided to try Papa John's for the third time. Luck was on her side and they were just about to put a notice in the window for a general helper. She starts next week. They didn't even mind about her hand. They said she could just wear a glove.

A little more unsettling has been the frequency of visits from people at the church. And not just any people – leadership people, or to be more specific, Frank and Pastor Littlemann in particular. First it was an offer of a lift to church on Sunday after they arrived. Sister Serenity had declined, due to the fact that they'd only just moved in and were unpacking. Frank accepted that, so no big deal.

But he turned up again on Tuesday to offer her a lift to evening prayer meeting. This time he's invited himself in and met Henry. Serenity supposed that was ok in principle, but Henry was, well, just a little suspicious of Frank, and they had metaphorically circled each other like a couple of New Forest stags getting ready for the rut. Serenity didn't much like the thought of being the subject of their testosterone-driven confrontation. She feels a deep debt of gratitude to both of them, but she is quite clear that she belongs to neither. She belongs only to God and His son that she is carrying. By the second Sunday, it was Pastor Littlemann who called round, ostensibly to check everything was ok with the flat. But Pastor's hard to resist. So, yes, she'd accepted the lift to church and, amazingly, Henry had chosen to accompany her. Fortunately, he had tolerated the service wordlessly, playing with his little egg-Talisman on his knee all through. But she could see that he wasn't really comfortable. Fortunately, it had been a subdued service. If it had been one of Pastor's calls to repentance, goodness only knows what Henry would have thought.

Saturday 5th July 2008 5.35 pm BST
So, now, Laura's worried. She's really, really worried. The girls at Papa John's have been great. Always willing to pull together to get the work done, standing in for one another when needed. But her address has come up in conversation with her new friend, Jodi, and Jodi's looked immediately dubious at her mention of the block Laura lives in. Then, Jodi's told her a story about a delivery to that block back in April… to a strange woman with purple hair. And by a process of elimination, Laura's established that the delivery took place while she was in the police cell and that it was made to the flat next door to theirs. And now, Laura's crying really, really hard and Jodi has texted her boyfriend to come take her home.

While they're waiting for him, Jodi tries to reassure Laura: she

, and the mad woman's probably moved her since that day. But Laura can't hear /'s arrived and she's too busy weeping ilder about how she can't go back to the ave a home again and how her baby's ɔn Christmas Day with nobody caring, :.

ilessly until, mercifully, the phone calls n-inch Neptune with two portions of f Pepsi for delivery up at the nurses' · Laura with Henry – 'cos if she really ıg, well that explains a lot about her ıs talk, doesn't it?

If you have enjoyed *Vicious* would please take a moment to review it,

at Amazon: http://tiny.cc/knywry

For special free offers: Michaelforester.co.uk

Thank you for your time. This will help others find and enjoy the book.

Best to you, Michael Forester

Philemon

Rule Twelve:

The free will of Nominated Proxies may be influenced but never withdrawn. Players must work through the inherent characteristics of their chosen Proxies.

Saturday 5th July 2008 10.35 pm BST

He's never been one for partying. Even in his youth he was never what you'd call an extravert. So, his indulgences, his pleasures, he commonly takes alone or with the very few friends he genuinely trusts. Friends like Frank. Friends like Gus. But Gus is on the other side of the world, and Frank's away for the weekend at his twin sister's wedding in Oxfordshire. He's considered paying a surprise visit to the girl and her boyfriend to cement the relationship a little further. But that's business and he doesn't want to work this evening. So, he's sat the evening away in *Bobbies*, on the waterfront near his apartment. He isn't enamoured with the nineteenth-century police theme of the décor (particularly since they should have called it 'Runners', not 'Bobbies', if that's what they meant – no bloody sense of history, these people) but it's a working day destination for the office workers and at the weekends he can rely on the evenings being quiet there. So, tonight has been pleasantly squandered on a series of single malts (not as good as his collection at home, but tonight he wants to be out of the apartment) and now it's time to make his way home to an empty bed. Not that he feels sorry for himself, you understand. It's just he's used to sharing. Used to another person lying next to him.

He gets up to leave and catches the eye of a young man whom he noticed earlier sitting in the corner on his own. The young man smiles that oh-so-knowing smile at him, the ancient and time-honoured signalling system common to all races, all cultures. One malt too many smiles back. As he turns to hand his credit card across the bar, the young man rises from his seat and brushes past Philemon on his way to the exit. As he makes his way unsteadily towards home, Philemon shuts out a thought of Frank. Philemon is adept at shutting out thoughts.

On Sunday, he wakes alone. The young man might have been a

dream. Except, also missing are his wallet, his credit cards, and worst of all, the Song of Songs ring.

Sunday 6th July 2008 7.35 am BST

If he were given to clichés, something like 'sick as a parrot' would probably have covered it. But few know the power of words as he does. And the pain of this loss is beyond the power of profanity to relieve. So, he bears it, this tangible pain, this ice knife slicing through his entrails, silently. Because he knows that today will not be a good day to permit others to judge him by his words, for the first time in years, he calls a Deacon, Adrian Pride, and tells him in an appropriately croaky voice that he has laryngitis and asks if he can preach in his stead that morning.

Pride is both taken aback at the offer (Pastor has so rarely let anyone preach instead of him) and irritated to be interrupted from his preferred early Sunday morning activity. Putting down the phone, he switches the laptop from the pornography site he has been using as a masturbation aid and clicks onto one of ready-made sermons. Here, he selects something that will befit the 11.00 am homily a little more than his own preferred choices of the flat chests and hairless crotches of kiddy-porn.

By the time Pride is printing off his sermon on sexual purity (like most of the depraved, he sees no irony), Philemon is in the car and on his way to the riverfront and the near-completed Southampton Tabernacle. He has loved to come here over the last year, watching his cathedral rising, block by block, the majestic proportions he had always visualised steadily emerging, an edifice fitting to his own greatness, never mind the glory of God.

The building was topped out in January and now they are well into second fix. Now, he wanders the un-plastered corridors and the yet-to-be-floored break-out rooms, dreaming of the future. Now, he stands in the centre of the main hall, leans his head back and looks up at walls that soar without interruption to a glazed atrium roof and a pinnacle that rises still further up to a cross placed so high that God can see it and reach down to shake hands with Pastor Philemon Littlemann. At least, He could, if there were a God.

If anything, the builders are going to beat the completion deadline of 31st August. The first use of the building has been pencilled in for Sunday 28th September. It will be a simple service of thanks to the Lord for the Tabernacle, Internet broadcast of course, but nothing heavy. Now the loans are secure, there is no particular rush to bring in funds. He can build his empire methodically upon the momentum of *SecondCome*, particularly now the girl has confirmed that she is pregnant. Who the father actually is is entirely unimportant. Who people believe the father is is everything. He finds himself wondering about the first so-called virgin birth – who the father might have been that time. Joseph, he presumes – which of course puts him in agreement with just about everyone in Nazareth at the time.

He has set the Tabernacle's official opening ceremony for Christmas Day, when, according to his calculations, the girl will be all but ready to drop her bastard. He knows he can't predict the moment exactly. But if the publicity is handled properly it could just be the biggest religious event since... since... well, since *FirstCome* of course.

The ring is all but forgotten now, soothed away by narcissistic dreams of fawning sycophants falling at his feet, dreams stirred deep by a wispy presence that floats unseen behind him.

Wednesday 23rd July 2008 8.15 pm BST

"Hey, Jen. How was Bali?"

Frank leans across the table and gives his sister a kiss. She turns her cheek to receive it.

"A perfect honeymoon, thank you. Conrad is everything a

husband should be. He speaks when spoken to and does everything I tell him to first time."

He ignores the jibe, considers making some lewd reference to the normal nocturnal activities of honeymooners and decides against it. He has a purpose for being here this evening and doesn't want to risk a family row frustrating it.

"Sounds like he's quite the 'Gentleman' too."

She smiles at the play on their surname.

"And by the way, I shall indeed be retaining my maiden name for professional purposes. 'Jenny Gentleman' will continue to grace the pages of the Southampton Echo for some time to come yet. So, tell me, to what do I owe the honour? I was impressed enough that you took the time out to be at my wedding. Now, I see you again two weeks later. That has to be some kind of a record."

"I have a story for you."

"Oh, goodie! I love exclusives. And that church planning permission story you gave me was delightful."

"Yeah," he replies curtly. "Shame Harold Jowlett didn't see it quite the same way. Glad to see you're still just a teensy-weensy bit sad about it."

She shrugs. "Collateral damage happens in every war. So, what have you got this time?"

"Have you ever heard of something called *SecondCome*?"

Thursday 24th July 2008 6.15 pm BST

There is a total of four seats in the flat. Henry and Laura are sitting on the two-seat sofa. Jenny and Frank are on the upright chairs drawn away from the dining table. Jenny looks closely at the girl, only a few years younger than herself, but oh, so innocent in comparison. Later, alone in the bar, Jenny will think about those few years that separate them and how they have fashioned an experiential gulf between herself and the Lauras of this world. She will wonder if the gentler path might not have been kinder to her. But her course is set. Her brand of journalism affords no space for sentimentality. If there is a story here, her editor will expect her to get it, verify it, and write it for immediate publication.

"So, Laura," she begins.

"Sister Serenity," the younger girl interjects.

"Yes, of course. Sister… Serenity. I'm told you're pregnant with the second coming of Jesus Christ?"

Friday 25th July 2008 11.11 am BST

Nineteen years a sub editor gives a man a nose for a story. And Danny Harper's seen every story under the sun, true, false, false presented as true, true presented as false. Living and breathing journalism for the best part of 35 years has also gives him a nose for a reporter who has ambition. He'd marked the Gentleman woman out two years ago, when she first appeared at the paper. She was one who planned to go to the top and didn't mind what she had to do to get there. She'd made her availability clear to him within a week of her arrival. And a few years back, he might well have accepted the invitation. But a prostrate removal reins in such urges and gives a man other priorities. It also makes him reassess what he wants to do with his remaining working years. Harper had come down on the side of professional integrity. Newspapers, of course, have to be sold. And that means stories have to be found that make people want to read them. But those stories have to be credible to the readership and rigorously researched. So, he's looking at the words on the screen in front of him on the desk, periodically looking up to look at Jenny Gentleman as he does so. She sits silently, waiting for him to finish, her eyes never leaving him. Finally, he pushes his chair back.

"So, let's see. We have a girl who says she's a pregnant virgin. She's carrying Jesus Christ who has come back to be born a second time. And she has a stigma."

"Stigmatum," Jenny corrects, aware Harper does not like being corrected.

"Whatever. And what have you done to verify the story?"

"She won't let anyone examine her, Danny. She says the matter has to be taken on faith or not at all."

"Faith, huh? Hope and Charity as well, no doubt, when she's proven to be a fraud. I know it's the silly season, but come on, Jenny, this is no more credible than TV personalities eating hamsters! We're a serious newspaper. Some crap is too far-fetched to be bothered with, even in July. Bin it."

But she doesn't. She prints the story off and puts it in her drawer. She gets on with other assignments. She meets all her deadlines. A week later, on 1st August, she takes it out again. She's about to do as Danny said and bin it. But there's just something about it that nags her and won't go away. So, it goes back in the drawer while she thinks.

Over the weekend, Harper suffers a left side Grand Mal stroke. By Monday 4th August, Southampton General is saying he will survive, but can't predict whether he will gain mobility again, or if he does, how long it will take.

On Tuesday 5th August, Group Head Office phones to say it will be a week before they can get a temporary replacement out. Jenny is instructed to step into the vacant post temporarily.

On Friday 8th August, the paper carries a two-hundred-word story under a sixteen-point headline, *'Is this the Second Coming?* The name Jennifer Gentleman appears underneath.

On Monday 11th August, the call comes in from what the industry continues to refer to as Fleet Street.

On Tuesday 12th August, a London journalist appears unannounced at Laura and Henry's flat in Shirley. Henry answers the door. Laura refuses to be interviewed.

Sunday 17th August 2008 9.00 am BST

The News of the World carries a full-page article on page 6 under a banner headline, *'Cult declares Second Coming'*, accompanied by constructed picture of Sister Serenity cradling a baby, and Henry as Joseph, all standing under a stylised Christmas star. Other pictures show the new Southampton Tabernacle and an unshaven and surprised Pastor Philemon in his dressing gown at the door to his '£500,000 luxury waterside apartment'. Frank manages to escape the photograph.

Monday 18th August 2008 9.00 am BST

The Church of the Body of Christ issues its own formal press release confirming that a member of the congregation is pregnant whilst a virgin, in fulfilment of the prophesy of *SecondCome*, and that she also bears a healing stigmatum on the palm of her left hand. The New Messiah is expected to be born on or around Christmas Day, 2008. The church's new building, The Southampton Tabernacle, will be formally opened on that day. However, its first service will be held on 28th September. Sister Serenity, mother of the New Messiah, will be present at the service. She will give no interviews and on no account must be approached. Admission will be by invitation of the Church of the Body of Christ only. All enquiries should be directed towards Pastor Philemon Littlemann.

Wednesday 21st August 2008 6.24 pm BST

Pastor Littlemann makes his first appearance on national TV as the last feature on the early evening ITV news.

On Thursday 22nd August, the Church of the Body of Christ begins broadcasting on its new Internet TV Channel, *'Saviour s Body'*. The channel carries old sermons by Pastor Littlemann interspersed with appeals for money, stories about *SecondCome* and announcements of the date of Sister Serenity's first public appearance.

Serenity watches the broadcast in horror. No one has consulted her on the matter.

Henry phones Frank in considerable irritation. He is reminded curtly of where he is living and that unless Serenity really does want to give birth in a barn, she will follow the instructions of the Church.

Thursday 28th August 2008 8.00 am BST
UK house prices are reported to have fallen 10.5% over the preceding year.

Saturday 30th August 2008 9.00 am BST
The Guardian newspaper carries an interview with Chancellor Alistair Darling in which he warns that the UK economy faces its greatest crisis for 60 years. The word 'depression' is carefully avoided.

Philemon is not in the least bothered. Money is pouring in from the daily broadcasts. The church's call centre is booking new members at a 'voluntary' administration fee of £150.00. The balances in the Manx accounts are soaring. At this rate, they will have sufficient funds to repay the loans before Christmas.

Philemon is laying out his first five-year plan for the life of the New Messiah.

Tolly

Rule Eleven:

Players may make themselves visible or audible to their Nominated Proxies but must not intervene directly in the chain of events.

Monday 1st September 2008 9.00 am BST

Hathaway had done his job as professionally as any Tangible I know. He has pulled together a comprehensive file on Tolly Jones which left little room for uncertainty over a verdict. But the problem with being a copper is you don't get to make the decisions on how cases get processed. By the time CPS had trawled the file, they'd convinced themselves that a decent defence barrister would claim she was unfit to plead (and how very right that would have been) and likely have had the judge decide her actions were all out of character and due to concussion from her bang on the head (and how very wrong that would have been). So, in the great tradition of British Justice, a compromise was agreed and she was shunted off to secure psychiatric hospital to await a psychiatric report. Somewhere along the way (Tolly can't remember when and no one's owning up to it), her head got shaved, sacrificing that beautiful trademark purple Mohican we have all come to love so much. And what's more, the shock of being banged up has changed her eating pattern. So, by the time she arrived at the Riverdean Secure Unit some seventeen miles north east of Southampton, she had been sporting a full, if relatively short, head of naturally brown hair (albeit that the short style didn't suit her terribly well) and she had lost perhaps 25 kilos from her probable starting weight of 125. I say probable, since weighing scales had not been seen in the Shirley flat since she broke the last set back in 2002. The weight loss hasn't made her slim, but together with the brown hair, it has made her look, well, normal-*ish*. And Tolly's no fool. She knows her chances of release, whenever the possibility comes, will be all the greater, the more normally she appears and behaves.

So, here she, is in the waiting area outside the psychiatrist's office on the day of the evaluation. She's not being monitored. Manpower in the unit is stretched and she's not considered an escape risk. As the second hand of the clock on the wall touches 9.00 am exactly, she knocks and, without waiting for an answer, enters. The seated figure behind the desk looks up. Tolly is not too observant of matters that don't concern Sid, or Old Holborn rolling tobacco, or chocolate cake. But even she can't fail to notice the man's unkempt hair, his bright red sleeveless pullover, his shiny brown trousers.

He rises and unconsciously, clicks his heels together. "Guten tag," he says, stretching out his hand. "Schmetterling."

Monday 15ᵗʰ September 2008 9.45 am BST
"Gut progress, Fraulein Jones. Gut progress."

Schmetterling had requested to continue working with Tolly following the initial evaluation after diagnosing Anti-social Personality Disorder with a continuing risk to the public if Tolly were to be released. The court has yet to make a formal decision on her future – that may well take months yet. But it's pretty much a forgone conclusion that she will be detained at Her Majesty's pleasure. No one, of course, has explained this to Tolly, who would no doubt take considerably less pleasure than Her Majesty in the prospect of her indefinite detention.

Naturally, Schmetterling does not take every case he is asked to evaluate. The interest to him in this one is the effect of the combination of ASPD with Tolly's delusional tendencies. As he has worked with her, he has noted her remarkable ability to rewrite events in such a way as to fit her map of reality. She sees nothing abnormal in the idea of Sid Vicious reincarnating to be with her, nor in the need to eliminate Nancy Spungen if she is to keep Sid for herself this time. Indeed, she cannot conceive of why this perfectly normal approach to everyday life should in any way impede her release.

"Well, that's great, Doc. So, how long before I can go home?"

Schmetterling is sitting in one of two armchairs in his office. The 1960s building doesn't have the same character as his Georgian consulting rooms in Oxford. But he has attempted, nevertheless, to make it as patient-friendly as possible. Hence, the two deep armchairs on one side of the room that face each other at a 30-degree angle. He leans forward towards Tolly who is sitting opposite him, his elbows on the arms of the chair, his fingers laced.

"Fraulein Jones, I think you may need to consider the possibility of quite a long period of adjustment before your return to the outside world."

"Why, Doc? When will I be ready?"

He remains silent a while. "I rather think that depends on you. When you are able to accept that it is not normal for people to reincarnate, nor to attempt murder, then, I think we may be able to acknowledge a material change worthy of reconsideration."

She does not argue. She knows this man is the key to her escape. She returns to her room unsupervised where she opens the door to see me floating just above the bed.

"Sid?" she exclaims in surprise. I have to congratulate myself. It was one of the smoothest, most congruent incarnations I have ever undertaken. I adopt a dismissive expression to her and respond, "Fuck you, Doll." Then, I spit right across the room and into her face.

"Sid!" she squeals, and throws herself directly at me. I dematerialise before she reaches me.

"Godda go, Doll," I say, retreating towards the ceiling. "But we're gonna get you out of here. Soon, Doll; you'll be out really soon."

The key to winning this game, in my humble opinion, lies in knowing precisely when, and as whom, to incarnate. I may just have made the decisive move. Screw Gabe, as you Tangibles would say. This world is mine now and he's not getting it back.

Philemon

Rule Twelve:

The free will of Nominated Proxies may be influenced but never withdrawn. Players must work through the inherent characteristics of their chosen Proxies.

Monday 1ˢᵗ September 2008 11.00 am BST

He has begun dribbling tickets on to the secondary market on eBay at an opening price of £47.00, not really knowing what to expect. Bids have hovered for a couple of hours. Now, they're climbing.

Friday 5ᵗʰ September 2008 3.45 am BST

The FTSE has notched up its steepest one-day decline since July 2002. He doesn't give a toss. He's been out of the market for almost a year.

Sunday 7ᵗʰ September 2008 3.45 am BST

Mortgage lenders Fannie Mae and Freddie Mac which, together, account for half of the outstanding mortgages in the USA are rescued by the US government in one of the largest bail outs in US history.

In the UK, most people seem to think Freddie Mac is married to Fannie Mae.

He doesn't really give a shit about what happens in the US mortgage market. All his real estate is in the UK. All his borrowings have been switched to Icebanki. All his money, that's ALL his money, is safe offshore in Manx accounts where no one can get at it but him.

Sunday 14ᵗʰ September 2008 3.45 am BST

eBay is pricing tickets at £237.50.

Sunday 21ˢᵗ September 2008 3.45 am BST

Final market price on disposal of all tickets to the inaugural service of the Southampton Tabernacle (appearance of the 'Mother of God', as the press is referring to her, is guaranteed) reaches £501.22. Total proceeds lodged in the Manx account of the Church of the Body of Christ exceed £1,400,000.

Monday 22ⁿᵈ September 2008 9.05 am BST

Amelia Fotherington-Smyth telephones to make an appointment the following day for Sir Fredrick Dickinson to visit the Southampton Tabernacle. The call is put through to Philemon personally. "She sounds like melted chocolate," he thinks as he fondles his crotch and wonders just how right he really has been about his sexual orientation all these years.

Tuesday 23ʳᵈ September 2008 11.00 am BST

Sir Fredrick's Rolls-Royce stops outside the Southampton Tabernacle, impeding the delivery vans scurrying back and forth with carpet and stacking chairs and hymn books and crockery. Amelia Fotherington-Smyth alights from the offside rear door and scowls at Frank Gentleman to whom she has not been introduced, as he reaches the nearside rear door first and opens it to permit Sir Fredrick to alight.

Sir Fredrick and Amelia are conducted on a tour of the building by Frank, terminating in the kitchen where Pastor Philemon Littlemann, dressed in a new Nathan Road tailored suit and invisibly platformed shoes, is leaning nonchalantly against the worktop. He smiles involuntarily at Amelia and passes Sir Fredrick a cardboard cup of Costa coffee. Sir Fredrick smiles in amusement.

"Go play, children," he says without turning to either Frank or Amelia. They both exit the room scowling at each other. Then, he offers his hand to Philemon, nods and says, "Well done. You've impressed me. We will be doing more together."

Before he leaves, he has offered, and Philemon has accepted, the opportunity to participate in the underwriting of an Icebanki rights issue on 6ᵗʰ October. All of the church's liquid funds have been committed to the deal, including the £1.4 million raised from ticket sales on eBay. Sir Fredrick has told Philemon that the rights issue will be over-subscribed many times and he can expect to at least double his money. The proceeds of underwriting can be deposited under any name of Philemon's choosing, anywhere in the world.

Wednesday 24th September 2008 noon BST
Henry telephones Frank to tell him Laura is feeling ill and cannot attend the inaugural service on Sunday. Frank replies that Sister Serenity will be present regardless of how she feels about it.

Thursday 25th September 2008 12.15 pm BST
Laura is on her knees in the bathroom in the Shirley flat, vomiting uncontrollably into the toilet pan. Henry is kneeling next to her, trying to press into her hand what she thinks is a crystal egg and he insists is the Talis-man.

Friday 26th September 2008 12.42 pm BST
Philemon rings the doorbell of the Shirley flat, deli sandwiches in hand. Henry answers the door and tries to bar his way. Philemon pushes him aside, strides into the lounge where Serenity is drifting in and out of a light sleep on the couch and shuts the door on Henry. By the time he leaves, she is wide awake and has agreed to attend the service on Sunday evening. She will tell Henry only that he has given her very specific instructions for what she must do on Sunday and that everything will be alright.

Henry is not convinced.

The deli sandwiches remain uneaten on the table until they curl.

Saturday 27th September 2008 12.42 pm BST
Laura tells Henry she wants to go boating on the Hamble River. Afterwards, Henry is unable to decide whether she fell in the water, or jumped in, with a view to ending her life. He will never know for sure. He, of course, jumps in after her. There was never any real damage to her, him, the baby, or the Talis-man, who afterwards is

still in his pocket. He assumes it was a cry for help. He is already doing all he can to help.

Sunday 28th September 2008 6.17 pm BST

Frank calls at the Shirley flat to take Sister Serenity and Henry to the Tabernacle. On arrival, he hands Henry a VIP ticket at the door and walks away with Serenity.

Sunday 28th September 2008 8.17 pm BST

"I want so much for you to see what I am seeing now. With aaaall my heart, I want you to know what it means to be in the *arms* of the Risen Saaaaviour."

The short man is standing at the front of a darkened auditorium, capacity 5,224 (fire regulations forced the number down from the planned 5,500). Every seat is taken. The height of the room, somewhere way above in the darkness, creates cathedral echoes. Surely, God is in this place.

Monday 6th October 2008 4.45 pm BST

"One moment, please," intones the liquid chocolate voice. "You have a personal call coming through from Sir Fredrick Dickinson."

"Philemon? I felt I needed to telephone myself. In all my years in the city, I have never needed to make a personal apology on this scale before. I'm sorry to have to inform you that the rights issue has not been well taken up. You are currently out of funds, temporarily, of course. The good news is that you are the proud owner of some £4,378,292 worth of Icebanki stock. I'm truly sorry for the inconvenience, but I assure you that you will be able to release the stock onto the market over the coming weeks and regain your liquidity. I acknowledge, I owe you a favour. I never fail to return what I owe."

Tuesday 7th October 2008 2.00 pm BST

The Icelandic Financial Authority announces it is taking control of Icebanki. Share transactions and asset movements are frozen.

Wednesday 8th October 2008 2.00 pm BST

The British Government announces it is freezing all assets belonging to Icebanki under the terms of the Terrorism Acts 2000–2008.

Philemon knows all is not necessarily lost. His assets are in the Isle of Man, which is not subject to UK legislation.

Thursday 9th October 2008 2.00 pm BST

The Directors, Icebanki
To
The Trustees, The Trust of the Church of the Body of Christ.

Dear Sirs,

We write to inform you of the appointment of Worth, Dryhouse, Barrellman as Administrators to Icebanki (Isle of Man) Limited. If you are in any doubt as to the legal rights and obligations of the Administrators, please contact your usual financial advisors or the Institute of Chartered Accountants, IoM.

Sister Serenity

Rule One:

The rules of the Game must not be fully disclosed to Tangibles until the Game has been completed, and then, only selectively and by metaphor.

Wednesday 5ᵗʰ November 2008 7.00 pm GMT

When she was a child, he comforted her when she was hurt, explained to her when she was confused and made sense of the world for her in a way no one else could. Well, she still feels six years old in everything but her body, this body that God has chosen as his own personal incubator. She wasn't consulted. She didn't ask for this. Gabe didn't come to her one day and say, "Hey Babe, is it ok if God makes you pregnant with his son?" And Christ only knows (pun definitely intended) what she would have said if he had. She searches the flat daily for feathers in the forlorn hope he will just come and talk to her. A good talk is really all she needs to make it all ok again. But Henry's a scrupulous cleaner and they have man-made fabric in the quilt and pillows. There are no feathers to be found.

So now, every day is a day of pain. If they try to get outside the door, reporters mob and children jeer. Could it really have been this bad for Mary? She has to admit, it probably was. Granted, there were no reporters from the Jerusalem Herald lurking around every corner, but the gossip and derision aimed at a pregnant unmarried woman must have been near intolerable. "At least she had Joseph," Serenity thinks. "At least I have Henry."

Some nights the sense of isolation has been so bad, she has wanted him to make love to her, just so that she can go outside in the morning and tell the bloody reporters she isn't a virgin any more and it's all been a huge mistake and they can all go away. And the irony of it is that when she has reached for him, it has been he who has gently deflected her advances, then held her tightly in his arms from behind while she sobbed herself to sleep. In the morning her sense of integrity returns and she is glad of his strength. She could not conceivably get through the next nine weeks without his strength.

And after that, what? She is supposed to rear a child that she knows was conceived without sex? Without sin? There's no advice on the NHS website on how to rear a sinless child. Does a sinless child cry? Does he read the Bible before he's six months old? Does he bring dead butterflies back to life in the garden? Does he heal himself when he cuts his knee in the playground? Does he know all the answers to his GCSE questions without ever learning them? Do girls flock to him? Does he have sex with them? Does he get married and have a family of his own? Or is he destined from birth – no, from conception – to be nailed to a wooden cross and die of exposure? And what of the church's role in all of this? These people have been showing a more insistent, more forceful side of late. What will they be like when the child arrives? And to top it all, whatever is she supposed to name this baby? Jesus? That's a recipe for derision and bullying.

The questions have swilled round in her mind like black water in a foul drain as she wanders her way around the flat.

Henry is out… somewhere. She hasn't bothered to turn the lights on or draw the curtains. So she sees the little rockets and Catherine wheels of Guy Fawkes' night flash their momentary lives away in the darkness, fulfilling their design purpose, bringing joy to many a laughing child and screams of pain and terror to a few. "I am a Roman Candle," she thinks, "belching my brief little life into the darkness where no one is watching. I will bring joy to none and pain to many."

But they are watching. Mary is watching from the other side of the mirror, if Laura would but glance at it as she passes down the low-lit hall. Mary looks with concern and with love and with worry. Gabe, if she would only look for the shimmer of his ethereal form, hovers silently in the corner. But there are times when communication is permitted between the living and the dead, between Ethereals and Tangibles, between heaven and earth. And there are times when it is not. Some have called these the nights of the soul. They are times of solitude and silence, when the angels and the dead can do nothing but watch and care. And for those about to bear Messiahs, such soul-nights are long and dark and number above the stars in the heavens.

Philemon

Rule One:

The rules of the Game must not be fully disclosed to Tangibles until the Game has been completed and then, only selectively and by metaphor.

Thursday 6th November 2008 8.44 am GMT

There is a sound each city makes as it commences its working day, that is characteristic of that city alone. Of all the cities in the world, London's working cries are the most easily distinguished. The shallow will hear the accents of the cockney newspaper vendors, the chimes of Big Ben, the diesel engines of the black London Cabs. But beneath that, for those that have ears to hear, there is a substructure, a disharmonic wail of lost souls, its aria of passion and pain and of tears for the fabulously wealthy who have, for all eternity, sold their birthrights for a mess of pottage.

As he slips his ticket into the barrier, Philemon joins the choreographed dance of the heaving mass of mammon worshipers.

Thursday 6th November 2008 4.44 pm GMT

Deflated. Disappointed. Disgusted. Disarmed. Dismantled. But not deflected. And certainly, not destroyed. Not yet, anyway.

They wouldn't let him see Sir Fredrick. Resigned on health grounds, they said. He saw a couple of bean-counters from Worth, Dryhouse, Barrellman who are running what is left of Landsbanki IoM now; from here in London, of course. They wouldn't sully the soles of their shoes by getting Douglas dust on them, would they?

So, here's the drill. First, they make him wait 47 minutes just so he's clear about how unimportant he is. Then, they spend precisely 17 minutes and 40 seconds with him. No coffee. No chocolate-voiced PA. Just an empty room, two of them, him and a pile of manila files on the desk in front of them. Then, they rub his nose in it. How they now own everything and he has nothing. How they can kick him out of the Tabernacle, his rental properties, the Shirley flat, even the fucking waterfront flat he lives in, any time it pleases their sweet little hearts to do so. And when they're confident that he knows he's nobody and nothing and that he's their own personal fuck-dolly that they can bugger whenever the fancy takes them, then and only then, do they throw him a bone.

He's been waiting for it, of course. There would have been no need for a meeting if they hadn't planned to offer him something. And he's not forgotten what they've only just got round to realising. They might own every brick and all the mortar that joins it together. But he owns his tongue and he owns the girl. And the securitised value of those income streams, well let's just say, there's never going to be a sub-prime crisis when it comes to fleecing the particular kind of sheep he shears. Without the girl and without him, most of the assets are all but worthless. With him and the girl, their value is beyond the estimation of even a bean-counter from Worth, Dryhouse, Barrellman.

So, here's the deal, they said. He gets to go on using the assets while his little nativity play winds its way towards Bethlehem. They get 85% of everything he makes.

But that's a mistake, isn't it? They've told him they know he still has cards in his hand. So, by the time the train pulls out of Waterloo, he's carrying the deeds to the waterfront apartment and the Shirley flat and an undertaking from their solicitors to make immediate entries of satisfaction on the Land Registry Charges Register. And their share of the income has dropped to 50%. What happens after Christmas, no one has said. But Christmas is still seven weeks away. And 2009 is on the other side of eternity.

Before the train reaches Clapham Junction, he has phoned Frank. The TV channel and the call centre are back up and running, the eBay secondary market in Christmas Day tickets for the Tabernacle has opened. The bookies are giving 8 to 3 odds-on for the Mother of God to drop a child during the evening service.

Tolly

Rule Ten:

Interaction between Proxies is a matter of free will. Players will do nothing to stimulate or retard it.

Monday 8th December 2008 9.45 am GMT

"Gut progress, Fraulein Jones. Gut progress."

She's seen him nine times now and every time he's said the same thing. She has the little German weed completely convinced she means what she says.

Internet privileges have given her access to sites where she's gained a working knowledge of what the therapeutic process is supposed to achieve. That's been helpful in maintaining the masquerade. It has also given her access to other sites such as the news and the official site of the Church of the Body of Christ. Putting two and two together, she knows Nancy Witchbitch is Laura Spungen, is Sister-fucking-Serenity. And she knows that all this Mother of God stuff is just something Nancy's cooked up to get to be with Sid again.

Sid explained it all to her the day he materialised in her cell: how he's Sid in Spirit but Henry in body, and how the Yankee witchbitch has cast a spell over his Henry-self so he can't resist her. Sid's managed to get away from his body twice more since then to materialise with Tolly, to reassure her that he loves her and that he's making it so they can both be free and together. He also swears the witchbitch's baby isn't his and she believes him, to both their relief. He's also coached her in what to say to the German weed in the therapy sessions. But she's frustrated. All she can ever seem to get out of him is "Gut progress, Fraulein Jones. Gut progress."

But at Sid's suggestion, today, she has an answer of her own.

"Really, Herr Professor? It doesn't feel that way to me."

Schmetterling leans forward in his armchair and contemplates Tolly with a slight raise of the eyebrow.

"Warum, Fraulein Jones? Warum?"

"Well, this is our ninth session, Herr Professor, isn't it? We seem to cover much the same ground each week. I tell you about Henry, Laura and Sid and Nancy and you nod at me. I feel better for it. I feel like I'm facing up to what I've done. I feel clearer now about the difference between right and wrong. But I feel I need something more powerful to stimulate a more profound change." These are not her own words, of course. They are the words in which I have coached her whilst appearing to her as Sid. They are Internet site English. They are psychobabble. "I have an idea, Herr Professor, that is... if you think it's a good idea."

He looks at her from behind interlaced fingers, both eyebrows slightly raised in question.

"Something from the past, Professor. Something uniquely anchored to my delusions. First, I thought of ash from Sid's urn, but it's all blown away. Then, I thought... that is, if you think it's a good idea... I thought... I thought to be confronted with my hunting knife."

He looks at her without moving. She looks back at him, equally static. Not an eyebrow of his shifts. Not a finger of hers shakes. Until finally, he speaks.

"Ja, ist gut idea. I will have knife with me next time we meet."

"Oh, Danket, Herr Professor, Danket-shine," she fawns. She all but backs out of the room, bowing. She closes the door behind her and shuffles forward until she is sure she is out of his line of sight. Then, she straightens and picks up her pace. It's all she can do to stop herself letting out a cheer. Nevertheless, she brings her fist down through the air, clenches her teeth and whispers "Yes!" Two weeks. In only two weeks she will be free.

Wednesday 24th December 2008 9.16 am GMT

"May I touch it?" She looks at him questioningly. He nods, barely perceptibly.

Today, they are sitting on either side of his desk. She assumes it is because of the knife. Presumably, he has a panic button on the other side of the desk. She reaches out a shaking hand, index finger foremost. She is a Sistine Adam, reaching for the finger of God. Her finger traces the polished steel of the blade, the smooth carved wood of the handle, the jaguar's sleek form. "I had this made by a mate of a mate from the union club. Incredible carver, he is. Look at the detail, Professor. Have you ever seen anything like it? I reckon it might be better than the original. But who knows?"

He watches her in silence. She puts the knife back on the desk and pushes it towards him.

"Can we go back to the armchairs now, please, Professor?" She stands and walks towards the armchairs. He follows, visibly relieved that she has left the knife on the desk.

"Ja, sure. Gut progress, Fraulein Jones. Gut progress."

She smiles at him as she reaches for his wrist. "I knew you were going to say that," she says as she twists it back and snaps it. Then, she spins him round, her left arm around his neck, and up over his mouth. She takes his chin in her right hand, twisting his head to the right until his neck snaps. Then, she eases him down into the armchair with its back towards the door and arranges his arms in their characteristic interlocked fingers pose. She pockets his keys, cash and credit cards from his jacket. Then, she pulls the telephone cord from the wall, slips the knife into her belt inside her jeans and exits the room, careful to ensure she is not seen. In the car park, she identifies his car by pressing the remote control and looking for the flash of indicator lights, just as Sid has instructed. If she is lucky, he may not be missed until someone at home reports him missing and that could be Christmas morning or later, depending on his lifestyle.

Getting into the 5-series BMW, she fails to notice the child seats in the back.

At home in Abingdon, Frau Schmetterling is preparing stollen for the Christmas Eve celebration, whilst tending to two very small, very excited children. Later, her mother will telephone from

Stuttgart. She's sad not to be seeing her this year. But at least her husband is stopping work for the whole holiday period through until the New Year. That, at least, will guarantee them some much needed family time together.

Henry

Rule Four:

The Arbiter will initiate the Game by establishing a bond with a Nominated Proxy.

Wednesday 24th December 2008 7.12 pm GMT

Life has become dramatically more serious since we left Oxford. I can't believe how quickly I've gone from being a carefree student to an overburdened partner of a pregnant girlfriend. She's still not told me who the father is. Maybe one day she will, maybe not. It really won't matter to me. But I do wish she'd not come up with these stories about angelic visitations and Holy Spirit impregnations. I'm sure she didn't mean for this, but the consequences have been devastating. We can barely go outside now, without reporters mobbing us. The only way we're getting out of the building is when one of her Church people collects us for Sunday service or prayer meeting. Not exactly my favourite activities, but without them, I'd not be taking a breath outside the flat. So, yes, I'm looking forward to 2009 when the baby's born with the same number of fingers and toes as everyone else and no halo round its head. Hopefully, at that point, all the fuss will die down. Then, with that deranged woman, Tracey, behind bars indefinitely, we could finally get on with living the same kind of life that everyone else leads.

Everything had been continuing normally (well, as normally as it ever does under the circumstances). I was stuck into Sky Sports, Laura was icing the Christmas cake in the kitchen, when the music started up next door, loud enough to shake the walls. The volume was ludicrous. I marched straight round to complain and knocked loudly on the door. A voice called out, "We're having a party." I kept knocking vigorously. Finally, I heard a shuffling and muttering (yes, even over the volume of the music). When the door opened, the new hairstyle did nothing to disguise Tracey.

I had three thoughts at once.
1. Oh, fuck, it's Tracey.
2. God, she's lost a lot of weight.
3. Oh, fuck, it's Tracey.

Despite being roaring drunk, she clocked me immediately. "Sid! Henry! You're here at last." She grabbed me by the sleeve and dragged me in.

I then had another thought.

4. If this crazy woman gets any idea that Laura is next door, she will go for her.

I couldn't let that happen. So I thought to humour her until she fell asleep, then be out of the building as quickly as I could manage with Laura. But that was two hours ago. And that would be the two hours I've just spent dancing with her to 'God Save the Queen', 'Sid Sings' and other similarly tuneful seasonal melodies. Two bleedin' hours of shuffle dancing, Tracey slobbering all over my neck to tuneless ear-shattering punk rock. Why does it always happen to me? Finally, she flopped down on the sofa. "I can't dance any more, Sid. Oh, Sid, I love you so much," she slurred. "Come here and take me, Sid, take me."

"Bear with me, Tracey," I replied. "I need the bathroom." And I bolted in the direction of the hallway. By the time I came out three minutes later, she was snoring soundly, her head thrown back on the upright part of the couch, her arms and legs splayed out, making her look remarkably like a five-pointed Christmas tree star. I dashed next door and explained our predicament rapidly to Laura. In two minutes flat, we'd thrown the minimum we needed in a suitcase and legged it straight out of there, hoping against hope that the mad woman wouldn't wake up.

I would have preferred that we spent the night with one or other set of parents. Hell, I would have preferred that we spent the night in a bloody stable. But Laura was insistent. She immediately phoned Frank, who, within half an hour, was picking us up from a spot round the corner that was not visible from Tracey's flat. To give him his due, he was very understanding and took us straight to the Tabernacle where he let us in and gave us access to what he said would eventually be a staff flat. As a result, we spent what felt like a very odd Christmas Eve night effectively in Church. I suppose I should be grateful that the baby wasn't born and no shepherds or wise men turned up. On Christmas morning, I was all for going to either Laura's parents or mine for a decent breakfast and Christmas lunch but she wasn't up for it. So, we simply stayed put and took in the atmosphere of Christmas on the TV and radio. The national media was pretty well silent about the long-awaited virgin birth. Not so the local radio, Wave 105, which repeated their standard news story about us on the hour. Laura spent a Christmas Day drifting in and out of sleep, mumbling almost deliriously at times. At noon Frank, and several colleagues of his to whom I'd not had the pleasure of an introduction, arrived to begin preparations for the big event at 7.00 pm. Given that they had to get over 5,000 seated by then, doors were to be open at 5.00 pm. Lines started forming outside from around 3.00 pm (did people really have nothing better to do with their time on Christmas Day?) That was about it for the afternoon, except for one odd thing – the weather. There seemed to be a lightning storm and continuous thunder, right over the Tabernacle.

Philemon

Rule Fourteen:

The winner will be awarded control of the field of play until such time as another random event creates a further tear in the curtain.

Thursday 25ᵗʰ December 2008 8.37 pm GMT

He's a high roller on the highest roll of his life. It's been getting better and better day by day. When he checked the eBay secondary market price last night for the last time, it was well into four figures. He could have sold the tickets three times over and still had the same queues for entry outside. He's also syndicated the Internet TV broadcast with the better known religious stations in Europe and America. Intriguingly, his highest audience figures are now coming from Central America. "But that's Catholicism for you," he supposes.

He's been speaking for almost an hour now. He's wowed them up ("With aaaall my heart, I want you know what it means to be in the *arms* of the Risen Saaaaviour.") and he's dragged them low ("My dear, dear child, can you not *see* that you are separated from the Risen One, from the Bleeding Lamb of God by a *chasm*? A chasm of darkness that is *your sin*?"). Soon it will be time to call them home – and then, of course, to pluck them clean.

For now, he simply enjoys the vibration, the sheer throb of the god, Power, pulsing through his veins ravishing the goddess, Opportunity, driving his seed deep inside her until, screaming, she births the progeny, Domination. And now, at last, it is that heinous progeny pouring forth from every pore of him, in his every word, through his every gesture.

His debts have become immaterial. Deposits in the Landsbanki IoM account are well into eight figures (US$ that is, of course. He's quickly learned that the real high rollers calculate everything in dollars). The proceeds from tonight will be flowing in for weeks yet, pumping the well dry through every press release, every unattributable leak, every piece of rumour-mongering he has initiated.

He has to fess up to it, though. None of it would have been possible without the gullibility of the girl herself. She's stuck absolutely to the story of a virgin pregnancy and resolutely resisted every attempt to have medical tests undertaken. Philemon doubts the boyfriend will ever admit to being the father, but so what? The job is almost done now.

And there the little darling sits, robed up like an icon, yet in such a way as to emphasise her late stage of pregnancy. He doesn't actually think she's going to drop tonight (despite having decided to blow a monkey at the bookies on the possibility she might) but he'd be more than happy to be proved wrong. He isn't even expecting any healings. Well, this is the twenty-first century, you know. It will be entirely enough that she stretches out that bloody little paw of hers and let it drip onto the hysterical. They will do enough re-writing of reality for themselves without needing any real healing.

It is nearly time. He nods to Serenity, signals to Frank. As he delivers his final few words and stands arms outreached to heaven with the spotlight silhouetting him from behind, the organ begins softly:

Just as I am, without one plea,
But that thy blood was shed for me.

Like the sun, Sister Serenity rises.

Tolly

Rule Ten:

Interaction between Proxies is a matter of free will. Players will do nothing to stimulate or retard it.

Thursday 25th December 2008 9.05 pm GMT

She almost didn't get in. We tried several who wouldn't be parted from their tickets for love, nor money nor threats. And it took all my ingenuity to spot and direct her to the geeky little teenager in the hoodie. She convinced him his first fuck with her would give him better titillation than watching the mother of God give birth. It worked. We finally persuaded him to come round a corner into a dark alley where, behind a 1100-litre Eurobin, Tolly does indeed fuck him – but not in the way he'd anticipated. He will wake up eventually – tomorrow in Southampton General – sans eye, sans teeth, sans wallet and, most important of all, sans ticket for tonight's big event.

So, with the uncertainty over, Tolly pockets his cash and credit cards, tosses the wallet in the bin and, clutching the ticket in her hand, elbows and stamps her way rapidly to the front of the queue, where her new hoodie and my influence will conceal her recently restored (albeit fairly short) Mohican from prying eyes until it's too late.

Amazingly, it is Frank himself who inspects her ticket and fails to see who she is. She is seated half way down the rows and about half way in on the left-hand side.

It is there I leave her to take up my own place, entirely confident she will execute her pivotal role in the proceedings perfectly. Execute. Yes, what an appropriate word that is.

So, Tolly waits. She waits through the opening hymn. The readings. Philemon's sermon. She waits while the call to sinners is made. She waits while the line builds from the front, until it reaches her row. Then she slips into the line and waits her turn. She can see the witchbitch, complete with full-term pregnancy. She knows exactly where she's gonna bury that shiny silver blade and it's gonna get her two for the price of one – the witchbitch and her unborn bastard she's been using to manipulate poor darling Sid all these months. Like as not they'll bury them in the same grave. Then, she and Sid can finally get away and be together without a worry in the world.

Now, the main light has come up behind Nancy. The line is shuffling forward, slowly forward. Nancy's holding out her bleeding hand over a man with one arm shorter than the other. If she wasn't fully sober, Tolly would swear she must be drunk, because she's just seen the short arm grow to the length of the long one. The Yankee bitch is obviously even more of a witch than Tolly's given her credit for. Then, it's the turn of the girl in the wheelchair in front of her. The bitch lets her bloody hand hover over her. Then, the girl gets out of her chair and walks away. The chair rolls back into Tolly. She shoves it aside sharply and steps in front of the Yankee witchbitch, her head still covered with the hoodie. As Laura reaches forward to lay her stigmatum upon the hooded head, Tolly throws the hood back and draws the knife. She smiles a thin smile as she sees recognition in the girl's eyes. She grabs the outstretched hand and pulls her towards the upturned blade. "Merry Christmas, Witchbitch," she says.

The jaguar pounces.

Sister Serenity

Rule Twelve:

The free will of Nominated Proxies may be influenced but never withdrawn. Players must work through the inherent characteristics of their chosen Proxies.

Thursday 25th December 2008 9.06 pm GMT

She has been slipping between this world and the next all day. She wonders why Henry has not seen it. She wonders if it is happening because of the impending birth of God's son. She wonders how long it will be before she enters the presence of God permanently. She wonders when she is going to die.

At a time of their choosing they led her to the dressing room. Women of the church, including some former friends from *Sisters*, helped her undress, showered her, dried her in soft towels, answered her requests with "Yes, Sister Serenity," and "No, Sister Serenity," as if she were royalty. With reverential care, they gently dry her long, flowing hair and dress her in a robe of purple, hemmed with gold thread. It is tied with a golden cord under her baby so as to emphasise her pregnancy. They lift the golden hair carefully out from under the robe and tie a chiffon emerald headscarf over her head.

Then, they stand around her in a circle, considering their handiwork. One of the women spontaneously drops to her knees in front of Serenity. Serenity does not understand what the woman is doing until she bows her head and begins to speak quietly. "Hail Serenity, full of grace." Others fall to their knees around her, continuing "Blessed art though among women." Now, they are all on their knees. "And blessed is the fruit of thy womb, Jesus." She suppresses a sob. She is not her own any more. She belongs to such as these. She is no longer Laura. She is Sister Serenity, Mother of God.

The organ plays softly as the auditorium fills, 5,224 seats. Standing room of 277 places is also filled, in breach of the fire regulations. It is the fire of the Holy Ghost that will be upon her tonight. She knows not whether it will consume the Tabernacle, 5,224 seated spectators, 277 standing illegally in breach of fire regulations. But she knows beyond a doubt there will be fire, fire unquenchable and holy, in this place tonight.

Laura searches one last time for her love for Henry and locates it precisely in the place it should be in – her heart. Then, Sister Serenity releases Laura and rises, rises, rises inside her body and out of it and up, up, up, to the Heavenlies. She is Mother of God and there is no room in her for anything else now.

Serenity prays softly and unceasingly while the Pastor speaks: prays of matters we cannot be party to. It is Heaven's business she transacts tonight, not ours. Then, in a moment, he is finished and the organ is starting up with the old familiar tune:

Just as I am, without one plea,
But that thy blood was shed for me.

The halo light comes up slowly behind her, seemingly hovering just over her head. She waits a moment, then moves to the front of the rostrum and down the steps to the auditorium floor. The main lights come up. The lines form. Her fallen headscarf lies about her neck, an emerald river cascading through the golden cornfields of her hair, and down onto her purple robes. She un-bandages her stigmatum and reaches out over the first in line. The man falls to his knees, weeping, then is led away past a line of orange buckets. There is a rustle as he drops a sheaf of notes into the nearest. The next continues forward, a child of, perhaps, 7. Sister Serenity reaches her hand out again over a twisted body that slowly straightens before the eyes of her astounded parents, who are simultaneously terrified and overcome with gratitude. The family walks away past the buckets. More notes fall. The line moves on. Each arrival is treated the same. She knows, now, what the Lord meant when he said "Virtue has gone out of me", for with each healing, she feels an outflow of energy from her hand and an inflow into her crown chakra from Heaven.

Her concentration slips into a heavenly trance and she misses the detail of the next few healings until she returns to consciousness to find her arm stretched out towards a hooded figure. Her hand is grabbed. A jaguar leaps. There is a rush of air; a loud crack; an angry voice screaming from somewhere above in the darkness.

Serenity rises.

Thursday 25th December 2008 6.57 pm GMT

She rises up and back, back to where Henry is seated at one of two wicker chairs at a café table floating just under the glass roof of the Tabernacle's atrium. On the table is a bottle of white wine and two glasses, one containing freshly poured wine, the other empty. Henry watches Gabe float in through the glass roof then calls to him. "Gabe! Beautiful day for the final round, don't you think? Come and join me in a glass of wine – I have your favourite – Marlborough Grey Ghost."

"Get out of that body please, Lu. You know it isn't yours."

"Oh, I don't know. I think it's been mine since 1946 when I took this reality off you last time. You do remember Hiroshima, don't you, Gabe? The last breech of the space-time continuum in this universe? You do remember I won, don't you? That after almost two thousand years of abominable rule by your pestiferous 'Christian' values, I finally won this world back from you? You do remember the earth is now mine, and the fullness thereof, don't you, Gabe? But I'll tell you what, just to humour you…"

Henry morphs into Schmetterling, complete with neck twisted at an impossible angle for a living person.

"Is this any better for you?"

"I really would prefer you took your own incarnate form, just like the rest of us," replies Gabe in measured tones.

"Spoilsport." Schmetterling melts away into an angelic form, similar in size and bearing to Gabe in all respects but colour. She is golden and unutterably beautiful.

Gabe floats forward, pours wine into the second glass. He takes a sip and nods approvingly."

"You play the Game your way, Lu, I shall play it mine. The Arbiter will decide on the winner."

Around them Ethereals are materialising with increasing frequency. Each arrival is accompanied by a flash of light and a melodic sonic disturbance. It could easily be called the music of the heavens. Viewed from floor level below, the sky seems lit by an electrical storm accompanied by an unknown form of music. It being Christmas Day and the expectation being for a birth, the presumption whispered around the hall is of a heavenly choir and a star to guide the Magi. Perhaps it's not surprising, since many of the Ethereals present today had also looked down over Bethlehem that night.

Thursday 25th December 2008 9.47 pm GMT

From the floating table and chairs, they peer over the scene below where Serenity reaches out to Tolly. Tolly grabs her hand and draws the young woman forward towards the point of the knife, aiming for it to penetrate directly into the baby. Behind Tolly and to her side, Henry (the real Henry, that is,) has seen what is happening, but is prevented from reaching them by the lines of healing-seekers. He does the only thing he can do. He reaches into his pocket and throws what he finds there. Witnesses will later say it was a stone about the size of an egg. The Talis-man hits the blade of the knife side on with surprising accuracy, deflecting it upwards and away from the baby.

Immediately, Lu roars as if the knife has penetrated her, her colour changing from gold to black and back again. "Foul by Arbiter! Foul by Arbiter! Freeze Action. I appeal to the Game Maker."

The scene at floor level freezes, like a paused 3D movie.

Gabe looks at her in surprise. "Are you sure, Lu? I hardly think you would wish to draw the Game Maker's attention to yourself, given your track record for stretching the rules."

The Talis-man floats upwards, growing in size and changing form as he does. By the time he reaches the table, he is the same size and shape as the other Ethereals.

"Who called foul?" he asks. "And pass the wine." He pours from the bottle into empty air. The wine takes on the shape of a glass, though there is no glass. Talis picks up the glass that is not there and sips the wine. "Grey Ghost," he says, nodding approvingly, "I admire your taste, Lu."

But Lu isn't feeling conversational. "I won the game in 1946 following the tear in the curtain caused by the Hiroshima explosion," she declares, clearly angry, "and I am *not* prepared to lose this reality back to him," she says, pointing at Gabe, "due to a foul by you, Arbiter."

The Arbiter pauses. "I appreciate that you may think I am in contravention of rule 15, Lu. However, had I intervened to avoid that, I would have been guilty of contravention of rule 12. Rule 12 is precedent."

The Arbiter looks at Gabe, questioningly. "The game is not yet over, Arbiter," he says. "But I have a suggestion. Let us explore rule 13 first. Then, and only if I have acceptably fulfilled the requirements of the first half of that rule, will we proceed to the appeal to the Game Maker over the alleged breach of rule 15. Then, depending on the outcome of the appeal, we can return to the second half of rule 13 as required."

The Arbiter looks enquiringly at Lu.

"Very well, Arbiter, I agree," she says.

Gabe speaks again. "I offer in evidence the events in Deacon Road, Southampton, tomorrow afternoon."

"Fast Forward," commands the Arbiter. The three disappear, leaving time still frozen below them. Serenity follows, though she knows not how.

Paula

Rule Thirteen:

The Game will be deemed won either:
    when a verified Immaculate Conception is followed by a verified Virgin Birth
    or
    when either or both of the two events is rendered impossible.

Friday 26th December 2008 3.47 pm GMT

In Deacon Road, Paula is sitting on the sofa, singing softly to a newborn child. Haddon sits by her, his arm around her. Jamie is in an armchair to their left. All three are crying.

They do not see the Rolls-Royce glide silently round the corner. Nor do they see the peak-capped chauffeur get out and deposit a small package and a letter in their letterbox. They do not see him get back into the car and drive away.

Later, Paula will retrieve both items from the box. She will first open the letter. It reads:

> *My dear Paula,*
>
> *I do not imagine that a communication from me will be welcome after an angry parting and so many silent years. However, I do ask that you at least read to the end.*
>
> *I have been diagnosed with an aggressive cancer that has spread beyond operability. I have very little time left to live. I am using such time as I do have, to put right some of the wrongs I have done. And God knows, I did you wrong back in Liverpool all those years ago.*
>
> *The enclosed item turned up in the course of my work. I recognised it immediately and am quite certain that you will not have parted with it willingly. I hope that you will be able to consider its return as some small recompense for my abuse of you all those years ago.*
>
> *There are two further matters I would like to draw to your attention. Firstly, for what it is worth, whilst I have been much doubted and by many over the matter of my participation in the Falklands War, please be aware that everything I ever told you (and for that matter told others) on this subject was true. Secondly, and more importantly to you, I need you to know that I am not the father of the child you were carrying when I left you. Shortly after we parted I was diagnosed as being incapable of fathering children.*

I wish you, your daughter, and her father, whoever he may be,
the very best for the future. Live well. Live happily.
Yours,
Fredrick Dickinson.

Later she will open the package to find the Song of Songs ring.

For now, she simply stares at the letter incredulously, for she has had sex with just three men during her life – Fredrick, Denny and Haddon. None of them, it seems, can be the father of her daughter.

Sister Serenity

Rule Fourteen:

The winner will be awarded control of the field of play until such
time as another random event creates a further tear in the curtain.

Thursday 25th December 2008 9.55 pm GMT

"All satisfied as to the fulfilment of rule 13, then?"

The Arbiter is looking directly at Lu.

"I acknowledge the first half of rule 13 fulfilled, Arbiter. Whether Gabe is permitted to attempt to fulfil the second half depends on my appeal to the Game Maker."

The Arbiter turns to Gabe. "Satisfied with that?" Gabe nods his assent.

Right then, we stand before the Game Maker to lodge the appeal."

They dematerialise once more, leaving time still frozen below them.

Thursday 25th December 2008 9.56 pm GMT

"I'm sorry that took so long, players. But we do now have a decision. We play on. Unfreeze."

The Arbiter drifts back down to the floor of the Tabernacle, gradually changing back into the Talis-man form. He arrives back in his place just as motion recommences. Tolly draws Serenity forward onto the knife, which itself is deflected upwards by the impact of the Talis-man upon the blade. It penetrates her left breast up to the hilt.

Lu looks enquiringly at Gabe. "Care to concede?"

Sister Serenity

Rule Eleven:

Players may make themselves visible or audible to their Nominated Proxies but must not intervene directly in the chain of events.

Thursday 25th December 2008 11.02 pm GMT

They are leaving now, in a more ordered fashion that she would have expected. It makes her think of queuing for a bus. Each departure into the light is accompanied by a flash that marginally diminishes the collective brightness of the remaining Ethereals. Each departure is accompanied by a musical note that is the reverse of their arrival, and somehow more sombre for being so.

To the Tangibles, it will look like the Bethlehem star is going out. And it will sound like Heaven is sad for this death.

She looks down at the child in her arms: newborn, but nevertheless so old while still so young.

She thinks she understands at least a little of it now, a little of what it has all been for. "We make a world of meaning out of our representations," she thinks, "for we are meaning-making creatures. We build about it an impenetrable wall of certainty to render our beliefs about ourselves inviolable. It is a reality that is uniquely ours, populated with people and places of our own creation, the juxtapositions, causes and effects, from which we order our existence. We carry this version of reality with us all our lives as we go to and fro upon the earth. And we are surprised, or irritated, or angry, when it collides with the perceived realities of others. Nothing – not fact, nor event, not death itself – will ever permit us to unmake this world of meaning we have conjured."

She looks again at the child: this child with the shining eyes that make her want to dance. "Hello Eve," she says, and smiles at the baby.

It is love that permits us to face up to the psychological catastrophe of discovering that our reality is not unique, and to acknowledge that there are others out there who experience their reality differently. The risk of facing danger on this scale results in most of us choosing to erect shrines to the concept of love rather than to experience love for what it really is. Most choose forever to dissociate, never to experience what it means to prefer another above the self.

Looking down one final time at the baby in the arms of her own dying body, Serenity smiles a last smile at Gabe and follows him into the light.

The Game Maker

Rules of the Game
(abridged for use by inaugurated Tangibles)

1. The rules of the Game must not be fully disclosed to Tangibles until the Game has been completed and then, only selectively and by metaphor.

2. The Game will be initiated upon the occurrence of an event, outside the control of the players, that establishes a tear in the curtain ("a random tear"). Players are free to observe the occurrence of the event if they wish. A player who initiates a tear in the curtain will forfeit the Game and may, at the discretion of the Arbiter, be excluded from any future Game.

3. The Arbiter will confirm the existence of a randomly established tear in the curtain by passing through the tear onto the field of play.

4. The Arbiter will initiate the Game by establishing a bond with a Nominated Proxy.

5. Players will not commence play until the Arbiter has made physical contact with a Nominated Proxy of each player's choice. The Arbiter will then declare the Game open. Prior to this point, players may initiate contact with their Nominated Proxies ONLY in non- incarnate form. Any physical manifestation before the Arbiter declares the Game open will result in immediate forfeiture of the Game by the offending party.

6. Players are free to invite Tangibles to observe play. Observers will not interfere with the chain of events.

7. Players are free to move around in time and space at will.

8. Players will undertake play through Nominated Proxies and other Tangibles only. Any player who compromises this rule will account to the Game Maker for their conduct.

9. Players may choose more than one Proxy if they so wish.

10. Interaction between Proxies is a matter of free will. Players will do nothing to stimulate or retard it.
11. Players may make themselves visible or audible to their Nominated Proxies but must not intervene directly in the chain of events.
12. The free will of Nominated Proxies may be influenced but never withdrawn. Players must work through the inherent characteristics of their chosen Proxies.
13. The Game will be deemed won either:

    when a verified Immaculate Conception is followed by a verified Virgin Birth

    or

    when either or both of the two events is rendered impossible.
14. The winner will be awarded control of the field of play until such time as another random event creates a further tear in the curtain.
15. Should a player question the objectivity of the Arbiter, an appeal will be made directly to the Game Maker.
16. In all other matters, the decision of the Arbiter is final.

At a time when there is no time

If you think of me as God, then you have understood neither of us.

He is the conductor who orchestrates the music of the spheres.

I am he who writes the songs sung by the whales.

It is she who choreographs the dances of the galaxies.

It is we who decreed the circumlocution of the quarks.

To us your 'Big Bang' was but a whisper on the wind and each time it repeats, it is but the ticking of a second hand, measuring the respirations of eternity.

She stands, one foot upon each universe, drawing her bow across the strings of your authenticity.

I singing sweet lullabies to civilisations past, who treasured and lost greater knowledge than yours will ever hold.

He dwells where parallel lines meet.

I abide where the fireflies write poetry on the fading brightness of red dwarf stars.

We dwell where Gaia and her sisters make burnt offerings of petrified egocentricity upon the temple altars of the alchemists.

In the shadow of his milky wings will He hide the victims of oppression unmerited from the perpetrators of crimes too long unpunished.

And all the while I gaze upon the never-to-be-seen and hold close the souls of the abandoned.

We guarantee the freewill of the predestined.

I am the dream of choices yet unmade.

He am the writer of the rules and righter of wrongs

Us be the historians of the yet-to-come.

She are the Alpha and the Omega.

I am the Game Maker.

Epilogue:

Handwritten letter addressed to Henry Tallison found on a circular table in the Southampton Tabernacle, underneath an empty bottle of Marlborough Grey Ghost, 26th December 2008, 5.14 am

Dear Henry,

My work is done and soon I will be leaving. I will close the curtain behind me on my departure and hope that it is never opened again. But I have to be honest and say I cannot be wholly confident that my outcome will be achieved. Your technology seems to be taking you in the directions of further rifts. You will understand, of course, that I am under no obligation to explain myself to Tangibles. You are dramatically less important in the greater scheme of things than you give yourselves credit for, you know. Yet, I am not without compassion, and I have greatly enjoyed our time together, so much that I can honestly say I have come to love you.

It is in the nature of your race to seek for certainty. And since it is painful to you to move forward in your time here without it, let me see if I can be just a little merciful and help you achieve the closure you crave. Consider, for a moment, if you will, if you can conceive of the following as a plausible reconciliation of the irreconcilable.

If you check the newspapers or the Internet, or any other public record, they will show that the Large Hadron Collider was switched on on 10th September 2008. Shortly prior to that date, a group of what you might wish to call alternative thinkers had attempted to use the force of European Human Rights legislation to prevent the machine being activated, for they believed it would create a black hole that would swallow your Universe. In evidence to the court, the established body of informed scientific opinion expressed the contrary view, that no such event could conceivably occur.

Consider for a moment, if you will, why the greatest scientific brains of your age could be so certain of the outcome of an event that was yet to take place. After all, you people have enough trouble agreeing about what happened yesterday, let alone what might happen tomorrow. Consider, for a moment, the possibility that these minds could be so certain, only if they were speaking not of possible future events, but of past events they had already experienced. Consider the possibility that by 10th September 2008, the LHC had already been switched on for some time. Consider that, for example, it might first have been switched on on Saturday 6th April 2008 at precisely 9.00 pm. Consider the possibility that the result of switching on the machine was the creation not of a black hole, but of a rift in the space time continuum, a 'worm hole' or a 'tear in the curtain' to use the vernacular from my own home, in what you would refer to as a parallel universe. Consider the possibility that the exact location of the rift was the first floor of a house in Brockenhurst in the New Forest, UK, the home of a rather nervous young man who was out celebrating his twenty-first birthday. Consider whether you believe it plausible, that through such a rift, it was possible for energy, matter and personality to pass from realities other than your own. Consider whether you find it plausible that some of such entities hold a benevolent intent for your Universe, whilst others are malevolent. And then, consider the possibility that there is an Ethereal always in oversight of your universe, so that it may evolve naturally, without interference from other places, other entities. Could you then conceive that competing Ethereals, some of whom might have a less benevolent intent, might seek the prize of holding that position of oversight? Could you believe that from time to time such malevolent entities manage to gain control? And, is it possible, within your map of the world, that there is a higher creature, one we might perhaps call a Game Maker, responsible for the equilibrium of all the realities? An entity who oversees Ethereal influence over such realities by use of predetermined rules? By, perhaps, Arbitration?

But then again, perhaps all this is beyond the plausible. All you can say with certainty, Henry, is that philosophers after the Renaissance saw epistemology differently. All you can say is that some regarded knowledge as the product of your senses and therefore, only as reliable as those senses, whilst others considered it to be the product of rational reflection. All you can say with certainty, is that several current philosophers consider that, though knowledge has to be developed by observation, it is still absolute. All you can say is that, in the end, all have to acknowledge that there is no entirely reliable means of proving that knowledge or information is consistent, any more than there are means of demonstrating your actions are entirely free and of your own choice.

So, Henry, consider very, very carefully the reality in which you choose to believe and to live by, for the rest of your life. And consider the possibility that all the above was so, is so and will be so, world without end, or at least until Final Countdown begins.

Alternatively, you might wish to consider the possibility that you are very, very ill. Indeed, Henry, can you be certain you actually exist?

With affection.
Your friend,

Talis
The Arbiter

Other Books By Michael Forester

If It Wasn't For That Dog

IF IT WASN'T
FOR THAT DOG!

"A delightful and hugely enjoyable true life story of how an assistance dog changed a life – I loved it!" Sir Anthony Jay
Writer of Yes Minister

Dr. Bruce Fogle MBE
Vet and co-founder of Hearing Dogs for Deaf People "A humorous and heartfelt chronicle about two individuals learning to dance together in perfect harmony!"

MICHAEL FORESTER

It's amazing what you can achieve with persistence, a bit of chopped liver and a second hand teddy bear...

In 2002 Michael, a deafened man from the New Forest, lost his home, his marriage, his business and his father– but then again, he always was a tad careless. However, in the same year someone suggested that getting a dog might be a good idea–not just any dog, but a hearing dog from Hearing Dogs for Deaf People. And when, in 2004, Michael was presented with a Hearing Dog of his own called Matt, he just knew life would be so much easier. Amazing how wrong you can be, isn't it!

If It Wasn't For That Dog is the story of Matt's first year with Michael, the challenges and accomplishments of climbing the Hearing Dog learning curve, the profound changes he stimulated and the inestimable joy he confers magically on everyone who meets him. But most of all it is the story of the strange power of meaty treats to work miracles in doggie behaviour.

Dragonsong

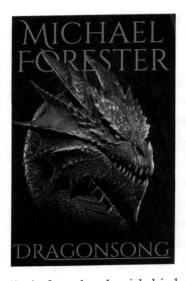

Sometimes nothing but the death of your father will do

Rebekah, noblewoman of Albion, has been driven to madness by the murder of her lover Vidar. In her torment she bargains with the Prince of Demons to turn her into a dragon. Thus transformed, she seeks to take revenge upon her father, Merlin, whom she is fooled into believing is responsible for Vidar's death. To save the world from the ravages of Dragonsong, Merlin is forced to banish his beloved daughter to hell, regardless of the consequences for him personally. Behind the subterfuge stands Oberon, Captain-King of Elves. He does not foresee the devastation his jealousy and unrequited love for Rebekah will unleash upon Gaia when he frees her from Merlin's spell and summons her from hell to support his war against Albion. To save Gaia a second, Merlin is forced to travel back in time to prepare a warrior capable of overcoming the dragon through the power of the Sleep Stone. But he does not foresee the bond that will develop between the dragon and his own assistant, the Seer, Michael of Albion. If Lady Attie and Michael prove unable to return the Sleep Stone to the mouth of Hell in time, the Demon Army will be swarm out of Hell and overrun Gaia. Time. Time is the key. Time is the only solution to Gaia's destiny – but only if the gods of Asgard can find a way to stop it.

The Goblin Child

Well hello there.

Why don't you step inside and take a look round? You remember this place, don't you? That's right. You've been here before. And us. Surely you remember us. We're old friends. This is where the light in your eyes glimpses the darkness in your mind.

Sit down and stay a while – if you can face the risk finding out who you really are, that is. I'll introduce you to some friends of mine:

- Meet the man who remembers his birth. He wishes he didn't.
- And the goblin child – if his mother is to be believed.
- Or how about the boy who takes his god to school?
- Here's Madeleine, the author who can't get beyond chapter seven – because of the raven with white eyes, that is.
- And Santa. Yes, you really must meet Santa.
- But really it's all about David who spent his like circling the moon – just like you and I do, in fact

Come with me. Come with me now.

A Home For Other Gods

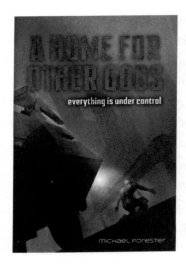

It's 2117.

A country where everything you do has to be approved by the State; a State that tells you what to eat, when to shower; when to make love, what to think.

As the waters start to rise in the city, the fish people begin to arrive. Ultimately compliant, obedient without question, they open and close their mouths incessantly, saying nothing.

When Greg dares to think for himself, the Departmental Republic seeks to draw him into their elite to keep him quiet, to force his compliance. But if he agrees to be elevated to the level of the shadowy 'Gods,' it's going to cost him his home and the life of his family.

People are saying this ground-breaking novella reads like a follow-on to 1984.

You yourself live in a regulated, bureaucratically-controlled state. Can you afford not to read it?

Forest Rain

Spiritual Learnings for a New Age

Your spiritual journey is unique to you. But it is in mindfulness of the journeys of those who travel with us that we learn more of our own purpose and how we can draw energy and meaning from the challenges and events on our road.

This collection of Spiritual Learnings in prose and poetry form a unique meditation that will support you in exploring your own journey, and the life events, both great and small, that will offer themselves to you as you travel forward.

These meditations will move you to joy; they will move you to tears. They will help you give yourself permission to experience the depth of learning to be found within, to experience fully what you have come into the world to learn and to teach. In so doing, they will support you in discovering the astonishing and profound messages meant for you alone, for *Forest Rain* truly is your Heart's Home.

Biographical

Michael Forester is a deafened writer who lives in Hampshire's New Forest with his hearing dog, Matt.

He can be contacted at michaelforesterauthor@gmail.com

Michael Forester with hearing dog Matt